DATE DUE			JUN 0 6
7-10-06			
NOV 01 '06			
JAN 19 08			
4-6			
10-20/20 18			
GAYLORD			PRINTED IN U.S.A.

THE ISLAND

**Center Point
Large Print**

**This Large Print Book carries the
Seal of Approval of N.A.V.H.**

THE ISLAND

HEATHER GRAHAM

CENTER POINT PUBLISHING
THORNDIKE, MAINE

This Center Point Large Print edition
is published in the year 2006 by arrangement with
Harlequin Enterprises, Ltd.

The text of this Large Print edition is unabridged. In other
aspects, this book may vary from the original edition.
Printed in the United States of America.
Set in 16-point Times New Roman type.

ISBN 1-58547-754-0

Library of Congress Cataloging-in-Publication Data

Graham, Heather.
    The Island / Heather Graham.--Center Point large print ed.
        p. cm.
    Novel
    ISBN 1-58547-754-0 (lib. bdg. : alk. paper)
    1. Large type books. I. Title.

PS3557.R198I85 2006
813'.54--dc22

                                                2006001013

To Rhonda Saperstein, with lots of love and thanks. And to Coral Reef Yacht Club and its members, with deepest thanks, especially Fred and Marian Davant, Teresa and Stu Davant, Dr. Michael and Kelly Johnson, Jock and Linda Fink, and the Commodore & his wife: Eric and Elise Thyree.

Prologue

"YOU'RE GOING TO FEED them *again?*"

Molly Monoco looked up at the sound of her husband's voice. She had been busy in the galley, putting together a goodie bag filled with substantial meals. Ted, speaking with a growl in his voice, had been at his workstation. Apparently he had just noticed how industriously she had been preparing food.

Her husband appeared both aggravated and disgusted.

He knew what she was up to.

She couldn't really blame him for his feelings. Ted had worked hard all his life, and had earned every bit of the income they were now enjoying after his retirement. They both came from Cuban families who had made the move to Florida long before the refugees had begun fleeing the little island. While Molly's maiden name had been Rodriguez, her first name had always been Molly, just as Ted had been Theodore from the start. Their parents had brought them to the States, believing in the American dream, and teaching them a work ethic that would allow them to achieve that dream.

Ted had started out playing the drums at nightclubs in Miami, not unlike a man who had become a lot more famous, Desi Arnaz.

7

He had worked as a busboy, as well, then a waiter, a host and a dancer. From his playing, he had fallen in love with salsa. So he had kept playing the drums, kept dancing, kept bussing tables and being a waiter and bartender until he had made enough money to buy his first studio, totally dedicated to the art of salsa. Eventually he had owned several studios, then sold them for a nice fat profit.

Work. Ted had known how to do it well. He had little patience with those who would not or could not help themselves.

And she did understand.

But she had her goals, too, trying to look after others who perhaps didn't deserve help, but then again, who might turn their lives around with a little assistance.

Now, as a retired man of means, he also had his hobbies, like all the sonar gadgets and other equipment on the boat. After all, he would have noticed what she was up to earlier, if he hadn't been playing around so intently with one of his computers!

She smiled. Even miffed, as he was right now, he was still as attractive to her as the young man with whom she had fallen in love forty-odd years ago. Tall, but not too tall, still fit. The hair on his chest was now gray—like the thinning strands on top of his head, but she didn't care. After all those years of marriage, the ups and the downs, she loved him now just as much as she always had—even if he had decided to name the yacht *Retired!,* despite the fact that she could have thought of a dozen more charming names.

His current displeasure with her wouldn't last. It never did. Just as she loved the fact that he was always tinkering with some new kind of technology, he was secretly pleased that his wife was concerned for the welfare of others.

"Ted, what else can I do?" she asked softly.

"Quench the maternal instincts," he said, rolling his eyes. "We may well be talking criminals here. Hell, we're *definitely* talking criminals."

"Or misdirected young people who just need a helping hand," she said firmly. All her life, Molly had been involved. Blessed with Ted, her high-school sweetheart, she'd worked alongside him at many a club. Then—when she hadn't been able to produce the family she would have loved—she'd tried to help out where she could, at the church, with the homeless, and for various good causes, raising funds, even working soup kitchens. She could afford to, once Ted began making good money.

And she remained blessed. At sixty-five, she was no spring chick. But she was in good health, good shape, and pleased, mainly for Ted's sake, that people would say what an attractive woman she was.

"It's food, Ted. Nothing but a little food," she assured him. "And the last handout we're giving, since we're setting off on our own excursion."

He sighed, and a small smile crept over his face. Coming to her, he wrapped his arms around her. "How did I get so lucky?" he asked.

"Chance?" she teased, smiling.

He gave her a swat on the bottom. She giggled. Flirting was fun. They were older now, so a pat on the behind didn't lead to an afternoon in the handsome master cabin. Forget Viagra. He had a heart condition; she wouldn't let him take it. When there was this kind of amazing affection and closeness after so many years, nothing needed to be pushed.

In his arms, she thought with wonder what a great life they'd had together, and how wonderful it was that they still had each other—and the *Retired!* They could go anywhere, live out their dreams, explore—wherever the whim took them—and do it all in luxury.

"Okay, woman, we're moving on, so go and be lady bountiful, and then we'll get cracking," he said firmly.

"Right."

Molly headed for the ladder that would take her to the deck, her bag of goodies in her arms. She hummed softly as she emerged topside.

For a moment she just stared, confused. She even started to smile.

Then the tune she had been humming abruptly halted, broken on the air.

Her mouth began to work.

No sound came.

TED HEARD, OR THOUGHT HE HEARD, a slight sound from topside.

"Molly?"

No answer.

"Molly?" he called, a little louder this time.

He felt a little thud against his heart. Maybe she had fallen, taking the dinghy, getting on or off the main boat. Hurt herself. Worse. They were neither of them young. What if she'd suffered some kind of attack? Fallen—maybe unconscious—into the water?

He leaped up, some instinct suddenly warning him of danger.

He ran up the steps to the deck.

And froze.

Two thoughts occurred to him.

What an ass he had been!

And then . . .

Molly, oh, Molly, Molly . . .

"Time to talk, Ted," snapped an angry voice.

"I can't tell you what you want to know," he protested, tears in his eyes.

"I think you can."

"I can't! I swear, before God, I would if I could."

"Start thinking, Ted. Because trust me, you *will* tell me what you've found."

1

IT WAS A SKULL.

That much Beth Anderson knew after two seconds of dusting off bits of dirt and grass and fallen palm debris.

"Well?" Amber demanded.

"What is it?" Kimberly asked, standing right behind Amber, anxiously trying to look over her shoulder.

Beth glanced up briefly at her fourteen-year-old niece and her niece's best friend. Until just seconds ago, the two had been talking a mile a minute, as they always did, agreeing that their friend Tammy was a bitch, being far too cruel to *her* best friend, Aubrey, who in turn came to Amber and Kimberly for friendship every time she was being dissed by Tammy. They weren't dissing anyone themselves, they had assured Beth, because they weren't saying anything they wouldn't say straight to Tammy's face.

Beth loved the girls, loved being with them, and was touched to be the next best thing to a mother for Amber, who had lost her own as an infant. She was accustomed to listening to endless discussions on the hottest music, the hottest new shows and the hottest new movies—and who did and didn't deserve to be in them, since the girls were both students at a magnet school for drama.

The main topic on their hot list had recently become boys. On that subject, they could truly talk endlessly.

But now their continual chatter had come to a dead stop.

Kimberly had been the one to stub her toe on the unknown object.

Amber had been the one to stoop down to look, then demand that her aunt come over.

"Well?" Kim prodded. "Dig it up, Beth."

"Um . . . I don't think I should," Beth said, biting her lower lip.

It wasn't just a skull. She couldn't see it clearly, there was so much dirt and debris, but despite the fact that it was half hidden by tangled grasses and the sandy ground, she could see more than bone.

There was still hair, Beth thought, her stomach churning.

And even *tissue.*

She didn't want the girls seeing what they had discovered any more closely.

Beth felt as if the blood in her veins had suddenly turned to ice. She didn't touch the skull; she carefully laid a palm frond over it, so she would recognize the spot when she returned to it. She wasn't about to dig anything up with the girls here.

She dusted her hands and stood quickly, determined that they had to get back to her brother, who was busy setting up their campsite. They were going to have to radio the police, since cell phones didn't seem to work out here.

A feeling of deep unease was beginning to ooze along her spine as vague recollections of a haunting news story flashed into her mind: *Molly and Ted Monoco, expert sailors, had seemed to vanish into thin air.*

The last place they'd actually been seen was Calliope Key, right where they were now.

"Let's go get Ben," she suggested, trying not to sound as upset as she felt.

"It's a skull, isn't it?" Amber demanded.

She was a beautiful girl, tall and slender, with huge hazel eyes and long dark hair. The way she looked in a bathing suit—a two-piece, but hardly a risqué bikini—was enough to draw the attention of boys who were much too old for her, at least in Beth's opinion. Kimberly was the opposite of Amber, a petite blonde with bright blue eyes, pretty as a picture.

Sometimes the fact that she was in charge of two such attractive and impressionable girls seemed daunting. She knew she tended to be a worrywart, but the idea of any harm coming to the girls was . . .

Okay! She was the adult here. In charge. And it was time to do something about that.

But they were practically alone on an island with no phones, no cars . . . not a single luxury. A popular destination for the local boat crowd, but distant and desolate.

It was two to three hours back to Miami with the engine running, though Fort Lauderdale was closer, and it was hardly an hour to a few of the Bahamian islands.

She inhaled and exhaled. Slowly.

The human mind was amazing. Moments ago she had been delighted by the very remoteness of the island, pleased that there weren't any refreshment stands, automobiles or modern appliances of any kind.

But now . . .

"Might be a skull," Beth admitted, and she forced a grin, lifting her hands. "And might not be," she lied.

14

"Your dad isn't going to be happy about this, Amber, when he's been planning this vacation for so long, but—"

She broke off. She hadn't heard the sound of footsteps or even the rustle of foliage, but as she spoke, a man appeared.

He had emerged from an overgrown trail through one of the thick hummocks of pines and palms that grew so profusely on the island.

It was that elemental landscape that brought real boat people here, the lack of all the things that came with the real world.

So why did his arrival feel so threatening?

Trying to be rational with herself, she decided that he looked just right for the type of person who should be here. He had sandy hair and was deeply tanned. No, not just tanned but *bronzed,* with the kind of dyed-in-deep coloring that true boat people frequently seemed to acquire. He was in good shape, but not heavily muscled. He was in well-worn denim cutoffs, and his feet were clad in deck shoes, no socks. His feet were as bronze as his body, so he must have spent plenty of time barefoot.

Like a guy who belonged on a boat, cruising the out islands. One who knew what he was doing. One who would camp where there were no amenities.

He also wore shades.

Anyone would, she told herself. She had on sunglasses, as did the girls. So why did his seem suspicious, dark and secretive.

She needed to be reasonable, she told herself. She was only feeling this sudden wariness because she had just found a skull, and instinctive panic was setting in. It was odd how the psyche worked. Any other time, if she had run into someone else on the island, she would have been friendly.

But she had just found a skull, and he reminded her of the unknown fate of Ted and Molly Monoco, who had been here, and then . . .

Sailed into the sunset?

An old friend had reported them missing when they hadn't radioed in, as they usually did.

And she had just found a skull at their last known location.

So she froze, just staring at the man.

Amber, at fourteen, hadn't yet begun to think of personal danger in the current situation. Her father was a boat person, so she was accustomed to other boat people, and she was friendly when she met them. She wasn't stupid or naive, and she had been taught street smarts—she went to school in downtown Miami, for one thing. She could be careful when she knew she should.

Apparently that didn't seem to be now.

Amber smiled at the stranger and said, "Hi."

"Hi," he returned.

"Hi," Kim said.

Amber nudged Beth. "Um—hi."

"Keith Henson," the man said, and though she couldn't see his eyes, his shades were directed toward her. His face had good solid lines. Strong chin, high-set cheekbones. The voice was rich and deep.

He should have been doing voice-overs for commercials or modeling.

Hey, she mocked herself. Maybe that was what he *did* do.

"I'm Amber Anderson," her niece volunteered. "This is Kim Smith, and that's my aunt Beth." She was obviously intrigued and went on to say, "We're camping here."

"Maybe," Beth said quickly.

Amber frowned. "Oh, come on! Just because—"

"How do you do, Mr. Henson," Beth said, cutting off her niece's words. She stepped forward quickly, away from their find. "Nice to meet you. Down here on vacation? Where are you from?"

Oh, good, that was casual. A complete third degree in ten seconds or less.

"Recent transplant, actually a bit of a roamer," he told her, smiling, offering her his hand. It was a fine hand. Long fingered, as bronzed as the rest of him, nails clipped and clean. Palm callused. He used his hands for work. He was a real sailor, definitely, or did some other kind of manual labor.

She had the most bizarre thought that when she accepted his handshake, he would wrench her forward, and then his fingers would wind around her neck. The fear became so palpable that she almost screamed aloud to the girls to run.

He took her hand briefly in a firm but not too powerful grip, then released it. "Amber, Kim," he said, and shook their hands as he spoke.

"So are you folks are from the area?" he asked, and looked at the girls, smiling. Apparently he'd already written Beth off as a total flake.

She slipped between the two girls, feeling her bulldog attitude coming on and setting an arm around each girl's shoulders.

"Yep!" Amber said.

"Well, kind of," Kim said.

"I mean, we're not from the island we're standing on, but nearby," Amber said.

Henson's smile deepened.

Beth tried to breathe normally and told herself that she was watching far too many forensics shows on television. There was no reason to believe she had to protect the girls from this man.

But no reason to trust him on sight, either.

"Are you planning on camping on the island?" Beth asked.

He waved a hand toward the sea. "I'm not sure yet. I'm with some friends . . . we're doing some diving, some fishing. We haven't decided whether we're in a camping mood or not."

"Where are your friends?" Beth asked. A little sharply? she wondered. So much for being casual, able to easily escape a bad situation, if it should prove to be one.

"At the moment I'm on my own."

"I didn't see your dinghy," Beth said. "In fact, I

didn't even notice another boat in the area."

"It's there," he said, "the *Sea Serpent*." He cocked his head wryly. "My friend, Lee, who owns her, likes to think of himself as the brave, adventurous type. Did you sail out here on your own?"

It might have been an innocent question, but not to Beth. Not at this moment.

She had been swearing for years that she was going to take kung fu classes or karate, but as yet, she hadn't quite done so.

She always carried pepper spray in her purse. But, of course, she had been wandering inland with the girls, just walking, and she wasn't carrying her purse. She wasn't carrying anything. She had on sandals and a bathing suit. Like the girls.

"Are you alone?" Keith Henson repeated politely.

Politcly? Or menacingly?

"Oh, no. We're with my brother. And a whole crowd."

"A whole crowd—" Amber began.

Beth pinched her shoulder.

"Ow!" Amber gasped.

"Lots of my brother's friends are coming in. Sailors . . . boat people . . . you know, big guys, the kind who can twist off beer caps with their teeth," Beth said, trying to sound light.

Amber and Kim were both staring at her as if she'd lost her mind.

"Oh, yeah, all my dad's friends are, like, big, tough-guy nature freaks," Amber said, staring at Beth. "Yeah

19

right, the kind that open beer bottles with their teeth."

"They are?" Kim asked, sounding very confused.

"At any rate, there will be a bunch of us. A couple of cops, even," Beth said, realizing immediately how ridiculous that sounded.

Time to move on!

Tugging at the girls' shoulders, she added, "Well, it's a pleasure to meet you. We'd better get back to my brother before he misses us. We're supposed to be helping with the setup."

"We'll see you, if you're hanging around," Kim told him cheerfully.

"Yes, nice to meet you," Amber said.

"Bye, then," Keith Henson said.

A plastic smile in place, Beth continued to force the girls away from the man and toward the beach where they'd come ashore in the dinghy. And where they would find her brother, she prayed. Surely he hadn't gone wandering off.

"Aunt Beth," Amber whispered, "what on earth is the matter with you? You were so weird to that man."

Kimberly cleared her throat, "Um, actually, you were pretty rude," she said hesitantly.

"He was alone, he appeared out of nowhere—and we had just found a skull," Beth said, after glancing back to assure herself that they were out of earshot.

"You said you weren't sure if it was a skull or not," Kim said.

"I wasn't sure—I'm *not* sure."

"But it looked like he just got here, too," Amber

said. "And the skull—it *is* a skull, isn't it?—had been there a while."

"Criminals often return to the scene of the crime," Beth said, quoting some program or other, and anxiously moving forward.

Amber burst out laughing. "Aunt Beth! Okay, so you got the heebie-jeebies. But puh-lease. Did you see a gun on him?"

"Or anywhere he could have stuffed one?" Kim asked, giggling.

They weren't such bad questions, really.

"No," Beth admitted.

"So why were you so rude?" Amber persisted.

Beth groaned. "I don't know. I guess when you think you might have found a skull, you become very careful about your own health and well-being, okay?"

"Okay," Amber said after a moment. "He looked like a decent guy."

"He probably is."

Kim giggled suddenly. "He was *hot*."

"He's way too old for you guys," Beth replied a little too sharply.

"So is Brad Pitt, but that doesn't mean he's not hot," Amber said, shaking her head as if it was a sadly difficult thing to deal with adults.

"Right," Beth murmured.

A thud sounded from behind. Beth jumped, ready to cover the girls with her own body against any threatened danger.

"Aunt Beth," Amber said, "it was a palm frond."

Beth exhaled. "Right," she murmured.

The girls were looking at one another again. As if they had to be very careful with her.

As if she were losing her mind.

"Come on, let's find your dad," Beth said to Amber.

THE WOMAN HAD TO BE ONE OF the strangest he'd ever come across, Keith decided, watching as the three-some walked away.

She'd acted as if she'd been hiding something.

As if she was guilty of . . . something.

He shook his head. No, not with those two teens at her side. They were far too innocent and friendly for anything to have been going on. Not that teens couldn't be guilty of a lot. But he had learned to be a pretty good judge of character, and those two were simply young and friendly, like a pair of puppies, fresh and eager to explore the world, expecting only good things from it.

But as for the woman . . .

Beth Anderson. She and the tall girl were obviously related. Both had the same very sleek dark hair. Not dead straight, but lush and wavy. And Beth had the kind of eyes that picked up the elements, that could be dark or light, that held a bit of the exotic, the myste-rious. Very nicely built, which was more than evident, since all three were in two-piece suits. She appeared to be in her mid to late twenties, naturally sensual and sexy, though not in an overt way. Athletic. With shapely legs that went forever . . .

She was compellingly attractive.

And a little crazy.

No. *Frightened.*

Of him?

This was his first trip to Calliope Key. But he surely looked the part. So why had he appeared so menacing to her?

She wouldn't ever have come to the island with the girls if she had been afraid of something from the get-go. So . . . ?

They must have found something.

He looked quickly around the clearing. There was nothing immediately evident that would have disturbed anyone, whatever they'd found had to be right around where they had been standing.

For a moment everything in him seemed to tighten and burn; his jaw locked. The heat of anger filled him, the raging sense of fury that the world was never just, and no effort on his part could change that.

And that was part of the reason he was here, he reminded himself, though he kept that fact private. Keep your eye on the prize—that was the standing order. There was one objective. Find what they were seeking, and do it discreetly. Then the rest would fall into place. He hoped. He wasn't certain anyone else really believed that, and he would be damned if he even knew what he believed himself.

He heard his name called. It was Lee.

He forced a deep breath, aware that he had to tamp down his emotions over his current situation.

23

He shouted back, "I'm over here."

A minute later, Lee Gomez and Matt Albright appeared in the clearing. "What's going on?" Lee asked him. Half-Ecuadorian and half-American mutt, Lee had brilliant blue eyes and pitch-dark hair, and skin that never seemed to mind the sun.

"Not much. Met a woman and two girls—they're with the woman's brother, maybe some other people, camping on the island tonight," Keith said.

Matt shook his head, swearing. He was the redhead in their group, quick to anger, quicker to apologize, but at all times easily irritated. "There's more. Two more good-size boats, both anchored not far from us. I saw a dinghy coming in with several people."

"Well, what are you going to do," Keith asked with a shrug. "Boaters have been coming out here since . . . well, hell, probably since forever."

"Yeah, but dammit, they shouldn't be here now," Matt muttered.

"Hey, we knew we'd be in public view, working around whatever happened and whoever appeared. People are here, so let's make the best of it," Keith said. "And think about it. It's not much of a shock. It's a weekend, the perfect time for boaters to take a little break."

"You don't think we could dress up as pygmies and scare them all off the island, do you?" Lee murmured dryly.

"Pygmies?" Matt said.

"Some kind of tribal islanders, maybe cannibals?" Lee teased.

Keith laughed. "Oh, yeah, that would make us really inconspicuous. Besides, while they're on the island, they're not out on their boats, checking out the reefs. It's a weekend. Let's do like the others. Play tourist. Get to know the folks. Check out what they know— and what they're thinking." And what they're afraid of, he thought, but he kept the possibility that anyone on the island might suspect them of something to himself.

Lee shrugged. "All right."

"So we roll out the cooler and the tent and make like party people," Matt said. He laughed suddenly. "Not so bad. One of the people on the boat was a woman, and man, she sure as hell looked like a hottie. From a distance, anyway."

One of the people on the boat? Keith thought. You should have seen the woman in this very clearing, just minutes ago. And I wasn't any distance from her. None at all.

"Doesn't matter if she's hot as blue blazes, no getting too close to the locals, not tonight," Lee warned sternly.

"Hey, I'm just going to be a party boy. A friendly guy, just looking for fun, a good ole boating fool," Matt assured him.

"Well, you can be a good ole boy later. I'm not hauling stuff off that boat by myself," Lee said. "If we're turning into Boy Scouts and doing the camping thing, you guys can do some of the lugging, too."

"Actually, camping isn't such a bad idea," Keith said.

"No, and getting to know folks from the area isn't a bad idea, either," Lee said. He grinned. "I think I'll own the boat."

"Hey!" Matt protested.

"Someone has to own the boat, right?" Lee asked.

"You can own the boat," Keith said.

"I get to own it next time," Matt said.

"With any luck, there won't be a next time," Keith said. He stared at the other two, and he couldn't help feeling an edge of suspicion.

Lee stared back at him. His eyes were enigmatic. "Ever the optimist, huh?"

"I just know what I'm doing," Keith said.

Lee assessed him for what seemed like an eternity. "I hope," Lee said. "I hope to hell you're focused on what we're doing."

"I'm focused. You can count on it," Keith said, and he knew his tone was grim.

"C'mon, then, let's go play tourist," Lee said.

"Sure. Be right there," Keith said.

"Hey, we're all in this together, you know," Matt reminded him, his eyes narrowed.

"Yup."

They *were* in it together, true. But the other two didn't know that he'd been warned specifically to keep an eye on them.

"Damn, Keith, you're acting bizarre," Lee said,

staring at him. "Think of what's happened. Focus is the most important thing here."

More important than human life? Keith wondered. "I'll be right with you."

"He's working on that instinct thing he's got going for him," Matt said, shrugging. "Come on, Lee, let's get started. Wonderboy will be along."

Keith waited until they walked back toward the northern shore.

And then he began to search the clearing.

Oh, yeah. He was focused.

There were certain images a man could never quite get out of his mind. Dead men. Dead friends. Friends who'd had everything in the world to live for. Young. The best of the best.

He stiffened, listening. People were coming. The island was becoming more crowded by the minute. He swore softly.

"Hey there," came a throaty, masculine voice.

A man of about sixty, followed by a petite young woman and two men about his own age, was entering the clearing.

"Hey," Keith replied, stepping forward, a smile on his face.

Ah, yes, the masses had arrived. He didn't know why he was suddenly so certain that he and his associates weren't the only ones traveling incognito.

BETH AND THE GIRLS EMERGED from the lush greenery in the center of the island to reach the beach. It was

27

beautiful. Once upon a time there had been a very small naval base on Calliope Key, a research center. It had been abandoned, but back toward the interior the ruins of the old buildings remained, allowing a safe haven of sorts if the weather turned really foul. Today, though, the sun was streaming down, a soft breeze was blowing, and the sea appeared incredibly serene.

Ben was on the beach, barefoot, in cutoffs and shades, dressed remarkably like the man who had just scared Beth. He glanced up when he saw them coming. "Back so soon? I thought you were exploring, seeing if there was anyone else around."

At thirty-four, Beth thought, her brother was in his prime. He had, however, taken the task of raising his daughter to heart. Despite the fact that he had lost his wife years ago, he was still far more prone to spend his nights at home rather than out at the boat clubs—though he did belong to Rock Reef, where she worked as a social director—seeking companionship. Beth actually wished he would be more of a sinner at times. She knew how much Amber meant to him, but she was afraid that he wasn't allowing much room in his life for the future. He had been madly in love with Amber's mom, his high-school sweetheart, and nothing had ever changed his desire to see that Amber had everything he could provide, including his company—whether she wanted it or not, since Amber had reached that age where she wanted to spend her nights prowling the malls with her friends, rather than bonding with her dad. She adored him. She was simply being a teenager.

"We *were* exploring," Beth said.

"We met a guy," Amber said.

"Wicked cute," Kimberly added.

Beth groaned.

"Wicked cute young, or wicked cute old?" Ben asked, a sparkle in his eyes.

"Wicked cute your age, or Aunt Beth's age . . . well, I don't know," Amber said. "He's not a kid, anyway."

"Ah." Ben winked at Beth. "They trying to play matchmaker?"

"I hope not," she said too sharply.

"So, he wasn't wicked cute?"

"Oh, no, he was good-looking."

"But . . . ?" Ben teased.

"Not my type," she said quickly.

Amber sighed dramatically. "The two of you are hopeless."

"He's a total stranger, and you don't go around trusting total strangers," Beth snapped.

Ben arched a brow. She tended to be the one who nagged *him* to lighten up on Amber.

"Girls, go grab the barbecue equipment, will you?" Beth asked.

"She's going to tell you about the skull," Amber said.

"Skull?" Ben had been fiddling with one of the tent poles. He went still, staring at Beth with a wary question in his eyes.

"Kim stubbed her toe on something, and . . . I think it's actually a skull," Beth said.

"Did you . . . pick it up?" Ben asked.

"No, I thought you and I should go take a look. And then, if it's what I think, radio the authorities. I didn't want to dig it up with the girls there," Beth said. She bit her lip. "Except . . . I'm not so sure we should leave them alone on the beach."

Ben shook his head. "Beth, this island has been a boaters' paradise forever."

"I know that."

"The naval base has been closed for decades— people who come here have boats and are . . . well, boat people."

"I know that, too."

"So . . . ?" he said softly.

She cleared her throat, glancing at the girls, who clearly weren't about to leave.

"Ben, damn it! Remember that couple . . . Ted and Molly Monoco?"

"What about them?" Ben asked, frowning.

"They were last seen here, on this island."

He sighed, shaking his head. "So what? They had a state-of-the-art yacht and intended to sail around the world, Beth."

"They disappeared. I heard it on the news several months ago," she responded stubbornly.

Ben let out a deep sigh. "Beth, a friend called in, worried about them, that's all. They might be any-where. The news loves to turn anything into a tragedy." He caught Amber's eyes and grimaced. "Maybe your aunt does need to meet a tall dark hunk, huh?"

"Ben!"

"He was blondish!" Amber said, laughing.

"Okay, girls, you stay here and set stuff up, and Aunt Beth and I will go check out that skull."

"I don't think we should leave them alone," Beth said.

"She's afraid of the guy we met," Amber explained.

"I'm not afraid of him," Beth protested.

"It's all right," Ben said. "I just saw Hank and Amanda Mason, and her dad and a cousin, I think. They're just down the beach. Girls, scream like hell if anyone comes near you, all right?"

Amanda Mason. Great. Normally, the concept of Amanda—who could be totally obnoxious—being around on the weekend would have bugged Beth to no end. At the moment, though, she was glad that the Masons were there on the beach.

Within screaming distance.

"You bet," Kimberly said.

"Unless it's a really hot guy with a beer," Amber said.

That brought her father spinning around.

"Just kidding!" Amber said. "Dad, I'm joking. Aunt Beth? Tell him."

"She's just teasing you, Ben. Give it a break," Beth told him.

He rolled his eyes, starting off ahead of her. "Why

does she do that to me?" he demanded.

"Because you tend to be completely paranoid, and you're on her tail like a bloodhound most of the time," Beth told him, following him through the brush, pushing palm fronds out of her way.

"Right, and you're not being just a little bit paranoid?"

"Ben, I honestly think we found a skull. I'm worried with reason. If you make Amber crazy enough, then you'll have reason to worry, too."

"You wait 'til you have kids," he warned her, stopping and turning back to her. "She's everything I've got," he said softly.

Beth nodded. "So let go a little bit."

"She's only fourteen."

"Just a little bit. Then she'll come back to you and tell you all the wild stuff going on with her friends. You've got to let her live a little."

He nodded, serious then.

They reached the clearing. It was empty.

"Okay, I don't see any guy."

"I hardly thought he would just stand around waiting," Beth said.

"All right, then. Where's the skull?"

"Right here . . . I pushed a palm frond over it."

She walked over to where they had been. Tentatively, she moved away the fallen debris.

There was nothing there. Nothing at all. It didn't even look as if the earth had been disturbed. "I . . ." She looked at her brother. He was staring at her with skepticism. "Damn it, Ben, the girls saw it, too!"

"So where is it?"

"I don't know!" She stared around the clearing. There was plenty of debris about; area storms could be fierce, blowing hard against fragile palms and pines.

But though she kicked up every inch of the clearing, dragging away every palm frond and branch she could see, there was no sign of anything that so much as resembled a skull.

Then . . .

"Aha!" she cried, and dug, only to dig up a conch shell.

"There's your skull," Ben said.

"No, this isn't it. Ben, I'm telling you, I saw a skull. And I didn't dig it up while the kids were here because it looked like there was still hair attached, even rotting flesh."

"Come on, Beth. You're too into *CSI* and *Autopsy one-two-three-four-and-up-to-fifty-or-a-hundred-or-whatever-it-is-now*. I'm heading back to the campsite."

"Ben!"

"What?" he demanded, turning back to stare at her.

"I'm telling you, there was a skull. And then there was that guy—"

"You know what, Beth? I'm a guy, a lawyer, and yes, I tend to be a little nervous because I know the kinds of people who are out there in the world. Hell, I have a gun, and I know how to use it. But think about it, Beth. You just saw the guy a few minutes ago. And what you thought was a skull had to be down to the bone."

"Not completely," she murmured, feeling a little ill.

"Beth," Ben argued, "how could a guy who just got here be responsible for a skull that may or may not exist, and, if so, is almost down to the bone? I am not going to ruin this weekend with my daughter and her friend, so please . . ."

She stood up, dusting off her hands again, lips pursed. She nodded. "I know it's the weekend. I know that it's bond-with-your-daughter time. Yes, we'll have a good time. I promise."

He started back along the trail to the beach.

Beth hesitated. She felt night coming, felt the breeze whispering through her hair.

Could she have been mistaken?

No!

Damn it! She had seen it, and it had been a skull. A human skull. So where the hell was it now?

A chill settled over her.

Had *he* taken it?

Was the skull the reason he had come to the island?

The palm fronds around her began to whisper. She turned quickly toward the trail. "Ben?"

Her brother didn't reply.

She glanced around quickly, then called out again, "Ben! Wait for me!"

With those words on her lips, she raced after him, clinging to the words he had said to her.

I have a gun, and I know how to use it.

But did he have it with him?

And what if the other guy had a gun and knew how to use it, too?

2

"THERE'S YOUR GUY," BEN SAID as they walked back onto the beach. He pointed down a stretch of sand.

And indeed, there he was. Along with two other men, one dark and Hispanic looking, the other a blazing redhead, he was securing a large tent pole in the sand. They had respected the silent privacy rule all boaters who used the island obeyed, staking out their territory a distance away from anyone else. From where they stood, Beth couldn't make out the expressions of any of the men.

The redhead stopped working, however, elbowed Keith, pointed toward them, then waved.

Ben waved in return.

"You're not waving to your new hottie," Ben teased.

"He's not *my* anything," Beth retorted.

"The girls were impressed."

"The girls are young and impressionable," she snapped.

Her brother looked at her quizzically. "What is the matter with you?"

"Nothing. It's just that, no matter what, I know I saw a skull."

"Which we couldn't find."

"No," she admitted. "But I'm telling you, there was *something* there. That guy was there, too. And now the thing isn't there, and the same guy is on the beach!"

"I can walk over and ask him if he just dug up a skull," Ben said.

She glared at him. "And if he did, he's just going to say yes?"

"Beth, what do you want me to do?" Ben demanded, shaking his head.

"Be careful."

"All right, I'll be afraid. Very afraid."

"Ben . . ."

"Beth, honestly, I'm not ignoring what you said. But don't ignore what *I* said, either. I'm capable of watching out for my own family. I never forget that I have two teenagers in my care when I take the girls out. Okay, you got spooked and you remembered that missing couple. But I read the stories, too. They wanted to explore the world, take off by themselves. They planned on an endless trip, on going wherever they chose."

"But still, they just . . . disappeared," Beth said stubbornly.

"Beth, it's legal for adults to disappear, if they want to."

"Their friends were concerned."

"Maybe they wanted an escape from their friends," Ben suggested.

"Who would do that?" Beth demanded.

"Beth, please. This is a weekend. We're here to have fun. Just let it go, okay?"

She exhaled loudly in exasperation, spinning away from him and heading toward the girls. The were studying a Hollywood-gossip magazine and seemed to have forgotten that they might have stumbled across human remains.

But Amber looked up when Beth hunched down and joined them in the little outer "room" of their tent.

"Was it a skull?" she asked.

"I don't know. It wasn't there anymore."

A strange look filtered through Amber's eyes.

"Do you think *he* took it?" Kim demanded.

"Shh," Amber commanded. "He's *here.*"

Beth's head jerked around. The man who had introduced himself as Keith Henson *was* there—standing just outside the tents, where Ben had been building a small fire to cook their evening meal.

The other two were also there: the tall, lean, redhead and the darker man with the stockier, well-muscled build.

Beth overheard introductions and realized her brother was telling Keith that she had mentioned meeting him earlier.

Beth sprang into action, hurrying out. The girls followed her quickly. More introductions were made. The other two were Lee Gomez and Matt Albright.

Keith was still wearing the sunglasses, allowing no insight to his thoughts. He was smiling, however, and Beth had to admit that he was gorgeous, with classic bone structure that also offered a solidly sculpted strength. Lee Gomez was also striking, with his dark good looks, and Matt, though freckled, gave the initial impression of the charming boy next door.

"Keith was just saying that they brought a portable grill and have enough fresh fish to feed an army," Ben said.

She stared at her brother. He wanted them to join these strangers?

"I've also made a mean potato salad," Lee offered, grinning.

"We must have something to offer, don't we?" Ben asked Beth.

"The salad," Amber answered for her. "We have chips, too, tons of soda and some beer."

"Sounds great. We're right down the beach. Hopefully the alluring aromas will bring you right over," Matt said.

"Well?" Ben asked her.

"Of course," Beth said, seeing no graceful way out of it.

"We met some other people, down the beach on the other side," Keith said. "They said they know you. They'll be joining us, too."

"Oh, the Masons," Ben said.

"That's right. The Masons are here," Beth murmured. She could see Hank's yacht, *Southern Light*, out on the water. She was a fine vessel, forty-five feet, forty years old, but her motor had been completely rebuilt and the interior redone. She was often referred to as the Grand Dame at the club.

"Actually, I'm not straight on exactly who's who yet. Except for Amanda," Keith said.

Of course he'd gotten Amanda right. She was five-five, shaped like an hourglass, with blue eyes and light blond hair. Few men ever missed Amanda.

"There's an older man," Lee said.

"Roger Mason, her dad," Beth said.

"Hank has to be here," Ben said. "Amanda's cousin. The boat's his."

"Yes, right. Hank. And the other guy is . . ."

"Probably Gerald, another cousin," Beth said. "He lives just up the coast from the rest of the family, in Boca Raton."

"So . . . they're all cousins?" Matt asked, a hopeful note in his voice.

"Hank, Amanda and Gerald are cousins—second cousins, I think," Ben said.

He hadn't seemed to notice the hope in the question. He wouldn't, Beth thought. He was always too busy being a father.

"There's a young couple camping just beyond them," Keith said. Even though Beth couldn't see his eyes, she knew he was staring straight at her. "Maybe you know *them,* too. Brad Shaw and a woman named Sandy Allison?"

She shook her head. "The names aren't familiar." Again she looked out to the water.

She had missed the fourth boat because it was anchored just beyond Hank's *Southern Light.*

The last vessel was a small pleasure craft. She looked as if she needed paint, and she probably offered no more than a small head, galley, and perhaps room enough for two to sleep in the forward section. There were lots of small boats docked at the club, and some of those—especially the motorboats—were incredibly expensive.

On the other hand, some of them weren't. One of the things Beth had always liked about working at the club was the fact that the people there were honestly dedicated to the water. They came from all life's corners, just like their boats did. The initial membership fee was steep, but after that, the annual dues were reasonable, so people from all different social strata could afford to join, once they saved up the initial investment. She was also proud that the club specialized in lessons in sailing, swimming, diving and water safety.

At the club, though, no matter how inexpensive any of their boats might be, the members, even the broke ones, took pleasure in caring for them—unlike the sad little vessel out beyond *Southern Light*.

"Four boats," Beth murmured.

"Anyway," Keith said, "we've asked everyone over to our little patch of beach."

"Great," Ben said.

"Come on over whenever you feel like it," Keith said. "We're not far," he said, indicating the short stretch of sand that separated the two camps.

"Want help?" Amber asked enthusiastically.

Beth was tempted to grasp her niece's arm.

"I think we've got it under control," Keith said gravely. "But if you need help hauling chips and salad, you let us know."

He had dimples and a pleasant way with the girls. He wasn't inappropriate or flirtatious—as some older men would have been, just nice. He should have seemed charming, Beth knew, but she was too suspicious of him for that.

"We'll see you down there in a bit," Lee said.

The three men waved and started off down the sand. Ben turned to Beth. "Feel better?" he asked her.

She stared at her brother, shaking her head.

"What? Still scared? Nothing's going to happen. Some of the other members from the yacht club will be with us," he reminded her.

Ben was a member. She was the social manager, and she loved her job and most of the members, who were always pleasant and appreciative.

Then there was Amanda.

Luckily she wasn't there on a daily—or even weekly—basis. Hank was the real boat fanatic. It had been his father who had first joined the club, which had been formed back in 1910. Originally it had been just two lifelong friends, Commodore Isaak and Vice Commodore Gleason, who had gotten together to drink and chat in their retirement. By the 1920s, there had been ten members, rising to nearly a hundred before World War II. With far too many able-bodied sailors in the navy, the facility had been used for a

41

while as rehab for returnees. The 1950s had seen a resurgence in membership, and it had become a casual place in the seventies. When the hippies became yuppies in the nineties, the price of membership had soared. At the moment, there were about two hundred members, a hundred of those with boat slips, and at least fifty who could be considered fairly active. Ben and Beth's father had been a commodore, and with his passing, Ben had taken up the family participation in the place.

Beth, with a degree in public relations, had taken a job.

Had she realized that she would be dealing with the Amandas of the world, she might have thought twice. Amanda was the type to drop a letter on her desk and, without looking at her, tell her that she needed copies. She complained at the slightest mistake made by any of the help. Two waitresses in the dining room had quit in tears after serving her.

Ben didn't jump when Amanda was around; he seemed to be immune to her wickedly sensual charm and oblivious to her frequent vicious abrasiveness.

There was no use trying to explain Amanda to her brother. He would just think it was feminine envy.

"Having them here makes everything just perfect," she assured him dully.

"Amanda," Amber said, making a face.

Ben rolled his eyes. "Is something the matter with her?" he demanded.

"Dad, she's a bitch."

"Amber!"

"It's not really a bad word," Amber said.

"Not like a four-letter word or anything," Kim added hastily.

"Beth," Ben said, "aren't you going to say something?"

She shrugged. "They're calling it as they see it," she told him.

He frowned. "I don't like that language."

"Amber, your father doesn't like that language. Please don't use it."

"All right," Amber said, "Miss Mason is a rude, manipulative snake, how's that?"

"With really big boobs," Kim added.

"Kim . . ." Ben protested.

"Sorry," Kim said, without meaning it in the least.

Ben pointed a finger sternly. "You will be polite."

"Of course," Beth said. "I mean, she's always so polite to me."

Ben groaned out loud and turned away, walking to the spot where he had pitched his own tent, his back to them. "Maybe you'll like the new people better," he said irritably over his shoulder.

She could hardly like them any less, Beth thought.

It wasn't exactly as if they were going out, but Beth chose to throw a cover-up on over her bathing suit, and the girls did likewise. They hauled their coolers with sodas and beer, and their contribution of salad and chips, down to the meeting point before any of the Mason family appeared but just after the arrival of the new couple, Sandy Allison and Brad Shaw.

She had sandy hair that matched her name and pleasant amber eyes, a medium build and was of medium height. She wore a terry cover-up and sandals, while Brad, about six feet even, with the same sandy hair but green eyes, was still in swim boxers with a cotton surf shirt over his shoulders. They were both cheerful and hailed from the West Coast, according to Brad.

"Love it here, though," he assured them. "When we're diving, I feel like I could stay down forever."

"Absolutely gorgeous," Sandy agreed, slipping an arm around his waist. "There are areas here when you can practically walk right from the beach to the reef."

"Dangerous for ships. Well, at one time," Keith put in, handing Brad a beer. "The area is very well charted now."

"Well, it *has* been a few years since the first Europeans made landfall," Beth murmured.

Keith looked sharply at her. She should have guessed. His eyes were a deep, dark, true brown, rimmed with black lashes that were striking against the light color of his hair and the bronze of his face.

"A few ships did miss those reefs," he murmured, and turned back to the men. "Lee has some equipment on his boat that would do the navy proud."

"So you're not a boater yourself, Mr. Henson?" Beth asked. She hadn't meant for it to sound as if she was heading an inquisition, but it did.

"I am. We're just here with Lee's boat," he said.

Here from where? she wondered.

She could just ask the question, of course, and immediately spoke before she could think better of it.

"So where are you three down here from?" she asked, hoping she didn't sound as suspicious as she felt.

Lee looked at Matt and Ben, then shrugged. "We're from all over, really. I was born here."

"On the island?" she teased.

"Vero Beach," he said.

"I'm your original Yankee from Boston," Matt said.

"Great city," Beth said, looking at Keith.

"Virginia," he said.

"But you must know something about these waters," Beth said. "This island isn't exactly on the tourist routes."

"I told you, I'm originally from Vero Beach," Lee reminded her. "The locals use the island a lot."

"It's our first time camping out here, though," Keith said.

"So how do you know each other?" she asked, unable to stop herself from probing. "Are you business associates?"

"Dive buddies," Keith said. "Hey, here come your friends."

Whatever her opinion of Amanda, Beth had to admit that the Masons were one attractive family. Roger was fiftysomething but had the build of an athlete, and, so she had heard, competed with the young studs at the nightclubs on the beach. Hank was blond and blue-eyed, like his cousin, but he was all man, with a broad bronzed chest and shoulders. Gerald was a shade darker, but obviously a family member.

"Ben!" Amanda cried, sounding as delighted as if she'd met a long-lost relative. She hadn't bothered with a cover-up and was clad in only a small bikini.

A string bikini at that.

Her hair was loose and falling around her shoulders in a perfect golden cloak.

"She's indecent," Amber whispered from behind Beth.

"Totally," Kim agreed.

"She does it awfully well," Beth murmured, watching the woman.

While Amanda was greeting Ben, Hank looked over her head and saw Beth and the girls. He offered a real smile. "Hey there."

"Hi, Hank," Beth called.

"Hey, you remember our cousin Gerald, right?" Amanda said.

"Absolutely." By then the two men had walked over to her. Hank gave her a kiss on the cheek and greeted the two girls. Gerald took her hand. "Small world, huh?"

"Not really, considering how close we are to home," she told him.

"True," he said with a laugh, then turned to the girls. "Amber, if you get any taller, you'll be giving me a run for the money. And . . . don't tell me, it's . . . Kimmy, right?"

"Kim," the girl corrected.

"Kim," he agreed. She blushed slightly. He was nice, not condescending, and it was apparently appreciated.

"Fish all right for everyone?" Keith called out. "We've got hot dogs and hamburger patties, as well, for any landlubbers."

"I'd love a hot dog," Kim called out, hurrying toward the barbecue. A pleasant aroma was already beginning to emanate from the portable cooker. Amber followed her friend, leaving Beth behind with the other adults.

"Beth, how nice to see you here," Amanda said. She walked over, perfect smile in place. "You have the weekend off?" she asked politely, as if surprised.

"Hello, Amanda. Yes, I have the weekend off."

Amanda looked disapproving. "I would have thought they really needed you, what with the tourists and all. I suppose the club really does run itself. Still, I'm surprised the commodore didn't want your lovely face around."

"I'm sure he can manage on his own for a few days," Beth said sweetly. "Have you met Sandy and Brad?"

"Briefly," Amanda said, turning.

It was enough for Beth.

She escaped.

To get anywhere, though, she had to pass the barbecue, since the three men had their tents set up in the other direction, and if she made a point of going around the barbecue, she would be heading inland, into the dense foliage, rather than along the sand.

She had nearly made it past when Amber caught her arm. "Aunt Beth, come see. Everything looks perfect!"

She smiled weakly as Keith expertly flipped a fillet, then shook a mixture of seasonings onto it.

"That looks great," Amber told him, though her enthusiasm sounded forced.

"Are you sure you wouldn't rather have a hot dog, like Kim?" He laughed at her grateful expression and put another hot dog on the grill.

"You guys are ready for all occasions," Beth murmured. She was wedged between her niece and Keith Henson. They were almost touching. Almost. Not quite.

"Well, it's not that I can't—we can't—rough it, but a few conveniences are nice," he said. He looked at her. The sun was slipping lower toward the horizon, and in the deepening shadows, his eyes seemed darker than ever. She felt as if he was staring at her with the same suspicion she felt for him.

"We have two-bedroom tents!" Amber said.

"I'm not really sure you could call them bedrooms," Beth murmured.

"Well, I only have a one-bedroom tent," Keith said. "But it's still a convenience when it rains. What I really like is just to sleep on the sand and stare up at the stars."

"Yeah, that's cool," Amber agreed.

"I think your dad wants you in the tent tonight," Beth said, once again afraid her words sounded sharper than she'd intended.

She saw Keith's lips tighten as he tried to hide a smile. Yes, she was definitely on edge, and it was showing.

"Amber?" Ben called, and she scampered off, Kim following in her wake.

"So, have you got padlocks on those tents?" Keith asked.

She flushed, but stared defiantly back at him. "You're strangers," she said, feeling that no other explanation was needed.

The smile he had been hiding turned into a deep grin that brought out his dimples once again. "So are Brad and Sandy."

"They're not three guys."

"Are you sure we're not going to poison the fish?" he asked.

"I hadn't thought of it," she admitted, but stared at him with a grim smile. "Maybe I should have."

"Ouch. That's a challenge. I can take a bite of yours first, if you want."

"I'll live dangerously."

He looked out across the sand, then at her. "Do you come here often?"

"Yes. Well, usually. Not this year. This is the first time this year." She didn't know why she was stumbling around to explain. She didn't owe him any explanations. She kept talking anyway. "We spent our vacation in the Bahamas this year. This used to be the last weekend of summer vacation. Now, the girls have already been back at school for a few weeks. And for Christmas, we all went to Denver. Even though it's so close, this is the first time we've been out here this year. And you?"

"I've dived the area dozens of times," he said, turning his attention to the fish once again. "But there was never really any reason to stop at the island."

"I thought Lee was the one who knew the area," she reminded him sharply.

He smiled. "Lee knows it best. But I *have* been here before. Just not to this island."

"So why now?" she demanded.

He arched a brow. He was answering slowly, she thought. Too slowly. "Well . . ." He laughed. "Because it's here, I guess."

"So you're really here for the diving? Not the fishing?"

"Obviously we've been fishing." He smiled and nodded toward the grill.

"But you're mainly here to dive."

"Has it suddenly become illegal?" he queried, laughter in his eyes again.

"Of course not."

"I love diving here," he told her, and she felt that he was being totally honest at that moment. Actually, she couldn't think of anything he'd said that hadn't sounded honest. Was she being ridiculously suspicious? Even if she had seen a skull, Ben was right.

There was no reason to suspect that a man appearing *then* would have anything to do with a skull that had been on the beach for days, maybe longer. So why was she so suspicious?

Because he frightened her in too many ways?

"Excuse me. I think I'll get a beer," she murmured, slipping past him, but she intended a smooth exit. She stepped a little too quickly and a little too close. She felt the tension in his muscles, then nearly careened sideways into him.

"Excuse me," she murmured again, afraid she was blushing. She hurried away and walked right past the cooler, then remembered she had said she was going for a beer. She quickly secured one, then went to stand by her brother's side.

Sandy and Brad were telling stories about diving the Great Barrier Reef. She had to admit that she'd never been.

Amanda, however, could agree with them on the beauty of the dive.

"Such a long flight, though," Sandy said.

"Oh, it was really a lovely jaunt for me," Amanda gushed. "We went with some of Father's associates, sailed for months and saw zillions of islands, and then went on to Australia. The week in Fiji was my favorite, I think. Though Tahiti was fabulous, too. We had such a darling little place there. While the yacht was being cleaned, we had charming and very private rooms right on the beach. The sunrises were exquisite, the sunsets even more so."

"Hey, all we have to do is step out of our tents tomorrow morning for the same effect," Keith said, arriving with a large plate of grilled fish. "There are some fantastic sunrises right here." He offered Amanda a broad smile. Flirtatious? Or intended to take some of the sting out of his reminder that their own home offered a world-class beauty.

"Oh, yes, this area is fabulous, as well." Amanda smiled meaningfully at Beth. "Especially when you really can't go anywhere else."

Beth smiled back, all the while envisioning dumping the ice in the cooler over the woman's head.

"Soup's on!" Matt announced cheerfully.

There were a few camp chairs, and Matt had spread blankets out on the sand. A looped palm offered a few seats perfectly created by nature, and with her plate filled with fish and potato salad, Beth found herself claiming the tree as a chair. Hank took the seat next to her, but when Amanda called to him, begging him to get her something to drink, he left, and she found herself being joined by Keith. She wondered if he was seeking her out on purpose. And then she wondered why. She didn't have a lack of confidence, it was just that . . . well, Amanda Mason was there, and she was the far better flirt, on top of being an undeniably alluring woman.

"So you work for a yacht club?" Keith asked.

"Yes." She waved a hand in the air. "*I* work for it. *They* belong to it."

He laughed. "Are you supposed to be the poor little

rich girl or something?"

She shook her head, looking at him. "I like working there. It's fun." She hesitated, wondering why she kept feeling compelled to explain things to him. "My brother is a member, so if I weren't working there, I'd have all his privileges. Working there pays well, and I get free dockage, which Ben uses, since employees get that perk and members don't, and he owns a boat and I don't. I see some of the most luxurious and beautiful yachts in the world. And meet some of the nicest people. Mostly."

"Mostly?" He offered her a slow, wry smile.

"Mostly," she repeated, refusing to say more. Had the tension in her relationship with Amanda been so evident to a stranger?

"It's always interesting when you get around boats," he said. "Some people are as rich as Croesus and you'd never know it, they're just so down to earth. Some are as poor as church mice, putting everything they have into staying on the water. And they're just as nice. But don't ever kid yourself. The sea can breed demons."

She looked up at him, startled, but he was rising, looking toward the group that had drawn around the fire.

Had he been warning her about something?

Maybe himself?

The light had faded in earnest. No more deep blues, purples, streaks of gold or any other color. Night had come.

In the far distance, a faint glow could be seen, coming from the lights along the heavily populated coast of south Florida. But on the island, there was nothing except for the glow from the fire. Around them, the foliage of the inner island had become blanketed in shadows.

The wind stirred, creating a rustle.

"The girls want to hear some ghost stories," Lee called out to Keith.

"I said pirate stories," Amber said, laughing.

"Pirates would be ghosts, by now," Ben told his daughter, amused.

"Most of the time," Keith said, moving toward the fire. "Except that there *are* modern-day pirates. All over the world."

"Too real," Amanda protested with a shiver. Of course, she was still clad in nothing but the skinny bathing suit. Sure, they were on a semitropical island. But the sea breezes at night could be cool.

Keith noticed her discomfort. He slipped off his shirt and draped it around her shoulders. She flashed him a beautiful smile. He smiled back.

It was a simple gesture of courtesy, but it made Beth lower her head, wondering how she could allow someone like Amanda to irritate her so much.

"Okay, so we want an old-fashioned pirate ghost story, right?" Keith asked. He didn't remain behind Amanda but strode toward the center of the group, closer to the fire. He hunkered down by the flames, forcing Beth to wonder if he was aware that the flames added a haunting quality to his classic features.

"I'll tell you the tale of the *Sea Star* and *La Doña*. Both were proud ships with billowing white sails! But one was English, and the other sailed under the flag of Spain. The *Sea Star* sailed from London in the year of our Lord 1725. Her captain was a fierce man, loyal to the core to the king. England and Spain were hardly on the best of terms, and Jonathan Pierce, the captain, was eager to seize a Spanish ship full of gold from the New World.

"Captain Pierce, however, wasn't sailing alone. Along with his crew, he was carrying a party of nobility. One of them was the Lady Marianne Howe, daughter of the governor of one of the small islands, and he was unaware that a year earlier, her ship had run aground on coral shoals and she'd been saved by a handsome young Spaniard, Alonzo Jimenez. Of course, under the circumstances, despite the fact that the young Spaniard and his crew had simply returned the Englishmen and women he had rescued to the governor in Virginia—asking no ransom, no reward, and ignoring the hostilities between the countries—there could be no happy ending for Marianne and Alonzo. Not only was he a Spaniard, but an untitled one, at that.

"Still, Marianne had managed to keep in contact with him, smuggling out love letters. She was ready to cast aside her title, her fortune and her family, all for Alonzo. He had arranged to hide his ship here, around the curve of Calliope Key—"

"Calliope Key?" Kim interrupted. "Where we are now?"

"Of course. What good would a ghost story be if it weren't about this island?" Keith asked, smiling slightly.

His voice was perfect for the tale, Beth thought. It was a rich, deep voice. She had to admit that she was as seduced as the others.

"Oh, right," Amber murmured.

Beth looked at her niece with a certain amusement. Amber was—and always had been—capable of sitting through the scariest horror movie. Now, however, her eyes were very wide.

Keith Henson—whatever he was really up to—had a talent for storytelling. With the strange fire glow on his face and the deep, intense rasp of his voice, he held them all enthralled.

"Go on," Ben said, his profound interest surprising Beth.

"Well, the young lovers never intended harm toward anyone. Marianne was a strong swimmer. She simply meant to get close enough to her lover's ship to escape into the sea, then find refuge on the island until he could come to her. With any luck, the *Sea Star* would have been long gone before anyone noticed she wasn't aboard.

"But while Marianne was conducting her daring escape into the sea, Captain Pierce was sending spies out in his small boats to get the lay of the land—well, the sea. Just as Marianne was reaching shore, news reached Pierce about the Spaniard hiding past the reefs. He manned his guns. Meanwhile, Alonzo had taken a boat to shore . . . this shore, right here, where our fire now burns. Just as he and Marianne met, the first cannons exploded. It was a fierce battle, and Alonzo was brokenhearted, watching his friends lead the fight . . . and die. His ship, *La Doña*, was sunk. Many of his men tried to swim to shore but were cut down by the English before they could reach landfall. Marianne was desperate that her lover not be caught, but Alonzo was brave to a fault. When Captain Pierce came ashore, following the Spanish crew, he prepared to fight. Their swords clashed so hotly that sparks flew. Then Captain Pierce was unarmed. He had lost the fight. Alonzo, however, refused to deliver the *coup de grâce*. He stepped back, and said that all he wanted was a small boat for himself and Marianne. Captain Pierce showed no gratitude for the fact that his life had been spared. His men came upon them, and he ordered that Alonzo should hang. Marianne was hysterical, heartbroken, and ashamed that her countryman could behave with so little honor. As Alonzo was dragged away, Pierce assured her that she would forget their enemy, and that he would be her new lover and her husband. Marianne wiped away her tears and approached him, and no doubt Captain Pierce assumed she was ready to accept his offer. But she reached into his belt and drew his pistol. She shot him dead, but too late to save her lover, for even as the shot rang out, Alonzo swung from the hangman's rope, crying out her name and his love—right before his neck snapped. Marianne, desperate in her grief, turned the gun on herself.

"And as that shot went off, the *Sea Star* suddenly moved . . . drifting out to sea. The Englishmen on the island, stunned and frozen by what had occurred before their eyes, moved too slowly. They raced for their longboats and made to sea. But neither they nor the *Sea Star* were ever seen again. Sometimes, they say, at night, the ship can be seen, riding the wind and the waves, only to disappear into the clouds or over the horizon."

"Oh . . ." Sandy breathed.

"And what about Marianne, Alonzo and Captain Pierce?" Amber asked.

"They haunt the island, of course," Keith said. "At night, when you hear whispering in the breeze, when the palm fronds move, when the wind moans . . . what you hear is their voices as they roam the island for eternity."

"Oh, jeez," Kim groaned.

"Oh . . ." Amber breathed.

Keith looked at Ben apologetically, afraid that his story had been too effective.

"You're not scared, are you?" Kim demanded.

"Of course not," Amber protested. She laughed, but it was a brittle sound. "Don't be silly. Sandy, you're not scared, are you?"

"About staying on a haunted island?" Sandy asked. "No. I mean, the tents are all pretty close together on

58

the beach when you think about it, right? Of course, I do wish Brad and I were one of the groups in the middle."

"I'm sure we're just fine," Amanda said.

"I think it will be fun," Brad teased. "Sandy's going to be all cuddly tonight, I assure you."

"Oh, my God!" Amber exclaimed.

"What?" Ben demanded.

"Dad . . . we might have found one of them today. One of the ghosts!"

"It's just a story," Keith said. "You asked for a ghost story and—"

"No, no, there was a skull. At least . . . we thought it was a skull," Amber said.

Ben groaned loudly. "Girls, one of you stubbed a toe on a conch shell. There was no skull. Enough with the scary talk, okay?" he said firmly.

Beth kept her mouth shut, wincing. And not because Ben was annoyed, but because she was suddenly more frightened than ever herself. The girls had just let everyone know they had seen a skull.

And someone here, someone sharing thc island with them, had taken that skull for reasons of their own. Reasons that couldn't be ignored.

"It's easy to imagine things out here," Matt said easily. "I promise you, there are no ghosts here."

"But lots of ghost stories supposedly have some truth to them. There were shipwrecks all around here. I'll bet the story is true, and that the ghosts whispered it in your ear," Amber said.

"Okay, that's a scary thought!" Sandy said, shivering.

"It's getting better and better for me, girls. Please, go on," Brad said, laughing, but also trying to ease the fear the girls seemed to feel.

"We're in the Bermuda Triangle, too, aren't we?" Amanda asked, rising. "Luckily, I don't have a superstitious bone in my body." She stretched, and Keith's shirt fell from her shoulders. She reached down languidly to pick it up and slowly walked—or sashayed—over to Keith to return it. "Besides," she said softly, "there are a lot of handsome, well-muscled men around here to protect us if we need it. Well, good night, all."

Her cousins and father rose to join her, saying their thank-yous as they rose.

The group began to break up, everyone laughing, promising to see each other in the morning.

As they returned to their tents, Beth was silent.

"Aunt Beth, are you afraid of ghosts?" Amber asked.

"No," she assured her niece.

"Then what are you afraid of?" Amber persisted.

Beth glanced self-consciously over at Ben. "The living," she said softly.

Her brother sighed, shaking his head. "Just like good old Captain Pierce, I carry a gun. And I won't let anyone close enough to use it against me," he assured her.

A few minutes later they had all retired, Ben and

Beth to their "one-bedroom" tents and the girls to the large "two-bedroom" Ben had recently purchased for his daughter. None of them were more than ten feet apart, with the girls situated between the adults.

Amber and Kim kept a light on, and Beth found herself hoping their supply of batteries would be sufficient. She could hear the girls giggling, probably inventing ghost stories. She told herself that people were simply susceptible to the dark, to shadows, whispers on the breeze, and the dark intent of a tale told by firelight.

But she was uneasy herself. She reminded herself that she had been uneasy long before Keith's ghost story.

It's just a story, he'd said. A good story, told on the spur of the moment.

And it hadn't scared her. Not a silly—even sad—ghost story.

Yet . . . she *was* scared.

Despite her unease, she eventually drifted off to sleep. Her dreams were disjointed, snatches of conversation, visions that seemed to dance before her, never really taking shape until she saw, in her mind's eye, a beautiful young girl in eighteenth-century dress, a handsome Spaniard and a sea captain, sword in hand. . . .

The sea captain—arresting, exciting, masculine—took on the appearance of someone familiar . . . Keith Henson.

Sadly, even in her dream, the beautiful young girl

looked like Amanda.

She tossed and turned as the dream unfolded, more like a play with the director continually calling, "Cut!" than a real dream.

And then she heard the wind rise, a rustling in the brush . . .

She awakened, a sense of panic taking hold of her. Her palms were clammy, her limbs icy.

It was just a nightmare, she told herself.

Except it wasn't just a nightmare.

Nearby, the foliage was rustling. Someone was creeping about in the stygian darkness.

Pirates had definitely frequented this area, once upon a time.

Spanish galleons *had* carried gold.

Had Keith truly only been telling a tall tale?

Because human nature never changed. Piracy still existed. She wasn't frightened by anything sad that might have occurred in the past, because the present could be frightening enough.

Someone was out there. Not a ghost.

Someone very much alive.

3

NIGHT MOVES.

He had expected them.

Someone on the island was playing games.

Innocent games? Searching for legends?

Or games with far more deadly intent?

Keith rose silently and waited just inside his tent, listening, trying to determine from which direction the noises were coming. There was a breeze, so the trees continued to rustle. But he had heard far more than the subtle movement of the palm fronds in the soft, natural wind of the night.

Whoever it was, they had slipped across the sand and into the dense foliage of the interior.

Looking for a skull?

Or was there something more, something entirely different, going on? Perhaps he shouldn't have told his ghost story. But he had told it on purpose, watching the others closely for their reactions. In the end, though, he'd learned nothing except that everyone seemed awfully easy to spook.

But had he caused this movement in the night?

He eased slowly, silently, from the tent and started across the white sand. Just ahead, barely discernible, the rustling sound came again.

Suddenly there was a light ahead, as if whoever was there felt they had gone far enough not to be noticed.

With the appearance of the light, he knew for certain he wasn't chasing some nocturnal animal through the trees.

He followed, quickening his pace as he left the beach behind.

FEAR KEPT BETH DEAD STILL for several seconds until

her instinct to protect the girls rose to the fore.

She almost burst from the tent, to find . . .

Nothing. Nothing but the sea by night, the soft sound of the gentle waves washing the shore, a nearby palm bent ever so slightly in homage to the breeze.

She went still, looking around, listening.

Still nothing. She told herself she needed to get a grip. She had never been the cowardly type, and stories were just that: stories. There were real dangers in life, but she had always dealt with them. She didn't walk through dangerous neighborhoods alone at night. She carried pepper spray, and she'd learned how to use it. She even knew how to shoot, since their friends included several cops, who'd taken her to the shooting range and taught her how to handle a gun, though she didn't choose to keep one, since her house had an alarm system.

So why was she panicking?

Because in her heart of hearts, no matter what anyone said, she was certain she had seen a skull. And it hadn't belonged to any long-dead pirate.

No one nearby, no sounds now. She still had to check on the girls.

First she looked down the beach. All the fires were out, and she could see the tents, silent in the night. Keith and his buddies had tied a hammock to a couple of palms, where it swung ever so slightly in the breeze. Down from them, another group of tents, and farther still, a larger tent, all of them quiet and dark.

She hurried over to the girls' tent and looked in, her heart in her throat. But both of them were in the second of the two little rooms, and they were soundly sleeping. Their light was still on, turning their small bedroom into an oasis and everything around it into a black hole.

She exhaled in relief and started backing out—straight into something solid, large.

In her, terror rose and she screamed.

KEITH HEARD THE SCREAM and froze, his blood congealing at the terror in that shrill sound.

In a split second, he was back in action.

The scream had come from the beach.

Beth!

The light ahead went out, but he ignored it and turned, tearing through the brush, desperate to reach her.

SHE LET OUT A SECOND, terrified scream; then she swung around, ready to fight to the death on behalf of the girls.

There was no need.

"Dammit, Beth," a voice swore fiercely in the night. "What the hell are you doing?"

She blinked, drawing back with just seconds to spare before giving her brother a black eye.

"Ben?"

"Who the hell did you expect?"

"You scared me to death," she accused him.

"What's going on?" Amber asked nervously, rubbing sleep from her eyes as she crawled from the bedroom.

Kim followed, and the four of them wound up in the small outer room of the tent, tripping over one another.

"Nothing," Ben said irritably.

Just then, as Amber tried to stand, she bumped one of the poles and the tent collapsed on them.

Ben tried never to swear around his daughter, but tangled in the nylon, tasting sand, Beth could hear him breaking his rule beneath his breath.

"It's all right. The tent just fell," she heard herself protesting.

But when she twisted to free herself, she only became more entangled.

Then the fabric was lifted from her, and, looking up, she saw the face of Keith Henson, tense and taut as he stared down at her.

"What the hell is going on?" he demanded curtly.

"Nothing," she snapped.

"You screamed."

By then Ben had managed to escape the mess of poles and nylon and make it to his feet. He was shaking his head disgustedly.

"Sorry, everyone."

When she looked around, still on her back, she saw that everyone was there, flashlights shining. Had she really screamed that loudly?

Well, of course she had.

And she was still flat on her back in an oversize T-shirt riding up her thighs, staring up at everyone. Just as the thought occurred to her, Keith reached a hand down to her. At that particular moment, she didn't think twice about accepting it.

His grip was powerful. She was on her feet before she knew it.

"What is going on?" Amanda demanded, swiping back an errant piece of blond hair. Even at night, Beth noticed dejectedly, Amanda looked great. Like a soap-opera character who awoke in the morning with perfect makeup and shiny teeth.

"Are you all right?" Hank asked, polite as always.

Roger, definitely the oldest in the crowd, set an arm on his daughter's shoulder and looked over at Beth, smiling, as well. "Maybe we should avoid ghost stories at night," he said easily.

She tried to smile. And then apologize. "I'm really sorry. I woke up, and went to check on the girls. And then, backing out, I ran into my brother, who was apparently checking on why I was checking on the girls. There were too many of us in too small a space. I guess I woke everyone. I'm sorry." Except, of course, she was certain that she hadn't awakened *everyone.*

Someone had already been up and creeping around the island.

Who?

It was impossible now to tell, because all of them were there. Staring at her.

Amber started to giggle. Beth stared at her, brows raised.

"Oh, Aunt Beth, I'm sorry, but it *is* funny."

"Yeah, a real hoot," Ben muttered.

"Hey, let's just get the tent back up, huh?" Keith suggested.

Kim stared at him, obviously fascinated. "Oh, sure, thanks."

"I can manage—" Beth began.

"Take the help when it's offered, honey. Then maybe we can all get some sleep." For once Amanda spoke without malice. There was even a teasing tone to her words.

Ben smiled. "Keith, if you'll give me a hand, we'll have this back up in two minutes." He cleared his throat. "Beth, you're in the way."

"Excuse me."

"Me, too," Amanda said, and yawned. "I'm going back to bed. Dad, want to walk me back? Hank? Gerald?"

"If you guys are all set, we'll go catch a little more sleep, too," Sandy said.

"We're fine. Good night all," Ben told them.

Once again they parted for the night. Or what was left of it. Glancing at her watch, Beth saw that it was around four in the morning.

The girls' tent was quickly repositioned, and their group, too, was ready to try for a few more hours of sleep.

Ben thanked Keith, as did the girls. "Hey, Aunt

Beth. You could bring your sleeping bag in here, and then you wouldn't have to worry about us," Amber said.

"I'll give you guys your privacy," Beth told her, smiling.

Keith was staring at her, his gaze intent, as if he was trying to read something in her expression.

Then he smiled easily, without suspicion. "You all right?"

"Yes, fine."

"I'm sorry if I scared you with my story."

"Don't be ridiculous. I'm not afraid of ghosts." She couldn't help the feeling that her eyes were narrowing. And she wondered if he realized she was telling him that she *was* scared, but not of any story—of him.

"Well, then, good night."

With a wave, he started off for his own tent.

"Girls, go to bed," Ben said firmly.

"Good night," Amber said.

"Good night," Kim echoed.

They went into their tent again. Beth winced as she heard them giggling.

"Beth, what the hell was going on?" Ben demanded.

She sighed. "I heard a noise. I was worried about the girls."

He let out a sigh. "What's the matter with you? You never used to be paranoid."

"I'm not paranoid."

"Listen, Beth, we're surrounded by people here, half of the people we know. Nothing is going to happen."

"You scared me," she protested. "Creeping up behind me like that. You might have made yourself known."

"I didn't know who you were," he told her.

"Aha!" Beth declared. "You *were* worried. Admit it."

He sighed. "Beth, nothing's going to happen," he responded. "Trust me, huh?"

"I do trust you," she told him.

"Then act like it."

"Okay."

"Can we go to sleep now?" he asked hopefully.

"Yes."

"Okay. Good night."

"Good night."

Beth realized that he was waiting for her to be safely tucked back into bed. She smiled and nodded ruefully, then crawled back into her own tent and into her sleeping bag, where she lay staring at the fabric above her in the deep darkness of the night.

She rolled over. It was better in that direction—the girls were still sleeping with the little lantern flashlight on.

She tried to close her eyes and sleep.

She had heard something.

Or had she? Maybe it *had* been only the natural rustling of the wind in the leaves. Had she simply made up something in her mind, and become truly paranoid?

Or, on the other hand, was she just being sensible?

Trust me. . . .

She did trust her brother. He would gladly die for his daughter, she knew, and would probably do the same for her, and for Kim.

She just hoped to hell he was never called upon to do so.

She tossed again, yearning to go to sleep.

It was a long time coming.

AMANDA MASON WAS DEFINITELY a flirt. She made a point of crashing into one of the guys every time she hit the ball.

Usually himself, Keith decided wryly. He wasn't letting it get to his ego, since she also liked to tease Lee—she'd seen the boat, and they'd all said it was his. She didn't much mind brushing against Brad, either, even though he was here with his girlfriend. But so far, no one had taken their makeshift volleyball game too seriously. So far, everyone was laughing.

He, Amanda, Brad, Lee and Kim were one team. Sandy, Amber, Gerald, Matt and Ben made up the other. Roger Mason sat on the sidelines, being the ref.

So far today, they hadn't even seen Ms. Beth Anderson.

"Outside!" Matt yelled in protest of Keith's serve.

"It was not outside—you just missed it," he returned.

"Where's our referee?" Matt demanded.

"Sleeping, despite the noise," Amanda said, chuckling affectionately as she pointed to her father.

It was true. Roger had leaned back in the hammock and gone straight to sleep.

"It was definitely outside," came a voice.

Keith spun around. She was up at last, yawning despite her late appearance. She held a cup of coffee. Sunglasses covered her unique marble-toned eyes, and she was in a bathing-suit top and chopped-off Levi's pedal pushers.

His serve hadn't been outside, and if she had been watching, she had seen that. He wondered why she had decided that they were enemies from the first moment she had seen him.

Other than the fact that she'd been trying desperately to hide her discovery from him.

He forced a smile. "Hey, Matt, the lady says you're right."

"Beth Anderson, you're blind!" Amanda protested irritably.

"It's just a game, isn't it?" Beth asked politely.

"I'm going to have to speak to the commodore and make sure you don't ref any games at the club," Amanda said, a teasing note in her voice that was meant to hide her still-obvious dislike.

Beth managed an icy smile and an easy laugh. "You do that, Amanda," she said.

"Aunt Beth, come play," Amber urged.

"I think I like Roger's idea best," she said.

"Sure—wake the rest of us up in the middle of the night and then sleep all day," Matt teased. "I don't think so."

"No, of course not, come play," Hank urged. "And you can ref my game any old day," he teased.

"Come on, Beth, play," Ben urged.

"I'd make the teams uneven," she protested.

Roger, who had appeared to be so peacefully sleeping, rose. "I'll join in and make it even," he offered.

He walked past Beth, smiling. "Fifty-eight, and I guarantee I can take on you kids."

It was interesting, watching the group dynamics, Keith thought. Everyone seemed to get along fine except for Amanda and Beth.

Was Beth jealous?

Or was it vice versa? Amanda was petite, ultrafeminine. Beth seemed . . .

Elegant, he found himself thinking. A strange adjective, since she was in beachwear, as casual as any of them.

The teams readjusted. Beth took the serve.

It was wicked.

From the rear corner, he barely returned it. Ben caught the ball, and Roger, bless him, attempted a slam. Amazingly, Beth caught it low, setting it up for her brother, who went in for the kill.

"Point," Beth said calmly, reclaiming the ball.

The game was neck and neck from then on. Sandy was the weakest link, but she made up for it with her good humor and refusal to give up.

Beth was a superb player, in excellent physical condition. She wasn't just shapely, she was sleek. Perfectly toned. She played not so much to win as simply to play hard. There was a vibrance about her, a love of life, of activity, a passion that seemed to come through in everything she did and said, in the way her eyes seemed to burn like a crystal fire when they met his across the net. She clearly loved a challenge.

He had the feeling she would always meet one head-on.

At last Beth's team took the final point, and they all collapsed, laughing.

"What's up next?" Hank asked, lying flat on the sand in exhaustion.

Lee was up and staring at Keith. "Fishing?" he suggested.

"Yeah, fishing," Keith replied.

They were fishing, all right.

"Not me, boys. I'm for lazing in the sun now," Amanda said, rolling sinuously to her feet.

Ben nodded toward Lee's yacht. "You asking us out on that?"

"Would you like to see her?" Lee offered.

Keith looked at Lee and knew just what he was thinking. Keep the current denizens of the island with them, occupied. Keep an eye on them. Know what they're up to at all times.

Keep them fishing, not diving.

He stayed silent. In the end, there wasn't anything they could do about people diving these waters. Still, if discoveries here had been easy . . . well, they wouldn't be here now.

"You bet," Ben said enthusiastically. "Looks as if she's got every new electronic device known to man."

"I like my toys," Lee said with a shrug.

"I'm with you," Ben said.

"Hell, I'd like to see her, too," Hank said, grinning.

"Me, too," Gerald agreed.

"Little boys, little toys, big boys, big toys," Amanda teased.

"Me, I'd like to see the hammock again," Roger said.

"I think Sandy and I are going to take a walk, explore . . ." Brad said. "But thanks for the offer."

"Beth?" Lee inquired. "Girls?"

"I'd love to see the boat," Amber said.

"Yacht," Beth murmured beneath her breath.

"But actually," Amber admitted a little sheepishly, "I hate fishing."

"That's cool," Lee told her.

"Beth?"

"I'll stay with the girls," she said. "But I do appreciate the offer."

"You don't care if I go?" Ben asked his sister.

"Not at all!"

But she did. She cared like hell.

"Maybe I will join you men," Amanda said with something like a purr. "The sun is actually much better on the water. And I can always escape below if all the testosterone proves to be a bit too much. I'll just get my things." She started to walk away, then turned back. "I am not, however, cleaning any fish."

Keith watched her sashay toward her tent.

When he turned to study Beth again, she was studying him. The way she was looking at him caused a little pang to creep into his heart.

She was so suspicious of him.

Well, she had every right to be.

But this was a game he played often. And he knew how to play it.

And he knew damn well that he couldn't let her get in his way.

Her eyes swept over him. Cool. Still assessing him.

Then she turned.

He had been dismissed.

BETH WAS DEFINITELY ANGRY with Ben, although she wasn't sure he knew it. And she wasn't about to lash out at him in public—certainly not with the public that was surrounding them.

He was so big about protecting his family, but show the guy a new yacht with all kinds of cool toys, and he was gone in a flash.

To be fair, he thought she was being paranoid and there was nothing to protect his family from. Maybe she couldn't blame him. There had been nothing in the inland clearing, and last night she had awakened the entire island by screaming because she had run into him.

At this point she wasn't even sure herself just what she had seen. Maybe it had been a conch shell, and what she had imagined, in a stomach-churning moment, to be human tissue only sea grass and debris.

It was so easy to question oneself, especially in the bright light of day. Except that the afternoon was waning.

Sitting on the beach with the girls, she looked out to sea. The dinghies were long gone, bearing the fishermen—and woman—out to sea. Roger was sleeping in the hammock. Brad and Sandy were laughing, and running in and out of the waves, being romantic, being a couple.

Good for them. It seemed odd that they were the only couple among the groups. That Amanda had come on a family outing seemed amazing to Beth, but then, she disliked the woman. Roger and Hank were always decent enough, and though she really didn't know Gerald well, he seemed okay, as well. Was she jealous of Amanda? She probed her own psyche in a moment of introspection.

No. She really, truly simply disliked her. And she really, truly liked most people.

So that, she decided with a wry grin, really, truly made Amanda a bitch.

"Aunt Beth, what are you smirking at?"

"I am not smirking," she protested, turning to her niece. "I'm just . . . smiling at the day."

"It really is a cool weekend, huh?" Kim said, looking up from her star-studded magazine. "I was afraid of being bored, but . . . well, those guys are cool."

"Those guys are way too old for you two," Beth said sharply.

"Aunt Beth," Amber groaned. "We know that. Can't they just be nice guys?"

"We really don't know them," Beth reminded them.

"You sound like a schoolteacher."

"Right, well, schoolteachers teach you things you need to know."

Beth stood up, stretching, eyeing the water again. Lee's yacht was almost out of sight. Brad and Sandy were still happily cavorting. Roger was sleeping.

She hesitated, looking at Amber and Kim, and then she headed for her tent. Returning, she dropped the little black pepper-spray container on the towel next to Amber. "If anyone comes near you, you know what to do."

Amber looked at the pepper spray, then up at her. "Really, Aunt Beth. Are you expecting a giant grouper to leap out of the sea and accost us?"

"Don't be a wiseass. Wiseacre," she quickly amended. But not quickly enough. Both the girls were laughing at her.

"Amber, Kim, I'm serious."

Amber forced herself to look somber. "We're taking you very seriously."

Beth really didn't think there could be any trouble, not with the yacht out at sea. She offered a dry smile and started to walk away.

"Hey," Amber called. "Where are you going?"

"For a walk."

"You're going back to look for the skull, right?" Amber pressed.

"No." She stepped back toward them. "And don't go talking about the fact that we might have seen a skull, do you understand?"

Amber let out a great sigh. "No, Aunt Beth. I mean, yes. We won't mention it again, okay?"

"Good. And scream like hell if anything happens."

"Like you did last night?" Amber teased.

"Behave or I'll tell your dad that every young guy in the theater department *isn't* gay!"

"Hey, have a great walk, Beth. We'll be little angels, sitting here. Ready with the pepper spray," Kim vowed seriously.

Shaking her head, Beth started off.

The island was such a strange paradise, she thought, heading toward the path through the pines and scrub brush just behind the area they had chosen to stake out their tents. The beach was pristine, the water clear and beautiful. Of course, just beyond there were dangerous, even deadly, reefs. But those who knew the area and could navigate those reefs knew how to reach a real Eden. But behind the beach, the island became a very different place, the dense foliage creating little nooks and crannies, shadows and an eerie green darkness.

She had always loved it.

Until now.

Today it seemed the island itself was working against her. She lost the trail and almost emerged at the other end of the beach. Retracing her steps, she swore softly.

A large mosquito decided to take a good chunk out of her arm, and she slapped it furiously, taking inordinate pleasure out of the fact that she managed to kill it.

At last she wound her way back to the clearing where she had stood the day before with the girls.

She looked around, trying to assess the area. Fallen palm fronds seemed to be everywhere.

Had there been that many yesterday? She tried to remember exactly where they had been standing.

And then where Keith Henson had emerged from the trees.

In the end, because there were so many palm fronds down on the ground, she decided to examine them one by one.

She tried to make sure she didn't miss an area. She had gotten to her fourth frond when she heard footsteps.

Someone else was heading for the clearing.

She forced herself to pause and listen. After determining the direction from which the sounds were coming, she headed across the clearing. As soon as she reached the shelter of the trees, she spun around, afraid that whoever it was had already burst into the clearing and seen her.

Through the trees, she could see something glinting.

She narrowed her eyes and swallowed hard. Whoever was coming was carrying a knife. A big knife.

A machete.

Staring intently at that deadly glint, she backed farther into the trees.

Suddenly she felt an arm reach around her middle, pulling her deeper into the foliage.

A scream rose to her throat.

But a second hand clamped tightly over her mouth, and no sound escaped.

4

STRETCHED OUT ON THE SAND, Amber watched her aunt disappear into the foliage, then rolled again to face Kimberly with a sigh.

"We've got to do something!"

"About what?"

"Beth, of course."

"You're calling her 'Beth' now?" Kimberly queried with a brow arched high in a semblance of mature disapproval.

"No . . . it's just, we've got to do something."

"She's so cute," Kim agreed.

"And so is he," Amber said.

"Which one?" Kim asked, frowning.

"The cute one."

"Even your dad is cute," Kim said.

Amber laughed, shuddering. "Ugh. Dads are not cute."

Kim shrugged. "I'm sure he is to lots of people."

"I know, but . . . ugh. No, I'm talking about *him*. And I know you know which one I'm talking about."

"Keith Henson," Kim agreed sagely.

"We need to get the two of them fixed up."

"Amber, they're both here. If they want to get fixed up, they'll do it." Kim giggled. "I mean, they're older than we are. They've got to have some smarts."

"Do you think he has a wife somewhere? Or a girlfriend?" Amber asked worriedly.

"I don't think so."

"He better have, like, a real job. I don't want my aunt working her whole life to support some beach bum."

"Amber, we're not getting them married off or anything."

"But we should get them together," Amber protested. "Seriously, she's so pretty, but she never goes out. She needs a date."

Kim blushed. "You mean she's not getting any?" she asked with a giggle.

"Kim!" Amber nudged her hard.

"Well?"

"We need to set her up. But first we have to check him out."

"How are we supposed to do that?"

"I'm not sure yet. We'll have to see when we get home. Dad has lots of cop friends. We can talk to one of them."

"Amber, we may never see these guys again once we go home."

Amber sat up, grinning, and did an amazing Alfred Hitchcock impersonation. "Have you ever had a premonition?"

Kim laughed. "All right. We'll do a real investigation when we get home. Meanwhile, I'll find out a few things about him."

"And how will you do that?" Amber demanded.

Kim smiled smugly. "Silly. I'll just ask him."

THE YACHT WAS STATE OF THE ART. Ben loved it the minute he stepped aboard.

"Wow," he said simply to Lee.

He worked hard and earned decent money as an attorney, and he'd been proud of his own boat, but in comparison, *Time Off* was small.

And simple.

What the hell does this guy do for a living? he wondered, though he was too polite to ask. None of the guys seemed like dope dealers, and he'd learned that in Miami, lots of people were simply independently wealthy.

Hank Mason wasn't quite so hesitant.

"How the hell do you afford a puppy like this?" he demanded.

"Family money, I'm afraid." Lee's pride was justified when he grinned and said, "She's something, huh? She's a Hatteras, top of the line, and she's been customized, since most of these ladies aren't set up for real fishing."

Customized to a T, Ben thought. Topside, there was

the kind of rigging that made deep-water sport fishing fun. The flybridge offered every convenience from a global explorer to sonar and radar equipment, along with a stereo system and the more mundane racks for drinks and snacks. The upper deck offered complete comfort, and the decking was exquisite, with teak trimming. There was even a small refrigerator. The stern afforded racks for at least twelve diving tanks, and a lift-top seat bore a small sign that read Diving Equipment.

"Come into the cabin. You'll like her even more," Lee told Ben.

"I like her already," Amanda said. She smiled up at Ben and linked an arm through his. "Now this, I must say, is a boat."

Ben had known Amanda for several years, though never well. She was definitely beautiful, capable of stirring his senses, but also making him uncomfortable. He'd learned a long time ago that when someone you loved died, you lost a part of yourself, but you were still among the living. And being alive, he definitely had sexual urges. Amanda gave a man the impression that she could fulfill those urges beyond his wildest dreams. It would be a lie to say she didn't have an effect on him. The problem was, she gave the same impression to every man. He would never trust a woman like her if he so much as blinked. For some guys, it would be okay. They were players. It was curious, though, that she seemed to be hanging on to him. He knew he was decent looking, fit and made a good living.

But the island, as Amanda had said herself, was chock-full of testosterone. Lee, Matt and Keith were the kind of men women always seemed to go for—well-muscled, tall, with the slightly rough good looks and hard-adventure attitude that seemed to draw women like moths.

So why the hell was Amanda clinging to him?

He wasn't a player. His life focused—maybe too much, as Beth was always warning him—on his daughter. And he had a great career. So unless he found himself falling head over heels in love again, he kept his social life discreet. It actually did exist, which might surprise his sister.

But then, a lot about him might surprise his sister.

"Cool, huh?" Amanda murmured, snuggling a little closer. She was wearing sexy perfume, and she knew how to press her anatomy against a guy.

He smiled and shrugged, looking down at her. "It's one hell of a boat," he agreed.

"Come below," Lee urged, and the rest followed.

Only Lee and Matt were hosting their excursion. Keith had chosen not to come, and despite his impatience with Beth, Ben had to admit that the guy staying back had caused him a bit of concern. But Brad and Sandy were on the island, as well, as was Roger. Though he vaguely felt he should be concerned about Keith, he just couldn't believe the man had any real evil intentions. He didn't like to believe in instinct—he'd worked in the D.A.'s office long enough to learn that it was unreliable at best—but no matter what logic told him, he didn't fear for his daughter, her friend or his sister when they were with the guy.

"Oh, wow!" Amanda exclaimed, hugging his arm. "This is beautiful!"

The cabin utilized its limited space with sleek elegance. A turn to the left of the steps led straight to an aft cabin, while the steps themselves led into a galley that seemed to offer more appliances than his home kitchen. The galley spilled into a main salon with a desk that held a computer, a radio and a number of electronics he couldn't even name. A table looked as if it could hold up to eight diners, and a hallway led to a forward cabin and the head. Everything was leather, teak or chrome.

"Can I get anyone anything?" Lee asked.

"Beer," Ben said.

Lee moved into the galley, grinning. "Amanda?"

"You have any white wine back there?"

"Sure. Hank . . . Gerald?"

The other two men settled on beers. After the drinks were served—even Amanda's wine was in a small bottle—Lee led the way through to the aft cabin. The master stateroom held a large, comfortable bed. "It's a trundle," Lee explained proudly. "When you need more space, you just pull it out. Of course, you lose your floor space that way. But it allows for a lot of sleeping space. There are a couple of 'closet bunks' in the hallway, as well. There's a private head here in the master stateroom, too, with a shower. But it's the fishing we're out for. Let's head back up."

Ben thought Matt might have gone topside already, to fire up the motor. But he hadn't.

He had remained in the cabin by the computer desk, radio, and Ben had the oddest feeling that the guy was guarding them.

Amanda was still glued to his arm, but Ben had a feeling she, too, was aware that although the saying here seemed to be *Make yourself at home,* there were certain areas of home that were off-limits.

Why?

His instincts were kicking in again. There was something askew with this picture. But what? For a sick moment he wondered if these guys were involved in a modern piracy ring, if they hadn't acquired the yacht illegally. Then again, if a vessel like this had gone missing, he would have heard about it. The members of the club had associates all over the world as well, and the theft of a craft like the *Sea Serpent* wouldn't have gone unnoted.

So much for his instincts. On the one hand, he was convinced that Keith, back onshore, would never cause the least danger to the people Ben loved. And on the other hand . . .

"C'mon," Lee urged. "Come see the fish finder on this beauty. We'll be hauling in our dinner at turbo speed."

Amanda disentangled herself from Ben, yawning. "You know, I was thinking maybe I'd take a little snooze." She laughed softly, looking at Ben. "We were all awakened in the middle of the night," she reminded them.

"No way," Lee protested. "We're striking out to sea, all for one and one for all. Everyone topside!"

Amanda pouted prettily. She would have spoken again, Ben was certain, except that Lee was striding toward them, ready to herd them all up, as if he were a friendly sheepdog keeping the masses together.

He wondered if he was just creating a sense of something that wasn't there, more spooked by Beth's unease than he'd realized.

She was worse than he was, worrying about Amber, worrying about him, spending the majority of her time at work. For most young women, the club would be a smorgasbord of rugged, tanned, athletic professional men. But not for Beth, who didn't date where she worked. It was as if she was oblivious.

Tall, tanned, perfectly fit in a feminine way—stacked—with her dark hair and exotic eyes, she was probably the greatest catch on the island. But even here, she was proving adept at keeping her distance.

"You're mean," Amanda teased Lee, and clasping his arm, a pretty moue on her face. "I'm just so sleepy."

"I'll set you up on deck. You'll love it," Lee assured her.

At that moment Ben knew for a fact that his suspicions were correct.

No one, for any reason, was going to be left in the cabin alone.

So just what were they up to?

"Shh!"

Beth found the sound absurdly reassuring. Though she couldn't see the man whose hand was on her mouth, she knew it was Keith Henson. Was it the feel of him? A certain chemistry? It didn't matter. She just knew.

She felt his other hand spanning the bare flesh of her midriff. He was tense but no longer forceful, and the hand on her mouth eased, then moved away. She could feel the thud of both his heart and her own.

As they stood there, silent, strangely bonded, Brad and Sandy appeared in the clearing.

And Brad was the one wielding the machete.

It was a wicked-looking weapon, and yet . . . boaters planning to put ashore on an island might readily have one. In fact, he was using it for the exact purpose one might expect in such a circumstance—chopping away at the heavy growth.

"I think it was here," Sandy said wearily.

"Here is an awfully damn big space," Brad said irritably.

"Don't be ridiculous. It's a small island."

"Way too small, at the moment. We should have realized. It's a weekend."

"Should we just quit moaning and start looking?"

Beth adjusted her footing ever so slightly. Behind

her, Keith did likewise. He seemed to have no intention of letting her go, accosting the pair or letting his own presence be known. She could feel the coiled tension in him. He was listening intently.

Were they looking for a skull?

And if Keith Henson didn't know about the skull, why would he be so worried about a young couple searching a clearing on the island?

She turned slightly, looking up at him as Brad hacked away at overhanging fronds and branches. He shook his head, warning her that she shouldn't move, shouldn't give herself away.

A fly buzzed near her nose. She began to wonder just how long she could stand so perfectly still. Yet, her own heart continued to race, and her suspicions were hiked to the limit, every fiber of her being attuned to danger.

"I hear something," Sandy announced suddenly.

"Don't be ridiculous," Brad told her.

"No, no, I hear something. From the beach."

"They're fishing."

"They're not *all* fishing."

"So what? We're just walking around the island."

"I don't like this, Brad. Let's go back."

"Are you scared?"

"You bet." She looked at him pleadingly. "Come on, they all have jobs. They'll have to get back to work in a couple of days. The island will be all ours again. Please, let's just get out of here for now."

Brad let out a long sigh. Then he slipped his arms

around her, letting the machete dangle.

"Ooh, nice sword," Sandy teased.

"You bet, baby."

He started to kiss her. Then, with his free hand, to fondle her.

Beth held her breath, feeling acutely uncomfortable. She could still feel the hand on her own midriff, and watching these two get more and more intimate . . .

I thought you were scared, Sandy! she longed to shout.

Then things got worse.

"Want to really fool around?" Brad whispered.

"Maybe."

"Then you won't be scared? Worried about getting caught?"

"There's something kind of exciting about it," Sandy whispered in return. Her hand slid from his chest.

Lower. Lower.

Beth could feel her cheeks flaming to a bright pink.

"Then again . . . I should be punishing you," Sandy said huskily. "You were all over the blonde today."

"The blonde was all over *me* today," Brad protested.

"You didn't seem to mind."

"Hey . . . she was determined to let me know she was full-bodied."

"You and every other guy there."

"Um, true, but you shouldn't let her worry you."

"No," Sandy agreed. "It's the other one I'm worried about. You were looking at her."

"I was looking at her?"

"Yeah, you know. *Looking.*"

"Well, she *is* really sexy. Legs that go on forever. Imagine what she could do with those legs."

Beth could feel the flames deepen in her cheeks, and she imagined that Keith had to be aware of it, too. She couldn't stand much more of this. Self-preservation had kept her silent so far. Embarrassment might well send her flying from cover.

"Hey," Sandy protested.

"Am I turning you on yet?" Brad demanded.

"Seriously . . . I keep hearing something."

"What happened to the idea of being caught in the act of being so hot and sexy?"

"Those girls are underage."

"Yeah?"

"Well, the last thing we need now is to be arrested for contributing to the delinquency of a minor," Sandy said.

"Good point," Brad agreed seriously. But then he quickly returned to his lighter tone. "Hey . . . the tent is exotic and hot, you know."

"So let's get back to the beach—please! In a couple of days, they'll all leave. It will be our island again, Brad. Then we can take care of things."

At last the two of them left, disappearing across the clearing, taking the same trail Beth had used.

Behind her, Keith remained still for what seemed like an aeon. It was all she could do to keep from wrenching away. And yet he was right—they needed to let Sandy and Brad put some distance between them.

Finally, however, she could stand it no longer. He was still touching her, his hand still on her midriff, her body backed flush against his.

She stepped away and turned, staring at him, tense and wary.

"What was that all about?" she demanded.

His eyes were as dark as ebony. He wasn't wearing his sunglasses, but his eyes still gave no clue of what thoughts lurked in his mind.

"Shh," he warned her.

"They're gone," she reminded him.

"The trees may well have ears," he said quietly, studying her.

She lowered her voice. "What were they looking for?" she demanded.

"I don't know."

"Why didn't you accost them?"

"Do you really think it's a great idea to accost a man carrying a machete?" he cross-queried.

"But . . ." She shook her head. "Now we'll never know what they were doing."

"Maybe, maybe not."

She backed away another step, frowning. "What are *you* doing here?"

"Looking."

"Looking for what?" she demanded sharply.

He leaned back against a tree, crossing his arms over his chest. "Whatever you were trying to hide when we met."

Startled, she hesitated, then came back at him far too late. "Don't be ridiculous. I wasn't hiding anything."

"Then I wasn't really looking for anything, was I?"

She let out a sigh of irritation and started to turn away. Then she swung back and collided with him once again. Embarrassed, she braced her hands against his chest and regained her footing quickly.

"Why aren't you out fishing?" she demanded. "I thought you went out on the boat."

"Obviously I didn't."

"Why not?"

"There was a full crew."

"But you snuck around to come back here," she accused him.

"I didn't sneak anywhere."

"Then why didn't I see you before?"

"Probably because you weren't paying any attention. There was no secret about me staying behind. I didn't jump off the boat when no one was looking and swim back."

She stared at him, shaking her head. "There's something wrong with you."

That brought a wry smile to his lips. "I'm not exactly sure how you mean that, but . . . You should certainly hope not. You're alone with me on an island, and all help is far away."

She took a step back again.

He sighed, reaching for her. She jumped; he let his arm fall, shaking his head.

"I'm going to give you some advice, whether you

94

want it or not. Stay away from this area of the island. Obviously it's of interest to someone, and we don't know why. Keep your mouth shut about seeing Sandy and Brad looking around here. In fact, if you have any suspicions about anyone, pretend that you don't."

She narrowed her eyes, staring at him hard. "Someone might have been killed here."

"And you wouldn't want to join them."

"Is that a threat?"

"Good God, no. It's a warning."

"Right. And *you* should be trusted?"

"Actually, yes."

She studied him long and hard. He was a man in the prime of his life, muscled and hard. She was suddenly certain that, if he had chosen, he could have wrenched the machete away from Brad without breaking a sweat.

To her discomfort, she also remembered the strength with which he had held her.

She spun around, striding for the trail.

He caught her arm, swinging her back. She didn't open her mouth to protest, only narrowed her eyes at him in serious warning, arching her brows slowly as she gazed from his eyes to the place where his hand rested on her arm.

"I was serious. Keep your mouth shut."

"You know something, so you'd better be planning on talking to the police," she warned him.

"If I knew something, I wouldn't need to eavesdrop on other people's conversations."

"I think we should call the police."

"And tell them what?" he demanded.

She faltered. "That . . . that . . ."

"That there *might* have been a skull on the island? That a young couple was scrounging around, looking for something? So far, they haven't done a thing that's illegal. And so far, you haven't got anything at all to tell the police. Guess what? You need to get your nose out of it. You need to keep your mouth shut and pretend that you haven't seen a single thing on this island."

"You *are* threatening me."

"I'm not the threat!" he protested angrily. "But just maybe there *is* a threat out there."

"Then we need to stop them. Now."

"There's this little thing called the law. You think you can just tie up Sandy and Brad and call the Coast Guard, and they'll arrest them for acting in what you've decided is a suspicious manner?"

She felt herself flush. He was still holding her. She swallowed, strangely far more afraid now than she had been at any time before. Odd, it felt far too good, especially under the circumstances. She wanted to close her eyes. Lean against him. Let the moment go on. She loathed the concept of basic instinct, but she realized that she was feeling one right then. There was something so right about feeling his touch. She told herself it was just because she hadn't so much as dated in a very long time, but inside she knew it was because she had simply never felt anything so right.

He released her suddenly. "All right, you don't trust me. Stick with your brother. Tight. And keep your mouth shut."

He wasn't touching her anymore. That should mean that sanity would return. Instead she felt startled, like a doe caught in the headlights.

She stiffened, determined to follow a course based on sense and reason.

He started to walk past her, but she wasn't done with him.

She found herself running to catch up with him, then caught his arm, swinging him back to face her.

"What does all this have to do with you?" she demanded.

"Nothing. I came to this island to camp, just the same as you," he told her.

"Then why were you searching the clearing?"

"I told you. It seemed obvious you had hidden something." He had been impatient, almost ready to pull away. But suddenly he became the one determined to carry on the conversation. He moved toward her. There was a tree behind her, and she backed up against it. He set a palm on the trunk to trap her, leaning close.

"What were you hiding?" he demanded.

"Nothing."

"A skull?" he queried.

"Of course not!"

He pushed away from the tree and once again started back toward the beach. She followed him, irritated and uneasy.

And oddly determined to keep up with him.

To remain close.

They reached the trail. For a moment Beth was afraid they would run straight into Sandy and Brad, but the couple was nowhere to be seen.

Amber and Kimberly were lying on the beach, exactly where they had been when she had left them. Roger, too, seemed not to have stirred from the hammock.

"Hey, girls!" Keith called out.

Amber rolled over and looked back, seeing Keith. "Hi," she called, smiling.

"Hey, guys," Kimberly said.

The girls looked at him, then Beth, then one another. They smiled.

No, she thought. They *smirked*.

"Did you find any good coconuts?" Amber asked him.

It was Beth's turn to look from him to the girls and back again. Obviously the girls had known that he hadn't gone on the boat. Where the hell had she been?

Not paying attention. A mistake she didn't intend to repeat.

"Hey . . . that looks like a decent coconut right over there." He pointed in the direction of the hammock where Roger lay sleeping.

"I'll get it," Amber volunteered.

Beth bit her lip, not allowing herself to protest. The girls liked Keith. Trying to draw them away and tell them to be wary would only send them flying to his defense.

Kim jumped up to run after Amber.

Beth's pepper spray lay forgotten on Amber's beach towel.

Staring at Keith, she went and picked it up. He smiled, shaking his head.

"What's that smile for?" she demanded, moving closer to him so the girls wouldn't hear her.

"Pepper spray . . . machete. Hmm."

"Don't kid yourself, this stuff can blind a man."

"I wouldn't dream of mocking your strength, Ms. Anderson," he told her.

Then he turned and went to accept the coconut Amber had picked up. Beth watched as he slammed it against a tree.

The coconut broke at his bidding. He didn't look back at her, just offered the pieces to the girls. Only then did he turn.

"Sorry—is it all right if they have fresh coconut?"

Amber giggled. "Silly. Aunt Beth doesn't have anything against coconuts."

Beth forced a smile.

She was relieved to see the first of the dinghies sliding smoothly onto the shore, just a hundred feet down on the beach.

The others were back.

"Mahimahi tonight!" Ben shouted. He jumped from the dinghy and dragged it farther up the shore, then reached back to give a hand to Amanda. She accepted it with her usual innate sensuality, managing to bring her whole body against Ben in her smooth effort to step to the sand.

"My recipe tonight," Ben called to Beth.

He sounded so pleased. Their fishing expedition had clearly been a great success.

Once again, she forced a smile, then waved and slipped into her tent.

She hoped her brother was having a good time.

For herself, it felt as if she had taken the night train to hell.

And, she realized, it could only get worse. She was suddenly longing for something she shouldn't have.

Perhaps couldn't have . . .

But the really scary thought was that he was feeling just the same.

5

BETH SAT ON THE BENT TRUNK of the palm tree, eating Doritos and watching.

It might have been a family reunion.

The light was gone, but three separate fires blazed, and the portable barbecue was working away, as well. The fires, she decided, were mainly for show, for warmth and light, though the moon was full, and the sky was clear, studded with stars. The fires were still nice, she thought.

Ben was talking to Keith and Matt by the barbecue, explaining the secret to his perfect mahimahi, she suspected. A coffeepot was set over one of the fires. Brad was the coffee brewer. Hank, Gerald and Matt were hanging out with him, probably talking about their day on the water.

As she watched, Amanda joined the group, giggling, laughing and, judging by her gestures, telling a story about the way someone had caught a fish. The men were laughing, obviously entertained, and equally obviously enthralled.

Beth was startled when Sandy sat down at her side.

She had a beer in her hand, and she was watching the group at the fire, as well.

"She's got a way with her, huh?" Sandy said a little glumly.

"She's very pretty," Beth said judiciously.

Sandy turned to her, a half smile in place, a wry expression in her eyes. "You're much better looking. Actually, so am I. She just really knows how to turn it on and use everything she has."

"Two of those guys are her cousins," Beth reminded her. Sandy seemed so normal at the moment, but Beth couldn't forget what she had seen and heard in the clearing.

"And two aren't," Sandy said flatly. She shrugged. "I guess some women are just like that. They can't keep their hands off anything in pants."

"She comes from a . . . a world of privilege," Beth murmured, wondering why she was even attempting to excuse Amanda Mason, who tended to make her skin crawl. Still, she'd made it a point to make sure she never talked badly about any member of the club. She offered Sandy the bag of Doritos.

The other woman sniffed. "Think those boobs are real?"

"Um . . . I've never asked."

"Enhanced," Sandy assured her.

"Well, lots of people . . . enhance."

Sandy sighed. "True. It's just that . . . I mean, she uses the damn things like business cards. And men are so easy."

Beth laughed. "I guess sometimes they are."

"She can't have many friends."

"I don't really know," Beth murmured. She felt like she was ragging on the most popular girl in high school, and it felt more and more uncomfortable. She decided to change the topic. "So how long have you and Brad been together?"

"Three years," Sandy said. "A long time, huh?" She paused. "I'm still madly in love with him. More or less."

Beth wasn't certain how "madly in love" and "more or less" could actually coincide, and again she felt she'd gone back to high school.

"Well, it's great that you're together, then," she said.

Sandy chomped a Dorito. Amanda had her hand on Brad's arm. Sandy shook her head unhappily and looked at Beth. "You don't think it's too long?"

"Too long for what?"

"Shouldn't we be getting married?"

"Oh. Um. Well, I don't know. I guess it's good to really know a person first. I'd much rather be with a person and know that he's the one I want to spend the rest of my life with than marry in a hurry and have it all fall apart. The divorce rate is so high today."

"Is your brother divorced?"

"No. His wife passed away."

"That's terrible."

"Yes."

"So . . . you don't think it's a bad thing that I stay with Brad even though it's been this long and we're not married yet?"

Beth hesitated. She hadn't begun to imagine that Sandy would come to her for advice on her relationship, certainly not after what she had seen and heard in the clearing earlier.

"I'm not qualified to give advice," she said. "I don't think there's anything wrong with staying with someone, no matter how long, if that's what *you* feel is right."

Sandy stared at the group by the fire, eyes level on Amanda. "Do you think he'd cheat on me?"

Beth was beginning to feel acutely uncomfortable. "Sandy, I just met both of you. I have no idea."

Sandy didn't seem to hear her. "She's moving on. Who is she after, do you think? Your brother? Or Keith?"

Amanda *had* moved on. Now she stood between Ben and Keith at the barbecue. She was still laughing, charming, flirtatious.

And once again, she seemed to have enthralled her conquests.

"My brother is in his midthirties," Beth said. "He has to take care of himself, make his own decisions."

Sandy sighed. "Yeah, I guess Keith is all grown up, too. Hey, if Amanda is going to be all over Brad, maybe I should be making a few moves of my own." She stared steadily at Beth again, then shook her head. "You're so moral."

Beth laughed. "How do you know that? We've only just met."

Sandy shook her head. "There are things you just know. Things you see. No matter how long you've known someone." She laughed softly. "Like chemistry. Don't worry. If I make a play for someone, it won't be Keith."

"What?"

"There's chemistry going between you two, and if you say it isn't, well, then you're a liar."

"I'm too moral to be a liar, aren't I?" Beth queried lightly.

Sandy still seemed caustically amused. "Well, he feels attracted to you. I see his eyes when you just walk by. And to be truthful, that's why I'd never make a play for him. Why bother? He's preoccupied. Actually, I don't play games. And I don't think Brad would, either. She just really pisses me off."

"It seems as if you and Brad do have something . . . special," Beth said, feeling a little lame but also really uncomfortable. When she looked at the woman, she wanted to shout, What the hell were you looking for today? A skull?

Both women turned to stare at Brad then. Apparently his coffee was perked, and he had gone to the trouble of making Irish coffee; he had a bottle of Jameson's out, as well.

"Hey, I'd actually like one of those," Beth said, ready to get up and end what was becoming too intimate a conversation with someone she didn't know—and didn't trust. She rose. "Come on, we'll both head over there, and it won't look like you're worried in the least."

Sandy flashed her a quick glance, and she realized that the woman *had* been worried. But Brad hadn't done any instigating, and Amanda was being just as flirtatious with every available guy there.

Beth headed over to the fire and told Brad, "That's definitely a different drink for a night on an island. I'd love one."

"Sure. Sandy?"

"Sounds good to me, too. I'd love one."

Brad mixed up two mugs. "Club Med has nothing on us, huh?" he teased, sliding an arm around Sandy's shoulders.

"No, we're just a regular party," Beth agreed.

"Food's ready!" Ben called out. "Someone grab some plates, please."

Roger was the first one to oblige, and he became the official hand-'em-outer. Everyone found seats, in the hammock, on blankets or towels on the sand, or in the few folding chairs they'd brought out. For the next several minutes, compliments to the chef rang out.

"Hey, how about me?" Lee teased. "I led the fishing expedition."

"I know, and it was a hell of a good time," Ben told him.

"Maybe we should have gone along," Sandy told Brad.

"Yeah, maybe," Brad said, grimacing.

"There's always tomorrow," Matt offered.

"Tomorrow. Sunday," Sandy said, and shivered. "Just Monday and then back to the real world. Work on Monday."

"What do you do?" Beth asked her.

"Do?"

"For a living," Beth said.

"Oh, I'm a consultant."

Maybe it was the fact that Sandy had brought up going back to work on Monday when Beth knew she didn't plan on doing any such thing, but Beth didn't believe her for a minute.

"Back to work for you, too, Beth, right?" Amanda asked sweetly.

"Thankfully, I love my job," Beth replied pleasantly.

"I'm not always so fond of mine," Ben admitted.

"Ben's a lawyer," Roger explained.

"What kind?" Keith asked.

Ben laughed, a slightly dry sound. "Criminal. I used to work for the D.A.'s office, but now I get the scumbags off. It's a good living, but . . . well, I don't know how long I want to do it." He hesitated, glancing over at his daughter. "I'd like to get away from some of the ugliness. I'm thinking about making a real switch into entertainment law or something like that."

Beth turned to Keith and asked pointedly, "What do you do for a living?"

She thought he hesitated for just a second before he said, "I'm a diver."

"And you make a decent enough living?" Hank asked.

"Decent enough for what?" Amber piped in.

Hank laughed easily. "Well, enough to have friends like Lee with a boat like that."

"Hey, the boat is his," Keith said.

"Well, what do *you* do?" Amanda asked Lee.

"Nothing remarkable," Lee said. "Family money."

"I like that," Amanda said, and everyone laughed. The sound, however, had an edge to it, Beth thought.

Apparently Amanda had decided that Lee offered the best opportunity to go on living in the style to which she'd become accustomed. During cleanup, she hung around him, flirting, giggling.

Later Ben sternly vetoed the idea of ghost stories, and the others agreed, staring at Beth. Someone suggested music, and a boom box appeared from somewhere.

As the music played and the conversation went on around her, Beth found herself thinking about the Monocos again. Was there some connection between them and the maybe-a-skull she'd found? Or was she getting carried away worrying? As Ben had said, they were adults, and they could travel the world without reporting to anyone, if they chose.

Whether she'd seen a skull or a conch shell, she was absolutely certain that people were behaving strangely.

The feeling of being in the middle of something she didn't understand sat heavily over her. The rest of them were acting like the world was a great place and everyone just loved everyone. Well, except Ben. Her brother seemed to be brooding, for some reason.

And Keith.

He had managed to hang back and avoid conversation.

He was watching, she thought. Watching everyone.

The thought gave her chills. And yet . . . despite *his* strange behavior, she was still drawn to him. She should have been wary, but, ridiculously, she sensed in him a kind of strength, an . . . ethic. Was she crazy? Was it only because she couldn't remember when she had met someone who so attracted her? But if he'd wanted to hurt her, he'd certainly had the opportunity, and he hadn't. Instead, he'd protected her.

She decided that she wasn't going to say anything more to Ben or anyone else about the skull or her sense of uneasiness. But when she got home, she was definitely going to start finding out more about the Monocos.

On the other hand, maybe the need to know that

seemed to fill her every waking minute now would ebb once they returned to real life. She would see Amanda and Hank again, and Roger and Gerald. But there was no reason to believe she would ever cross paths again with Sandy and Brad, or the independently wealthy Lee, Matt—or Keith Henson.

The group split up late. Beth tried to act nonchalant as she made her way back to their site, but when she was curled up in her own tent, she realized that she still felt uneasy.

If he hadn't had any idea what Brad and Sandy were up to, why had Keith been so determined not to reveal their own presence?

She felt a hot flush rise within her when she remembered the way they had stood, listening, for what had seemed like aeons.

She lay awake, just listening, for a long, long time.

Then, just when she was finally relaxing into sleep, she heard something. A rustling. The wind in the trees? She strained to hear.

Great weekend. She should have been suntanned and relaxed. Instead she was a nervous wreck, more tired than when they'd started out.

In the night, she imagined that she was hearing all kinds of things.

At last, with a sigh, she untangled herself from her sleeping bag and carefully stuck her head out through the opening of her tent.

There was nothing around. No one to see. The night was silent.

She crawled out of the tent to stretch, then froze.

She wasn't alone.

Looking down the beach, she realized that what had appeared to be a shadow against a tree was a man.

The realization sent a flurry of fear snaking along her spine. She stood still, staring.

The shadow lifted a hand. Said, "Hey."

"Hey," she responded automatically.

It was Keith.

Barefoot, in her oversize T-shirt, she walked down the length of the beach to him. The night wasn't especially dark. In fact, it was beautiful. The moon was out, along with dozens of stars. The breeze was gentle, and it wasn't too humid.

"Enjoying the weather?" she asked.

"It is nice, isn't it?" he asked. He sat down and patted the sand by his side. "Join me?"

She hesitated, then sat. "What are you doing?" she asked him.

"Enjoying the weather, just like you said."

"It's the middle of the night."

"I have strange sleeping habits."

"I'll bet you do," she murmured.

He smiled, handsome face rueful. "Is there a hidden meaning behind that?" he asked.

She shook her head and looked away.

"You just don't trust me."

"No, I don't." She let out a sigh.

He laughed. "By the way, what happened to your brother's friends?"

"Pardon?"

"The guys who were supposed to be joining you. You know, the great big lugs who can open beer bottles with their teeth."

She stared at him with a deep frown, having no idea what he was talking about at first. Then she remembered what she'd said when they met.

"I guess they got . . . sidetracked. They're not coming."

"And they never were."

"Okay, so I don't trust you much now and I certainly didn't trust you at all when we first met."

He looked forward again and spoke softly. "Well, we're not pirates, if that's what you're thinking."

"I didn't suggest you were pirates. Pirates belong in ghost stories."

He shook his head, looking her way again. "No. Modern-day pirates are very real. Ask your brother. Sail in the wrong direction and you're asking for trouble. Think about it—the sea is vast. You can be close to civilization, but on the water, far, far from help. Don't ever think of pirates as being something from the past!"

She frowned, surprised that he had spoken with such passion.

"Pirates, because of the drug trade?" she asked him.

He shrugged. "Pirates because some men will always covet what other men have." He watched her intently, then turned away again. "And pirates because sometimes what another man has is knowledge that's worth its weight in gold."

The way he spoke sent shivers down her spine. She was sitting close to him, not touching, and she wasn't sure if she wanted to stumble quickly to her feet and say good-night, or move closer into the aura of his warmth. He was definitely a compelling man, built like rock and steel, with his strange easy smile and chiseled features. And chemistry.

She knew she should be drawing back just because she wanted to move so close. She realized in shock that she was envisioning sex with the man.

Not a good thing when she didn't trust him at all, much less what was happening here on the island.

He seemed to be warning her again.

"Go back to your life tomorrow. Forget anything you might have thought while you were here. And for God's sake, don't talk about it," he said softly.

She shook her head. "You're very scary, you know."

"Am I?" He looked away again. "I don't mean to be. It's just a good thing not to get involved."

"A good thing how? And involved with what, exactly?"

He let out a sound of impatience, flicking at a few grains of sand from his knee. "You're trying to make a mountain out of a molehill," he said, shrugging. "Just leave it alone. When you dig for one thing, you may find something else that you don't expect—or want."

The breeze seemed to grow chilly. She was silent for a moment. "Just what is it that you know, or at least suspect? Why were you so determined that Brad and Sandy shouldn't see us today?"

He groaned. "There you go. I don't know or suspect anything. Hey, I'm a diver, remember? I like the sea, the sand, the wind . . . going down deep where it's peaceful and calm and the world doesn't intrude. I like fishing, islands, Jimmy Buffett and the easy life. So I keep out of things that don't concern me. And that's what I'm strongly advising you do, too."

She stared back at him, shaking her head. "You're talking in circles, and the strangest thing is, no matter what you say, I don't believe you."

"Oh?" He arched a brow, features slightly tense, then easing as he offered her a rueful grin. "Is that a challenge? Or an accusation?"

"Neither. I'm just saying that I don't trust you."

"How amazing. I never would have realized—especially since we've just discussed that fact."

"You're sarcastic, to boot."

"Sorry. If I bug you that much, you might remember that I claimed this tree first."

She stiffened and started to rise.

He caught her arm. "I'm sorry."

"I'll leave you to your tree," she told him, teeth grating.

"I said I was sorry. It's just that you came over here and started attacking—"

"I didn't attack."

"You accused me of . . . something. I just don't know what you want from me."

113

She hesitated, feeling his hand lingering on her arm. His eyes were so steady on her. So sincere.

Why couldn't she have met him at one of her brother's small get-togethers? At the yacht club, or on a local dive trip? Why couldn't he have been an old school friend of someone, anyone, who could be trusted? His touch was the kind that made little jolts of electricity tease the bloodstream, and when she was close to him like this, all she wanted was to touch and be touched.

She gave herself a serious mental shake. He wasn't one of her brother's old school friends, and she had met him under very strange circumstances. And she seemed to be having trouble answering him, though he wasn't pressing anything. He was just looking at her, and they were very close. Close enough so that she knew she liked the arch of his brows, the strength of his features, the way his jaw could seem as hard as a rock until his smile changed everything about him.

"Beth, seriously, I don't know what you want—"

"The truth," she murmured.

He released her and leaned back against the tree, looking up at the night sky.

"The truth?" he asked, sounding edgy again. "I don't know anything about anything. My motto is simply to be very careful. That's the truth. I just think you should be careful, too, that's all."

"Because Brad and Sandy were behaving suspiciously?"

"Because you think you found a skull—and you're

pretty much letting everyone know."

It was her turn to be aggravated. "There you go— talking in circles again. I *think* I found a skull. If I didn't find a skull, then what is there to be worried about?"

"Maybe nothing. Probably nothing."

"Do you know you're incredibly exasperating?" she demanded.

That rueful smile slipped easily into place again. "Do you know the line that should come after that one? Let's see. 'You're incredibly beautiful. I don't think I've ever met anyone quite like you.' But that wouldn't sound much like the truth to you, either, would it? And it's probably something you've heard a million times before." The fact that he didn't touch her then, or move closer to her in any way, made his words seem all the more compelling. She felt the urge to move closer, but she forced herself to maintain her distance. She felt as if there was at least a grain of honesty in his compliment, and she doubted he was a man who got turned down often.

"Thanks," she murmured uneasily, and looked at the swaying palms against the night sky. She worked with the public herself, knew how to smile and play a part, how to manipulate—and when she was being manip- ulated.

She turned to him squarely, "Actually, it sounds like the kind of line you use when you're trying to change the subject."

"I've just offered all that I can on the subject that I'd

be changing," he told her.

Her eyes fell on Lee's yacht. "Quite a boat," she murmured.

"A seventy-five-foot motor yacht," he agreed. "You should have come aboard. She's one glorious lady."

She turned to him. "You could show her to me in the morning."

He seemed surprised by the suggestion. "I could, yes." He watched her curiously for a moment, a slow smile creeping over his lips. "Ah. You're going to check her out. Look for bodies or evidence of evildoing."

Beth averted her eyes. "No such thing. She's a beautiful boat. I work at a yacht club."

"So you see lots of beautiful boats."

"I love to be able to discuss them with the members."

He laughed easily. "You can check her out. No problem."

"Which means, of course, that if you were concealing something, it would be well hidden," she informed him.

"Did you study criminology?" he demanded. "Or do you suffer from an overdose of cop shows on television? If you've been paying attention, one more time, Ms. Anderson, it's smart to keep out of things that don't concern you."

"So I shouldn't go on the boat?"

He groaned. "You're more than welcome to see the boat. I told you—we're not pirates."

"Does that mean you're not pirates but you *are* some other kind of criminal, or that some people are pirates, even though you and your friends aren't?"

"If I say good-morning when I see you and the sun is up, will you be dissecting those words, as well?" he asked her.

She shrugged. "I don't know."

He stood, reaching a hand down to her. "Well, I suggest we get some sleep and find out," he said.

She hesitated before accepting his hand. As he helped her to her feet, she came up against him. The length of her body brushed against his. When she was up, she remained close, thinking—hoping?—he was going to touch her.

She thought she might lose all sense of reason and reach out and touch him, place her fingers on his face.

"No line," he said softly. "You are . . . like a flame. I'd give my eyeteeth to be the moth that was consumed."

She blinked. His voice was deep, sincere, and yet he was distant. He didn't even try acting on his words. If anything, they were wistful.

"Don't worry," he assured her, and a dry smile twisted his lips. "I know how to pine from afar." He hesitated. "You really don't need to be afraid of me," he assured her.

"I'm not afraid of you," she lied.

"You're not?"

"Only a little."

"Actually, you should be. I'm dying to touch you," he said.

The breeze whispered. The ghosts of the island, she thought. The cool air caressed her flesh. She was tempted to step forward and tell him that she *was* afraid, but willing to take her chances anyway.

Just to be touched.

To her absolute amazement, she heard herself say, "Maybe *you* should be afraid. Maybe I'm dying to touch you, too."

His hand rose. His knuckles and the back of his hand just brushed over her cheek. His eyes met hers. For once there seemed to be honesty in them. "You're like a dream, perfect in so many ways."

She swallowed hard. "Not perfect," she murmured.

He laughed, dropping his hand, easing back a bit. "Smart, gorgeous, sexy . . . and good on a boat. That's a dream to me. And I'm insane for saying this. I don't think that I'm what you want. I don't know if I can be." He drew a deep, shuddering breath. "And now we should get some sleep."

They stood there for what felt like forever but was probably no more than a dozen seconds.

"Still want to see the boat in the morning?" he asked.

"Yes. And I'm not a complete coward, you know." What did she mean by that? She wasn't certain herself.

He smiled and stepped back, and she could almost believe she had imagined a moment more intimate than any she had ever shared.

"In the morning, then," he said, and she wondered if his voice was as husky as it sounded, or if she only wanted to think so.

"Yeah . . . in the morning."

"Should I see you back to your tent?" he teased.

"I'll be fine. It's only a few feet away."

He smiled the rueful half smile that seemed to tear away sanity. "I'll just keep an eye on you from here," he assured her. "Apparently you didn't bring your pepper spray."

She shook her head, studying him, and lifted her hands. "No pepper spray. *Should* I have carried it?"

He groaned, then laughed. "Good night, Ms. Anderson. It's been a lovely evening."

"It *is* a lovely evening," she murmured.

Suddenly he pulled her close, and she thought he was going to kiss her, take her in his arms and really kiss her, and if he did, she didn't know what she was going to do.

But he didn't. He just held her. She felt the electric heat and force of the length of his body, not at all dissipated by the cotton between them. He brushed the top of her head with his lips, then pulled back again. "Go, go on back," he told her.

She stepped away, staring at him.

"Trust no one," he told her.

"Not even you?" she whispered.

"Not even me. Go on."

Husky had been replaced by something that resembled harsh. She backed away for several steps before turning to head to her tent.

When she reached it, she turned back.

He was exactly where she had left him.

Watching.

Somehow, she knew that when she went into the tent, he would remain there, watching—though for what, exactly, she had no idea.

But he would be there through the night. Of that she was entirely certain.

Just as she was certain she was the one who was the moth coveting the flame. In her life, she had never actually planned anything the way she was planning it now.

But there was an ache inside her.

Whether she burned to ashes or not, she had to touch the fire.

HANDS OFF.

That was what he had warned the others. They had business to attend to here.

But there was the other business, as well. And that kept him thinking, curious—and determined to find out everything he could about their fellow campers.

Clenching his teeth, he reminded himself that it was no surprise that tourists had come to Calliope Key for the weekend. But he couldn't allow anger to waylay him, nor could he allow himself any emotional involvement. All he could do was seek justice now. And put an end to it all.

Beth Anderson was a distraction he couldn't afford. Keith swore softly in the night.

Then he spun, instantly alert at the smallest sound.

Matt, stretching, looking as if his joints ached and he wasn't ready to pull a shift on guard duty, eyed him cautiously.

"Quite a conversation," Matt said.

"I couldn't exactly force her to go back to bed," Keith reminded him.

"She's something, huh?" Matt said, and grinned. Then the grin faded and he shook his head. "It's dangerous. I wouldn't want her to wind up . . . hurt."

"She won't," Keith snapped out.

"If she—"

"She won't," he repeated.

"Hell of a story you told the other night," Matt said, sounding somewhat sharp, as if the words were an accusation.

"It's a well-known legend."

"Did you tell it on purpose?"

Keith shrugged. "Why not? Throw it out there."

"Yeah, maybe." Matt shrugged, looking out to sea— and the yacht. "Nothing?" he inquired.

"All's quiet."

Matt nodded. "Actually, what else could we expect?"

"Nothing," Keith murmured. He looked at Matt. Neither one of them felt at ease.

"Well, I'm up. You can catch a few winks."

"Yup."

"You're not going to sleep, are you?" Matt asked.

"I'm damn well going to try."

"Don't worry. I know it isn't your lack of faith in me. It's just your nature."

"Trust me. I'm going to try to sleep."

"That's right. You've got a date in the morning, don't you?"

"What?"

"You have to show Beth Anderson the yacht."

"Oh. Right."

Great, just great. His entire conversation had been overheard.

"It will be fine. It's Sunday at last. The working world will return to work," Matt said. "And we'll have the place to ourselves again."

Keith murmured a disjointed, "Not exactly."

"I don't blame you, by the way," Matt went on.

"Blame me for what?" Keith said.

"If Beth Anderson had looked at me with so much as a slightly interested smile, well . . . I'd forget everything, too."

"I haven't forgotten anything," Keith said.

He left Matt by the palm and returned to his tent.

But Matt had been right.

He lay awake. And listened.

He couldn't help remembering a picture that was as vivid in his mind's eye as if he were back at the morgue again, staring down at Brandon Emery's face. He'd been so young. Twenty-four and so damn good at everything he did. One of the brightest newcomers, filled with all the right stuff, as they said.

Too damn good. He shouldn't have been out alone. Especially when he had seen something, known something. And he *had* known something. Keith could still recall the last e-mail he'd gotten from Brandon, word for word.

I think I've got it. Honest to God, you're not going to believe it. I'm going to check it out, and I'll let you know next time I write.

But there had been no next time.

No next time for Brandon.

Keith had never heard from him again. Not until he had been called to see the body. What had seemed like a fairly easy—even run-of-the-mill—venture had turned deadly, and the image of Brandon Emery in the morgue was one that would never leave his mind.

His body had floated up near Islamorada. His boat had been found drifting a few miles farther north. But he hadn't been anywhere near Islamorada when he had e-mailed.

He'd been here, working off Calliope Key.

And no matter what anyone said, he hadn't simply drowned.

He sat up in a sweat. Swore.

Ted and Molly Monoco. He hadn't known the couple, but he'd read about them. He'd never put them in the same arena as Brandon before. Brandon had been part of his work. Ted and Molly had been retirees, off to see the world.

But they'd been here, too. It might well have been damn stupid of him not to connect everything that had happened in the area. But what was the connection? Brandon's boat had been no great shakes, and it hadn't been stolen. Had the Monocos' boat been seized? He'd heard rumors that it had been seen. Rumors. And there had been similar incidents in the papers over the last year.

The Monocos had owned the kind of vessel any modern-day pirate might well envy.

Had they died for that reason?

How could that be connected to Brandon's death, or their own quest here? Had the island itself become deadly, or remained deadly through the centuries, a place near enough to civilization to attract visitors, and yet remote enough for anything to happen? A place to kill and . . .

A place to hide the dead?

He would never sleep. Because now Beth was on the island. Beth, who wouldn't let things rest.

It was chilling.

She would be going home soon. She would be in no great danger, once she returned to Miami. Once she forgot the island.

Forgot the fact that she thought she'd seen a skull . . .

Gotten over the idea of discovering just what had happened to Ted and Molly Monoco?

6

"Hey, Dad, where's Aunt Beth?"

Ben, who'd been stowing gear, looked up from the tent poles he was arranging as his daughter rubbed sleepy eyes and stared at him.

"Gone," he said gravely.

She frowned, shook her head and rolled her eyes. "Dad, where is she?"

"I'm serious. She went out to see the yacht with Keith Henson."

"What?"

His daughter's incredulous excitement gave him pause. "I said," he enunciated, "that your aunt went out to see the yacht with Keith Henson."

"Oh, Dad. I heard you perfectly."

"Then—"

"Oh, Dad, it's too cool." By then, Kimberly had come up behind her. "Did you hear that? She went with Keith to see the boat."

"Wow!" Kim agreed.

"I didn't think she had it in her."

"She's just so suspicious."

"This is awesome."

"Random."

"Wicked."

By then Ben was frowning. "What are you two

going on about?"

"Oh, Dad. He's a hunk."

"Really fine," Kim agreed somberly.

"I mean, there was . . . like, thunder."

"And lightning."

"Between them," Amber finished.

"We were trying to figure out a way to get them together," Kim admitted.

Ben scowled seriously then. "You two butt out, okay? She's a grown-up, and she's not going off any deep end over a guy just because he's got a six-pack, okay? Don't you two go pushing anything. She went to see the yacht because I raved about it, and that's it, do you understand?"

"Okay," Amber murmured.

"Seriously," Kim agreed.

Then they looked at each other and ruined the effect, bursting into laughter.

"Amber Anderson," he said firmly. "I mean it. Leave your aunt alone."

"He's acting like a male," Kim murmured to Amber.

"All touchy," Amber agreed.

"*He* is standing right here," Ben told them.

"Sorry, Dad," Amber said.

"I mean it."

"We know you mean it," Amber told him. She nudged Kim. "Hey, let's go explore."

He felt a frown furrowing his brow. "No exploring."

"What?" Amber protested.

"Stay on the beach."

"Why, Dad?"

Why? He didn't know.

"Because I said so."

"But, Dad—"

"Because I said so," he repeated.

He turned away, because he really didn't have a better explanation to give his daughter. As he paused to look down the beach, his frown deepened, and he tried to tell himself there was nothing to worry about.

But everyone, it seemed, was looking out to sea.

Not too far away, Matt was standing by one of the palms. His arms were crossed over his chest, and he was looking toward the yacht.

Down farther, Amanda Mason was posed in almost the exact stance, staring out over the water, hugging her arms around herself.

And even farther down . . .

It was Brad. Staring out at the water, at the little boat nearing the majestic yacht.

A sense of unease filled him, like a little inward shiver.

He literally shook himself, irritated.

He dealt with the scum of the earth, so why was he so bothered now?

With a slight groan, he turned away. Good God, Keith's buddies—including the owner of the yacht—were right there. The Masons were down the beach. Brad and Sandy were unknowns, but what the hell, they were there, too.

Beth was as uptight as an old schoolmarm, worse

than he was himself.

Everything was fine.

"Hey there!"

He turned. Lee Gomez was waving to him, heading toward the interior of the island.

"Looking for a few good coconuts," Lee called to him. "Want any?"

"I'm fine, thanks," he returned.

Down the beach, Sandy had moved to stand behind Brad. She slipped her arms around his waist and rested her cheek on his back.

Brad didn't seem to notice. He was intent on the yacht. Then he turned, as if aware that he was being watched, and saw Ben staring at him.

Ben waved.

Brad waved back, then turned his attention to Sandy.

It's all just fine, Ben assured himself.

And it was. They would be getting off the island.

He was amazed to realize he was glad the weekend was nearly over. He usually dreaded going back to work after a break. What the hell. There ought to be some saying about the scumbag you knew and the scumbag you couldn't quite recognize.

HE LOOKED GOOD ROWING, Beth decided.

She purposely turned her gaze to the yacht they were approaching, dismayed that she seemed to be doing little other than appreciating the physical assets of the man.

Around boats, guys wore trunks, cutoffs, T-shirts,

even no shirts. They tended to be bronze, and the club attracted a slew of well-toned, healthy, fit specimens of masculinity.

Keith Henson just seemed to have it all and carry it off just a little bit better.

This morning he was in blue-and-black swim trunks, the kind a million surfers wore, the kind that shouldn't have been the least bit erotic. He had eschewed a shirt, since the day was hot—nothing unusual in that. But his skin seemed to be an unreal masculine shade of bronze, and his muscles flexed with each tug on the oars. Shades hid his eyes from her view, and she certainly hoped her own hid her thoughts equally well. Suddenly she blushed. She had been thinking about how he was dressed, but now realized that she, too, was skimpily clad in a bathing suit and sarong—an outfit that she would have thought nothing of if she weren't with him.

But there was something between them.

She couldn't stop herself from thinking of it as chemistry, though she was sure she never would have felt such a draw if it hadn't been for his smile. Or the darkness of his eyes. Or the keen mind that seemed to lie behind his every word.

His every lie.

"Well, do you like her?"

They had reached the yacht. He stood, rocking the little dinghy, and tied on. The aft ladder had been left down, and he swung on, reaching out a hand to her. With the dinghy bobbing on the waves, she accepted.

She found herself noting the ease with which he helped her. The man was strong. Did that make him some kind of a criminal? And if he was, what kind of an idiot was she to be here with him?

She landed on deck with ease and looked around. She estimated the original price of the boat at more than six figures.

"Really, *really* nice," she assured him.

"Come on. I'll show you around."

He took her around the upper deck, then to the flybridge, and finally down to the cabin. She whistled softly.

"It's like a luxury-hotel suite," she told him.

"The great thing is that she can do anything. Despite her size, she's got top speed, and she's rigged for fishing as well as pleasure cruising."

"That's why there's the global positioning system, sonar, radar, communications—and whatever else is up there and down here?"

"We all like to fish," he said with a shrug. "What can I get you? Juice, soda . . . water? Want coffee? It will only take a minute."

"I'd love coffee," she told him.

He seemed to be involved in the task, but she had the feeling that he was watching her all the while. For her reactions?

Or to make sure that she didn't notice something she shouldn't?

"Make yourself at home," he said.

"Thanks." She took a seat on the sofa in the main

salon area. She might have been sitting in the salon of a resort. Beyond the windows, she could see the sea, the sky and a glimpse of the island.

"How long do you think you'll be in this area?" she asked him.

"Oh, a while."

She laughed suddenly. "Do you ever have a direct answer for anything?"

"What do you mean?"

"Okay, how long are you going to be here? A while. A 'while' can mean anything. If someone had asked me about this weekend, my reply would be clear and direct. I go home tonight."

He shrugged, pouring coffee into mugs. "I don't know how long I'm going to be in the area. When we're fished out, dived out and done, I'll head back."

She let out an exasperated sigh. "Back to Virginia?"

Even then, she thought he hesitated. "Yes."

"Do you have a house there?"

"Yes. There—is that direct enough?"

"What part?"

"Northern Virginia."

"Does your city or town have a name?" she demanded.

He came around and handed her a mug. "Whoops, sorry, did you want cream or sugar?"

"Black is fine, thanks. Well?"

"A fairly well known name, yes. Alexandria."

"There, see, it wasn't so hard. You have a house, it's in Virginia, in the city of Alexandria."

"Do you have a house?" he inquired in turn, perching on the arm of the sofa. Close again. The kind of close that made her wonder why she felt the need to analyze everything. Why not just take a chance? Why care so much about exactly who or what he was?

Just enjoy the simple things in life, she told herself. Everything doesn't need to last forever. She never just met a man and went with him . . . anywhere. It seemed that she had never been so emotionally confused before. Last night she had lain awake during all that had been left of the darkness, thinking, tormenting herself. She could . . . no, no, she couldn't, sure she could, she shouldn't, mustn't . . . and then, why not? This sense of something hanging in the balance was new to her. This kind of need, this kind of longing . . . She couldn't actually even remember ever being spontaneous, simply acting on instinct. And yet she was free and single, over twenty-one, always responsible, dependable . . .

Surely everyone had a right to a moment's insanity, to fulfill a fantasy. It was Sunday and she would head home, back to the real world, and most likely thought she would never see him again.

"Hey, are you still with me?" he asked, bemused.

"I, um . . . yes, of course."

"Well?"

"Well what?"

He arched a brow. "House. Do you have a house?"

"Oh! I have a town house, yes."

"And that would be where?" he asked.

"Coconut Grove, near the yacht club."

"Nice."

"I like it."

"However—"

"Yes?"

"I've heard that Coconut Grove can be a dangerous area."

"Any populated place can be dangerous. As you said yourself, even sailing the islands can be dangerous. But Miami has a bad rep. People are nice there. It's like any other city. You're most likely not going to be hit by a drug lord unless you're dealing or something like that." She shook her head suddenly, looking into her coffee cup. "You ask a simple question, and I give you a paragraph. I ask a question and get a one-liner. Maybe I'm the one with the problem."

She was startled to realize that he didn't laugh, or even smile, as she had expected he might. He was looking at her very seriously. He reached out and touched her. Light, totally casual. He just touched her chin with the tip of his forefinger. "I don't think you have a problem at all," he said very softly.

There it was. The moment when she was supposed to stand and say, "I have to go."

But she didn't. He eased down from the arm of the sofa, next to her, his scent a mixture of the wind, sea and salt, his flesh still reflecting the heat of the sun, emitting power from every pore, and she didn't move. She waited.

His sunglasses were gone, and his eyes seemed as

133

dark as ebony, as mysterious as an abyss, and he was studying her, long and intently. Once again she thought it was time to back away, because then he would rise, as well, and the moment would be broken.

But she didn't move, and his fingers slipped into her hair, cradling the base of her skull. Then, at last, his lips touched hers. At first it seemed like nothing more than a hot and teasing whisper of air; then the fullness of his mouth pressed over hers. She wasn't avoiding, wasn't protesting; she was set adrift in a sea of fascination and discovery, her arms rising, hands resting on his shoulders, fingertips awakened by the simple feel of skin. He kissed her hard and deep, and she felt an infusion of warmth and arousal.

It was he who broke the kiss, easing away, and his voice was definitely husky when he spoke. "I think you're supposed to tell me that you need to get back."

She nodded. "You should be telling me that this isn't your boat."

He nodded in response. "We should go."

"Certainly. Now."

"Remember, I told you that you should be afraid of me."

She shook her head, studying his eyes. "I should be. But I'm not. I mean, I am. But I'm not."

"Tell me to take you back," he said.

She shook her head slowly. "I guess I'm just not afraid enough."

"Still . . . we need to . . . not . . ."

"You're right."

But neither moved, and when he kissed her again, she let her fingers play down the length of his back, and she felt his hands on her. Then, he broke away again, his voice extremely deep as he said, "I really should take you back."

"If that's what you want."

"What you *don't* want is to be involved with me," he murmured.

"I don't recall saying that I was involved."

He moved away. "Ah, Ms. Anderson, you are far too decent, believe me. So if you'll just say . . .." His voice trailed off.

She smiled, her senses perfectly attuned, her mind suddenly set upon her course. She moistened her lips slightly, her smile deepening. "You want me to say I should go? I should. Do I want to? No. Am I going to? I don't think so, but then again, that's up to you now."

His groan was deep and shuddering, and then he stood with a suddenness that surprised her and swept her up into his arms.

"We shouldn't be doing this," he said.

"Absolutely not," she agreed softly as she linked her arms around his neck.

Her eyes locked on his, she was barely aware that he was heading for the elegant master stateroom. The bed was huge. He managed to rip off the black-and-white cover without losing hold of her, and when he laid her down, the sheets seemed cool against the sun-touched heat of her flesh. He quickly lay down beside her. Her sarong was a tangle around them both, quickly eliminated, and she would forever remember the contrast between the coolness of the bedding and the warmth and vibrance of his flesh. They met in a passionate, exploratory kiss, lips melding, tongues sliding, mouths locked. His hands were every bit as powerful as she had imagined, his fingers as gentle, his touch as magnetic. His lips fell to her throat, to spots just below each ear, to the center of her throat once again, and lower, the tip of his tongue teasing up and down her collarbone, then lower still. Her fingers slid into his hair, testing its rich texture, blond and then ash, where it had been bleached by the sun. She felt the pressure of his body against her. With his hips and legs pressed to hers, she felt the swell of his arousal, taut beneath the surf trunks. Then his hands, adept at manipulation, released the hook of the bikini bra, followed by his lips, firm against her breasts, and his hands, caressing, cradling. His lips teased after every touch, moving over her areolas, nipples, up the length of her throat again. The frenzy of caresses wet, hot, seemed to send streaks of pure fire sailing through her bloodstream, and rushing with ardent precision into the very heart of her sexuality. She didn't remember ever feeling as she did now, and knew that was because she had never actually felt anything this vital, this passionate, alive, tempestuous . . . ever before.

He paused, his eyes on hers, smile totally seductive. "This is insanity."

"We've agreed on that."

"You need to go back. You shouldn't be here."

"We've agreed on that, as well," she whispered.

"You shouldn't be involved with me."

"I wouldn't dream of being involved with you."

"One might call this involved."

"One might."

He shook his head. His lips touched down again. For a moment they teased a mere breath above her own. Then the kiss deepened, and their limbs entwined as their bodies met and melded. The naked length of his chest seemed glorious, the sound of his breathing filled her senses, along with the thrum of their hearts. His flesh felt like the sun and the sea, smooth, slick, hot. He moved erotically against her, her breasts crushed to him.

She clung to him, splaying her fingers down his back, along his spine, down to the waistband of his trunks, around in front to the ties. Her fingers weren't as adept as his, not quite as experienced. His hands covered hers, though he never broke the kiss. She was dimly aware when the trunks were gone, acutely aware when the naked length of his body pressed against hers. She felt his fingers slipping beneath the bikini bottom as he effortlessly did away with the last barrier between them, which in itself seemed an exotic ecstasy. She was pressed close to him again, and his fingers seduced a path down her spine, curved over her buttocks, brought her flush against his arousal. His lips continued to caress and assail. Then he moved, sleek, agile, shifting atop her, lips pressing against the hollows of her collarbone, teasing her breasts. His hand glided down the curve of her form, pressed apart her thighs. She felt the stroke of his touch first, and then the taunt of his tongue; felt as if she burned within, caught in a sudden, swift maelstrom of fire. Pure sensual ecstasy exalted her even as the rage of intimacy dismayed her, though for only a split second in the rush of sensation.

He was an incredible lover.

Subtle and bold. Teeth, tongue, lips, touch, all meshed in a passionate dance of sensuality that left her breathless, thundering, quivering somewhere between total vibrant ecstasy and simple delicious death. She arched, writhed, thrashed, cried out God-knew-what. . . .

Trembled, throbbed . . . begged.

Involved.

Good Lord, yes, she was involved, any more involved and she would be living in his skin. She had sworn to herself that she had sense and reason and knew what she was doing, but this was . . .

Involved.

She was more involved than she had ever been. More touched, elated, electrified, swept away, taken . . .

She tore at his hair, dragged him to her, and before she could even meet his lips again with her own, she shuddered with a new sense of sheer carnal elation as the force of his body thrust into hers.

The ship rocked.

God, the man knew how to coerce with the slowest, gentlest movements, and then to thunder and pulse with the force of a wicked gale in the North Sea. She knew there were moments when she literally forgot everything except the burning need to be with him, one with him, feeling the shudder and quiver, strength and power, the slick wet heat, the movement, the hunger. . . .

She must have shrieked, screamed . . . loud enough to wake the dead and half the ocean. She knew he must have felt the burst of the climax that violently seized her, so euphoric she thought she knew at last what they meant by a thousand little deaths.

Surely he felt, he knew . . .

And waited, his own climax erupting seconds later—or hours, she wasn't at all sure, she lay in such a damp bath of steam that she wasn't sure she was breathing, or that her heart continued to beat at all anymore.

She had thought she could just walk away. Congratulate herself on a mature affair. On allowing herself adult pleasure, denying the complications of real emotion.

But nothing came without a price, and she knew that. She'd told herself not to get involved . . .

Too late. This *was* involved.

Easing to her side, he held her, smoothed back her hair. She wondered desperately what their pillow talk would be after such a sudden and volatile interlude. When he rolled her to face him, his eyes were dark and intense, and the slightest smile curved his lips. Again he touched her hair, and she had to wonder what he was seeing in her eyes, how much he could read from her face.

God help her, she didn't know what to say or how to act. She was afraid she would start stuttering, try to explain that she never did things like this, that he'd been unique somehow, and that he'd been more than she had ever begun to imagine.

But there was no chance for awkward words, no reason to promise that of course they would see each other again.

Beth's eyes flew open as she heard the sound of a dinghy approaching, the sound of chatter and laughter.

The girls!

His eyes widened and his brows arched as he heard them at the same time.

"Dear God," she swore, flying up even as she spoke, stunned, horrified.

Feeling like an idiot. Anyone could have come aboard at any time. What in God's name had she been thinking? She *hadn't* been thinking. She'd been reacting, and feeling. . . .

She hadn't wanted to get out of pillow talk *this* badly!

"Hey!" He was up, too, and reaching for his trunks in the blink of an eye. She looked in panic at the condition of the bed, and wondered about the state of her hair at the same time.

"Got it," he assured her, tossing over a brush from

the nightstand and reaching for the sheets. She tripped back into her bathing suit, fingers shaking so hard she couldn't get the bra top fastened.

"Don't panic, you're a grown-up, you know," he said calmly, fixing it for her.

"That's my niece!" she exclaimed, running the brush viciously through her hair. "*And* her friend, and they're at a horribly impressionable age. I'm supposed to be a role model. You don't understand. Her mother is dead—"

"Don't panic," he repeated softly. "I *do* understand, and we're fine. Get topside. I'll finish making the bed."

She sped out of the cabin. There was a boating magazine lying in a wire rack by the table. She nearly ripped it apart in her haste to grab it. Then she sat on the sofa, her heart racing painfully again.

The girls—and whoever had come with them—were just coming aboard.

She stretched out and crossed her ankles, trying to look casual and comfortable. Then she decided she looked too casual and comfortable, and uncrossed them.

She crossed them again, smiling, as Amber made her way down to the cabin. "This is too cool. Way, way too cool," she said.

"Ohmygod," Kim breathed, coming down behind her.

"Like a floating hotel suite, huh?" she said, trying to sound cheerful and welcoming. She decided she was loud and fake, but apparently she sounded all right to everyone else.

Amber turned to her with wide eyes. "Like a floating palace."

"Not that lush," Ben protested, coming down behind the girls. He looked at his sister and grinned—apparently oblivious, she noticed gratefully. But then, he probably thought he knew her. Just as she had thought she knew herself.

Keith came striding breezily out from the stateroom. "Hey, kids. Want a tour? Or would you rather roam around on your own?" he asked.

Amber didn't get to answer. "Would you look at the kitchen!" Kim exclaimed.

"Galley," Amber corrected.

Kimberly laughed, running her hand over the counter and staring at the appliances. "No way. This is a full kitchen," she protested.

"Seriously, it's not a salon, either, it's a living room," Amber agreed, looking at Keith.

"You can go around the world in her, can't you?" Kim asked.

"You could."

"Have you ever?" she asked.

"No. But she does offer all the comforts of home," he said. "Speaking of which, would you like something to eat? Drink? You want a smoothie?"

"You can make a smoothie?" Amber asked.

"Yup. I'll see what we have."

He delved into the refrigerator, and the girls went to

join him. Ben looked at Beth. "You don't mind that I brought them?" he asked.

"Don't be silly."

"We didn't interrupt anything, did we?" he asked, a frown starting to crease his brow.

"Don't be ridiculous," she protested. Then afraid that she was about to blush the shade of a beet, she leaped to her feet, closing the magazine.

"Hey, did you get a good look at the upper deck and the flybridge?" he asked excitedly.

She smiled. Big boys, big toys.

"It's an amazing yacht," she said.

"And to think I thought I had the prize of the seas when I bought mine."

In the galley, a blender roared to life just as she started to answer, so she had to smile and wait.

"You have a wonderful boat, and I love it," she said loyally at last.

"Oh, I love it, too. It's just . . . well, who wouldn't want to own something like this, huh?" he asked.

"Dad, you want a strawberry smoothie?" Amber called.

"Sure."

"Aunt Beth?"

"Absolutely," she murmured. She followed her brother into the galley and accepted a large paper cup from her niece.

She couldn't help it; she felt wary of Keith. She had to keep her distance. She was afraid even to make eye contact, terrified that at any minute she was somehow going to give herself away. She was certainly over twenty-one, but she felt so responsible toward her niece. She'd always tried to teach her that sex should be special; that it was the most intimate act between two people and shouldn't even be contemplated without sincere emotion, the deepest respect, and a sense of responsibility and consequences.

Well, emotionally, she *was* involved, like it or not. Had she been in the least responsible? No. And as to thoughts of future consequences . . .

It terrified her to realize just how much she wished there could be one. That he would reappear somewhere in her world, that he would be a responsible member of the human community and not just a diver. Or . . . a common criminal. Or worse.

A murderer.

No. She knew instinctively that wasn't true. Or else she just wanted to believe it.

Keith didn't have any problem being entirely natural and casual. He chatted easily. Beth wasn't even sure what was being said half the time.

Then they heard the motor of the yacht's dinghy, returning with Matt and Lee and the supplies. Ben said it was time to go, and thanked Keith, then Matt and Lee. They all talked about what a pleasure it had been to meet, said they would undoubtedly run into one another somewhere along the line sometime.

"Beth, you can come back with the girls and me," Ben said. "Save Keith the bother."

"Of course."

"I can take you back—" Keith began.

"The girls and I have already packed up. We don't need to head back to the island, just straight to the boat," Ben said.

"Perfect," Beth murmured.

It wasn't perfect. Perfect would be if they all disappeared, if there didn't have to be any words, if she could just go back where she had been and pretend. Pretend Keith Henson was someone she would see again, someone she had known forever and ever . . .

Someone she trusted.

She had to trust him. She'd just gone to bed with him.

She felt more awkward than ever. She was at ease saying goodbye to Matt and Lee, but she couldn't meet Keith's eyes, and she only shook his hand, while she'd kissed the others goodbye on the cheek. So much for appearing completely casual.

She couldn't escape quite that easily. He stopped her and took her hands. His eyes met hers. Amused but affectionate, she thought. *Affectionate?* She wanted so much more.

She still felt so ridiculously awkward.

"We'll talk soon," he said.

She nodded, hoping she looked casual, carefree.

"I will find you," he said softly.

"Finding me won't be very difficult," she murmured.

"Strange timing, huh?"

She didn't know exactly what he meant. And she

couldn't ask him. She couldn't stand being so close to him any longer, with so very much unsaid.

She had to escape, and she did, reaching her brother's dinghy before the others.

As Ben revved his little motor to life, he laughed with the girls as they raved about the *Sea Serpent*. She was grateful she didn't have to speak. She kept a smile plastered to her face as she lifted a hand in farewell to the men standing on deck.

Soon Ben had set their course for home. She reflected that she hadn't even said goodbye to the others—any of the Masons, or Brad and Sandy. The Masons she would see again, and as for Brad and Sandy . . .

Thinking of the pair still gave her an uneasy feeling.

She looked away from the yacht at last and turned her gaze westward, toward the Florida coast. It would all come into perspective, she told herself.

She would get home. She would believe she had been silly, that she couldn't have seen a skull. That nothing had been going on during their stay on the island. No one had lurked around with evil intent.

And as for Keith . . .

She would stop thinking about him eventually. In her mind, he would lose the charismatic appeal that had all but obsessed her. She would remember him as a man. As someone special she had once met. Handsome, virile, exciting . . . but too laid-back, too ready to enjoy good times with his friends, too lacking in ambition.

It would all come into perspective. . . .

But things always came back around to one fact.

She was certain she had seen a skull.

Just as she was certain there was something about Keith. No matter how appealing the man might be, he simply wasn't what he seemed.

There had been an honesty in the way he'd touched her, but only lies had fallen from his lips.

7

"I ADMIT TO STILL BEING confused," redheaded Ashley Dilessio said, easing back in her chair at Nick's, her uncle's restaurant on the bay.

Nick's was everything good about the area, Beth thought. Boats came in to dock, houseboats were moored nearby, and anyone was welcome. The tables were rough wood, an overhang sheltered the outside seating from the sun, and it felt like a continuation of island living in the midst of a hectic, overpopulated, multicultural community.

Not to take anything away from the yacht club, she decided a little defensively. The two establishments were just different. And of course part of Nick's appeal was that she'd known Ashley most of her life.

Now Ashley was with the police force, in the forensics department, and her husband, Jake, was a homicide detective.

"Okay, you got to the island. You walked with the kids. You thought you saw a skull. A man showed up—you hid it. You went back with Ben, and there was no skull," Ashley said, her green eyes studying Beth with a slight frown wrinkling her forehead.

"That's the gist of it, yes. Ben thinks I saw a conch shell," Beth said, her tone a little sheepish. "It might be nothing, it might be something. But I couldn't stop thinking about Ted and Molly Monoco."

"I remember the story, but . . . I thought they were sailing around the world," Ashley said. "No wonder no one's seen them."

"But what if it *was* a skull?"

"You said that whatever you saw was gone when you went back."

"Maybe I just couldn't find it," Beth persisted.

Ashley stirred her straw around in the large glass of iced tea in front of her. "This isn't my jurisdiction, or even Jake's, you know."

"But you have contacts," Beth reminded her.

Ashley nodded thoughtfully.

Beth let out a deep sigh. "Shouldn't someone check it out?"

"Yes," Ashley agreed. "We can get the Coast Guard out there to take a look, if nothing else. But . . . why would the skull—if it was a skull—have disappeared? Did any of the other boaters seem suspicious?"

Beth groaned. "All of them."

Ashley smiled. "Okay, tell me."

Beth began describing the other campers on the

island: the Masons, who Ashley knew casually, Brad and Sandy, and the three men in the exquisite yacht.

"Three hunks, huh?" Ashley teased.

"Um. They looked the part."

"What part?"

"Oh, you know, the type who would be out fishing, diving . . . boating."

"You mean they had beer bellies and could open the bottles with their teeth?"

"Ashley!" She flushed slightly, remembering the way she'd described Ben's mythical "friends" who were due to arrive on the island.

"Sorry, just kidding. But they don't sound like modern-day pirates. Not if they already had such a fantastic boat themselves."

"So there really are pirates out there?" Beth asked, keeping to herself the thought that maybe Lee hadn't been the legitimate owner of that boat after all.

"You bet. There's lots of money—and very little law—once you're out on the ocean," Ashley said seriously. She was doodling idly on a napkin. "Describe your guy."

"Which one?"

Ashley grinned. "The one you're talking about the most, seem the most suspicious of—and the most attracted to."

"Ashley . . ."

"Beth, just describe the guy. Tall? Dark? Face shape—round . . . long . . . ?"

"Um, really good bone structure. Cheekbones

broad, chin kind of squared, really strong. Eyes . . ." She watched as Ashley sketched on the napkin. Her friend was good. "Farther apart. And the brows have a high arch. The nose is a little longer, dead straight. The lips are fuller. And the hair . . . well, depends on whether it was wet or dry."

"Just go for the face."

"A little leaner there, below the cheekbones," Beth said. Then she exhaled, leaning back, staring at Ashley. "You'd think you knew the guy. That's incredible."

Ashley shrugged, sliding the cocktail napkin with the perfect likeness to the side of her plate. "Let's hope so. I'm being paid to do it."

Beth shook her head, staring at Ashley, thinking of the man whose likeness her friend had just drawn.

"Hey! Look what the summer wind brought along," a masculine voice said, breaking the moment.

They both looked up. Jake had arrived. Winking at Beth, he kissed the top of his wife's head and pulled out a chair. He was a rugged-looking man; he either looked his part as a cop or could be taken for one of her boat people. In fact, he was both. He'd spent years dealing with the hardest, darkest, ugliest secrets of a big city, and still knew how to come home and smile, play with his toddling son and baby daughter, love his wife and enjoy his friends.

"Beth thinks she might have found one of the missing Monocos," Ashley said.

Beth was startled when he looked at her sharply,

150

then at his wife again. "I'm not sure they *are* missing. I just heard a rumor that their boat was seen recently."

"She might have found a skull on Calliope Key," Ashley explained further.

"It disappeared," she murmured, then shook her head. She couldn't be hesitant. "Actually, I'm sure I saw a skull. But I got scared and tried to hide it. Then I couldn't find it. And—"

She broke off, then plunged back in. "Well, if someone else had hidden the skull, it didn't seem like a good idea to make a production of digging it up."

Jake grimaced, looked at Ashley again, and then smiled at Beth. "Don't worry, kid, we'll get on it," he assured her. "I'll call Bobby—Robert Gray, a friend with the Coast Guard. I'm sure he'll help. Will that make you feel better?"

"Yes, and thank you," she told him.

"Hey, are we invited to your next big event at the club?"

"Absolutely," she assured him. "You can come in anytime, you know that. Just use my name. No, better yet, use Ben's. He's the paying member." She grinned.

"Want to hear more about Beth's excursion on Calliope Key?" Ashley asked her husband. "Some of her new acquaintances sound fascinating."

"Oh?" Jake said, and looked at Beth curiously.

"She met three hunks. Rich ones, maybe."

"Ohhhh," Jake said.

Beth groaned and stood. "You two are cops—you're

supposed to be taking me seriously. I'm out of lunchtime. Call me."

Ashley grinned, shaking her head. "We're taking you seriously, really. The thing is, your hunks do sound intriguing." Ashley paused, her expression turning serious. "I promise we'll find someone—the right someone—to look into what you saw."

"And we *will* call you," Jake promised.

Shaking her head, Beth turned and left them. But she smiled as she did so. She could trust them. If they said they would see to it that the Coast Guard checked out the island, it would be done.

As soon as Beth had gone, Ashley pulled the cocktail napkin from the side of her plate, setting it directly in front of her husband.

He frowned and stared at his wife.

"He was out at Calliope Key. Where Beth thinks she saw a skull."

Jake picked up the napkin, but hardly bothered to study it.

"She sounds as if she's paranoid already," Ashley murmured.

Jake shook his head.

"Perhaps," Ashley began, "I should—"

"No," Jake said firmly. "No. She's back here, and she's safe. There's no reason to say anything."

"We both know—"

"Yes, we both know. But we don't know what the hell else is going on. Leave it. I'll call Bobby, they'll

152

check out the island. Other than that, there just isn't a hell of a lot we can do."

"Jake—"

"Ashley, it's out of our hands. And besides, since we don't really know anything for certain, what the hell are we going to say?"

She sighed, still unsure that silence was the right course.

KEITH SURFACED, lifting his mask, spitting out his mouthpiece. He saw Lee on deck—his binoculars in his hands, looking toward the island.

Hand on the ladder, Keith kicked off his flippers and crawled aboard.

"What?" he asked Lee, shedding the rest of his equipment.

Lee shook his head slowly. "I'm not sure what they're doing."

The day before, they had caught sight of Sandy and Brad on their old scow of a boat—and the couple had been watching them through their binoculars.

"What does it look like they're doing?" Keith asked.

"Stashing, stowing . . . getting rid of something. In a hurry."

Keith took the binoculars from Lee and turned slowly, scanning the horizon. *Damn!* He thought as he sighted a Coast Guard cutter. *Beth.* She just wasn't going to let it rest. She'd gotten the authorities involved. The problem was, they weren't going to find anything.

"Take a look," he said softly to Lee.

Lee took the binoculars back and followed Keith's line of vision. "Coast Guard," he muttered. He looked at Keith. "Anything we need to worry about ourselves?" he asked. "This isn't the time to be making explanations."

Keith shook his head.

"Nothing down there?" Lee asked tensely.

"Not yet."

"What was on the radar?"

"An old tire iron."

Lee swore. "Well, hell, let's get ready for guests, then, huh?"

Keith nodded.

He turned, moving down the deck to find the freshwater hose and rinse down his equipment before stowing it. Lee hurried down to the cabin.

As he worked, Keith was startled to see that Brad had gotten in his dinghy and was motoring quickly away from his anchored boat.

He chose the direction away from Keith and his group, disappearing around the island.

He was gone for only a matter of minutes, back long before the Coast Guard cutter approached.

Brad hadn't even turned on the dinghy's motor, he thought. He had used the oars, but had moved with incredible haste.

Why?

The answer was obvious. To try to go unnoticed. And to get rid of something.

Or some*one?*

• • •

ON MONDAY BETH HAD BEEN hopeful, by Tuesday she had been mad, and on Wednesday she was morose, then angry again, this time with herself.

Keith Henson knew her name, where she came from and where she worked. She realized that she'd had it in her head that he was going to find her, that he was going to say he had to see her again, that he was as mesmerized, fascinated, and in love or lust with her as she was with him.

But obviously he hadn't made any effort to locate her—she was simply too easy to find.

Every time the phone rang, she answered it eagerly, then was disappointed. Since she had come home, she realized, nothing had changed.

She still thought about two things: Keith Henson and the skull on the island.

She realized that she was becoming obsessive, but she couldn't seem to help herself. Despite the fact that Ashley and Jake had been true to their word—they had taken her seriously and gotten a friend to order the Coast Guard to search the island—nothing had been discovered. She should have been happy—there had been no corpse on the island, no body parts.

But she couldn't help wondering where the skull she had seen had been hidden, or whether at this point it had been removed entirely.

At home—and even at work—she had spent hours online, looking up everything she could find on the Monocos. There were pictures of them alongside their magnificent yacht. There was even an old photo of them—from perhaps fifteen years ago—when they'd been at her club. That meant some of the older members might have known them.

She'd also searched the name Keith Henson on the Internet. She found a dozen men of that name who had Web sites or were mentioned in articles.

He was not one of them.

She was thinking about both the island and Keith now, as usual, tapping a pencil idly on her desk, when there was a knock on her office door and George Berry, the current commodore of the club, poked his head in.

"Beth?"

"Hi, Commodore."

"May I come in?"

"Of course, please do."

He sat in the chair across from her. "I've been worrying about the Summer Sizzler."

"Oh?" She smiled questioningly.

The Summer Sizzler was an annual event, and all new members were seriously encouraged to attend. It was an important date on the club's social calendar. The food had to be the best. The entertainment was expected to be the same. And it was coming up in less than two weeks. She, along with the entertainment committee, had it well in hand.

"Chef Margolin has been working hard," Beth assured the commodore, when he didn't say anything further. "He hasn't given me his final menu yet, but

I'm willing to bet that once again, he'll completely outdo himself."

The commodore waved a hand in the air. He was a man in his early sixties, with a head of the most remarkable silver hair she'd ever seen. His wife had the exact shade. They both had twinkling blue eyes, and in Beth's mind, they were adorable. They'd had no children, and for as long as she could remember, they had put their time and efforts into their various boats, charities and the club.

Like the Monocos, she found herself thinking.

"You *are* planning something very special, aren't you?"

She arched her brows, looking at him. *How special?* The Summer Sizzler was like an end-of-the-season party—not as major as New Year's, Christmas or the Grand Ball, when the new commodore was installed each year.

Special?

Of course, there was going to be a great menu. And she'd ordered torches, and wonderful light and flower arrangements for the outside bar area, hired a band. . . .

"Really special," Commodore Berry said insistently.

His concern gave her an idea. "I think you're going to be very happy with my plan," she told him.

"You do have a plan for something special?" he asked.

She saw no reason to tell him that her plan had just come to mind. "Give me a day or two, and I'll lay it out for you, all right?"

"It's going to be incredible, right?" He smiled anxiously. "It has to be, you know. I want to go down in history as the best commodore this club has ever had."

"We'll see to it," she vowed.

As soon as he had left her office, she jumped up and headed for the stairs that led down to the first level, with the dining room and, beyond glass doors, the patio. Just a little while earlier, she had noticed a member she had been anxious to talk to—Manny Ortega.

Manny was in his sixties, just like the commodore. He was a fascinating man, who'd come over from Cuba in his teens—lying about his age in order to enter the States with a conga band. He had worked clubs all over Miami in his day.

She was certain he must have worked with Ted Monoco at some time in his life, and she was more than certain he knew the couple, because, according to an item in the paper, he had called the police about the Monocos, suggesting that they were missing.

"Hey, gorgeous," he said to her as she approached his table. He was sitting, Cuban coffee in front of him, smoking and staring out at the different vessels in their berths.

Manny loved his Cuban cigars. He always had the real thing. She wasn't at all sure how he got them, but she never asked.

"Hey, yourself," she said. "And thank you. Can I join you?"

"Absolutely. What's up? Need an aging drummer?"

She laughed. "You never know when I'll take you up on that, Manny. Actually, I was curious. I happened to be reading some old newspapers the other day. Are you a good friend of the Monocos? Ted and Molly?"

"Yes, I am."

"Have you heard anything from them?"

He shook his head slowly, his mouth downcast. "Not a word."

"Do you think something happened to them?"

"Well, I did. But the police told me the other day that their yacht had been spotted, so I guess I have to respect their right to privacy. Seems odd, though. They've always kept in touch with me before."

"It does seem odd. Do you know who actually saw their boat?" she asked.

He tapped his cigar, studying the smoke. Then he looked at her. "Is there a reason you're asking all this?"

"Oh, we just came back from Calliope Key, and it made me start thinking."

Manny lifted his hands in a fatalistic gesture. "Who knows about people? They tell me that Ted and Molly can do what they want, that they are adults. So . . . did I offend them somehow? I don't know. Could they show up tomorrow? I suppose."

"But . . . don't they have bills to pay and stuff? Taxes?"

"Everything is done automatically from Ted's accounts. He set it up when they started planning to sail around the world. I just hadn't realized he was planning on closing the door on old friends."

"So no one has talked to them?"

He looked upset, and she wondered if she was treading on dangerous ground. Manny's feelings had evidently been hurt. He might have started off worried, but whatever the police had said to him must have made him believe that his old friends just didn't care anymore.

She leaned forward. "It doesn't sound like the Monocos to me," she said.

He arched a brow. "You knew them?"

"No, but . . . they were—or are—nice people, right?"

"The best," Manny agreed.

"Then it doesn't seem right."

"No, it does not seem right. But it is . . . what is." He stood and stretched. He was a man of about five-nine, compact and wiry, his features weathered. He set a hand on her head. "You're a sweet person. Kind to worry, but don't. It will do nothing but frustrate you, I promise."

But they were your friends, she longed to remind him. She managed not to say anything, in the interest of remaining employed.

She nodded, then, on a whim, asked, "Manny, have you ever met a man named Keith Henson?"

He frowned. "I do seem to recognize the name. In what context, I'm not sure. I don't think I've ever met him, but the name rings a bell." She waited, he frowned. After a minute, he shook his head again.

"How about Lee Gomez?"

"Hey . . . this is Miami. I know dozens of Gomezes."

"But a Lee?"

Again he shook his head.

"Matt Albright?"

"No . . . can't say I know that name."

"How about Sandy Allison or Brad Shaw?"

He stared at her, frowning and took a puff of his cigar. "What is this today, Beth? Twenty Questions? All these names? There are three million people living here."

She flushed. "They're just people we met on the island."

"Honey, people have been going to that island for centuries. Lots of them. From all over."

"I know. But the name Keith Henson rings some kind of bell?"

"Yeah. But I don't know what."

"Thanks, Manny," she murmured. "Sorry for bugging you."

"I have to go, big date this afternoon," he said. She had always thought of him as a dapper man, rather an old-fashioned word, but one that fit him. He inclined his head toward her. "Thank you for the lovely company, Beth. See you later."

"Oh, Manny, I'm sorry. One more question. A man named Eduardo Shea bought the studios from the Monocos. Do you know him?"

"Sure."

"Is he . . . a nice guy?"

"Thinking of salsa lessons?"

"Maybe. Mostly I'm planning something for the club."

"The studios are doing well under his ownership, I have heard. He's a decent fellow, a good teacher. Is that what you need to know?"

"Yes, and thanks for the help."

"My pleasure." He stood, ready to go, then paused. "You are a very nice person, Beth. It's your job, I know, to be nice to people, but there's a real kindness behind everything you do. Don't make life miserable for yourself. Trust me. I don't know if Ted and Molly are alive or dead. I know that my fears make sense, and that the explanations I hear from the police make sense, as well. I've learned that there's nothing I can do. You should learn from my experiences."

"Thanks, Manny," Beth said. "You're pretty nice yourself."

He winked. "You're cuter. Have a good day, Beth."

He left. Beth waved, then rose. Walking back inside and through the dining room, she noted that Amanda was seated at a table with a group of women. She was wearing a white skirt suit and a broad-brimmed white hat.

Only she could carry it off, Beth thought, hoping to pass through unnoticed. But Amanda looked up, and Beth groaned inwardly. She was going to be asked about something. Amanda would do her best to make it appear that she wasn't doing her job.

But Amanda only stared at her for a long moment,

then she turned away, as if she had assessed Beth and dismissed her entirely.

Beth returned to her office. As she reached it, she hesitated. Her door stood ajar. She could have sworn that she had closed it. A sense of unease raked along her spine. She gave herself a mental shake. Ridiculous. A member had simply come up to talk to her, then not closed the door all the way. The commodore had come back, perhaps.

She smiled, thinking she was really becoming absurd.

But as she walked into her office, she was convinced that things were . . . wrong. It seemed that the papers on her desk had been moved slightly. Frowning, she began looking through her things. Nothing seemed to be missing.

She glanced at her computer.

It was off.

Her frown deepened. She hadn't turned it off.

A chill shivered through her. And yet . . . there was nothing really frightening here. Maybe there had been a power surge. Maybe she had hit the off button without realizing it.

But she never turned it off during the day.

Still . . .

It was broad daylight. There were dozens of members and employees in and around the club. There was absolutely no reason to feel a sense of danger.

Yet she sat down slowly, the icy hot trickle of fear refusing to abate.

It remained with her throughout the day, and even followed her into the darkening parking lot when she finally left that night.

THURSDAY.

Morning dawned.

Keith and Matt stood on the aft deck, looking across the water.

The disreputable vessel belonging to Brad and Sandy remained where she had been at anchor.

Matt let out a long sigh. "Guess they have no jobs to get back to," he said.

"They don't know what we're doing," Keith said with certainty, though their presence had disturbed him, as well. He had explored the area where he thought Brad had dumped something, but he hadn't found anything. Still, the ocean was huge, and water and sand shifted. He hadn't known exactly where to look—or what to look for. He was still convinced, however, that Brad had thrown something into the sea.

Something he hadn't wanted the Coast Guard to find.

"I still don't like it," Matt said.

"I don't like it, either. Frankly, I don't like anything about the two of them. But as far as what we're doing goes . . . Matt, one of us stays on board as lookout, all the time. We can't stop our work completely just because other people are anchored nearby."

"They've been anchored nearby for too long," Matt pointed out.

"Maybe they're saying the same thing about us."

Matt snapped around, looking at him sharply. "I don't want to leave," he murmured.

"Maybe we should, though. Spend a night among the masses. See if we can pick up any idle gossip, any rumors."

Matt stared at him, eyes narrowed, and shook his head. "Keith, I think you're going off track. I'm upset that Brandon is dead, too. But now you're convinced that some old couple's disappearance is somehow connected, but I don't see how."

"They might be dead, too."

"Lots of bad things happen. Lots of people die. They're not all related."

"Nope, not all of them. But I don't think it would hurt to do a little investigating."

Matt looked like he was about to argue, but then he shrugged. "You might be right." Then he smiled. "I imagine you want to try to get an invite into the domains of a certain yacht club?"

"There are plenty of places to put ashore," Keith said.

"I repeat—"

"Yeah, I think we *should* head to that area. Other than Brad and Sandy, those were the people hanging here."

"We'll talk it over with Lee," Matt agreed. "And you're right," he murmured, sounding a bit disgruntled. "It's just damn convenient for you, huh?"

Keith shrugged. Hell, yes, he was anxious to get over there.

He was worried about Beth Anderson. She was home, but he knew in his gut that the Coast Guard had been out here because of her. Still, Brad and Sandy were the suspicious ones, and they were out here, while Beth was safely on the mainland. He shouldn't feel uneasy. But he did.

What the hell were Brad and Sandy up to? Hanging around forever, tossing things into the water.

He wanted to just go over and ask them what they were doing, but he didn't want to arouse suspicion against himself. He reminded himself firmly that a boatload of Coast Guard sailors had arrived on the island, stayed a good long time and searched the interior—and found nothing.

Beth had not given up. She had gone to someone with the power to make things happen, and what was to say she wouldn't push the issue again?

His smile faded, and he shook his head. She was like a dog with a bone, refusing to let go.

And that could be really dangerous for her. Because something *was* going on out here. He was sure of it.

Brad had been afraid they would search his boat, so he had gotten rid of something in the ocean.

So why were he and Sandy still there, watching them all the time?

It all kept coming back to one thing.

The skull.

8

ASHLEY SURPRISED BETH AT THE club on Friday.

"Hey! What are you doing here?" Beth asked when Ashley appeared at her door.

"Letting you take me to lunch."

"Cool."

Ashley slid into one of the chairs in front of Beth's desk. "I don't know why, but now you've got me going."

Beth pushed back the menu she had been going over and looked up, waiting for her friend to go on.

Ashley shrugged a little sheepishly. "Well, I told you the Coast Guard found nothing."

"Yeah. So . . . ?"

"I tried to find out if the Monocos' boat really had been seen."

"And?"

"Your friend Manny actually made inquiries up in Palm Beach County. I checked with the officials there, and no one ever made an official report about their boat having been sighted. And no one ever officially filed a missing persons report."

"I thought Manny did."

Ashley shrugged. "Nothing official. According to the police up there, there were inquiries made, that was all. An officer might have talked him out of

167

making an official report, because when you're over twenty-one, it isn't illegal to disappear, as long as you choose to do so."

"So where does that leave us?"

"Nowhere. Just that you've made it into a mystery that intrigues me. Now let's go eat, or I'll run out of lunch break."

Beth nodded and rose, and they went downstairs to the restaurant. They both ordered the mahimahi, which, the waiter assured them, had been caught that morning by some of the staff. As he started to move away, Beth suddenly caught his arm. "Henry, who is that, third table down, her back to us?"

"Ah. Maria Lopez. You've met her, right?"

"Yes, but only once."

"She's beautiful, isn't she?" Henry said admiringly. "She was an international dance champion. They called her the queen of salsa."

"I know. Didn't she work out of the Monoco studios?"

"I believe so. She danced all over the world. She's sixty now, if she's a day. She has the figure of a young girl, yes?"

"A well-endowed young girl," Ashley murmured, grinning. "She's striking."

"Excuse me," Beth said. She glanced at Henry and explained. "I have an idea about the club and salsa lessons. Maria Lopez being here today is too perfect. Be right back."

She was obsessed, Beth realized, but it was all right,

because she *knew* she was obsessed. Hell, even Ashley admitted that her curiosity had been piqued. "Ms. Lopez?" Beth said, feeling comfortable, because it was perfectly within her duties to greet the woman. "How very nice to see you."

The woman, as beautiful as Henry had said, turned to her.

She frowned slightly, trying to determine just who Beth might be; then a smile, soft and lovely, warmed her face. "Hello, Miss Anderson, isn't it?"

"Beth, please."

"Will you have a seat?"

"It's so wonderful to see you here," Beth said, sitting down.

"I like to come down by the water," Maria said. "The sea and sun can be so rejuvenating, don't you believe?"

"Definitely," Beth agreed. Where, and how, did she plunge in? "In fact, I was just out at Calliope Key, and that made me think of an old friend of yours. Didn't you work with Ted Monoco?"

Maria's dark eyes flashed, and for a moment, Beth was afraid she had made the woman angry. But then Maria said, "Oh, yes. Ted and Molly. Such wonderful people. Those were the days. The studios he ran were the best. He gave people the gift of movement, the gift of dance."

"How wonderful," Beth murmured. "I guess now . . . he's giving himself the gift of the sea and the sun."

Maria Lopez sat stiffly for a moment, then shook

169

her head. "No, I fear not."

Beth swallowed carefully. "What do you mean?" she asked, careful not to give away her own thoughts.

"I believe something has happened to them. I would have heard from them otherwise, and there has been no word. I miss them," she said softly. "And the worst is . . . there seems to be nothing I can do." She forced a smile. "So here I am. Lunching near the sea."

"I'm so sorry," Beth said. She paused for a moment, then asked, "Tell me, do you still dance?"

"Sometimes, yes," Maria said.

"I was wondering if . . . perhaps . . . you would consider dancing for our Summer Sizzler here at the club."

Maria arched a delicate brow.

"I'd love to do something extraordinary," Beth explained.

Maria was clearly flattered but not yet convinced. "To dance, one needs a partner. Perhaps you could speak to someone at Ted's old studio, the main studio, on South Beach. All the studios were bought by a man named Eduardo Shea. He does well."

This was too perfect, Beth thought, everything falling into place so casually and naturally.

"So I've heard—Manny told me," she explained. "You know Manny Ortega, I'm sure."

"Oh, yes, of course." She offered Beth a full smile. "Manny is very talented, a lovely man. He knows Eduardo, as well. Eduardo is also quite an interesting man, half Cuban, half Irish. I can dance for you—with a partner, of course. But you should bring dance to your members, as well."

"That's what I've been thinking. That we should offer lessons here."

"Your members will have so much fun. And the single men will do much better with the ladies."

"Maria, what a wonderful idea."

The older woman flushed slightly. "Thank you. Call Eduardo. Tell him that I suggested you speak to him. And if you go through with this, I will dance with his instructor, Mauricio. We will need to rehearse, of course. And if you wish your party to be a real success, you'll need at least two male and two female instructors. I will work with them, of course."

"I don't know how to thank you."

Maria laughed. "You will receive a bill."

"Of course."

"Truly, it will be my pleasure," Maria said, inclining her head, something regal about the movement.

As Beth rose, Maria reached for her bag. "Give me a moment. . . . I have Eduardo's card, and also my own, so that you may call me with details."

Beth accepted the cards and reminded Maria that if she needed anything, to please let her know. As she left the table, she stopped Henry and told him that she would sign the tab for Maria's lunch. Then she hurried back to Ashley.

"The fish was wonderful," Ashley said.

Beth apologized swiftly. "I'm sorry. It's just that—"

"There was Maria, who knew the Monocos, and

you're still obsessed with their disappearance, so . . ."

"Ashley, I saw a skull."

"Beth, you're not a cop."

"So I should feel in my gut that a murder—no, murders—have taken place and just forget it?"

"The police are on it," Ashley said.

"I hope so," Beth said. "Anyway, I needed something special for the Summer Sizzler. Now I've got it."

Ashley groaned, took a last sip of her iced tea and rose. "Jake and I will be at your Sizzler thing, by the way."

"Thank you."

"God sometimes needs help looking after fools," Ashley told her.

Beth grinned and waved as her friend left the dining room.

WHEN KEITH WOKE UP THE following morning, Brad and Sandy's boat was gone.

Even though he'd been bothered by their presence, he found their absence alarming.

Once again, he headed out to dive the area where he was certain that Brad had cast something overboard, though he was aware that both Lee and Matt, back on the boat, were convinced he wouldn't find anything.

He was close to shore, and there was a lot of seaweed in the area. Though the seas were relatively calm, the sand seemed to be rising; the area was murky.

A large grouper came quizzically toward him, stared

172

at him, apparently found nothing of interest and moved on. A small horseshoe crab, sensing danger, dug more deeply into the sand. A tang, far from the reefs, shot by.

Hands clasped behind his back, fins barely moving, he went over and over the area, trying to follow a grid. He wasn't deep, maybe twenty-five feet, so he could have stayed forever. But he began to wonder himself if he wasn't crazy. Maybe Brad hadn't really dumped anything. Or maybe the guy was a pot smoker and had tossed out his stash. Fish miles away could be chewing it up by now.

The sound of his own breathing was getting monotonous. He usually liked the sound. It was peaceful, just like diving, but now, he was aggravated, looking for what he couldn't find—just as it seemed he had been doing day after day.

A clown fish darted past his mask. A small eel slithered up from the sand and made a hasty retreat.

Though it seemed pointless, he retraced the area for the tenth time, even as the water began to turn chilly.

Just when he was about to give up in total disgust, he saw it.

At first he wasn't quite sure what he had found. He saw it in the sand. He reached out, dusted sand away, picked it up.

Stared.

Stopped breathing, the cardinal sin in diving.

Gulped in air again.

And knew what he had found.

• • •

IN THE MORNING, BETH DROVE out to the beach to keep an appointment with Eduardo Shea.

He was a striking man, not particularly tall, perhaps five-ten, no more. His eyes were a brilliant blue, and his hair seemed to be pitch-black. He was tanned, with fine bone structure and quirky, flyaway brows. He had a smile in place long before he reached her.

"Miss Anderson, welcome."

"Mr. Shea," she murmured.

"Come in, come in. We'll talk in the office."

She nodded, walked into his office and took the chair in front of his desk. The walls were lined with plaques, and the shelves held all kinds of trophies. Her heart quickened as she saw a large picture on the wall of Eduardo Shea shaking hands with Ted Monoco, Molly at her husband's side, beaming.

"I see you like that picture," Eduardo said.

"He must have been a very fine man," she murmured.

Eduardo frowned. "He *is* a fine man, talented, and also a good businessman. You don't always get the two together."

"Very true," she agreed, then changed the subject so he wouldn't think she was unduly interested in the Monocos. "How long have you owned the studios?" she asked.

"Not quite a year. But we are doing very well. Ted Monoco established a legacy of excellence, and we do our best to preserve it," Eduardo said proudly.

174

"I had a conversation with Maria Lopez yesterday, and she—"

"Yes, I've spoken to Maria. And I'm prepared to offer you an excellent deal."

"Oh?"

"Maria will dance with Mauricio, though she says she won't teach. But I know Maria—she won't be able to stop herself. We'll send four more teachers. As to the music, I must approve the band, because if the beat isn't right . . ."

"Perhaps you'll suggest a band," Beth said diplomatically.

"I'll be happy to. Now, as to the cost . . ."

He laid out a rate scale that was more than fair. She thanked him, a little curious that he was willing to let his teachers work so cheaply.

"I have faith in their abilities. Your people will be coming to the studio to go on with their lessons, I promise you."

"I hope so," she murmured, finding herself looking at the wall again.

"You know the Monocos?" he asked.

"I've seen them," she said vaguely.

"They were so excited to be off on their boat. Ted loved two things—dancing and his boat. After Molly, of course. They're a great couple, still in love, after so many years. So few people mean 'till death do us part' anymore."

"Some people do," she said.

"Ah, a dreamer. Well, I like dreamers. Though

175

dreams won't come true if people don't create them. Think of Ted. With nothing but his talent, he built up this business—and a fine retirement income."

"Were you friends before you bought the business?" she asked politely.

"Of course. I bought the business because I learned from Ted," Eduardo said. He glanced at his watch. "I have a lesson coming up. I'm delighted we'll be doing business together. In fact, I'll teach you myself on the night of your party. Next thing you know, you'll be taking lessons yourself."

She smiled. He and Maria seemed to have the same cheerful confidence. Nice.

"We'll see. I'll talk with you about final arrangements," she told him.

As she rose, he walked around the desk and in an old-fashioned manner, kissed her hand. She tried to decide if he was sincere or just slick.

On the way out, she paused, looking again at the pictures on the office walls. They had all evidently been taken at various competitions. The men were in tuxes. The women wore ball gowns, elegant, formfitting, beautiful.

And in one of the pictures, smiling at the camera, looking her most devastating, was Amanda Mason.

Beth scanned the rest of the pictures. Yes . . . there, in one, Amanda's father, Roger. And in another, Hank and a lovely young blond woman. Even Gerald, though he was merely in a group shot where a trophy was being handed to a woman.

"Are you interested in competitive dance?" he asked her. Before she could answer, he said, "Of course. You know the Masons. They're boaters."

"Yes, I know them. They belong to the club."

"Well, they won't be needing any basic instruction."

"I hope they'll enjoy the evening especially, since they already dance," Beth said. "Thank you again, and we'll speak soon."

She hurried out, her mind spinning.

What did it mean?

She groaned aloud. It meant that the Masons enjoyed dancing. Big deal.

She shook her head, wondering what she was doing, what she had accomplished. Eduardo Shea didn't seem worried about the Monocos. Eduardo had known them. The Masons had undoubtedly known them.

So?

She could meet a dozen people associated with the Monocos.

Those who had known them, worked with them, sailed with them, liked them.

And it all came back to . . . so?

None of it was bringing her any closer to the truth.

THE MONORAIL TOOK AMBER to school and home again. It was a ten-block walk from the Coconut Grove Station. Usually she got off and walked straight home, then called her father—Mr. Paranoid—who generally got home not long after.

This was an early-release day, though, and she had forgotten to tell him. Since Kim was with her, and she wasn't expected anywhere, Amber decided that they should walk down to the club.

It was a long walk. They stopped at a fast-food joint near the highway for a soda, but by the time they reached the entrance to the club, they were both sweating.

"Straight to the café," Kim said.

"We should tell Aunt Beth we're here first," Amber said.

"Why?"

"So she knows. Then she can call my dad."

"Water, water. We need water," Kim said.

"Okay, water, then Aunt Beth's office."

"Your dad is a member, right? So we're allowed in with or without Beth."

True, Amber thought, but she felt uncomfortable not letting her aunt know she was there first thing. It was going to be bad enough when Beth called her father to tell him that she'd forgotten an early dismissal.

When they approached the gate, Amber waved to the guard, who waved back.

"Beat you inside!" Kim said, and started running. Amber didn't have the energy to run, and by the time she entered the club and walked through to the restaurant, Kim had disappeared.

Amber went up the stairs, but Aunt Beth wasn't at her desk.

Kim *was* there, a look of pure mischief in her eyes.

"Look—her computer is on. She's getting an e-mail."

"Kim, you can't use my aunt's work computer," Amber protested.

"No, no, you have to look! This is totally awesome. It's him. I'm sure it's him."

"Who?"

"What do you mean, who? The hunk from the island."

"Keith?"

"Yes. Would you get over here and look!"

Amber exhaled a little nervously but couldn't resist temptation. She walked around the desk and stared at the computer. The e-mail read:

Beth, I got your address from the switchboard. This is Keith, from the island. I'm asking you again to forget anything you think you saw. Let it go, please. There's a new twist. I'll see you soon and explain.

"Should we answer him?" Kim asked.

"No!"

Kim hit Reply and started typing anyway.

Will I really see you soon? I'll be waiting anxiously.

She turned to Amber and asked, "What do you think?"

The two of them started to giggle.

"We shouldn't be doing this," Amber moaned.

"Oh, come on. She needs a life. Don't you want a

really hot uncle?" Kim demanded.

They looked at each other and started to giggle again. Amber smiled slowly, then started to type herself. If I'm not at the club . . . Once again, she hesitated.

Then she typed in her aunt's address, added Or Private message me and gave her aunt's screen name. With one last determined look, she hit Send.

"Oh, yes." Kim applauded.

They heard a noise that seemed to be coming from one of the nearby offices. Kim jumped up. "We need to get out of here now."

"Let's go."

They crashed into each other in the doorway in their eagerness to escape the office and their guilty endeavors, then ran down the stairs.

THE MAN REVELED IN HIS OWN strength and a sense of superiority.

Kids, he thought with a sniff. Thank God they were so into themselves, so silly, so unobservant.

He wondered briefly what he would do if a child got in his way. He smiled grimly. He had decided once that nothing would stop him. Still, one simply had to hope that certain snags never entered into a picture, since it was impossible to truly know exactly what one would do until the occasion arose.

He entered Beth Anderson's office in practiced silence and looked around slowly at first. He wasn't afraid; he could easily explain his presence there.

Then he walked over to the computer and pulled up the e-mails, curious what the girls had been up to.

For a moment he felt as if ice was running through his bloodstream. But then he relaxed as he realized there was nothing there that could be held against him. Nothing. He was certain of it.

There were tissues on her desk, the box held in an elegant gold wire basket, the metal filigree artistically designed into the shape of sailboats.

He grabbed two tissues and carefully, slowly, meticulously wound them around his forefingers. Then he wiped the keys he'd just touched and began to type himself.

BETH WAS THOUGHTFUL as she returned to the yacht club, worried that all her plotting and planning would come to nothing. Maybe everyone was right. Not that she'd been imagining things. She was too sure of what she'd seen for that. But that nothing she did would change anything. Even nature was against her. The ocean was vast. The truth of that was never more apparent than when you were out on the open sea in a small boat. It was easy to imagine that the sea could swallow a boat and leave no trace.

Then again, the sea had a habit of flipping a finger at humanity. Flotsam and jetsam usually washed up somewhere!

But not always.

She waved to the guard at the entrance, not really paying attention, and pulled into her space, close to the main building. Inside, she hurried upstairs. In her office, she tossed her handbag onto a chair, slid behind her desk and sat down. She closed her eyes, leaning back for a minute.

Forget it. Just get back to work, she charged herself.

With a shake of her head, she rolled her chair forward and touched the space bar on her computer to turn off the screensaver.

She nearly flew back in the chair.

A giant skull appeared on the screen, then flashed off as if it had never been there.

It was followed by the words *I'll be seeing you soon. In the dark. All alone.*

She jumped up and ran out of her office, ready to run down the stairs and find the manager or the commodore or anyone.

But as she reached the foyer and looked into the dining room, she came to a sudden halt.

Kim and Amber were there, just inside the doors, heads together as they sipped sodas. They looked up and saw her.

Both girls were talented actresses onstage, but in the real world, neither one of them was much at deception. The eyes that met hers were wide and filled with guilt.

She stared at them. "What are you doing here?" she demanded.

"Early-dismissal day," Amber said, swallowing hard.

The girls exchanged glances.

Beth crossed her arms over her chest, furious. She was sure they hadn't really intended to do anything awful, but she had been scared. Really scared.

"Early dismissal," she choked out.

"I . . . forgot to tell Dad," Amber said. "So, I, um, came here," she finished weakly.

"To my office," Beth said icily.

Both girls gulped.

"You were on my computer, weren't you?" Beth asked accusingly, forcing herself to keep her voice low, since she was at work.

"Aunt Beth . . ." Amber began, then trailed off guiltily.

Beth tried hard to control her temper, but she still felt frightened, and that didn't help matters.

She always tried so hard with Amber. It was such a delicate balance. She wasn't Amber's mother and could never hope to fill that void. She wanted her niece to know, though, that someone was always there for her, as a mother figure.

Her real mother would have had the luxury of real fury and the ability to punish her without losing her, but Beth had to tread a milder path.

"I suppose you thought you were very amusing," she began.

"I—just thought—" Amber began.

"I don't want to know what you thought!" Beth exploded, good intentions forgotten.

"Please don't tell Dad," Amber begged. "I'm sorry, really sorry. I'll make it up to you. Somehow. If you tell Dad, then he'll tell Kim's parents, and then . . ." Her voice faded. She looked at Beth and whispered, "Please. We really didn't mean to be terrible."

Beth didn't answer her. She had to calm down. She turned around and walked back up the stairs, not knowing if the girls would follow or not.

In her office, she sat down again, shaking.

She looked at the computer, then started to laugh. She had apparently tripped over the cord on her way out. The only thing that greeted her now was a blank screen. After a moment she rose, found the displaced plug and returned it to its rightful lodging.

A week ago she wouldn't have been scared, she would have been puzzled.

Her anger had already begun to fade, probably because she had been so frightened, then so relieved.

She weighed the situation while she logged on and opened up her art program, working on plans to promote the Summer Sizzler and make sure she got everyone in the place excited about the dance lessons.

Do I tell Ben about this or not? she asked herself, returning to the question of the girls and their prank.

Amber would hate her.

Amber would have to get over it.

Maybe she should give the girls a second chance.

She forced her mind back to business. She was going to need a picture of Maria Lopez, which should be easy enough to find online. She pulled out Maria's card to call her for permission.

She found a picture that was sensational and was

also able to reach Maria immediately. In an hour her flyer had come along perfectly and was ready for printing. With that accomplished, she sat back in her chair—just as her brother made an appearance at her door, his daughter right behind him.

He was frowning. "You knew you had the girls?" he asked.

She could see Amber's eyes. Pleading.

She shrugged, not willing to outright lie when the girls had done something so wrong.

"They never cause any trouble here, Ben." She stared at Amber. "Almost never," she added with a grim smile.

She saw him relax. She hadn't lied, though she hadn't exactly told the truth, either.

"All right, but I'm supposed to know as well when it's early dismissal," he told his daughter.

"Dad," Amber said, and there was a slight note of reproach in her voice. "You have the school calendar. You just don't always pay attention."

Ben opened and closed his mouth. "Yeah, I have the school calendar," he said finally. He sounded gruff. He turned and walked away.

Amber stared after him, thinking he was still angry. Beth knew better. He was just feeling as if he'd somehow failed as a parent.

Amber stared at Beth again, and Beth was startled to see tears rising in her eyes. "I'm sorry, Aunt Beth. Really sorry."

"Don't do it again," Beth said softly. "And your dad

lives for you. Give him a break."

Kim slipped an arm around Amber as they walked off together.

"Hey," Beth called. "Kim—what's the story? Am I driving you home later, or are your folks coming?"

The girls turned back to her. "I'm getting picked up at five-thirty by the guardhouse," Kim said. "Thank you," she added quickly.

"Right," Beth murmured. "Amber, after Kim's folks have come, we'll find your dad and have dinner before we leave, okay?"

Amber nodded and took off with Kim.

Beth watched them go, forgetting her own anger. This aunt thing wasn't easy, she thought. Of course, life never was.

She smiled slightly, turning back to her work, writing herself a mental note that she should be checking up on Amber's school schedule more than she had been.

BEN WASN'T ANGRY; he felt depleted. He was actually a pretty good father. He just sucked at trying to be two parents at once.

He sat at the outside bar, sipping a beer. "Hey," came a call.

Looking around, he saw Mark Grimshaw. As kids, they'd taken sailing lessons together. Then they'd wound up at law school together upstate, and, like their fathers before them, they'd both become members of the club.

"Hey yourself."

"Your latest case is sure making headlines," Mark told him.

Ben must have winced, because Mark quickly apologized. "There's a group of us—and not all attorneys, honest—at the pool. Why don't you join us?"

Ben lifted his beer. "My daughter's here. I think we'll just grab a bite and go home."

"It's early. They're not even serving dinner for another hour. Maybe your daughter wants to hop in the pool, too."

No, his daughter wouldn't want to hang with her old man. But maybe a few laps would tire him out, if nothing else.

"Sure. Let me go to my locker. I'll join you in a few minutes."

Mark nodded, smiling. He was a pleasant guy. Worked on civil cases, had a great reputation. Ben had tried to set Beth up with him. Beth liked him well enough but insisted there was just no chemistry.

In the locker room, Ben shed his coat, eased out of his tie and began to turn the wheel of the combination lock on his door. As he did, he thought he heard a noise and hesitated, looking around.

He wouldn't have been surprised to see someone. Lots of guys came straight from work, changed and headed out to the pool or their boats.

What surprised him was that he didn't see anyone.

He was certain that he hadn't been alone a moment ago.

Working too hard, too much. Worrying too hard, too much. Hell, if life was just a jaunt out on the boat, days on an island . . .

Hell. He suddenly wanted to give Beth a good shake. He was jumpy because of the stinking island!

With a shake of his head, he turned back to his locker and started the combination over.

Click . . . click . . . click.

The lock opened.

He changed and went out to the pool.

It wasn't even dark yet. He'd been ridiculous, thinking he'd heard something. Someone.

Disgusted with himself, he strode out to the pool and dived in. Strong-armed, he did lap after lap. When he came out, dripping, his friends were waiting with a beer.

Amber had come out. She smiled, waving to him. Apparently Kim's folks had picked her up. She walked over. "Dad, think Aunt Beth would mind if we ate burgers out here? I was thinking about hitting the pool, too."

"Sure. Aunt Beth won't care. It's a nice night, and you're right—we should just be casual out here." He left it at that, but inside he was inordinately pleased that she'd wanted to spend some time with him after all.

She smiled again, then scampered off to change. His heart took a sudden plunge.

It was hard to love someone so much and not smother them with that love.

As he watched his daughter walk away, he felt again the pinpricks that had haunted him in the locker room.

Fear.

Irrational but all too real.

He was scared. And he wasn't at all certain why.

It just seemed that suddenly a shadow, something dark, had entered his life, stealing away comfort and ease. . . .

He looked up.

The sun was still out, brilliantly shining.

The shadows, he tried to tell himself, were all in his mind.

9

BETH WAS GLAD SHE HAD KEPT her mouth shut about the girls messing with her computer. When she joined her brother and niece out at the pool, she found a number of families engaged in a game of chicken.

Ben, with Amber on his shoulders, was trouncing the opposition. There was a lot of laughter and camaraderie going on. Nice.

She sat on the sidelines, watching, until Amber saw her and waved, then tapped her dad on the top of the head and alerted Ben to her presence, as well.

The competition tried to take advantage of Ben's distracted state, but Amber turned back, ready to take on the world. Her opponent went down, and Amber laughed delightedly.

Like a child.

Then the two of them, after high-fiving each other in victory, laughed and left the pool, joining Beth on the sidelines.

"Congratulations," Beth said.

"Thanks," Amber said. "You're cool with this, right? Hamburgers okay with you? I'll go put our orders in. Would you rather have fish, Aunt Beth, or the salad bar?"

Beth shaded her eyes to stare at her niece. "Are you suggesting I *should* choose the salad bar?"

"No!"

"I'm going to have a hamburger and fries and iced tea," she told Amber. "Ben?"

"The same."

Amber nodded, grinned and went off to the counter to order.

Ben stared at his sister. "Dancing?"

"You could learn to dance," she said defensively. "Salsa, I've decided. For a party—'Summer Sizzler.' "

"I think it's great," he assured her. "Summer Sizzler—salsa. What's not to like?"

"Good."

"But are you sure that's all you have in mind?" He leaned closer. "Tell me you're not still trying to find out more about the Monocos."

"I happened to see Maria Lopez at lunch. She's a salsa queen. I spoke with her. It will be fun, good exercise, and Eduardo Shea gave me a great deal, because he thinks some of the members will sign up for dance lessons."

Ben let out a sigh, shook his head and leaned back in his chair again.

To Beth's dismay, one of the members, a woman named Tania Whirlque, came over and immediately brought up the same subject.

"Hey, Beth, I hear we're having a dance workshop at the Sizzler."

She hadn't even put the flyers out yet.

"Do you like the idea, Tania?"

"Love it, especially if they're going to arrange for a few teachers. I'm not so sure I'll get my husband out on the floor, though."

"We'll have to work on the guys," Beth said.

"You know, when I heard Eduardo Shea's name, I got thinking about the Monocos," Tania said. She took a seat next to Beth.

Beth couldn't keep from casting a slightly guilty glance at Ben. "It seems that no one has heard from them."

"Quite frankly, I fear the worst." Tania hesitated. "We have friends from Virginia who lost a boat to pirates."

"Really? What happened?" Beth asked, all her suspicions on the alert again.

"They were off Chesapeake Bay, in a forty-five-footer by themselves. They were anchored, sunning . . . I think Betty was cooking dinner. They were attacked by thieves who climbed aboard in dive gear. They thought the divers were in trouble at first, lost . . . whatever. Anyway, turned out they were armed. While Betty and Sal were being welcoming, the divers pulled knives, forced them overboard and stole the boat."

"How horrible! But they survived?" Beth said.

"They're both strong swimmers, and they were able to reach another boat in the area. They called in the Coast Guard, but the thieves got away."

"When did it happen?" Beth asked.

"About a year ago now. The boat has never been found. But then, you can disguise a boat just like you can disguise a car."

A year ago. Before the Monocos disappeared.

"Could they describe the . . . pirates?" Beth asked, finding she still couldn't quite wrap her mind around such a crazy concept.

"One was male, one was female," Tania said. "And that's about it. They both had on wet suits and head covers. I talked to Betty about it. She says when she looks back now, it all happened so fast that she can't really remember much about the incident. Frankly, she's just glad to be alive. Where they were . . . well, even though they're strong swimmers, they could easily have drowned."

"The thieves probably meant for them to drown," Beth murmured.

Ben moved uncomfortably, obviously disturbed. She wondered if it was because of the story Tania had told or because he thought it would fuel her desire to find out the truth about the Monocos.

"Ben is always armed," Beth said.

"Ben has good reason to be armed—he put away a few unsavory characters when he was with the D.A.," Tania reminded them. "You're a crack shot, right?" she asked him.

He nodded grimly. Then he said, "Let's drop this, please? Amber is coming back with our burgers. I don't want to scare her."

Despite the fact that he laughed and teased his daughter as the evening wore on, Beth could see that he remained uneasy.

Finally she realized it was getting late. "I've got to go back to my office before I go home. I left my stuff up there. See you tomorrow sometime?"

"Probably. Are you working?"

"For a bit. I usually come in just to see how things are going on the weekends. You know that."

"Want me to walk you out to the parking lot?"

"You guys have to change, and I'm tired. I just want to go home, and we have a security guard in the parking lot, remember? But thanks. And, Ben, I'm okay—I haven't gone off the deep end."

Beth said good-night to Amber, then left, hurried up to her office for her handbag and jacket. After scooping up her things, she turned out the light, and headed downstairs and out the front door.

The club hadn't completely shut down for the night. The dining room would still be serving until around ten or ten-thirty, and then it would take another hour to an hour and a half to close down completely. And that night, out by the pool, the snack bar was serving late, as well.

There were still plenty of people around, talking and laughing. Even so, Beth heard her heels click on the concrete.

As she walked, she could hear the breeze as it rustled through the trees and bushes that grew around the borders of the club and the reflecting pool by the front steps.

Suddenly she thought she heard footsteps coming up behind her.

She told herself there was no reason for the sound of footsteps to frighten her. The club was still full of people, one of whom might have chosen to leave at the same time.

Was it in her own mind though, or were these footsteps echoing her own almost perfectly?

She paused, turning back.

The breeze lifted her hair and felt cool against her neck.

No, it felt chilling.

"Hello?" she called. "Anyone there?"

There was no reply.

The bushes, which seemed so benign by day, suddenly seemed thick and dark, able to hide a million dangers.

She straightened her shoulders and gave herself a mental shake. "Hello?" she called again. Once more there was no reply.

She started walking again, looking toward the front of the lot, where the security guard should have been in his little glass-windowed booth.

She couldn't see him. He might have been sitting, with his head in a book, perhaps.

Or someone might have taken him out.

"Oh, right," she murmured aloud, disgusted that she was letting her mind go off in such a paranoid direction. He was there somewhere. Or maybe he had gone off to help someone who was having car trouble.

Her car was only another fifty feet or so away.

She stared at it, hugging her purse against her side, reaching inside until she found the comforting shape of the pepper-spray canister.

The parking lot was well lit, but bright lights always allowed for shadows.

And those bushes, so big and lush, admired by everyone who came.

She didn't like them anymore. Not one bit.

Aim for the car, she told herself. She had to get over this feeling.

The sounds from the club had faded completely. Click, click. She could hear her heels against the asphalt again, and then . . .

Footsteps, following.

She turned back once more.

This time she was almost certain she saw a shadow go flying behind a tree.

"Hello?" she called.

No one answered.

The car was nearly in front of her, and she made a hasty decision.

Screw rationality.

Run.

She did, and she was ready, keys in her hand, to click open the lock and jerk open the door as she reached the car.

Quickly she slid into the driver's seat and slammed the door shut. She started to exhale, then remembered to hit the automatic lock.

She let out a sigh and leaned back, allowing herself to feel a little ridiculous. When she looked to the side, she could see the guard in his little booth.

She closed her eyes again, took a deep breath and opened them. She frowned. The guard was gone again. She leaned to look out the passenger window to see where he had gone.

That was when someone loomed up in the driver's window.

BEN KNEW THEY SHOULD LEAVE, but he was really enjoying the evening. Amber was smiling and playful, almost like she had been when she was younger.

She was a good kid, he reminded himself. Talented, driven. He was lucky.

"Did you notice that yacht anchored on the other side of the *Sea Witch*?" Mark asked Ben.

"Huh? Sorry . . . I was drifting, I guess," Ben apologized.

"It's a night for that, isn't it?" Mark said.

"I don't think I've noticed any new boats around," Ben said.

"She's a real beauty. I'd love an invitation on to her!"

"What is she?"

"Motor yacht. Looks like she's fitted for anything in the world you could think of doing out on the water," Mark said.

"Oh, yeah? Some guys out on Calliope over the weekend had a boat like that," Ben said.

"Were you on it?"

"You bet. It really was fitted out for anything in the world."

"Well, if it's the same guys and you know them, get me an invitation," Mark said.

Ben nodded. "There were three of them. A guy named Lee Gomez owns her. His friends were Keith Henson and Matt Albright."

"Yeah? What do they do for a living?"

"Family money bought the boat."

"There you go. Can't beat family money."

"Nope. Better to earn it yourself," Ben protested.

Mark laughed. "You see it your way, I'll see it mine. Doesn't matter—I don't have any family money coming my way, so I guess I'll have to go with that damn earning it thing. Well. I'm going to change and get out of here. If you see those guys, though, hang on to them and call me."

"Sure thing," Ben said. He looked over at Amber. She had been lying on one of the nearby lounges, but

197

now she was staring at him. She looked a little ashen, or maybe it was just the light.

"You think it's them?" she asked.

He shrugged. "Could be. I think somewhere along the line I said they were welcome here anytime. I thought you liked them."

"Uh, yeah. I'm going to shower and change, Dad. You about ready?"

"Yup." He rose and set an arm around her shoulders. "Let's go home."

She didn't shake him off. She suddenly seemed glad of his arm.

SOMEHOW BETH REFRAINED FROM screaming, then was glad she had.

It was just Manny, tapping at her window.

She turned the key in the ignition, then rolled down the power window. "Hey, Manny."

"Hi, gorgeous. I hear we're having a salsa night at the Summer Sizzler." He sounded pleased.

"Yes, do you like the idea?"

"Love it. Maria will be dancing?"

"Yes."

"Wonderful. Well, sorry, I didn't mean to startle you." He started to walk away, but before she rolled the window up, he turned back to her.

"Did you go out to the beach and see Eduardo Shea?" he asked.

"I did."

"What did you think?"

She was startled by the question. "Um, he seemed to have a lot of love and respect for the Monocos, and he also seemed to like my idea. I think he likes the fact that most of our members can afford dance lessons if they like the taste they get at the Summer Sizzler."

Manny was studying her strangely, she thought.

But everything that night had seemed strange. It was definitely her, she decided.

Manny shrugged. "Sounds good."

"I hope so. Actually, some of our members have already taken lessons at the studio."

She was curious to see if he would ask her who—or if he would already know.

"Oh, of course. The Masons dance."

"Right."

"I'm sure it will be a fantastic evening. Good night."

Nothing suspicious there, she told herself dryly. "Good night," she returned.

He walked away. She rolled up her window and, shaking her head, started out. The guard was in his booth as she drove past.

A creepy feeling crawled up her neck, and she threw her car into Park at the entrance to the main road.

She turned, almost dreading what she might find, and looked carefully into her back seat.

There was nothing there.

Her car was an SUV, with plenty of room in the back. She actually got out, circled to the rear and stared into the back, then breathed a sigh of relief when she saw that it was empty of everything other than her mask, fins and a towel.

Feeling like a fool, she hopped into the driver's seat and headed home.

BEN OPENED HIS LOCKER and frowned. He wasn't obsessive-compulsive in any way, but neither was he a slob, and something seemed . . . out of order, somehow.

He looked over everything. His jacket was hanging on the hook. His shoes and suit pants were on the first shelf, his toiletries on the middle shelf. The things he kept on the upper shelf were there, just as they had been. Stuff he kept at the club that was only used at the club. His silly St. Patrick's Day T-shirt, his Halloween glow sticks and vampire teeth were there, along with the plastic eggs that members put pennies in for the little kids to find at Easter. His schlocky vampire cape was folded over everything else.

He couldn't think of a thing that was missing.

He checked for his wallet and found it right where it should have been, in the pocket of his trousers. His keys were there, as well. There was nothing missing.

He still had the feeling someone had been in his locker.

With a little oath of self-disgust, he got his clothing, slammed the door and headed for the showers.

BETH LOVED HER HOUSE. It was a row house, right on Mary Street. Although it wasn't really that old—no more than thirty or so years—it had been built in the old Spanish style. She had a little front yard to go with it, and a matching backyard. The entire diminutive community was enclosed by a high iron fence, with each house possessed of an individual gate for its front walk.

Her yard boasted a palm and a lime tree, and in the little garden area, she had different kinds of flowers in a brick plant bed. Her porch area had a swing seat.

It was no problem to leave her car overnight on the street, since pay parking ended at midnight and didn't begin again until nine the next morning. The Grove was one of those places that wasn't in a hurry to get up in the morning. Few places— other than banks— opened before ten o'clock, and lots of the shops didn't open until eleven.

She parked in front of her house, then opened her unlocked gate and headed for the door, only to discover that whatever paranoia had gripped her at the club had apparently followed her home. As she headed up the little walk, she was suddenly certain she saw a shadow on the street.

A shadow that was there, then gone.

The streets here—absolutely beloved by day—suddenly seemed eerie by night. Coconut Grove was famous for the lush foliage so many home owners encouraged, but by night, especially when there was a moon, there were shadows. And rustling leaves. Always. It was something she didn't usually think about.

But tonight . . .

She hurried up the steps to her door. On her way, she dropped her keys. She bent to retrieve them and looked back toward the street, certain she'd heard footsteps.

There was a huge oak just down the street.

It seemed that—just as they had in the parking lot at the club—a smaller shadow suddenly merged with the larger one of the tree.

As if someone had slipped behind the oak.

She quickly retrieved the keys and cursed when her fingers shook.

She got the key into the lock and twisted it. The door opened. She stepped inside, slammed it shut and leaned against it, quickly turning off, then resetting, the alarm, and locking the door.

The prickling of unease at her nape remained. She didn't turn the lights on but eased around to the window, kneeling on the couch and just touching the drapes, determined to look out. Her eyes widened.

She hadn't imagined it.

There had been two shadows.

A man emerged from behind the tree.

She could make out nothing about him, other than the fact that he was tall.

And that he was watching her house.

She sat back quickly in the dark, amazed and, oddly, not as terrified as she might have been.

At least she wasn't crazy.

She looked out again quickly, realizing that she

needed to watch him, needed to see where he went, what he did.

But when she looked out again, he was already gone.

It was then that fear set in.

Had he already moved closer to the house? Was he trying to find a way in . . . ?

Was he out there, closer still, nearly breathing down her neck?

What to do . . . call the police?

And say what? There had been a man standing on a public street?

She shook her head, got up and suddenly went into speedy motion, running around the downstairs first, checking every window, running through to the back, checking to see that both bolts were secure, then heading upstairs and assuring herself again that all her windows—and the glass doors to the upstairs balcony—were securely fastened.

She was certain she was never going to be able to sleep that night.

She dragged a pillow and blanket downstairs. In the living room, she set up a bed on the couch, then stood still in the middle of the room.

She had lights on everywhere. That was probably stupid—in fact there was no "probably" about it.

But she didn't want to sit in the dark.

At least she had heavy drapes. Coconut Grove was the kind of place where people walked all the time, where they took out their bicycles and ran with their dogs. She loved living where she did, but she also liked privacy, so her drapes kept her safe from the public eye.

She turned on the television. If she was going to sleep tonight, it would be with the television on and every light blazing. Fine.

As a last precaution, she dragged one of the heavy end chairs from the dining-room table and set it in front of the front door. Foolish? Maybe, but she couldn't help remembering the skull jumping out at her from the computer, and the words that had been written there.

I'll be seeing you soon. In the dark. All alone.

She knew she was being foolish. Amber had written the words. She had admitted it.

Still . . .

Someone had been out there, and there was nothing wrong with being careful.

Finally satisfied, she lay down on the couch, and hit the channel changer until she got to Nickelodeon. There was little likelihood of anything coming on that might scare her into a further fit of unease.

A vintage sitcom was playing, just as she had expected.

She eased her head against the pillow, smiling a little wryly at herself. This was all absolutely ridiculous. No reason to be afraid.

Then something thudded against the front door.

Sharp, hard, startling.

She bolted upright.

$\bullet \quad \bullet \quad \bullet$

"DO WE REALLY HAVE TO GO BY Beth's place now?" Ben asked, puzzled. "I'll see her tomorrow."

"I have something of hers, Dad," Amber explained. "Something—personal."

He assumed his daughter had taken some of his sister's female necessities and was in a panic to give them back.

Whatever.

It had been a great night, but he was tired.

"Dad, she's only two minutes away," Amber said.

He forced himself to grin at his daughter. "Liar," he accused with fake ferocity. "It's at least five minutes."

"Dad," Amber groaned.

"All right, all right, we're going."

They turned onto Beth's street, and he pulled his car up behind hers.

He frowned. Something seemed to be lying on the porch. A dark . . . lump.

"Um, Amber, stay in the car for a minute, huh?" he said.

He opened the gate and hurried along the walkway. His heart sank. It was an animal. Bending down, he saw that it was a cat. A black cat, and one that had evidently been in an accident. Poor thing; it had probably crawled off the street and on to Beth's porch. Maybe it had somehow known that a softie lived inside, a woman who would have rushed a strange animal right to the vet, no matter what the cost, if the creature had lived.

205

He hesitated. He didn't want his daughter or his sister seeing the badly mangled creature.

Amber was starting to get out of the car.

"Stay back!" he told her.

He returned to the car himself and opened his trunk. He tended to keep extra supplies for the boat in the trunk. Paper towels, toilet paper, dish detergent and, luckily, trash bags.

He went back for the cat.

"Dad?" Amber called.

He picked up the dead animal, deciding he would get rid of it without either woman knowing what had happened. "It's all right, honey. Just a mess of foliage," he called to his daughter.

He bagged the cat and walked around to the trunk. As he dropped it in, Amber emerged from the car.

With his daughter in his wake, he headed up the steps again and rang the bell. There was no answer. He rang again, then pounded on the door, which flew open.

Somehow, instinct warned him, and he ducked—right before a burst of pepper spray could hit him in the eyes.

"I'm calling the police, you pervert!" his sister swore, just before the door slammed shut.

10

THEY PULLED THE DINGHY UP to one of the club docks. Matt leaped out first, ready to secure the small boat.

"Nice place," Keith murmured, following behind him.

Before Lee had even joined them, Keith heard a cry. "It *is* you!"

Lithe and sleek as ever, Amanda Mason was sashaying down the dock. "How delightful."

"Amanda," he murmured.

She hugged and kissed all three of them, as if they were long-lost relatives.

"I wondered when you all would make it in," she said. She was in a sundress, the kind that showed off the perfection of her figure but also seemed fine for a casual night out.

Her sandals were studded with rhinestones. Her toes were painted perfectly.

"We decided we needed a little civilization," Lee said.

"Oh, honey, no one ever promised to be civil," Amanda said. "Come on in. We were about to leave. Thank goodness we waited. Daddy is here, and both my cousins are here tonight, too. It will be just like old-home week on Calliope. Well, minus Sandy and Brad. And I think the Andersons all just went home, too. But come on, Daddy would love to buy you guys a drink."

"We should buy your father the drink—we're invading his territory," Keith said. He wanted to remain polite and friendly, even flirty. But it was difficult with Amanda. A bit too much encouragement and she would be all over a man. Under different circumstances, he might not have minded, but right now, he had business to see to. He had an address, and Lee had called ahead for a car. It should be arriving within the next half hour.

"So, the Andersons just left, huh?" Lee said.

Amanda pouted as if that was the saddest news in the world. "Just a little while ago. Come on."

She linked arms with Lee and Keith; Matt was left to trail behind.

"Actually, you're in luck. Do you know who's here tonight?" she whispered.

"Who?" Lee asked.

"Maria Lopez, the award-winning dancer. If you stick around for our big event—the Summer Sizzler—you'll get to see a real salsa queen in action." She shrugged. "An aging queen, but the woman *can* dance. We're in the dining room," she said.

She led them into the dining room, with its teak trim, polished bar, sea-blue carpeting and white marble tiles.

"There they are," she said.

The three men rose as Amanda returned. They had evidently just eaten. Waiters were clearing the table.

Except . . .

It didn't look as if Roger had eaten after all. His spot was crumb free, there were no used plates, and the silver remained wrapped in a linen napkin.

Apparently Roger had just arrived as well, Keith thought, though that didn't have to mean a thing.

As the plates were swept away, coffee was being served.

"In from the sea at last," Roger said. Tonight, the patriarch of the clan was in a white suit. He wore it well.

Hank was more casual in a calypso shirt, and Gerald was wearing perfectly starched trousers and a tailored shirt, looking as if he had just shed his jacket and tie.

"So how's life been going out on Calliope Key?" Hank asked politely.

"Fine," Matt said. "What's not to enjoy about beautiful days out on the water?"

"Are you staying on the boat now, or still camping?" Roger asked.

"Mainly on the boat," Lee told him.

"Diving, diving, diving, huh?" Roger said.

"Nice life when you can get it," Keith admitted.

"Discovered anything out there?" Roger asked.

"Clown fish, angels . . . rays—saw a huge ray yesterday," Lee said.

"No sign of any wrecks?" Roger asked.

"No. Should we have seen something?" Lee asked.

Roger shrugged. "It's shipwreck city in these waters," he said.

"Did you see my girl out there?" Hank asked the newcomers. "The *Southern Light* has her berth here."

"We saw her," Keith said, thanking the waiter who was bringing over more chairs. "She's a beauty. Your club is great, too."

"I've actually been here before," Lee said. "And it is great."

"So, are you vacationing in Miami for a while now?"

"Taking a room anywhere?" Roger asked. "I can recommend some great places."

"Daddy, they could stay with us," Amanda said.

All three men in her group stared at her hard. Lee quickly said, "Thanks, but we're going to stay out on the boat. It's easy to get in and out."

"What are you drinking?" Roger asked them.

"We'll join you for coffee," Hank said.

"Excuse me, I'm off to the facilities," Keith said, rising. "Coffee would be great," he added, determined to escape before he could be followed.

"There's one by the front entry," Roger assured him.

Keith nodded, made his way through the tables out to the foyer, trying to get the layout of the club straight in his head. He looked back. Lee had risen with Roger Mason. The two seemed to be thick in conversation. Amanda had been left to flirt with Matt. Their conversation seemed to be intimate. Hank and Gerald were left to speak with one another. Keith watched the dynamics for a long moment, then hurried up the stairs. Curious that Gerald was here tonight. He'd been under the impression that the man lived farther north along the coast and wasn't around that often.

It didn't take more than a few minutes to find her office. He let himself in and closed the door.

THE DOOR FLEW OPEN a second time.

Beth stood there, looking horrified. She swallowed hard and said worriedly, "Ben?"

"It's all right," Ben grated out. "You missed me. Barely."

"Dad? Aunt Beth, what did you do?" Amber cried out indignantly.

"It's all right," Ben said, straightening. He stared at his sister, stunned. Beth was pale, in shock. Mortified.

"What?" he demanded.

"You scared me," she said. "Oh, Ben," she apologized again. "I'm so sorry." Then she straightened her shoulders. "What the hell were you doing out there? What did you throw against my door?"

He let his shoulders fall as he shook his head. He noticed the large dining-room chair, now moved over to the side of the entry. "Beth, kitchen," he said.

"Hey," Amber protested.

"Get in and lock the door, Amber," Beth said as Ben took her by the shoulder, prodding her toward the kitchen.

He sighed as she stared at him. "Beth, I didn't want to have to tell you—there was a dead cat in front of your door."

"A dead cat?"

"The poor thing had obviously been hit, and it crawled up on your porch to die," Ben told her.

"Ben, someone threw something against my door," she informed him.

"It probably fell against it," he said. "Dammit, Beth. You might have blinded me," he told her.

She exhaled. "Yeah, sorry. The sound just scared me."

He set his hands on her shoulders. "Let go, Beth. Let go of this whole thing with the Monocos, okay? You'll turn both of us into idiots jumping at our own shadows."

She nodded, touched his face. "I didn't get you?"

He shook his head. "Man, I'm tired. Good night, okay?"

She laughed suddenly. "What are you doing here?"

"Amber said that she had to give you something back. Do me a favor—don't tell her about the dead cat."

"Where is it?"

"In my trunk."

She shook her head. "I won't say anything."

They walked back to the living room. Amber was standing there, arms hugged around her chest. "Leave whatever you brought for your aunt and let's go, huh?" Ben said.

Beth stared at Amber, frowning. Amber stared back at Beth.

She wanted to say something to her aunt, Ben realized. Something she wouldn't say in front of him.

It was just going to have to wait until tomorrow.

He swore softly. "Amber, just call Beth in the morning, huh? Let's go."

He walked out the front door. He heard Beth say softly, "Amber, it's all right. We'll talk in the morning."

His daughter followed him. He heard his sister lock her door behind them as Amber headed for the car.

A moment later, exhausted, he drove away.

WHEN KEITH RETURNED TO the table, Amanda was just rising. "I was about to show Lee and Matt around the pool area. Join us?"

"Absolutely," he said. He took a sip of the coffee that had arrived in his absence and arched a brow to Roger. "Coming?"

"I'll let her show you the way," he said.

"We've seen it," Hank added dryly.

Keith nodded and followed the others out. Amanda caught hold of his arm. "I really want you to meet Maria Lopez. She's outside."

The woman was in conversation with a wiry-looking, older Hispanic man. She was animated and spoke quickly in Spanish, her tone hushed.

Realizing that someone was approaching, they both fell silent. The man rose.

"Manny, how delightful," Amanda purred. As she stepped forward, he took her arms and kissed her cheek.

The woman, very elegant in a dignified, old-world way, waited.

Amanda stepped back. "I'd like you to meet Maria Lopez, a very famous member of our little society, and Manny Ortega, a musician and a talented man! Maria, Manny, let me introduce Keith Henson, Matt Albright and Lee Gomez."

Keith thought he saw a flicker of recognition in the man's eyes. But the older man said nothing, merely exchanging handshakes with them all.

"I'm trying to convince them to come to the Summer Sizzler," Amanda said.

"Yes, you must come," Maria murmured politely.

"Will you be in the area that long?" Manny asked.

"We can arrange to be," Lee said in reply.

"If you're dancing, we'll certainly arrange it," Keith assured her.

She assessed him carefully, her beautifully defined features giving away nothing of either appreciation or dismissal. "It will most certainly be my pleasure," she said.

"Well, I'm showing my friends around," Amanda said. "Will you excuse us?"

"Certainly," Manny said.

As they left, Keith noticed that Manny and Maria didn't resume their conversation.

He was certain it was because they both suspected that Lee's Spanish was excellent.

He followed the group around for another few minutes, then glanced at his watch and excused himself.

As he had expected, his car was waiting.

· · ·

"I'VE SHOWN YOU MINE," Amanda said huskily. "Aren't you going to show me yours?"

Matt stared at her blankly. She'd been gone for a while. Said she'd had to feed a dog or something like that. Her cousins had disappeared, too, Gerald taking Lee for a trip around a few of the South Beach bars, Hank claiming to have a date. He'd been left talking to the salsa queen, Maria, and the older fellow, Manny, who had insisted he have a real Cuban cigar.

But then Amanda had returned, anxious to show him Hank's yacht.

The words she had just murmured were a come-on if he'd ever heard one. He was somewhat shocked. It wasn't that he didn't have self-confidence. It was just that in the company of Lee and Keith, he usually came out on the short end. Some men—or women, for that matter—just had an air that attracted the opposite sex. It was sad to admit, but in the company of the other two, he came in last. Like tonight. God knew what Keith was up to. Keith had the leeway to do whatever the hell he wanted; he was the leadman on the job. Lee had taken on the role of getting to Gerald Mason.

Frankly, he'd been feeling like the odd man out.

But now . . .

Here she was, cute as a button. No, not just cute. Sexy, provocative, petite and yet voluptuous. Her fingers rested on his chest. Stupidly he said, "Show you mine?"

"We've taken a look at Hank's yacht. I'd love another look at yours."

"She's actually Lee's," he reminded her.

"But I'm sure you have all the rights of ownership," she teased. "You don't mean to tell me that you can't ask me aboard? Your friends are gone for the night, right?"

How did she know that? It seemed important to know what this woman was all about. And with both of the others gone, it was his job to watch the yacht. "You want to go to my place?" he queried.

She pressed against him. "I do."

He wasn't a fool, he reminded himself. He could hold his own when he needed to. But . . . sometimes work and pleasure could collide.

She must have known that he was hesitating, because she grew even bolder. She ran her hand straight down his chest to his genitals. "I like risk and excitement," she whispered, standing on tiptoe to breathe the words straight into his ear.

"They, uh, they could return," he stuttered, testing her. "I can get a room."

"But I like boats," she insisted, pouting.

She didn't want him. She just wanted to get on the yacht. She thought she'd found a patsy. Well, two could play the game.

"Sure, the tender is right over there," he told her.

BETH LEANED AGAINST THE DOOR, shaking. She had nearly hurt her brother. Badly.

216

She let out a deep sigh, knowing she had to get a grip.

There was a firm knock on the door. She jumped, then caught herself.

Ben. What had he forgotten?

She threw the door open.

There was a man at the door. He seemed huge, looming in the darkness beyond the pool of light where she stood.

It wasn't Ben.

And she no longer had her pepper spray.

A scream rose in her throat as he stepped forward.

She screamed and tried to push the door shut. It met an immovable obstacle and stalled. Then she heard her name.

"Beth. Dammit, Beth. You told me to come!"

She went dead still, only then recognizing the towering form in the doorway.

She just hadn't been expecting him.

She stepped back in shock. She'd spent the first part of the week praying he would call.

The second half of the week, she'd simply been mad.

"May I?" he asked, still standing on the porch.

He was everything she had remembered and more. Dark eyes, a startling contrast to the sun-bleached lightness of his hair. Bronzed. In form-hugging jeans and a tailored shirt, open at the throat.

For a minute she couldn't find speech.

Then she was angry with herself, because she was

being worse than Amber and her friends, gawking, letting herself be thrown off-kilter by any man.

"What do you mean, I told you to come?" she inquired curtly.

He cocked his head slightly, a smile curving his lips.

"May I come in? The neighbors will be out soon, if they haven't called the police already," he teased.

She stepped outside, looking around.

She couldn't help but look over to the tree, then back at Keith.

Had he been stalking her? Hiding behind the tree while her brother was there?

Why on earth would he do such a thing?

Maybe he wanted her alone. All alone.

She lowered her head for a moment. To be frank, she wanted to be alone with *him,* too.

"Beth, are you all right?"

She stepped back and repeated, "I told you to come?"

He let out a sigh. "Today."

"I asked you to come today?"

"In your e-mail. Remember?"

Her brows arched; her mouth formed an O.

"I'm going to throttle her!" she said.

"Who?" he demanded, confused.

"Come in," she murmured.

He stepped into the house, frowning and looking around curiously. Then he turned to her, a half smile on his lips. "Great place. Amber, I take it?"

"What?"

"The one you're going to kill. Somehow she got on your computer and flirted with me, pretending to be you."

"I think so. The little rat tried to scare me, too."

"I see." He was silent a moment, surveying her place once more. Then he turned to her again. "Maybe you *should* be a little scared."

"Why?"

He hesitated again. Then he shrugged. "It's a scary world."

"Do you ever just answer a question?"

"When I can."

"You're a liar. You can answer right now. I should be scared . . . why?" She crossed her arms over her chest. "Because I *did* see a skull on the island?"

"I don't know what you saw on the island, Beth. But everyone there knew you saw *some*thing. And it's obvious that you're scared. Though if you *are* scared of something, it's not really all that bright to go ahead and just answer the door. Actually, you should never just open a door. That's why most of them have peepholes, you know."

"Yes, thank you for the lecture. I answered the door like that because I thought you were my brother."

"You scream when your brother arrives?"

She was glad when the phone began to ring then. She excused herself and went to pick up the kitchen extension.

It was Ashley.

"Hey," Beth murmured, watching Keith Henson in her living room as she spoke.

"I wanted you to know, there's an APB out for those people you met on the island."

She nearly choked. "Which ones?"

"That couple. Brad and Sandy."

She almost gasped in relief. "Um . . . why?"

"They're wanted for questioning. There's no proof of anything against them, and I probably shouldn't be telling you this, but I happen to know that the nameplate from the *Retired!* was discovered in the water just off Calliope Key. I thought you should know. I mean, I doubt they'll show up around here, and hopefully they have no idea they're under suspicion, but . . . well, you might have found the remains of one of the Monocos. The powers that be don't want that news getting out yet, because they don't want to scare them off if there's a chance of bringing them in for questioning."

Keith was still standing in the living room. She had the feeling that he could describe the place in detail if he was asked to do so later.

"Um . . ." She turned away, not wanting Keith to hear her. "Why do they suspect those two?"

"There's a reason," Ashley assured her.

"And that would be?"

Ashley didn't give her a direct reply. Instead, she asked, "Want to meet me at Nick's tomorrow? Breakfast, lunch, brunch—whatever works for you. Maybe you can give me a hand."

Her friend wasn't going to say any more over the phone, she realized. She was just glad for the information she *had* gotten.

If anyone was guilty, it was Brad and Sandy. *Not* Keith Henson or his friends. Not the man with whom she'd already slept, who was standing in her living room, surveying it with what appeared to be a practiced eye.

"Beth?"

"I'm here."

"You'll meet me?"

"Sure. I have to run into the office for a little while in the morning, and then I'll be out."

"See you then. Be careful, okay?"

Beth paused for a moment. "I will."

"See you tomorrow."

"Thanks."

She hung up and found Keith smiling at her. "It really is a nice place."

"I'm glad you like it." She was convinced there was certainly nothing evil about the man, so why did she feel uncomfortable?

She still didn't know why Sandy and Brad were the ones attracting suspicion when others had been on the island, as well, and the Monocos had been missing for roughly a year.

"Are you in Miami for long?" she asked.

"I don't know. We kind of go with the flow," he told her.

"Must be nice."

He studied her for a long moment. "You're acting very strangely."

"According to you, I'm always acting strangely."

"Sorry. And I'm sorry for just showing up, too. I honestly thought I was invited. Since that evidently wasn't the case—"

"It wasn't, but you—you don't have to go," she murmured quickly.

"You don't seem pleased that I'm here."

She smiled suddenly. "Actually, I am," she told him very softly. Then, because it seemed to her that the tone of her voice was way too intimate, she said quickly, "I'm the one who's sorry. I . . . well, to use one of Amber's words, I suck as a hostess. Can I get you a drink? I think I have wine and beer. Or coffee? Tea? Water?"

He grinned, walking toward her.

She was startled that she was still standing. She felt as if her bones had turned to liquid, destroying all hope of remaining upright.

Then he was there in front of her. He touched her chin, lifting it just slightly. She met his eyes and felt as if they could make her forget the world, melt into his being.

She shouldn't give so much to someone she had known so fleetingly, she knew. It was one thing to think she had every right to moments of sex, sensuality and lunacy. But this . . .

This was frightening.

"I can't stop thinking about you," he murmured

huskily, his thumb traveling a path along her cheek-bones. "When I should have been thinking about so much else."

She couldn't think of a thing to say to that.

"Should I leave?" he asked.

"Are we going to go through this again?" she asked very softly.

"I only—"

"If I didn't want you here, I wouldn't have asked you to stay. Yes, I know your speech. Don't get involved with me. Well, we're hardly involved."

"You're mistaken."

"We have different definitions of *involved,* then."

"So this means nothing to you?" he queried.

"I didn't say that," she told him. "But involved . . . that would mean I'd know where you were, not because you owed me explanations, but just because you'd want me to know. Wanting to see me again would be a priority for you, and seeing you would be a priority for me."

"Beth, right now I can't—"

"I didn't ask you to. I'm a grown-up. I've made my choice. I don't want you to go. It's already late. You'll leave too soon as it is, won't you?"

"Yes."

"Well, then . . ."

His movement always seemed unhurried, easy, as if he were a cat that had long studied its prey and seldom failed to reach its objective. It was in his eyes, as well, in his voice, that thing about him, always so casual, and yet . . .

What was his real objective?

Tonight, she decided, it was her.

Tonight there was nothing rushed about him. He studied her eyes again for a long time, as if waiting for a protest, knowing there would be none, but still giving her a chance to turn away.

She had no intention of doing any such thing.

At last his lips touched hers, and every remaining bit of resolve she might have felt fled. Her arms moved around him, fingers threading into his hair, and she tasted the kiss, explored the texture of his lips, felt the exhilarating sweep of his tongue.

His hands worked magic, cradling her nape, pulling her closer. The length of his body was a fire, rock-hard strength, something she wanted, needed. And where before it had been anticipation of all that was new, now it was memory of what was real, electric and compelling.

There had been a strange honesty in getting to know him . . . at least in this. She pulled away and said softly, "I do have a bedroom."

"I'm glad to hear it. And I'd love to see it."

She hesitated. He was giving her another out.

"Are you staying?"

"All night. I have to leave early. If that's all right."

"It wasn't a demand."

He lifted her chin again. "I think I would stay forever if I could."

Strange words. A line? At a different time, that possibility might have bothered her. But not tonight.

She turned, her hand in his, and started up the stairs. He followed close behind. She didn't put on the bedroom light; with him beside her, she liked the shadows, a realm where her own uncertainties could be hidden. With him in her house, she wasn't afraid of whatever lay beyond the door. The darkness offered no threat.

If he wanted light, he said nothing. She stripped the comforter from the bed and watched as he undressed, while she did the same. It seemed so bizarre. She had never had an affair like this before. She wondered vaguely if being together twice constituted an actual affair.

Then she didn't wonder about anything. He came to her in the shadows, touched her, and his naked flesh against her own seemed to be the most erotic splendor she had ever known. She allowed her fingers to play down his chest, feel the beating of his heart, knead the length of his back. The shadows gave her confidence, and from his back she slid the feathery brush of her fingertips lower, teased his buttocks, then stroked the rise of his erection. And then . . .

She found herself lifted, lying on the cool sheets, startled by the extreme difference between the crisp coolness of the bed and the heat of his body.

The pressure of his body aroused her. Their lips fused, hands stroked wildly. They broke apart, panting in the darkness, came together again. Her fingers moved through his hair. His lips moved to her throat, to her collarbone, below.

The touch of his fingers, the simmering, liquid heat of his lips and tongue, slowly trailed down her body. She writhed as if she longed to become part of him. She was in thrall to a brush, a stroke, a feathered sensation that left her yearning for more, a deeper, firmer exploration of fingers and tongue . . . acts of sheer intimacy that amazed her, exalted her, ever so slightly frightened her. She was barely aware of her own sinuous movements, flesh erotically sliding against flesh, the twist and curve of her body as she accommodated his, the sleek motion in which scent and movement, heat and pressure, combined, and it seemed that the world revolved upon the rise of her need and the climax he promised.

She let out a soft cry as the first little ripple of pure pleasure seared through her, a shot that catapulted, and continued, a slow tease that radiated. He rose above her, and in a corner of her mind she was ever so slightly afraid. Afraid because she had found the perfect fit, a man who thrilled and excited her, who captured her soul with the sound of his voice, his merest touch, the way he moved, in bed and out. A fear that he wasn't real, that this total consumption of body and soul would never come again.

Then he was in her and around her. She was striving, twisting, turning, hungry to become a part of his very being. Each thrust took her higher on a wave of eroticism, and the feel of his flesh, burning and powerful, beneath her hands, was almost more than she could bear.

Then there was the moment of ultimate climax, darkness shattered, a brilliant burst of light that shot violently into her mind, a feeling of sheer ecstasy so high and complete, that it shattered into a million pieces of crystal. There was one last powerful surge of his body, and then the collapse against her that signaled the volatility of his own climax, followed by the feel of his arms around her, the return of the shadows, the slowing thunder of her heart and a feeling of incredible completion.

His fingers, moving through her hair . . .

His arms, wrapped around her . . .

His words, soft and teasing. "Where have you been all my life?"

She moved against him. "Here. Right here." She tried to tell herself that no matter what had transpired between them, she barely knew him. Her feelings were insane. She didn't just want him, she was fascinated by him. Sex was incredible, but sex was not enough. She wanted to get beneath his skin, into his soul, know what made him tick, see his smile, feel wrapped in his laughter. . . .

She'd never been this foolish in her life, falling in love so quickly, so completely, forgetting all too easily that she needed to be wary. . . .

But wariness eluded her. Only one question formed in her mind but went unspoken.

Where will you be *the rest* of my life?

227

11

BETH WOKE WITH A START. Alone. She ran a hand over the side of the bed where he had been, feeling a sense of loss. He had said he couldn't stay late.

And yet . . .

Alone, with the morning light flooding in and washing away the shadows, she wondered why.

A meeting with the guys?

After a while, she rose, remembering that she needed to run by the club to pick up her design for the flyer so she could drop it off at the print shop to be made into a poster, then head down to Nick's to meet Ashley.

The thought of meeting Ashley jolted her into faster action. Now, more than ever, she was burning to know why Brad and Sandy were wanted for questioning.

If Brad and Sandy had stolen the *Retired!*, and if she had really seen a skull on the island, it seemed likely that the pair must have murdered the Monocos. The thought was chilling.

And had they also been the ones who attacked the couple in Virginia?

When she had showered and dressed, she hurried downstairs.

He had left coffee brewing for her.

Interesting. He was a man who took off at the first

light of day, but he left brewed coffee.

She drank a cup, still reflecting on his arrival and Ashley's phone call, then hurried out.

It took only a few minutes to drive to the club. She waved to the guard, parked, then ran up to her office and printed off the design she wanted.

She started down the stairs, ready to head out, when she paused, catching a glimpse of someone she shouldn't have.

Or, at least, someone she wouldn't have expected to see.

Not where he was. And with whom.

She didn't go into the dining room. She didn't need to. She could see just fine from where she was.

It was set for breakfast. In the morning, the restaurant manager used the colors of the flag—red, white and blue—and napkin holders in the shape of a captain's hat. Seated at the table nearest one of the paned doors—open that morning, in honor of the beautiful weather—was Amanda Mason. She wasn't there with her father, or either of her cousins.

Breakfast that morning was a buffet.

So was Amanda.

Keith Henson had apparently come for the buffet, too, though which buffet, Beth couldn't be quite certain. To his credit, he had food in front of him.

He just didn't seem to be eating it. Amanda was talking animatedly. Keith was listening. He was smiling; she was laughing.

There was a dress code in the dining room: shoes

and shirts, cover-ups for all bathing attire.

Amanda had followed the code, but just barely.

She seemed to be spilling from the bathing top she wore. Literally. True, she had on a cover-up, but it was sheer gauze.

Belinda, one of the breakfast servers, paused next to Beth.

"You should see the bottom."

"What?"

"Amanda Mason. Her bathing suit. You should see the bottom. Or lack thereof."

"A string?" Beth inquired, surprised. They frowned on such things at the club. This was a family place.

"A two-string. A one-inch square piece of fabric in front and another in back. The strings are on each side. Want coffee? Are you having breakfast?"

"Thanks, but I'm out of here," she said, flashing Belinda a forced smile. "I have plans."

"That's right, it's Saturday. You're off. I guess we're all used to you working so much overtime."

Beth shrugged. "It's not always work. When Ben and Amber are here, I'm just hanging with the family."

Suddenly, she realized that Keith had turned, that he'd seen her. Was watching her.

But he remained with Amanda.

"Well, have a good day off," Belinda said.

"What?"

"Have a good day off."

"Oh, yes. Thanks."

She hurried back out to her car, her head reeling. Once she was behind the wheel, she couldn't quite put the car in to Drive. She just stared out through her windshield.

What the hell was he doing? He hadn't just run into Amanda. He had said last night that he had plans in the morning. Amanda had been his plan? Then why come to her house?

She gritted her teeth. Maybe she was just mistaken about chemistry and some ridiculous inner sense of honor and decency. She didn't really know him. It wasn't as if he'd gone out of his way to seduce her. She couldn't actually blame him for anything. *She* had wanted *him.*

Angry with herself, she started to drive.

Her radio was tuned in to one of the local stations. The hosts were doing a segment called "Dial a Date." One DJ was telling callers to check out the "hotness" of their female guest on the Internet. Then one of the men dialing in asked her about her sexual experience. The guest purred that she knew what she was doing, and yes, if the guy was right—and the dinner good— she definitely slept with a man on the first date.

Beth was pretty sure the phone lines at the radio station were about to start ringing off the hook. She began to wonder if the entire world had come to think of sex as casually as they did breathing. Was that Amanda's take on it?

Was it Keith's?

Worst of all, was the whole thing about something

unique, special and honorable—and sheer chem-istry—all in her own mind?

MATT WOKE WITH A START. Alone.

He sat up, and his head started spinning. He felt ill. "Amanda?"

There was no response. He leaped up, then stag-gered, holding his head between his hands. Sweet Jesus. Had he really had that much to drink? They'd hit the Jack Daniel's on arriving . . . and she'd been with him every second. Aggressive, exciting, quite possibly the most purely carnal experience he'd ever had. Pushing him down, crawling on top of him . . .

"Amanda?"

He made his way out to the galley. She'd left coffee on, but no note. Matt reached into a cabinet for some-thing to kill the pain. He swallowed six caplets, drank a glass of water. His head was still spinning. He leaned against the counter, fighting the sensation. He needed coffee, a bagel, something.

He didn't bother to toast the bagel but ate it almost savagely. After a few minutes, his brain began to kick in.

He swore and went topside, where his voice rose as he cursed to the morning sun and the sea.

She'd taken the tender in.

He hurried back down to the cabin and searched it arduously. Nothing seemed disturbed. Nothing at all.

Still swearing, he judged the distance to the main-land, dressed in swim trunks and a tank, then went topside, furious with both the woman, and with himself.

He'd been had. Big-time.

He hit the water, glad the sea was smooth that day. As he swam, the salt, sun and sea began to clear his head.

But dull torture remained.

Did he tell the others?

"I'M SO GLAD THAT YOU ALL have decided to visit civilization for a while. Although . . ." Amanda smiled knowingly. "I can't say I'm all that surprised."

"You expected us?" Keith asked, smiling back. He didn't need to lean in close. Amanda had taken care of that all by herself. She was at a table but somehow nearly on top of him. There was no way out of the fact there was something naked and almost primeval about her raw sex appeal. She practically reeked of female hormones. She'd had money and position all her life, plenty of time and opportunity to hone the "bad girl who could do whatever she wanted" image.

So different from Beth. Everything about her was just as sensual, as gut level, as sexually, sensually appealing. But there was a touch of class inherent in her allure. She moved with supple grace, as sleekly as a feline. Her voice roused the libido. Her eyes seduced with cool intelligence and an underlying honesty that compelled and . . .

He locked his jaw. This wasn't the time to wax poetic—or simply sexual—about Beth. Or think of the way she had looked at him during their night together.

"What were three handsome, heterosexual men going to do out there forever?" Amanda asked huskily.

Her fingers—nails perfectly manicured—made a fluttering motion down his arm.

"I mean," she continued, "how long can you just dive and fish without some kind of a . . . break, shall we say?"

He shrugged and eased back slightly. "We were intrigued. So many of you had mentioned this place while we were on the island." He offered her a broad grin, moving in closer again. "So . . . this is it. And are you here all the time?"

"A lot of the time," Amanda said. "I love boats. The way they rock. Even when they're just tied up at the dock."

The older Cuban man he had met the other night was taking a seat at one of the tables, Keith noticed. Amanda cast him a brief glance, then paid him no mind.

Manny, Keith remembered. He was the friend who had reported the Monocos missing. He knew now that the Monocos were definitely missing and he was pretty sure he knew how and why. But a piece was still missing. He had a feeling Ted Monoco had known something about his own work out by the island. That nothing was as simple as it looked.

He looked back at Amanda, who was almost on top of him, despite this being a public place.

"You haven't been on board Hank's boat. She's

almost as nice as your friend Lee's."

"Where is Hank?" he asked. "And the rest of your family?"

"Oh, he and my dad have some business today. And Gerald doesn't come around as much as the rest of us. None of them will be around for quite a while."

It was as open an invitation as a man was ever going to get.

"You can tell me all about fishing . . . that rush you get when you land the big one."

She wasn't referring only to fish, he knew.

"And diving. Floating in a different world. A magical world. Making fantastic new discoveries."

Again her words were sexual, but he sensed something more. She wanted to talk. She wanted *him* to talk.

He glanced at his watch, forcing an expression of real regret to his face. "I can't see her right now. I have an appointment with a man about a boat."

Amanda pouted. She touched him again, delicately on the arm. "And you can't postpone it?"

"I wish I could. I'll be back, though."

He rose, made his goodbye.

She waved; he started out.

At the entry, he turned back.

Manny had risen. As Keith watched, he joined her at the table, and the two of them began to talk, heads close, voices apparently low.

He turned to leave again, then noted the dancer, Maria Lopez, at a corner table.

She was watching Manny and Amanda, as well.

BETH PARKED AND WALKED around the back, to the waterside. Ashley was seated at one of the tables there. She had her sketchbook out.

Though it was a public marina and boats came in and out constantly, it seemed to be quiet at Nick's that morning. A few people were down at the docks, working on boats. Friends chatted. Down one of the long piers, a fisherman was already in with his catch, cleaning it.

It was Saturday morning, a lazy time, except for those eager few who were anxious to get out on the water. The real early birds had already gone out and some had already come back in.

She noticed an old sailor, one of Nick's regulars, at one of the tables, smoking his pipe, sipping his coffee, reading his newspaper. Farther down, a mother fed a pair of toddlers, who seemed convinced all their food really needed to be given to the gulls by the water. Signs begged customers not to feed the birds at the tables—such generosity could lead to a scene straight out of Hitchcock. Once started, the birds did not give up.

There was a couple at another table, wearing sunglasses and looking as if they'd partied a little too hearty the night before. Probably why they looked vaguely familiar, she thought, then headed toward Ashley's table that was in the sun, but protected by an overhead umbrella.

"Hiya," Ashley said, seeing her arrive.

Beth slid into the chair opposite her.

"What's the matter? You look glum," Ashley said.

"I'm fine," Beth said.

"No you're not, but you can tell me the truth whenever you're ready."

"So what's up? Tell me what's going on. Why do they think Sandy and Brad went after the Monocos?"

Ashley thrust her sketchbook toward Beth. Beth studied the picture on top. It was of a couple, faces only, side by side.

"Recognize them?" Ashley asked.

"Are you kidding?" Beth asked.

"Look at the eyes."

She did, and hesitated. "It could be them, I guess."

Ashley looked disappointed.

"Who gave you these descriptions?"

"I started with a sketch done by a forensics artist in Virginia. Then I called the couple and got a little more from them. I didn't really think you'd be able to get anything from this, but I thought I'd give it a try."

"It could be them. But if I had to swear to it, I couldn't. There's just not enough there," Beth said regretfully. "But, please, tell me why the police are so convinced Brad and Sandy had something to do with the Monocos just because the boat's nameplate was found. There were a lot of people out there."

"They were seen dumping something where the plate was found," Ashley said.

"You couldn't tell me that over the phone?" Beth asked.

Ashley seemed a little uncomfortable.

"It was found by some boaters who saw Brad throw something in the water."

"Some boaters? The only other people out there when we left were Lee Gomez, Matt Albright and Keith Henson."

Ashley didn't reply. "Their names probably aren't Sandy and Brad," she said.

"Their boat was practically a derelict," Beth reminded her.

"If you were making money pirating exceptional boats, you wouldn't go running around in them while you were looking for more boats to pirate." She hesitated, turned to a fresh page in her sketchbook. "Describe them to me. One at a time. Start with Brad."

"All right, I can try," Beth said. She took her time, being as detailed as she could. She wasn't surprised when Ashley produced a startling likeness of the man, which became even better once Beth made a few adjustments for her.

"So that's pretty close to what he looks like?"

"Damn close."

"Okay. Now let's do Sandy."

When they were done, they had a good portrait of her, too.

"It's strange," Beth said. "They weren't . . . unattractive people. In fact, they were both . . . strangely wholesome looking. But I just realized something about them in these sketches."

"What?"

"They're . . . not remarkable in any way. Like his wasn't the chiseled face of a powerful man you'd recognize anywhere. She wasn't a raving beauty, she was . . . cute. I guess that would be the word. They were . . ."

"Nondescript," Ashley offered.

"Exactly," Beth said. "They were the kind of couple who could . . . well, blend in, disappear almost anywhere."

"Which is what it seems they've done," Ashley said. "Who knows where they've gone."

"I take it you know for a fact that they aren't on or near the island anymore?" Beth said dryly.

"I'm with Metro-Dade," Ashley reminded her. "But from what I've heard, no. The nameplate was found, but they were already gone. And the Coast Guard looked for them."

"How far could they get in their boat?" Beth mused.

Ashley shrugged.

"Maybe they found another vessel to steal and ditched the one they were on."

"Possibly. But I still don't think they're stealing boats and tooling around the seas on them."

"Then what the hell *would* they be doing with them?" Beth asked.

"Bringing them in to a boatyard, disguising them and selling them. It's just like a car theft," Ashley said. "You know, the way cars are stolen here, then sold down in South America."

"Ashley, a million people have a Ford or a Chevy. A luxury yacht is far more noticeable."

"Bigger risk, harder to really camouflage—but the rewards are worth it."

"I see," Beth murmured, then realized that Ashley was staring over her shoulder, looking uncomfortable.

"What?" Beth said.

"Nothing."

Beth let out a sigh of aggravation and turned around. She started.

There was Keith Henson. He certainly had a talent for showing up unexpectedly.

At least he was no longer with Amanda. And with that thought, she couldn't help but wonder if it had been . . . fast. Had Amanda gotten him out on her father's or cousin's boat?

She gritted her teeth, angry that she couldn't seem to get such thoughts out of her head.

Keith was standing on the dock, talking with the man who was cleaning his catch. When she looked farther down the same dock, she saw that Lee Gomez was there, as well, shirtless, in cutoffs, laughing as he spoke to a couple on a handsome catamaran.

Her eyes were drawn back to Keith, and she realized that she had only seen him because Ashley had been staring at him.

"You know him!" Beth accused Ashley, spinning back to stare at her.

"Who?" Ashley demanded innocently.

"That's Keith Henson you're staring at. You know it, and you know *him*."

"I don't know what you're talking about."

Beth stared at Ashley, convinced that for some reason, undoubtedly connected to police business, she simply wasn't being truthful.

"You've seen his face on an APB?" Beth demanded a little harshly.

"No," Ashley protested.

Beth frowned, watching her friend. "Ashley . . ."

"I don't know him," Ashley insisted. "But if he's your friend, you're more than welcome to ask him to come over and join us."

"You're lying."

"Beth, if you want to talk to him alone, go ahead."

"Ashley, what the hell is going on?"

"I don't know what you're talking about."

"You're an incredible artist, but you're a lousy liar," Beth said, trying to control her temper. "Is he a cop?"

"Who?"

"Ashley, stop it! Is he a cop?"

"Not that I know of."

"So you *have* seen his face on an APB!"

"Beth, stop worrying. I was looking at the guy because he's so damn good-looking. He'd be great to sketch."

"You are such a liar."

"You're obviously startled to see him. So go talk to him."

"I intend to," Beth said. She rose and headed

straight for the docks. Despite the sunglasses, she knew he saw her coming.

"Good morning," she said.

"Hey there." The fisherman who was cleaning his catch looked up, thinking she was talking to him.

She smiled, then turned to look expectantly at Keith.

"Friend of yours?" the man asked Keith.

"Beth Anderson, meet Barney. Barney, Beth. Barney here sails out early and sails back in early," Keith said pleasantly.

"Kind of the way you do?" she asked, still smiling and feeling as if her face would crack.

"So you're an early bird, too, huh?" Barney asked.

"He's a busy man, out at the crack of dawn, places to go—people to see," Beth told Barney.

"Sounds like a good life," Barney said approvingly. Keith was staring at her, thoughts and emotions hidden by the glasses, his expression just as friendly as her own.

"The best of everything," Beth suggested. "I'm sorry. Am I interrupting something here?"

"We were just talking about boats," Barney said. "Fine ladies, some of them around here. My own *Sheba* is just a rustic old girl, but I catch all the fish I want." He grinned nearly a toothless grin. "Sell 'em to old Nick up there."

"Good for you. Nick likes to make sure his fish is fresh. Would you like to try the catch of the day, Keith?" she suggested.

"Sometime. I've eaten," Keith said.

"Oh, yes. I did see you digging right into that buffet."

"I know."

"Well, excuse me, then," Beth said, her voice tightening. "You gentlemen go on and enjoy your conversation. Have a nice day."

With that she turned around and walked away. She was suddenly so angry—with him *and* herself—that she completely forgot Ashley. She walked straight to her car, got in and drove away.

KEITH WATCHED BETH LEAVE, frowning. No matter how cool her tone, how casual her words, she was angry, and he knew it.

And he was sorry.

Glancing at the tables, he saw Ashley watching as her friend left.

Then he saw that the couple who had been sitting near the wall of the restaurant in the shade had risen, as well.

They, too, were headed for the parking lot.

He frowned. He'd never seen them before. The guy was bald; the woman had really long dark hair.

He'd never seen them before, he thought again. They were just out for brunch. They'd eaten, and now they were leaving. Odd. He still felt there was something familiar about the pair.

Disturbed, he hesitated. Lee was going to wonder what the hell was going on, but that was just the way it was going to have to be.

Keith headed for the parking lot himself.

BETH DIDN'T KNOW EXACTLY where she was going as she drove out of the lot. Perhaps it was simple habit, but in a few minutes she was heading toward the club. Once she was there, she wondered what she was doing, but since she'd already waved to the guard and parked in her space, she went in. She regretted the fact that she'd walked out on Ashley. What she'd done was incredibly rude, but then again, Ashley wasn't being honest with her, and she knew it. Ashley knew Keith Henson. Or knew about him. Knew something she wasn't telling.

She was about to go straight up to her office, when she heard her name called. Manny.

"Hey, gorgeous. You're not working today, are you?"

"I'm . . . just working on the Summer Sizzler," she told him. "Commodore Berry wants it to be so good, so . . ."

"You've eaten?" he asked her.

"I'm not particularly hungry."

Manny frowned, studying her a little intently. "You look upset."

"No . . . a few things rushing around in my mind, that's all."

"You should get out on the water," he suggested.

She laughed. "Being out on the water doesn't solve everything," she told him.

He shrugged. "Out on my boat, the world is a better

place. I can smoke my cigars and sip my brandy . . . watch the sea and sky roll by. What's better? Lots of space. It puts everything into perspective!"

"I'm sure."

"You come out with me sometime," he told her gravely. "I promise, you'll feel much better."

"Okay," she told him. "It's a date. But I work all week, remember."

"Start work early, then leave early. We'll cast off around four, four-thirty."

"All right," she said.

"Sometime soon."

"Sure, soon." She smiled, gave him a wave and started up to her office.

As she climbed the stairs, she wondered again what the hell she was doing there. But she had arrived, and if nothing else, her office was a nice haven.

She had left it locked for the weekend. She dug in her purse for the keys, opened the door, walked in and tossed her handbag on a chair.

She closed the door thoughtfully as she reached for the light switch, then turned toward her desk.

Then she saw it.

Her heart seemed to stop in her chest.

Dead center on her desk.

A skull.

12

THE GUARD AT THE LITTLE outpost had seen Keith before. He tried a quick wave, but the fellow frowned and stopped him.

"Yes?"

"Hey," Keith said, offering an engaging smile. "You saw me this morning, remember?"

"Yes?" The man didn't smile. He waited.

"I'm a guest of the Masons."

"Your name?"

"Keith Henson."

"I'll have to call the Masons," the guard told him.

It wasn't as if the man were big and brawny, or as if he had a gun, Keith thought. If he had really needed to get through, he would have just gunned the engine.

But he wanted to keep his presence here on the level.

"Go ahead. Amanda is still here, isn't she?" he asked pleasantly.

The man stared at him again, then relented. "Yes, Miss Mason is still here. Go on."

Apparently Amanda had invited men to the club before. He must have fit the profile of her previous guests.

He wasn't sure that pleased him.

Didn't matter. He parked his car and hurried toward

the front entrance. He hadn't been able to move quickly enough to see what car the couple from Nick's had taken from the lot, nor had he managed to follow Beth and discover if the couple had been following her, as well. He wasn't even sure she was here.

As he walked in, he was startled when she came running down the stairs and directly into him.

"You!" she said, backing away as if he had suddenly become poison. He was startled. She wasn't staring at him with the simmering anger she had afforded him just a little while ago. She was staring at him as if he were some kind of heinous beast.

"What?" he demanded sharply.

"Henry!" she called, and he realized that one of the waiters from the restaurant had apparently heard them, and was hovering near the arch that separated the foyer from the restaurant.

"Yes, Beth?"

"Call the police. *Now.*"

Keith's heart sank. What the hell had she found out about him—or what did she think she knew?

"What is it?" he demanded.

"It's amazing, isn't it? I just found a skull on my desk—another skull—and look who's hanging around. Again. Henry, call the police," she repeated.

"Yes, Beth, immediately," Henry said.

"A skull?" Keith said, staring at her hard. Then he walked past her, heading up the stairs.

"Where do you think you're going? Don't you dare touch a thing. The police are on their way!"

He ignored her. She followed him up the stairs, nearly touching him, she was so close. But he continued to ignore her, reaching her office, stopping in the doorway.

"Where?" he demanded.

"On the desk."

He walked a few feet into the office. There was nothing on the desk that didn't belong there.

"Where?" he repeated.

She stood next to him and stared. "This is impossible!" she exclaimed.

By then they could hear sirens. Henry had obviously dialed 911.

"I'm telling you, it was there."

Footsteps were pounding up the stairway.

"What's wrong?"

Keith turned to see Ben Anderson striding into Beth's office. Several other men were behind him.

Ben gave Keith a seriously suspicious glare and hurried to Beth's side. "What is it? What happened?"

"There was a skull on my desk," Beth said heatedly.

"What?"

"There was a skull on my desk," she repeated.

Keith saw the emotions flickering through Ben Anderson's eyes. Dismay, worry, agitation—and a sense of weariness and annoyance.

"Not again," Ben said softly.

Beth glanced at her brother. "Dammit, Ben. What is the matter with you? When have I ever been a scared-of-her-own-shadow, paranoid storyteller?"

"What are you doing here?" he demanded of Keith, as if it somehow had to be the other man's presence that had brought this on.

"Guest of the Masons," he said softly.

"All right, what's going on?"

This time, the question came from a uniformed police officer, who parted the gathering crowd on the landing and came into the office.

The officer, a man of about fifty with clear green eyes and a very slight paunch, looked around, scowling. "Where's the emergency?"

"There was a skull on my desk," Beth said flatly.

"A skull?" the officer said.

Beth sighed deeply. "A skull, Officer. A human skull."

"Where is it?"

"It was there, now it's gone."

"I see."

"I swear to you, it was there."

"All right, folks. Clear out. Go back to what you were doing. This little lady and I need to have a talk," the officer said.

"I'm her brother. Perhaps I can help," Ben said. Beth looked indignant at the soothing tone of his voice, Keith noticed.

"Her brother. All right, the rest of you, please . . ." the officer suggested firmly. "Unless anyone else saw a skull?" he queried.

Some of the people who had gathered began to head down the stairs again.

Snatches of conversation rose to the office.

"Someone is playing a joke."

"It's not that close to Halloween."

"Hey, didn't we have a bunch of skulls as Halloween props?"

"Who are you?" the officer demanded when Keith remained.

"Keith Henson."

"Are you a brother, too? Husband? Boyfriend?"

"I'm concerned," Keith said.

"Look," Beth insisted, drawing the man's attention angrily. "There was a skull on my desk. Can't you look for fingerprints or DNA, or something?"

The officer looked wearier than ever.

"Miss . . . this sounds like a case of mischief to me, and that's all."

Beth appeared outraged. "You mean that you're not going to do anything?"

"I'm not sure what I *can* do," the officer said. "Look, you saw a skull, but it isn't there now. Your friends are probably right. Someone is playing a trick on you. Someone down there is laughing right now. Yes, I'd probably arrest 'em for it, if I could. This is malicious mischief. But I don't know who did it, and I have more important things to be doing than trying to find out."

"There was a skull on my desk," Beth said again.

"I'm afraid it isn't there now," the officer said quietly.

"So that's it?"

"What do you want him to do, Beth?" Ben asked in a conciliatory tone.

She stared furiously at her brother, then at the officer. She didn't even seem to remember that he was there, Keith thought—either that or she was still so suspicious of him that she didn't even want to acknowledge him.

"I want to file a report," Beth said. "I want someone to do something. My office had been locked. I cannot believe that I saw what might have been a human skull on my desk and you don't intend to do a thing about it."

Keith had the feeling that the officer—Patrolman Garth, according to his badge—had been involved in crank calls more than once.

Garth walked over to the desk, studying it carefully. "There's nothing here now. No sign of anything. And, I'm willing to bet, there *is* a master key."

A tall, gray-haired man burst into the office. "What's going on here?" he demanded. "What's this about a skull?"

"Commodore, Beth thinks there was a skull on her desk," Ben explained.

"Officer Garth," the policeman said. "And you're ... ?"

"Commodore Berry."

"Perry," Garth repeated, as if he was beginning to consider the entire place a joke.

"Berry. Commodore *Berry*," the man said, highly irritated. "Current elected head of the club," he explained. "Beth, what's going on?"

251

"There was a skull on my desk," she said.

"But there isn't now?" he asked.

"No," she admitted.

The commodore squared his shoulders. "Miss Anderson is not given to hallucinations."

"Beth," Ben said quietly, "don't you think someone might have been playing a little trick on you? A number of people—including me—have those skulls left over from last Halloween. They were part of the table decorations. And the master key does hang on a hook in the maintenance room. We should be more careful."

"Ah, yes, a *master* key. Hmm. You decorated your tables with skulls?" Garth asked.

"It was Halloween," Ben said.

"Beth, is it possible it was a prop skull?" the commodore asked.

Beth appeared torn. "It's possible," she admitted. "I saw it and . . . and panicked, then ran downstairs to call the police."

"Why didn't you just call from the office?" Garth asked.

Beth stared at him, lifted her hands, let them fall. "Because there was a skull on my desk! I didn't expect it to pick itself up and disappear."

"How many ways are there up to this level?" Garth asked.

"The stairway from the foyer leads up here," Beth said. "And there are restrooms up here, with stairs from the hallway in front of the office downstairs and from the south side of the dining room."

"I believe, Miss Anderson, that someone was playing a trick on you with an old prop. Whoever it was probably didn't think you'd react so quickly by calling the police. That person came up and took off with the skull after you raced down the stairs," Garth told her. "It was a prank."

"I want something done," Beth insisted quietly.

The officer let out a deep sigh. "We'll file a report," he told her. "May I use your desk?"

"Beth," Ben murmured, "you're actually going to make him do this? Fill out a report—over what was obviously a prank?"

"You bet," Beth said.

The officer sat down. Keith decided that, at that moment, he would definitely be more useful elsewhere.

Wanting to see what Beth had been talking about, he entered the hallway and saw the doors to the restrooms.

He hadn't realized that there was more than one way up here. Foolish on his part. He should have explored every inch of this place immediately.

The men's room was large and clean. At the far end of the hall there was a doorway that led to two ways out. A carpeted stairway led down into the club. Another door led to a balcony area, with an outside stairway.

If someone had been in Beth's office, there were plenty of ways they could have retrieved it after Beth went racing downstairs.

Had it actually been the skull she had seen on the island, though? Or had someone heard about her discovery on Calliope Key and decided to either tease her—or warn her—by putting a Halloween prop on her desk?

He followed the stairway to the balcony. From his vantage point, through the trees, he could see some of the cars in the parking lot. He could also see the acreage next door to the club. It was a public park. Anyone who was careful could come and go without being seen. All they would have to do was slip through the trees.

Had the couple from Nick's followed her, then left their car at the public park? Crawled through the bushes to the club grounds and, somehow, broken into Beth's office?

The scenario just didn't ring true.

He took the stairs down to the dining area. Roger Mason was having lunch with a man in a captain's hat. There was no one else he recognized in the dining room.

He walked out to the porch area. Amanda was at a table by herself, leaning back in her chair, broad white hat shielding her face from the sun, staring out lazily at the boats. He saw her cousin Hank at another table, having a beer with a group of men. Farther down from Amanda, he saw Manny Ortega involved in an avid discussion with Maria Lopez.

Without being totally obvious, there was no way to

eavesdrop on their tête-à-tête. He regretted the fact, but knew it was important that he not betray himself.

Looking to the left, he saw that Amber and Kim were by the pool. He wondered if they'd heard about what was going on.

Amanda called out to him.

He strode over to her table. She was grinning wickedly. "So what's going on up there? Has Miss Anderson finally snapped?"

"Pardon?"

"It's all over the club, of course. No one could possibly miss the arrival of the police." She indicated the inside dining room with a wave of her hand. "That's the commodore my dad is speaking with now, poor man. I'm sure he's beside himself with humiliation. We've never had the police here before. Ever."

"I don't think the man is humiliated. I think he's worried about Beth. It's a rather disconcerting thing, don't you think, to see a skull on your desk?" Keith said.

Amanda laughed. "I heard there was no skull."

"Even worse to see one and then have it disappear."

She made an impatient sound at the back of her throat. "Don't be ridiculous. She feels the stigma of her position here, you know."

"Pardon?"

"We're members. She's help. She's crying out for attention."

His temper flared at that, but he controlled it, forcing a casual glance around. "You know, Amanda,

I don't think anyone here feels like that. Her father was a member. Her brother *is* a member. I'm sure she could work somewhere else, if she wanted to."

Amanda laughed and picked up the frosted drink before her. "So you *are* sleeping with her. I thought so. Pity. I liked you best, you know." She spoke casually.

"Well, thanks for the compliment, but I'm just pointing out the fact that we're living in the twenty-first century," he said smoothly. "It's not an upstairs, downstairs world anymore."

"So you believe she saw a skull?"

"I believe she saw something, yes. She doesn't strike me as prone to histrionics."

"Please. A skull? A real human skull?" Amanda said disdainfully.

"I believe there was a skull on her desk. Whether it was human or a Halloween prop, I don't know. Are there any known pranksters here at the club?"

Amanda waved a hand in the air. "Who knows? People here like to have fun. Perhaps someone was playing a trick on her. Maybe even her own brother."

"There's an idea," Keith said, though he didn't really believe it. The more he thought about, though, the more he thought that the use of a skull had to be more than coincidence. The prankster had to be someone who had been on the island.

"Ben did keep one of the skulls in his locker, I hear," Amanda said.

"Don't you think he would have admitted that he'd done it?" Keith asked lightly.

"With the police called in already? Doubtful."
Amanda narrowed her eyes suddenly. "Why don't you
go talk to the little darlings over there?" She pointed.
"Amber and Kimberly. The girls are at that age . . . and
they do prowl around Beth's office."

"Maybe I *should* go ask them," he said lightly, and
rose.

"Do come back," Amanda invited, her voice husky
and amused.

He smiled, and walked over to the pool area. Amber
looked up, sensing the arrival of someone. When she
recognized him, she started, then smiled. "Hi."

"Hi yourself," he said. The girls were both seated on
lounges, but they weren't leaning back, relaxing; they
were sitting up, feet on the ground as they faced one
another. He sat at the end of Amber's lounge. "I hear
I had an e-mail exchange with the two of you."

They both blushed to brilliant shades of red.

He cut right to the point. "Did you put the skull on
your aunt's desk, as well?" he asked.

"No!" Amber said with horror.

He stared at her hard. "I'm not going to the police or
your father with the information, I swear. I just need
to know."

Amber shook her head, stricken. "I swear I didn't do
it. I would never do anything like that. Really."

"Honest, Keith, it wasn't us," Kim said.

He believed them. "Do you have any idea who
might have done something like that?"

Amber sniffed. "Amanda."

"Miss Rich-Bitch Mason," Kim agreed.

He smiled, lowering his head.

"Do you girls think maybe you have a little bit of prejudice going there?" he asked.

Kim looked away. Amber stared at him sagely. "You think? Or is it true that Miss Amanda Mason just takes what she wants and steps on anyone in her way?"

"Wow," he murmured.

"Good call," Kim said.

"Well, you tried to scare your aunt once."

Amber frowned. "No, I didn't."

"Oh, come on, you said that you were on her computer."

"Yes, I e-mailed you on her computer." Amber was frowning. "I didn't try to scare her."

He frowned in return. "Amber—"

His cell phone started to ring, and he excused himself, walking a few steps away.

It was Lee. Keith listened, his heart thudding, then standing still. "We'll talk later. I have to go," he said to the girls after he hung up.

He didn't wait for a reply but strode quickly toward the parking lot.

OFFICER GARTH WAS GONE. The commodore hadn't stayed while the policeman took the full report but had hurried down to play spin doctor about what had happened. Beth thought that he was a good man; he had some doubts, she was certain, but he also believed she had seen something, and meant to find out who had played such a trick and why.

When Garth was gone, she was left with her brother.

He was quiet, sitting in one of the chairs across from her desk, hands folded idly together, looking down.

"Beth," he said very softly.

"Oh, Ben, get off it. I have not lost my mind."

"I just don't believe it was a real skull."

"You don't want to believe me."

"Well, of course I don't," he said impatiently. "I don't want to think that danger is following me home."

"Ben, this is being done to me, not you."

He offered her a wry grin. "Basically, you *are* my home."

She had to smile at that. But she leaned on her desk, trying to reach him. "I swear to you, I have not gone mad."

"Okay, Beth. Whatever you say," he said skeptically.

To her surprise, he got up then and started out of her office.

"Ben?" She followed him.

He stopped and turned back to her on the stairway. "I need to check something, and you can't come with me."

"Why?"

"I'm headed to the men's locker room."

She frowned in earnest. "Why?"

"I'm just checking on something."

"What?"

"Beth, stop it. What are you doing in your office

today, anyway? Take the day off. Go home. Rest. Watch a movie. Do something."

"Ben, dammit—"

"Okay, Beth, I had a weird feeling in the locker room the other day. I think that someone was in my locker and stole my old Halloween skull. I'm going to go and see if it's still there."

"So you do believe me?"

"What I believe is that your wild story from the island has gone around and someone is playing tricks on you, okay? But just playing tricks, Beth. That's it. You can't keep running around as if you've suddenly become part of *CSI: Miami,* okay?"

"Me, *CSI!* You're a mess. You're acting as if you're frantic!"

"Because I think my skull is missing. . . . Don't you understand, I have to see if it's really gone. Okay, I am feeling a little déjà vu. It's weird. But I'm just checking my locker."

"Find out if your skull is gone," she said flatly.

"And then you'll leave, please?" he said. "I will, too. I was going to clean the boat, but forget that. I'm getting the girls, and I'm going home, or to a movie. Want to come?"

"I want to find out if your skull is gone."

He sighed. "All right."

She followed him down the stairs to the pool area. As she walked through the dining room, she felt herself reddening. People were staring at her. They weren't talking to her—they were just staring at her.

At least, when she passed Manny and Maria, they waved, though they looked at her strangely at the same time.

Amber and Kim leaped to their feet when they saw her arrive, while Ben headed toward the lockers. "Are you all right?" Amber asked anxiously.

"Of course I'm all right."

"But there was a skull on your desk," Amber said, no doubt in her voice at all.

"Yes."

Amber looked at Kim knowingly.

"*She* did it," Kim said.

"I'd bet she did," Amber agreed.

"Who did what?" Beth demanded.

Amber lowered her voice. "Amanda. Amanda Mason. She wants Keith, but she knows he's into you. She's jealous, and she's trying to make it look like you're crazy."

"Amber," Beth murmured, though she wondered if, catty as it sounded, her niece might not be right.

Except that Keith Henson certainly didn't seem to be denying Amanda Mason the pleasure of his company.

Amber groaned. "Aunt Beth, please stop trying to sound as if such immaturity is impossible among adults."

Beth had to smile. Sometimes her teenage niece seemed old far beyond her years.

"Amber, we can't just assume that Amanda did it, okay?"

Amber shrugged. She and Kim exchanged knowing glances.

"You two just continue to be polite or avoid her entirely, all right?" Beth said.

They nodded in tandem.

Beth looked over to the patio. Manny and Maria had gone to sit under an umbrella, heads close together. She wondered suddenly if they weren't kindling a few sparks. If so . . . good. She liked them both.

"She's gone," Amber said.

"Who?" Beth asked.

"Amanda," Kim said. She lowered her voice to a whisper. "She left right after Keith came over to talk to us."

"Yeah. Then his phone rang, and he took off," Amber said. Her eyes narrowed sharply with suspicion. "You don't think it was her calling him, do you?"

"Their whereabouts are not your concern, okay?" Beth said. Still, her teeth were grating. What the hell was the man's game?

Ben made his reappearance then, and he looked angry. "I'm going to talk to Commodore Berry and the board of trustees about this. Someone *was* playing a trick on you. The skull is missing from my locker."

"See!" Beth told him victoriously.

"Beth, it was a prank. I still don't think we needed the police."

"You're an attorney. You're the one who told me once that everything should be reported."

Ben sighed. "Girls, let's go to a movie."

"We've got to change," Amber said.

"All right, hurry. Beth, are you going to join us?" Ben asked.

"I think I'll go home," she said. Amber had been staring at her hopefully. "Honey, I'm really tired," she added. Then she realized Amber was afraid she was still angry with her. "Never mind. I'll go to the movies with you. But no horror movies, okay?"

"I can drive and bring you back here for your car later," Ben said.

"Thanks, but I'll take my own car. That way we can both head back home when we're done."

"Okay," Ben agreed. "Girls, go get dressed."

While the girls changed, Beth excused herself to make a phone call. When Ashley answered, Beth said, "Hey. It's me."

"So you have time for me now, huh? What happened to lunch?"

Beth inhaled. "Sorry. I was . . . angry."

"Great. Take it out on me."

"I really am sorry. It was inexcusable."

"As long as you know it," Ashley said, a teasing note in her voice.

"I need some advice."

"Oh?" She thought Ashley said the word very carefully.

"I found a skull on my desk."

"What?"

Beth explained everything that had happened.

"It does sound like a prank," Ashley said.

"Well, the guy you claim you don't know or recognize—Keith Henson—managed to be here right after it happened."

"I guess he followed you."

"Ashley, will you please tell me—"

"The baby is crying, I've got to go," Ashley said.

"Ashley!"

"Talk to him, Beth. Talk to *him*. I've got to go. Really."

The girls had changed and they were ready to go. Kim decided to ride with Beth, so she wouldn't be alone.

At the mall, they stared at the list of what was playing, argued over it for a few minutes, then chose a romantic comedy.

Beth decided she needed comfort food and ordered a hot dog, popcorn, Twizzlers and M&Ms. Her brother stared at her as if she had gone seriously crazy, but she ignored him.

The movie was good, but Beth was distracted. By the time the movie came to an end, though, she had decided that the whole thing *had* been a prank, and she was angry—determined to find out who had played such a twisted trick on her.

Maybe the girls were right. It could have been Amanda. She was definitely starting to feel more angry than scared.

They had an early dinner at a casual steak place in the mall, and walked to the parking lot together. Ben suggested that she come stay at their house. She thanked him but refused.

Kim looked serious when she said goodbye.

Amber threw herself into Beth's arms. "I would never hurt you, Aunt Beth. Ever!" she vowed.

Beth smoothed back Amber's hair. "I know that," she said, puzzled.

"I would never try to scare you. Really."

Beth frowned, remembering her computer. Amber had admitted to being the culprit who had been playing on it.

"Amber, honey, are we going?" Ben asked. "Beth, you sure you don't want to stay?"

"Yeah, I kind of need to be home."

"I think you're just being stubborn."

"I think I have things to do. Follow me home, if you want."

The girls went to Ben's car; Beth slid behind the steering wheel of her own. She made her way to the street, aware that Ben was behind her.

As she drove, she wished she was back at the movie. She had been diverted there, even though the thoughts of her panic were not too far away. Now everything seemed to be tormenting her at once.

If today's skull had been a Halloween prop, what about last week? Had she seen a skull? Or a conch shell. If she were seated on the witness stand in a court of law, could she really swear to anything? She'd been so sure, but now . . .

And what the hell was Keith Henson's part in all

this? One moment, so sincere, so real, she would bet her life on him.

And then . . .

She drew up in front of her house. Ben pulled up next to her. She waved him on and blew the girls a kiss, then got out of the car and started for her little gate.

It was then that it struck her like a blow to the head.

The shadow was back.

She wasn't imagining it.

There was the tree . . . the shadow of a tree . . . and someone emerging from that shadow.

Someone who was stalking her.

Someone who had waited.

But it wasn't the shadow that got her. The shadow was just a distraction.

She twisted her key in the lock, a wary eye on the shadow, ready to scream . . .

The attack came from the rear.

A sudden rush of wind from behind her, a gloved hand clamped over her mouth.

Only then was there movement from the shadows.

13

THIS TIME KEITH DIDN'T KNOW the man who lay on the sterile stainless-steel table.

Though completely antiseptic, the place had a smell.

It seemed that no matter what, a morgue had a smell.

"Victor Thompson, twenty-seven, been diving since he was fifteen, been on boats all his life, grew up in Marathon and knew the reefs like the back of his hand," Mike Burlington said. "Made a living taking out charter tours from Islamorada."

"Drowned?" he said, looking from Mike Burlington to the medical examiner, James Fleming.

Fleming had a reassuring appearance. In fact, he would have made a good family physician. He had a rich head of white hair, a pleasant, weathered face, and appeared to be in his early fifties. Old enough to have learned a lot, young enough to maintain his sharpness.

"Yes, his lungs are full of water," Fleming said.

"There was a good fifteen minutes left in his air tank," Mike said.

Mike Burlington was also the type to demand respect. He was tall, lean and wiry, in his early forties. He was the kind of man who had known what he wanted all his life. Coming from a sound but lower-income family, he'd joined ROTC in high school, gone into the military, gone for his degree on army funding, then headed straight into investigative work. He was tough, inside and out, but never lost sight of the fact that his purpose was to protect the living.

"There are no bruises, no sign of force on the body?" Keith asked.

Dr. Fleming shook his head. "Be my guest," he said softly.

Carefully, his hands gloved, Keith made his own inspection of the body.

Just like . . .

He studied the lividity markings and looked at Fleming again.

"Yes, I think he drowned, was taken out of the water, then thrown back into it. The blood settled forward, so he was transported face downward, then thrown in the water again, all within hours of his death. He washed up on Marathon."

"And his boat?" Keith looked at Mike again.

Mike shook his head. "Nothing like the kind of luxury vessels that have disappeared. He was out on a twenty-nine-footer. A decent enough boat. He took good care of it but it wasn't worth a fortune."

"Has the boat been found?" Keith asked.

"Not yet."

"He went out alone, I take it."

Mike nodded grimly.

"Any suggestion to friends that he was heading toward Calliope Key?" Keith asked.

"The police in Monroe County have done some investigating. Seems he and his friends talked a lot about sunken ships and the wrecks along the Florida coastline. I can give you a list. Anyone know where you are right now?" Mike asked him.

Keith shook his head.

"All right. Keep it that way. At the moment, since we don't know what the hell's going on, I want everything on a need-to-know basis."

Keith considered arguing the point. But Mike wasn't a trusting person. He'd been around too long. He'd seen the best of human nature, courage and loyalty. He'd seen betrayal, as well.

"There's a lot of weird shit going on here, and I'm starting to think it's connected," Keith said.

"Go ahead, explain," Mike said.

"Gentlemen? May we let this young man rest in peace?" the doctor asked.

"For the moment, but his body's not to be released yet," Mike said.

"I'm not sure if the local authorities—"

"I'll deal with it," Mike assured him. He looked at Keith dryly. "Come into my office and tell me everything," he said, leading Keith out to the hallway.

When Keith had given him a full report, Mike said, "Someone is leaking information."

"Not necessarily," Keith argued. "Too few people know about the operation."

"Too many people are dying," Mike said. "Someone knows something they shouldn't."

"That doesn't mean there's a leak. Hell, there are people who know who I am," Keith reminded him.

"Keep an eye on your co-workers, that's all I have to say," Mike said sternly.

"Right," Keith agreed tensely. Yeah, he would keep an eye on them, just as he'd been doing. But he couldn't believe either Lee or Matt was involved.

He looked down for a moment, then stared at Mike again. "We might have screwed this up. We can still change the procedure. Just do the whole thing up big, warn people, keep anybody else from getting hurt."

"Oh, great. Call the papers. What then?" Mike demanded. "Just forget everyone who's already died?"

"Doesn't look like we're managing to stop the flow of blood the way it is," Keith said.

"We're close, dammit," Mike insisted.

Close?

Close enough to prevent any more loss of life?

"You've got your orders," Mike said flatly.

"Right."

He left, and just as he exited the building, his phone began to ring. He answered, expecting Lee or Matt.

Certainly not the slightly accented voice that spoke to him.

"Mr. Henson?"

"Who is this? How did you get this number?"

"We can all do a little sleuthing, Mr. Henson. I'm talking to you because of a mutual friend."

"All right. Who are you?"

"Manny Ortega. You remember me, yes?"

"Yes. Why are you calling?"

"I need to speak with you. In person. I believe that I can help you. And you can help me. I believe that you will believe me."

He glanced at his watch, uneasy with the time but equally curious. "It's got to be quick, and I suggest you tell me first who gave you my phone number."

He was surprised by the answer, and more curious

than ever. "When? And where?"

"There's a boating store on Twenty-seventh. Huge place. Open late. Can you meet me now?"

"Give me an hour."

"I don't need much of your time."

"There's an errand I have to run first," Keith told him. "Then I'll be there."

BETH DIDN'T ATTEMPT TO turn around.

There was a knife at her throat. She didn't doubt for a moment that it was real.

Nor did she doubt that her attacker would use it.

Her pepper spray was in her purse. Worthless. The only thing she could do was stand there and pray. Even if she could somehow overpower the person with the blade, there was the other one to deal with after. If there was an after.

Because the "shadow" was armed, as well. And she was sure the gun pointed at her could stop her escape cold.

Her blood was racing through her veins; her limbs were rubber. She could make out nothing of the shadow's face, because he—or she—remained at a distance. She didn't even know if the shadow was male or female.

Just as she didn't know if she was being held by a man or a woman.

A man, she decided. The grip was powerful. She didn't think many women—no matter how deadly or well muscled—had that kind of painful strength. She also tried to tell herself that when someone went to the trouble of hiding their identity, it was because they didn't intend to kill. If she could see faces, *then* she would be in danger.

There was no way she could identify either person.

The whisper that slithered into her ear was no more helpful.

"This is a warning. Drop it. Forget Calliope Key. Forget you ever heard the names Ted and Molly Monoco. Next time, you'll die. Don't go to the police. Don't tell the police anything. If you even think about going to the police, remember this—you have a niece. That pretty little girl can die right in front of you, just so you'll know you killed her before you die yourself. Got it?"

Got it? She wasn't sure she had anything. She was frozen. She had been terrified enough—and then they had mentioned Amber.

Suddenly there were lights in the street. Lights from a car, coming to a halt in front of her house.

She was suddenly shoved hard. She went down on her knees, then fell flat. As she fell, she heard the sound of running footsteps.

Her attacker was gone.

So was the shadow.

"Beth!" It was Keith. He was by her side in seconds. "Are you all right?"

"Yes."

Then he was gone, running in the darkness.

Still stunned, she lay still for several seconds. Her

heartbeat slowed. She inhaled, and the air was ridiculously sweet. Her first realization was that she was alive.

Her second was that her knees hurt.

She managed to stumble to her feet and get the door open. She nearly screamed again when she heard running footsteps, and turned, ready to fight off any attacker.

But it was Keith.

"Call the police," he ordered.

"No!" She shoved him away and headed inside. He followed, and she locked the door, then headed straight for the kitchen. She poured a shot of brandy, ignoring him. She stood at the counter, aware of the pain in her knees, just staring.

He took her by the shoulders and shook her. "Beth, you have to call the police."

"No!"

"You were just attacked, and the bastards have disappeared. I can't search the neighborhood by myself."

"No," she repeated.

"Then I'll call them."

He reached for the phone. She grabbed his arm.

"No, I'm begging you—don't call the police."

"If they threatened you—"

"They didn't just threaten me. They threatened Amber."

He hesitated. "Beth, no matter who they threatened, you need to call the police."

"I will not put her life in danger. If you call the

police, I swear, I'll call you a liar. I'll say you're harassing me."

"You wouldn't."

"The hell I wouldn't. I mean it, Keith."

He swore, turning away from her, running his fingers through his hair. Beth swallowed a second brandy, and found that despite her anger and misgivings about him, with Keith there, she felt safer, with a renewed sense of determination. She was furious at herself for being so gullible, so vulnerable, such easy prey.

"I'm going to assume you're not a cop yourself," she said harshly.

He spun on her. "I'm not a cop. But I do know that you can't let people get away with threats."

She turned, reaching for the phone. She wouldn't call the police, but she would call a cop. Ashley. No. Maybe she was being watched. Ridiculous, she was in her own house, curtains drawn, the lock locked—and Keith inside, with her.

It was doubtful that the thugs who had attacked her had the resources to bug her phone, but even so, she didn't dial.

They had threatened Amber. That was terrifying.

Did she dare take a chance with her niece's life? And then there were the events of the day. A skull sitting on her desk and—an entire club full of people convinced she was overreacting to a prank. With her luck, she would get Officer Garth again. She could just imagine the conversation.

"As you know," she reminded Keith icily, "I already called the cops once today. Just imagine what will happen if I call them again. 'You're sure you didn't imagine there was someone behind you? In front of you? Why can't you say what they looked like? It must have been a prank.' Then I could speak in my own defense, 'Look, my knees are cut up.' And the friendly cop could tell me, 'I'm sure you were frightened of a bush, Miss Anderson. You must have fallen and hurt yourself.' "

"Beth, I was there. I saw them."

"Right. You saw them. You went after them, but they'd disappeared."

"This whole area is overgrown. There are a million places for someone to hide. But that's the point. They're cowards. Someone else showed up, and they ran."

"I'm not an idiot. But we're talking about my niece."

He put his hands on her shoulders. "Beth . . ."

She wrenched away from his grasp. "Even if the cops come, there won't be a damn thing they can do. I've had it with people doubting me. And my niece is in danger, too."

"Beth, you've been in danger since the day you saw the skull and the girls mentioned it when we were together as a group that night."

"So you're suggesting that someone on the island was responsible for the skull being there?"

"If there was a skull," he said softly.

"Not you, too!"

"Beth, I knew you were hiding something. I searched the area."

"And you knew what you were looking for?" she demanded.

"No, but I would have noticed a skull."

Beth stared at him hard, arching a brow.

He sighed. "All right, Beth, I didn't have a lot of time, I was interrupted almost immediately. But I had known where you were—I should have found something." Again, that implication. *If it had been there.* Then he shook his head, as if aggravated with himself for that admission, rather than her. "Beth, that night, there were people out and about when they should have been sleeping. I had even expected—been awaiting—that. Something was going on there. But . . ."

She stared at him. "I'll call my friend Ashley," she said. "She's a cop, and she knows I'm not insane, and that I'm not someone who tends to panic easily."

She hesitated, staring at him, then poured another shot of brandy. No, she didn't panic easily. But at the moment, she needed more fortification.

She drank down the shot, amazed to realize that she relished the burn when it went down her throat.

She still felt uncertain, with no idea what to do. She believed with her whole heart it was wrong to give in to criminals in any way, but . . .

They had threatened Amber.

She poured another brandy. Keith walked up behind

her, taking the glass from her. She spun on him, eyes filled with fury.

"That isn't going to help the situation," he told her.

"Really? And what is?"

"Calling the police."

She backed away from him. "Let me deal with this."

"Beth, listen to me—"

"No. And don't you have something to do, somewhere to go?" she demanded.

She wanted to beg him to stay with her, protect her. But she had a life to live—and obviously so did he. She couldn't ask him to be her personal bodyguard. That wouldn't help Amber. She felt furious, trapped and very afraid.

"I can't stay," he said in soft frustration, as if to himself.

His words reminded her that he seemed to be playing a million different games. "Excuse me, but I don't recall asking you to," she said.

He stared at her hard, then picked up the phone himself. She grabbed it, but his grip was firm. "Stop it. I'm not calling 911."

"Who are you calling, then?"

He took a deep breath. "Jake Dilessio."

She dropped his arm and took a step back from him, folding her arms across her chest. "So you do know Jake and Ashley."

"Yes," he said flatly.

He dialed. "Jake, it's Keith. Sorry for the short notice, but can you meet me at Beth's house?"

Beth narrowed her eyes, watching, listening. Obviously, he knew Jake well. Her sense of betrayal grew.

When he hung up, she stared at him. He stared back. "Want to explain?" she asked.

"You know I'm a diver," he told her with a shrug. "I've been called in to work this area before."

"With the police?"

"Yes," he said impatiently.

She shook her head slowly. "That's all you're going to say?"

"I'm afraid so."

"Were you on Calliope Key . . . looking for a body?" she asked.

"No."

"Then . . . ?"

"I have to leave when Jake gets here, but I'll be back."

She turned and walked away from him. "Don't bother. I've known Jake a while myself. He's married to one of my best friends. I think I'll rely on him for whatever help I need." And leaving him standing there, she headed upstairs.

IF BETH HAD BEEN AFRAID of being obvious by having a cop arrive at her door, she needn't have worried, Keith thought.

Ashley dropped off Jake, with both kids in the car, in their car seats.

Keith explained the situation briefly. "And you didn't make her call in a report?" Jake demanded.

"Apparently Miss Anderson is your good friend. You talk her into it. I'd love to see you succeed."

"I'll talk to her," Jake said firmly.

Keith mentally breathed a sigh of relief. He could safely leave—Jake Dilessio was there. Maybe the man could talk some sense into her.

"I'll be back as soon as I can," Keith told him.

When the door closed and locked behind him, he surveyed the area. He cursed, wondering how the hell the two attackers had disappeared so quickly and completely after assaulting Beth. He was fast, but in the seconds it had taken him to make sure she was all right, they'd disappeared. They'd headed down the block, turned the corner and been gone.

He knew he needed to get going to keep his appointment with Manny, but the speed with which the attackers had vanished disturbed him. He strode to the corner and looked down the street. There were more row houses. There was an old single-family residence, set back deeply in a large yard. Across the street, there were more houses. They could have taken off through any of the yards, and done so easily in the time it had taken him to bend over and see about Beth.

He headed for the yard of the house that was set back so deeply and crossed over the grass, his penlight on the ground before him. He traversed the area several times, but it seemed undisturbed. He turned his attention to the houses across the street and made a number of mental notes.

Then he walked back to his car, got in, and shifted

into gear to keep his appointment with Manny Ortega.

"YOU KNOW WHY WE'RE NOT finding anything?" Lee murmured, sitting at the computer console in the main cabin, his eyes darting from the screen to a book of charts.

"The damn thing isn't really there?" Matt asked wearily. He was on the sofa, his head on one of the throw pillows. A feeling of guilt and unease still plagued him. Lee had returned from his evening out with a full report—nothing. He'd gotten to see the clubs of Miami Beach. End of story.

That had been the time for him to speak up. Tell the truth. *I was taken for the ride of my life. Sorry, guys. I can't believe she used me as if I were a horny high-school kid.*

Lee turned and stared at him, shaking his head. "It's there. I know it's there. It's just broken up so badly that we're not getting anything. The coral's probably grown over a lot of the ribs and the hull."

"So why aren't we picking up the cannons?" Matt asked.

"That I don't know."

Matt felt a greater guilt. Still, he kept silent.

"Shit," Lee swore suddenly.

"What?"

The television mounted over the doorway to the aft area had been on, the sound muted. Lee reached for the remote and turned up the volume. The news was on. The tragic death of a local charter-boat owner and dive master was being reported.

"Another one," Lee said.

"They didn't say anything about him being any-where near Calliope Key," Matt pointed out.

"It's time we get our own asses back out there," Lee said. He shook his head. "Keith is crazy, thinking he can find out something at that yacht club. We need to be out there. Watching. Shit. Where the damn hell is he, anyway?"

WHEN KEITH RETURNED, Beth's house was dark.

He wasn't accustomed to even feeling uneasy, so it disturbed him to realize he was feeling something akin to growing panic. He dialed her number, but there was no answer. Where the hell was she—and, worse, where the hell was Jake? When the answering machine came on, he felt like an utter fool, but he started speaking. "Jake, dammit, answer. Beth, pick up. You don't have to see me or let me in, but pick up. I see your car. I know you're there, and I'm worried. If you don't answer, I'm going to get the police out here."

She picked up. "Yes?"

"You *are* there."

"Yes." The terms "icy" and "distant" wouldn't begin to describe the tone of her voice.

"Are you all right?"

"Yes. Is there a reason I shouldn't be? Jake is here, remember." If anything, her tone grew harder still.

"You guys didn't answer the phone," he said irri-tably.

"Jake is in the bathroom, and I'm fine. We don't need to talk right now. It's late."

"Beth, look, I'm sorry. I told you, I had some things I needed to do, and I knew you'd be all right with Jake there. But . . . we do need to talk."

"I'm not calling the police. And as for you . . . don't be sorry. You were around to run them off and now . . . now I'm with a friend. So don't be sorry. We all have an agenda, don't we? I just don't care to see you or talk about it any more right now."

"Beth . . ." He hesitated. There was nothing he was at liberty to say to her.

"Beth," he said, "it was a strange day."

"I just want to be alone, all right? Jake is here. I'm fine."

She hung up.

He sat there, his phone in his hand, for several seconds, just registering the fact that she had cut him off so coldly.

Well, what the hell had he expected?

It didn't matter. He was loath to leave. Nothing had been solved. Jake had a job and a family. He couldn't just turn his life over to keeping tabs on Beth.

His phone rang. He expected it to be Jake, and he answered quickly.

"Where the hell are you?"

It was Lee, and he was aggravated.

"Busy. What's up?"

"The noose is tightening. We really need to move." Lee was quiet. "They found another diver. The news just came out. We need to get back on the boat."

"I know we need to get back out there. I just need a little more time."

Lee was silent. "I told you before, we need to focus. There's the project, and that's it."

"I'll be there as soon as I can."

"Listen to me, Keith. We've got to get back out on the reef."

"I'll be there. I have something to solve first."

"Look," Lee said, sounding seriously pissed, "we need to talk. We have a job to do. You can't go taking care of the rest of the world. We have to be back on that reef by tomorrow morning."

"Where are you now?"

"Right where we've been. Waiting."

"I'll be there soon."

"Really soon," Lee said.

Keith hung up, contemplating the situation. He hesitated, then dialed Beth's number again. She had been attacked. And then there was the skull on her desk. That had to mean something, as well.

Why the hell couldn't he just find the connection?

He closed his eyes for a moment. There was money in this, big money. Maybe Mike was right. Money often meant corruption.

He called the house number, determined to tell her at least some of what was going on, and to hell with the consequences. The machine came on.

"Beth, I know you're angry. You have a right to be. But I'm worried about you. Jake can't stay there forever. Listen. I think that you were followed today, from Nick's to the club. A couple left right in your wake. That was why I followed you. A *couple,* Beth. It might have been Brad and Sandy, in disguise. If they're the pirates, they're dangerous." He paused. "Guilty of murder. Jake has to go home sooner or later. You need to stay with someone."

"What's happening?" she picked up and demanded. "Why did you leave, then, and come back so worried and determined?"

"I had a meeting, that was all. I said I'd be back. Put Jake on the phone, if you just want to fight with me. Please. Honestly, if I knew what was happening, I'd tell you," he said bitterly.

He heard her sound of frustration. "Listen, Beth, I'll explain everything to you as soon as I can, I promise. For now . . . please, pack a few things and go with Jake to his place." He was quiet. "I'm not leaving until I see you go with him."

"All right." She hung up on him.

He remained where he was, tense, pondering his next move. Then his cell phone rang. He looked at the caller ID and realized she had hit Redial. "Beth?"

"It's Jake. She's coming back to my place."

"Thanks."

"She still won't agree to filing a police report. I've tried everything but brute force," Jake told him.

"Just keep her safe, huh?"

"You bet," Jake assured him.

Keith remained where he was. He expected a long

wait, but it was no more than ten minutes before Jake and Beth appeared. She locked the house but didn't glance his way. Jake gave him a wave as he got into the passenger seat of her car.

Despite Jake's presence, Keith followed. He pulled out his phone and dialed when he realized she was going in the direction of Nick's.

Lee answered. "I'll be there in about another ten minutes," Keith told him. "You can bring the tender and get me at the dock at Nick's."

"Great. Glad you've had your entertainment for the night," Lee said sarcastically.

Keith hung up.

He waited in the car while Beth parked at Nick's, grabbed her overnight bag and headed toward the rear with Jake. Then he followed.

The place was jumping. It was a Saturday night. Nothing could go wrong with that many people around.

Please, God, he thought. Let that be the truth.

He saw Ashley, her youngest child in her arms, making her way through the tables to meet Beth and Jake.

Once they were all together, Keith circumvented the busy patio and headed out to the pier.

He heard the motor of the tender soon after. Lee had come. The stare he gave Keith spoke volumes.

"No involvements," Lee muttered with disgust. "Yeah, like hell. We came in for information. Not for your entertainment."

"Let's just go," Keith said.

"Hell, yeah. Let's just go. Eye on the prize, pal."

Keith swung on him. "Hey, swallow this, pal. Fuck you. The prize has changed."

IF NOTHING ELSE, it had probably been the longest, most eventful day of Beth's life. By the time she reached the privacy of Ashley and Jake's place, in an ell off the restaurant, she was so keyed up she was ready to scream—and not at all sure of where to start.

"You lied to me," she told Ashley.

"I'm not at liberty—" Ashley began.

"I've already explained that," Jake said, staring at Beth. "Over and over again."

"Oh, come on. You know I would never say anything to anyone else if you told me not to. What the hell is going on here? I can't imagine that you've become buddy-buddy with some kind of criminal, but he keeps denying that he's a cop." Beth stared from Ashley to Jake.

"Shh," Ashley pleaded. "You'll wake the kids."

She let out a sigh. "I'm sorry, I don't want to make your lives any harder, but—"

She broke off, wincing.

But Amber had been threatened. And Keith's words on the phone had hit disturbingly close to home. She had noticed the couple herself. She just hadn't realized they had followed her.

They had probably been following her all day, before staking out her house. She had to pray they hadn't waited around to follow her here.

She stood very still and stared at Jake. "I need someone off duty to keep an eye on my niece," she said softly. "And I mean now. That's the only reason I agreed to come here. You two can help me. I need Amber protected."

"Amber?"

She nodded. "Jake, you've got cop friends coming out of the woodwork. I can pay, but I want Amber protected. Without Ben knowing. I don't want him doing anything stupid." She was angry; her decision was made.

"Does someone want to explain exactly what's going on?" Ashley demanded.

"Beth was attacked," Jake said.

Ashley gasped.

"Threatened is more like it," Beth said.

"Keith showed up, they ran off."

"And you didn't call the police?" Ashley asked incredulously.

Beth groaned.

"I told her she should have called the police immediately," Jake said sternly. "So did Keith."

"They threatened Amber," she said. "And I'm not filing a report of any kind. I mean it. I'm not taking any chances. I want you to help me with this."

"Keith saw a couple here today, while you two were together today. They followed Beth when she left. I'm willing to bet they're the same two who are suspected of pirating the missing boats."

"Here?" Ashley said. "Beth, do you think it might have been them?"

"I don't know for sure, but it's starting to sound likely. And, oh yeah. I found a skull on my desk today, but the cop I called seemed to think I was a paranoid lunatic, so if you don't mind, I'm not speaking officially to any more police today. I think that someone got into my office, *then* followed me. The official cop couldn't see that. Okay? Wait! I don't care if it's not okay. You lied to me, Ashley. You said you didn't know him."

Ashley glanced guiltily at the floor.

"And if he's not a cop, what the hell is he?" Beth demanded, still angry.

"We don't have the right—" Jake began.

"Oh, Jake! What do you think Beth is going to do—post it on the Internet?" Ashley demanded impatiently. "He's not a cop. In fact—"

"Don't even try to tell me he's a scuba instructor," Beth snapped.

"Well, actually," Jake said, "he is."

Before Beth could literally scream with aggravation, Ashley spoke, explaining, "He's with a company that specializes in dive rescues and retrievals, salvage and maritime crimes."

Beth stared at her friends, perplexed. "Why couldn't you tell me that?"

"Because we don't know what he's doing," Jake said impatiently. Then he hesitated. "They contract their services to the government. He could be working for the feds or the state. When I see him, I don't ask. Whatever he's doing this time, it's important that people don't know who he is. He often works under-cover. So when he doesn't tell me what he's doing, I respect his position and don't ask. I don't want to jeopardize his work—or his life."

Beth stared at him, shaking her head. "Why wouldn't he tell me? Why wouldn't he trust me?"

Jake shook his head. "Beth, when you're under-cover, you tell no one. You pray that you don't run into the people who know you. And if you do, you pray they keep their mouths shut."

"Who on earth would I say anything to?" Beth protested.

Jake shook his head. "You wouldn't say anything on purpose, Beth, but what if you accidentally let some-thing slip to Ben? They've already threatened Amber."

"Get someone out there now, Jake," Beth demanded hotly, then added a soft "Please."

"All right."

He went away to arrange it, leaving her with Ashley. Beth still felt angry.

"You could have said something to me," she insisted.

"Beth, the point is, anyone can inadvertently say something. You just learn to keep your mouth shut."

"Fine," Beth said. "Then let's see what I can tell you. It seems that Sandy and Brad—or whatever their real names are—have been stealing yachts and mur-dering people. They probably changed their appearances and came here to scout for their next victim. They somehow decided that I had them pegged, probably when they saw me here with you, so they attacked me. They're out there somewhere, but Keith Henson—if that's *his* real name—has decided to go back . . . somewhere. I hope to find them."

"There's already an APB out across the country for them," Ashley said.

"Well, they were here. Right here, on land," Beth said. "And there *was* a skull on the island. Keith was in the clearing right after I discovered it. Did he take it? Did he bring it in somewhere? Did it belong to one of the Monocos?"

Ashley shook her head. "I don't know."

Beth shook her head in disgust. "Great detective I would have made. I figured Eduardo Shea must have had something to do with it . . . someone who was profiting off the dance studios. Or Amanda. I probably just wanted her to be guilty of *something*."

She fell silent.

Had Keith Henson been questioning Amanda? Had she misread that whole thing?

Jake reappeared. "Amber will be fine," he assured Beth.

"Jake, I don't care what it costs. I'll pay it. You called people you really trust, right?"

"Beth, I called people I'd trust with my own life, Ashley's life—my children's lives," he assured her. "And they're friends, doing me favors. You don't have to worry about it."

"Yes, I do," she said firmly. "But the point is, until . . . Brad and Sandy are brought in, Amber has to be kept safe."

She felt deflated suddenly. She'd been so angry, so frightened. And now she felt as if she were a balloon that had been suddenly popped.

"Beth, are you all right?" Ashley asked. "You look pale."

Beth lifted her hands in a shrug. "At least he isn't a criminal."

"Keith? No, he isn't a criminal," Ashley said.

"Beth, the FBI, the local police, the Coast Guard—everyone is looking for Sandy and Brad. They *will* be caught," Jake told her.

She forced a smile and nodded.

Sure.

But when?

That was the question of the hour.

WHEN JAKE AND ASHLEY HAD gone to bed, Beth found that she was still too restless herself to sleep. She went online and looked up the island. To her surprise, there was a great deal written about Calliope Key. Apparently almost everyone since Columbus had put ashore there. Ponce de León had stopped by. The Spanish had claimed it, then the English. Despite its proximity to the Bahamas, it had remained part of Florida after trades between the Spanish and English, the Spanish and the Americans, and the English and the Americans.

When the Spanish had held the island, they had often lain in wait to surprise English ships and lured them onto the reefs. Apparently the welcoming sight of the island, and the sound of the wind on the water and through the trees had beckoned them onward, and thus the name, Calliope Key. Sadly, the islet had been like a siren, enticing men to their deaths.

There had been too many wrecks to count, but as she read, Beth came across one very specific incident. A battle between an English ship and a Spanish ship, the *Sea Star* and *La Doña*. Captain Pierce had battled Captain Alonzo Jimenez. All had been lost, including the innocent travelers aboard, seeking to reach Spanish ports in Central and South America.

Beth stared blankly at the screen.

The ghost story, the tale that Keith had told that very first night around their campfire, had been true, or at least based on truth.

She was suddenly certain that meant something.

That it just might be at the base of everything else.

But *what* did it mean? Treasure seekers were always combing the coast of Florida. There were so many known wrecks that had yet to be found. The legend of the Bermuda Triangle had sprung up because so many had been lost and no trace ever found.

She hesitated, then began combing the article again. Both ships had been lost with treasure aboard, as had so many ships before their sad encounter. But these treasures had been worth millions, even at the time. Heaven only knew what they would be worth now.

Enough to kill and die for, certainly.

THEY WERE STILL ANCHORED in the bay.

Matt was pacing the cabin. "All right. Sandy and Brad are guilty. They've been stealing yachts. They have a base somewhere, and they've managed to get the boats to this base, where they're being done over. Every law-enforcement agency out there is onto them. So . . . what is the difficulty now? Why don't we just come out with the big guns—major league underwater equipment?"

"We've got to be back out there in the morning, and we have to find it," Lee insisted. "It's ridiculous that we haven't been able to."

"Maybe our coordinates are wrong," Matt said.

"I don't believe that," Keith said firmly. He was the one who had studied the accounts of the wreck, taking into consideration every storm that had ravaged the area since. He had also been the one to study and calculate what had possibly occurred after they had received the new records, only recently turned over to the United States by the German government. He had figured in time and tides.

Keith stopped pacing. "Why do you think they didn't try to steal *this* boat?" he mused.

"Huge boat, three men. Witnesses," Lee suggested.

"Just two of them," Keith mused. "Tough guys when they're armed, against a retired couple, one friendly diver . . ."

"But they hung around out there," Matt said.

293

"Maybe they were looking for the right opportunity," Lee said. "Hoping we'd eventually show some vulnerability."

"They won't dare show up out here again," Matt said. "They must know the law is onto them."

"Maybe, maybe not," Keith put in.

"I just don't get it. Why are we still tiptoeing around?" Matt said.

Keith rose. "Because we work for a company with a government contract and this is what we were hired to do. Not to mention that we've got another dead diver on our hands."

"Who might never have been anywhere near Calliope Key," Matt reminded him. "Plenty of assholes put on dive gear."

"This man was experienced," Keith pointed out.

"And didn't own a yacht," Matt added.

"Accidents happen," Lee murmured.

Keith kept silent on that score. He had seen the body.

There had been no accident.

ON SUNDAY MORNING, the newspaper carried an account of a diver found dead in the Keys.

Beth found herself obsessing over the article, reading it over and over again. When Ashley awoke, she stuck it beneath her nose.

Ashley shook her head. "Beth, everything in the world isn't related to a missing couple and pirated boats. Those two couldn't have been everywhere."

"It was idiotic of them to have been in Miami," Beth said.

"Not really. Think about it. The area is huge, boats everywhere. Hide in plain sight." She looked at Beth. "He didn't have the kind of boat our pirates have been stealing. And, Beth . . . Jake and I were out one day in the Keys, diving down to the *Duane.* A guy on our boat wasn't in the best shape and shouldn't have been doing such a deep dive. He panicked, popped up to the surface and died. It happens."

"I know."

"So do you have a plan for the day?" Ashley asked, carefully changing the subject.

"Besides just being worried sick?" Beth asked her.

Ashley leaned forward. "They *will* be apprehended. And Amber *will* be protected. Look, Beth, you have a right to be scared. And angry."

"I'm angry about having to be scared. I have a lot to do this week."

"We can get a man into the yacht club, as well."

"Ashley, you and Jake can't go calling in every favor you've ever earned. You have to let me pay these guys."

Ashley shrugged. "If you were to allow me just to report what happened—"

"No. I will not risk Amber."

"But, Beth—"

"Hey, I reported the skull. Lot of good that did."

"This is different."

"Maybe they'll be caught soon," Beth said. Her cell

phone rang, and she excused herself and picked it up.

"Where the hell are you?" Ben's voice demanded angrily.

"At Ashley's," Beth said.

"Why didn't you tell me? What were you doing, babysitting?" Ben asked.

"Something like that," Beth lied. She hesitated. Why not tell her brother the truth? Because he had doubted her over the skull? Because he would panic over his daughter? She didn't like lying to Ben. But for the moment . . . "So what's up? What do you need?"

Ben was silent for a minute, still angry. His voice was tight when he said, "Amber is anxious about you—I don't know why, and neither one of you seems to want to tell me. I have to clean the hull today, so I'm taking her to lunch at the club, and she's going to swim and sunbathe while I'm working. Will you come?"

She didn't want to do anything but fume and fret and worry, she realized. But that was a stupid course of action to take. She had to trust in her friends, and wait for Sandy and Brad to be apprehended.

They were probably hiding in plain sight, just as Ashley had said. And if so . . .

They were hiding around boaters. She looked at Ashley. "Want to have lunch at the club?"

"Sure. I just need to arrange a babysitter."

KEITH COULD HEAR THE LULLING sound of his own

breathing, at forty-five feet down, following the path of the reef. With breaks here and there, it stretched for nearly a mile.

Lee was topside. He and Matt were tracing a grid, with Matt perhaps twenty feet west of his position as they moved south.

Matt looked over at him and made the "okay" sign. He returned it.

They continued searching the area. In his mind, he ran over and over his conversation—conducted in the fishing rod aisle—with Manny Ortega.

"You had my name and number from Ted Monoco?" had been his own first incredulous and very suspicious demand.

Ortega had given him a shrug and a shake of the head. "You didn't know Ted, but he knew you. Four years ago, you were in the Everglades. A small plane had gone down. People he knew were on that plane. You and your crew rescued their daughter."

Manny continued. "I tried to reach you before. The number Ted gave me was for an office in Virginia, and when I called, they said you were away on assignment for an unknown length of time." He shrugged. "I contacted the police. I believe they tried with what resources they had. But the law in this country is that you may disappear if you choose if you're an adult and doing nothing illegal."

"Go on."

"The last time I heard from Ted was when he mentioned you and gave me your number to try to reach you. He thought he was onto something. He didn't say that he was afraid of anything, he was just very excited. I didn't think much of it until time went on and I didn't hear from him. Then I began to worry. That was when I tried to reach you but couldn't. I finally felt there was nothing I could do. Then you appeared here."

"So how did you get my cell phone number?"

"It wasn't as difficult as you think. You gave it to Laurie Green, the girl you pulled from the plane in the Everglades. I finally thought to call her and ask."

"I see. So what do you think I can do for you?"

"Find Ted and Molly. Dead or alive. Though I'm very afraid it will be dead."

A ray suddenly dislodged sand near the base of the coral, drawing Keith's mind back to the task at hand. The water was murky in the wake of the panicked fish. He nearly kept going.

Then he saw something.

Just the corner of something black that wasn't coral.

He circled, looked. The sand had resettled. Carefully, with just his fingertips, he explored the area. Dusted carefully, trying not to create such a cloud of sand that his vision would be impaired. Patience was needed for this kind of work, and he had learned to practice that kind of restraint through the years.

His efforts paid off at last. He found the object.

It looked like a crusted, big black button.

But it wasn't. His heart skipped a beat. He needed to

get it back up to the boat, but he was almost certain what he had found.

His hand curled around it. He looked over at Matt, who had realized he was onto something.

For a moment he was tempted to drop the object, to shake his head to show he'd been mistaken and come back later. Mike was so convinced that there was someone on the inside. . . .

And Manny Ortega believed Ted and Molly Monoco were dead. So did Keith, but he didn't believe they'd been killed for their boat.

He believed they had found something on or near Calliope Key, then died for their discovery.

Too late.

Matt swam over to him. He produced the object. Matt stared at it, nodded silently, then studiously began searching the area further.

Keith placed the object in a pouch and joined Matt in the search.

They were close. . . .

So close.

He had to wonder, though: Had others been this close before them?

But had those others even known just what it was they were really looking for?

IT WAS ON THE DRIVE to the club that Ashley looked at Beth and said, "You really do need to tell your brother what happened."

"You mean about being attacked?"

"Yes. You're in terror about filing a report because of Amber. He has a right to know."

"He'll tell me that I should file a report. And God knows—he might do something stupid and dangerous."

"You should file a report." Ashley lifted a hand in the air to silence the protest she knew was coming. "Make it official. If Sandy and Brad are what I think they are—tough-talking but only preying on the vulnerable—they're not brave enough to go up against real authority. They were at Nick's, a piece of real stupidity. The place is known for being a cop hangout. I doubt they really know what you're doing—it's unlikely that they have the time to continue to stake you out. They intended to scare you. That's all. Don't let them succeed."

Beth mulled over her friend's words. Then she asked, "They've killed before, so why did they just try to scare me?"

"We don't know that they killed the Monocos, and the couple in Virginia survived," Ashley said.

Beth shook her head. "I'm convinced the Monocos are dead."

"Maybe killing you was a risk they didn't dare take. I don't know, Beth. But I still think that you need to file an official report. Scare them in return. Hell, there's already an APB out on them, which they probably know, so what's the difference if you file a report, too."

They arrived at the club and easily found Ben and Amber at a table waiting for them. Amber still seemed anxious when she looked at Beth, who couldn't help but hug her too tightly. Then she smiled at her niece and tousled her hair, trying to defuse the moment. Ben and Amber both greeted Ashley with pleasure. The Sunday buffet was elaborate, the club filled with members in good spirits, and Beth wished she could go back to a time when all she did there on a Sunday was enjoy herself.

After lunch, Ben went off to work on his boat. Ashley, Beth and Amber went poolside. Beth was glad to see that it was busy, and that she couldn't for the life of her figure out who Amber's secret bodyguard was.

"Where's Kim today?" Beth asked Amber.

"I don't know. She just said she couldn't come," Amber said with a shrug. Then she hesitated. "Aunt Beth, I'm really sorry about the other day."

"You should be."

"I just . . . I want you to be happy."

"Let me be happy on my own, okay? Now swear

you'll never interfere in my personal life again."

"I swear," Amber said.

"And don't *ever* try to scare me again," Beth said.

"I didn't try to scare you," Amber replied.

"Oh? I remember what you wrote word for word. First the skull popped up and then, 'I'll be seeing you soon. In the dark. All alone.'"

"I never wrote such a thing!" Amber protested.

Beth frowned, feeling a new chill seep into her spine.

"Then Kim must have done it."

"No," Amber insisted. "All we did was write back to Keith on e-mail."

"Beth, it's time you reported this. Officially," Ashley said firmly.

"You're going to call the police about Kim and me?" Amber asked, stunned and horrified.

"No, honey . . . there's been more than that," Beth murmured. She looked around uneasily. There was no one around who might be listening to their conversation, she was certain. There was a group of children playing with a ball nearby, and a few members of the women's charities committee busily discussing their next fund-raiser.

She was startled to see that Maria Lopez was there again. She was elegant in a one-piece black bathing suit, straw hat and sunglasses, down at the other end of the pool. She couldn't possibly hear anything they were saying.

She looked down toward the docks, shading her

eyes. A number of the boats were out. She saw Ben, assembling his scuba gear—he meant to go down and clean the hull. As he gave his attention to his tank, a woman hopped to the dock from the deck of a boat farther down.

Amanda.

Dammit, didn't she have any other place to go? From being an occasional visitor to the club, she'd turned into a regular—a very unwelcome one, from Beth's point of view.

As Beth watched, Amanda approached Ben, lightly touching his shoulder.

Ben looked up and smiled.

Beth looked quickly away, but Amber had seen the direction of her gaze. She groaned. "Can we get her arrested?" she asked Ashley.

"Flirting isn't illegal," Ashley told her.

"Simply being that woman should be illegal," Beth said dryly.

"Beth . . ." Ashley persisted.

"All right, all right," Beth said. "But . . . let's get through the afternoon. Let Ben clean his boat. And I'm telling you, no one's going to be able to do anything."

THAT EVENING ASHLEY BROUGHT Amber to Nick's with her. Jake, Ben and Beth went to the station, where Beth filled out a formal report. Ben was a nervous wreck—and extremely angry with his sister. Beth continued to remind him that he was among those who had kept telling her that she was paranoid. Luckily, with Jake there, they couldn't fight too openly. Both he and Lieutenant Gorsky—the lead officer on the pirating case—tried to remain casual and calming as the two argued.

They left in a state of stiff tension. But it was done. Ben's house would remain under surveillance, and it had been suggested that Beth move in with her brother for the time being.

Great. He was barely speaking to her.

But since their lives might well be at stake, Beth agreed. She knew that the department didn't have the manpower to protect them all as they tried to get through their daily lives. At least, because of Jake and Ashley, extra protection, in the form of off-duty cops, would be afforded to them.

Still, the night was pure misery. Amber was confused, and her father warned her firmly that she wasn't to make a single move alone. Beth tried to be reassuring, but she had to reiterate her brother's words to her niece.

On Monday morning she drove Amber to school, glad to see the officer following them all the way.

He didn't follow her to the club. He was staying downtown, where he would be keeping an eye on the school throughout the day, so Beth was careful as she continued to work. At the club, she noted that the security guard was not alone.

She was nervous, wondering if anyone was inside the club itself or wandering the grounds to keep an eye on things. Midmorning, Commodore Berry came in and sat down gravely. He told her that he'd been contacted by the police and there was going to be at least one officer on duty inside the club or on the property at all times, keeping an eye on things. Since there were known pirates working in the area, he was grateful to have the assistance.

Beth wondered if he blamed her for involving the club. It didn't seem, however, that he even realized it had anything to do with her. There were so many exceptional yachts berthed there that he seemed to think that was what made them a potential target.

The rest of the day passed uneventfully. She made calls to confirm arrangements for the Summer Sizzler, contacting delivery services and the florist, and talked to the chef and the staff. She called Eduardo Shea's office, and he assured her that he had not forgotten, and told her that he would be in with Mauricio and Maria later during the week.

That afternoon a police tech came to inspect her computer. She went down to the cafeteria to allow him time to work on his own. The club was strangely quiet. There was no sign of any of the Masons.

The tech was a nice guy, encouraging in his expertise. He was convinced no one had hacked her computer from the outside. The sabotage had been performed right in her office.

Chilling information. Whoever had given her the warning had been at her desk, in her chair.

She left early to pick up Amber. The policeman followed them home. She waved goodbye a few minutes later, after he had inspected the house and she had locked the door behind him.

She spent the evening practicing scenes with Amber.

That night Ben kept his distance, and she found herself growing angrier with her brother. None of this was her fault, though he was behaving as if it were.

Tuesday was more or less a repeat of Monday. She felt the growing strain of the situation.

Wednesday was better. When she went down to lunch, she was startled to run into Eduardo Shea in the dining room.

"Mr. Shea," she said happily. "You're here."

"Miss Anderson, your party is this Friday night. I told you I would see you here."

"Yes, of course."

"Ah, there's Mauricio."

A handsome young man with dark hair and arresting green eyes approached, and Eduardo introduced him to Beth. A few minutes later Maria Lopez arrived in a stunning gown. Short, sequined, it fit her to a T.

"Where will the performance be held?" Eduardo asked.

"There will be a dance floor on the patio. It's being delivered Friday morning," Beth told them.

"That's not good," Eduardo said.

"Oh?"

"They should have more time to practice their number on the actual site," Eduardo said.

"Oh," Beth murmured. "I'm . . . I don't think we can

close off the area until then," she told them unhappily.

"It will be fine, Eduardo," Maria said. She smiled at Beth. "But for now, where may we rehearse?"

"The meeting room," Beth suggested. It was actually part of the dining room, but it could be closed off for committee luncheons and was sometimes rented out to corporations for special functions.

It also had a hardwood floor.

Eduardo wasn't pleased, but he seemed resigned. Disdainful, but resigned.

Beth managed to get Eduardo to allow her to attend the rehearsal. At first she simply watched the two dances in wonder. It seemed unbelievable that anyone could move their hips as fast as Maria did. On the dance floor, she was ageless. Her face glowed; her elegance was visible in every movement.

"Incredible," Beth murmured.

"Come on. I'll teach you," Eduardo said.

"Oh, no, no," Beth protested.

But she found herself standing up with him anyway. "It's all in the timing," he told her. The music was playing again. Mauricio came up to partner her under Eduardo's direction, while Maria stepped behind her to show her how to move her hips. She grew flushed and happy as she began to get the timing, so involved that, to her amazement, she forgot the current circumstances of her life.

Forgot that she had first thought of this because she'd wanted to meet Eduardo Shea, suspecting that he might somehow have been involved in the

Monocos' disappearance. To her absolute amazement, she was having fun.

Until Amanda Mason arrived.

Amanda greeted Eduardo with enthusiasm, kissed Mauricio, and did the continental kiss-on-both-cheeks thing with Maria Lopez. At that point Beth excused herself and returned to her office. She was startled when she reached her door to turn around and discover that she had been followed.

By Amanda.

The woman stood there, chin high, hands on her hips—looking much taller than her actual stature—staring at Beth belligerently. "Why do you do that to me all the time?" Amanda demanded.

"Why do I do what?" Beth demanded.

"I walk into a room, and you leave."

Beth stared at her, stunned. Then she replied honestly, "Let's see. Maybe because you treat me as if I were a servant or a lesser being of some kind?"

"I do not," Amanda protested.

"You do, too."

"If I do, it's only because of the way you act toward me."

"What are you talking about?"

"Let's see. You don't do anything overt. That nose of yours just goes in the air a little, and you look at me as if I were . . . the trash of the century."

Beth could barely believe the conversation.

"Amanda—" She broke off, shaking her head, not at all sure what to say. "Maybe it's the way you behave."

"And that would be . . . ?"

"I don't know! As if the world was your toy, as if men were there for your amusement, whether they're married, engaged or . . . taken."

"You're jealous."

"No, Amanda, I'm not jealous."

She expected anger, some kind of scathing retort. But Amanda just stared at her. "Am I that bad, really?"

Beth sighed. "I don't know, Amanda. Maybe it's me, too. I don't know."

She didn't know what she expected then. Certainly not the frown that furrowed Amanda's brow. "I . . . I'll try to be . . ." She paused, looking for a word. "Better."

Then she walked down the hallway, and Beth went into her office and sat down, stunned.

KEITH WAITED IN THE Palm Beach deli. At ten o'clock, Laurie Green walked in, just as she had promised. She saw him at the table, and a smile lit her face. "Keith!"

She rushed over and hugged him fiercely. He hugged her back, then disentangled himself carefully. She had lost her parents when the plane had gone down, and she herself had nearly perished in the muck soup of the Everglades. She had experienced agony and grief, but from the beginning, she had been grateful for her own life. Once on the verge of death, her sandy skin and light hair spoke of her health and well-being.

Slightly embarrassed by her show of emotion, he

managed to get her seated opposite him. "So everything's going okay?" he asked.

She nodded. "I graduate from Nova University next spring."

"That's great. I'm delighted to hear it."

She waved her left hand in front of him, showing him the diamond on her finger. "And I'm getting married in the fall."

"That's absolutely wonderful," he said sincerely.

Then she smiled. "That's not why you called me."

"No."

"What's up? You know that I'll help you any way I can."

"I know that, and thanks. . . . Do you know if your folks were friends with a couple named Ted and Molly Monoco?"

The smiled left her face. "Have they been found?" she asked.

He shook his head. "So it's true, they were friends of your folks?"

She nodded. "I didn't know them that well. My parents decided to take dance lessons for some event they were going to. Ted owned the studio they went to, and they got friendly. They were nice. *Are* nice. I hope. I don't know what to think."

Keith nodded. "Did you ever meet a man named Manny Ortega?"

"Oh!" she exclaimed, her cheeks reddening. "I gave him your number. I told him I'd gotten it a long time ago, that it might not be good. Did I do something wrong? I'd forgotten all about it."

"No, no, it's fine."

"Are you sure?"

"Absolutely. So you know Manny?"

"Yes, he was a friend of the Monocos. I went to a couple of dance parties with my parents, and he was there, playing with the band. I was sticking out like a sore thumb, and he was nice to me. I can't say that I've seen him in . . . well, in years. But when he called me, saying that Ted hadn't called in and he'd mentioned something about your name, well . . . I'm sorry. I didn't hesitate to give him the number."

"It's fine. I just had to make sure," Keith told her. "So tell me about this guy you're about to marry."

He had a firm destination in mind once he left Laurie, and with a two-hour plus—depending on traffic—drive ahead of him, he pulled out his cell phone and put a call through to Mike. "Manny's information checked out," he told his boss.

"Any more finds?"

"Not as of the time I left this morning," Keith told him. "I'm heading down to the Keys. Look, we're searching, doing the best we can with what we have. You need to haul out the big equipment for this one, Mike."

"You need to hang in there. They'll catch that couple soon. They're watching the roads, the airports, train stations . . . and boats."

"You know how big the damn coastline is, Mike?" Keith asked.

"Yes, I'm aware of the length of the coastline."

"I don't think that catching them is going to solve the entire problem," Keith said.

"It needs to happen."

"Yes, but, Mike, they can't be pulling this off alone."

"You don't think they'll squeal once they're caught?"

"Maybe, maybe not. Mike, you need to get the right people following the financial trail. Someone in the area is making the arrangements to take the yachts, and refurbish and camouflage them."

"We've been looking into every boat shop in south Florida."

"Start looking at people."

"Want to give me names?"

He did.

"What makes you certain any one of these people is involved?"

"Because I believe there was a skull on the island when we arrived. And I believe that someone who was there that weekend managed to remove it."

Mike was silent for a moment then he said, "You know, we're not really trying to catch pirates," he reminded Keith. "There are other people who do that. Our job is to find *La Doña*."

"I swear it's involved somehow."

"You know you gave me the names of your co-workers, right?" Mike asked casually.

"Hey, you're the one who said you don't trust

anyone," Keith said. "I don't have the resources to find out who's invested where. You do."

"I'm not an idiot, Keith. I've already spoken to the FBI. They've been working on the money angle. Thing is, people don't usually write down their ill-gotten gains on their tax returns."

"There's got to be a connection to some kind of boat shop somewhere."

"They're on it, Keith. What's your plan now?"

"First, can you get me a list of students and investors in the old Monoco dance studios?"

"Yes."

"I'm heading to the Keys. Islamorada. I'm going to hang around a few bars, see who knew Victor Thompson, try to find out what he was doing."

"The police have questioned at least fifty people."

"The police can't go down and hang out at a bar as well as I can," Keith said with a little smile.

A moment later he hung up. He hesitated, played with the thought of trying to reach Beth, then discarded the notion. She would just hang up on him, if he was even able to reach her. Of course, if she said hello and answered her phone, he would at least know she was all right. Still, he decided to call Ashley at work instead. She assured him that everything was all right: Amber was in school, Beth was well. There had been no more incidents. "Will we see you soon?" she asked.

"Of course. No news on Sandy and Brad?"

"Not yet."

"You're sure Beth is fine?"

"Yes, there's an officer on duty at the club. He calls in on the hour."

He thanked her and hung up.

MARIA LOPEZ WALKED INTO THE empty dance studio and looked around. A feeling of deep and poignant nostalgia swept through her.

She remembered the old days so clearly.

She could still outdo many a younger dancer, but the truth was, her glory days were over. No matter how hard they fought it, people got older.

Ted hadn't cared. He had wanted nothing more than retirement. He had always told her to cherish her accomplishments and enjoy life. She did enjoy life. But she had given up so much. Love, a real relationship. She had been too busy when she had been young, too eager to compete. Too determined to hold on to her title—until she had known it was time to bow out, rather than lose. Now she had no children to fill her life. She had traveled, of course. And then she had come back to see Manny at the club. And Manny . . .

Manny would not shut up about Ted and Molly.

She frowned, thinking she heard a loud voice from the office, and spun around.

Curious, Maria walked in that direction. The staff was gone. Not even the young receptionist was manning her station.

She moved closer to the office door.

And she listened, her eyes widening.

She had wanted to speak with Eduardo about the Summer Sizzler.

No more. She swallowed hard. At first she was afraid. Then she thought again of Ted and Molly and their kindnesses to her through the years, and she grew angry.

IN ANOTHER HOUR, Keith had reached Islamorada. He found the marina where Victor Thompson had kept his boat and run his charters.

The guy had clearly been well liked. At the spot where his boat should have been berthed, there was a cross, and flowers covered the pier and floated in the water nearby. He was standing there when a man walked up to him. "Friend of Victor's?" he asked.

"Fellow diver, paying my respects," Keith told him. "You were a friend?"

The man was in his late fifties, with a full head of silver-gray hair. Well built and bronzed, he was covered with tattoos and sported a gold skeleton for an earring. "I taught him to dive. I never taught him to go off alone, though," he said sadly.

"Doesn't make a lot of sense, an experienced diver like Victor," Keith said. "Where was he diving when it happened?"

"I didn't see him the morning he took off, so it's a mystery to me," the man said. He pointed toward a building near the docks, with a Keys-style thatched roof and an outside bar. "As far as I know, he didn't say anything to anyone. But we all hang out up there, at La Isla Bar-A. Some of us are up there now, drinking to Vic. Come join us, buy a round. Man, it's a sorry thing. I just don't understand how we lost Vic. It's a tragedy, and a waste, and I'm angry, I guess." He shook his head.

Keith thanked him for the information and headed for the bar. "I'll be up in a minute," the older man told him. "Name's John, John Elmer. You can buy me a drink, too."

"Sure."

The bar was typical of the area, with lots of tall stools and hardwood tables, chairs and benches. It had the neighborhood feel of Nick's. The woman behind the bar was attractive, but no kid. She was busy, but she handled the load with ease. He decided that the big group at the far end of the bar had to be Victor Thompson's friends. He didn't horn in on them immediately but sat a short distance away. When the woman came to take his order, he asked for a beer, then asked her about the group. "If those are Victor Thompson's friends, I'd like to buy them a drink."

"Sure. You knew Victor, huh?" she said. "So many people cared. He was a great guy. So sad . . ."

He saw the group at the end of the bar looking up after the drinks had been ordered. One of them lifted his newly delivered beer and called out to Keith, "Hey, thanks. Join us?"

Keith rose, taking his beer with him. He offered his hand around, and met Joe, Shelley, Jose, Bill,

Junior and Melanie. "Good guy, absolute waste," the one named Joe, who had summoned him over, told Keith.

"A real friendly guy. Never met a stranger. That's why we're all here right now," Melanie explained.

"He always said he didn't want a wake, people in black crying over his shell," Jose said.

"Yeah, Vic wanted a party," Joe said. "People remembering the good times, laughing. We're supposed to cremate him, take him out to the reefs he loved."

"Sounds like a fitting way to handle the end," Keith agreed. "Still . . ." He shook his head. "Funny thing. How could he know the reefs so well, and . . ."

"We can't figure it out, either," Shelley said, looking morose despite the fact that she was supposed to be partying. Keith's heart took a little plunge. The woman had obviously cried her eyes out.

He got them talking about Victor's destination the day he had died. But they were at a loss, as well. "As far as I know, the day before, he had talked about looking at some new places to take people," Joe said. "But no destination in particular that I know of."

"He wanted to get into a day-and-night thing. Like camping somewhere," Melanie offered. "The Middle Keys are filled with great places."

"Yeah," Keith agreed, thinking Calliope Key might be a great place, too.

"I think he headed south, but I don't really know," Joe said.

"Hey, remember the time he knocked the whole motor off John's dinghy?" Melanie said, and giggled.

"Yeah, and remember the time he fell in love with the Cuban girl in Miami and we all had to take dance lessons?" Bill said, snickering. "Man, did we suck."

"Victor took classes in Miami?" Keith said.

"We all did—he didn't want it to look as if he was chasing the girl," Melanie told him. "And speak for yourself. I was good," she told Bill.

"Where did you guys go?" Keith asked.

"Someplace on the beach," Bill answered. "It was changing hands when we were there . . . oh, man, I'm losing brain cells or something. Wait. Monoco. The Monoco Studios. They went missing, didn't they?"

"Sad, huh? That old Monoco guy was great. But I heard their boat had been seen," Melanie said.

"Where'd you hear that?" Keith asked.

Melanie looked at him blankly then shrugged. "I don't know. I think some people in here the other day were saying it."

Keith remained a while longer, bought another round of drinks, then left. On the way back, he put in another call to Mike.

It was late by the time he had taken the tender back to the *Sea Serpent*. Lee and Matt were in for the day, and neither seemed glad to see him, though they couldn't argue with his disappearance; since they had been informed by Mike that he was to come in with the coin and make a full report.

"You find out anything?"

Keith shook his head. "You?"

"Seems like we're beating our heads against a brick wall," Lee told him.

"Did you hear anything from your old buddy Hank?" Keith asked Lee.

"No, did you hear from any of your old buddies . . . like Beth Anderson or Amanda Mason?" Lee asked.

Matt made a choking sound. They both stared at him. "Sorry—swallowed wrong," he said, and turned away.

Keith and Lee stared after him, then Lee shrugged and turned away, as well.

A rift had definitely formed between the three of them. Lee went down to the cabin, while Keith remained on deck, staring out at the sea. His cell phone began to ring, and he was glad that he'd been left alone on deck when he answered it.

Manny. He listened to what the man had to say, weighed it, then replied, "I'll need Beth Anderson in on it."

"How will we manage that?"

"We have mutual friends," Keith said. "I'll check in with them. Beth will come," he added softly, "if you convince her brother and her niece."

He rang off, hesitated, then he put in a call of his own. He would be sticking his neck out in a big way, but he was convinced it was time. When he hung up, he stood very still in the night, listening, wondering if either of his co-workers had made an attempt to hear his conversation.

It seemed that he was alone in the dark vastness of the sea and sky.

Still . . .

When he went to sleep that night, it was with one eye open.

15

ON THURSDAY, BETH FOUND THAT she was well ahead on her work. Eduardo Shea, Maria and Mauricio were practicing, and the final rehearsal planned for the next afternoon, after the floor was in place.

She sat at her desk after lunch, going through all the last-minute arrangements. Then she found herself writing down a chronology starting with the day she had seen the skull on the island. She included a paragraph noting that the ghost story Keith had told had been based on a real event. She made a side note with the information about the couple in Virginia who'd had their boat stolen, along with the fact that—no matter what the rumor mill said—the Monocos hadn't been heard from since they'd last called in from Calliope Key.

A diver had turned up dead, which might or might not mean foul play.

Someone had messed with her computer.

Someone had put a skull on her desk.

She had been threatened at gun- and knifepoint, and

law enforcement everywhere was looking for Brad and Sandy, who were apparently pirates. They hadn't been at the club—at least, she was almost certain they hadn't been at the club when the skull had appeared on her desk. And she didn't see how they could have gotten there in time to place it there, anyway. She tried hard to remember if the skull had been real or a prop. Ridiculous question. She should have known. But the minute she had seen it, she had panicked, then run to get the police. Smart call, one would think. And since Ben's toy skull had turned out to be missing, it probably had been a fake, anyway.

Both Manny Ortega and Maria Lopez claimed to feel a real affection for the Monocos. Neither had been on the island. Eduardo Shea seemed like an up-and-up businessman with a love of dance.

She pressed her hands against her temples. Did any of it make any sense?

And why, in the middle of all this, could she not stop thinking about Keith Henson? She was so angry with him. . . .

And so suspicious and edgy. Had he just been attempting to get close to find out what she might know? What she might have set in motion.

Yes, she was sick with jealousy, too proud to ask certain questions —or too afraid of the answers? Had he slept with Amanda, as well, eager to know more about her, too?

Why did she wish she hadn't been quite so furious? Why hadn't she allowed a conversation? Why did she feel as if she had . . . cut away a part of her being? She prayed for a little more dignity. Praying didn't help.

She simply wanted to be with him.

"Hi."

She looked up, so startled that she nearly screamed. Her brother was standing in the doorway. She glanced at her watch. One o'clock. Way too early for Ben to be off work.

"What are you doing here?"

"Early-dismissal day," Ben said.

"Again? They just had one."

"Hey, do I control the Miami-Dade Board of Education?" he asked ruefully.

"You should have said something. I could have picked Amber up from school."

"I know. And I appreciate it. But I decided to get her myself. And now I'm getting you."

She arched a brow. "Getting me to . . . ?"

"We're going diving."

"Diving? I'm working."

"I've got permission for you to leave. Commodore Berry is thrilled to death with your plan for tomorrow night. He said you can take the afternoon off and come with us."

"Who's 'us'?"

"Amber, me, the Masons, Manny and a few others. Actually, Manny was the one who came up with the idea of a nice social afternoon."

"I should go down and watch the rehearsal," Beth said.

"You're too late. They've already finished. In fact, Maria is coming out with us."

"She is?"

"Um. With Manny."

"Ben, I'm not so sure—"

"Ashley and Jake are coming."

"Oh?"

"Beth, I'm not an idiot. My daughter's life has been threatened. I think Brad and Sandy are violent but cowardly, and we've taken precautions, but even so, we're going out with a pair of cops, okay? We're going in a big group. Amber wants to go out on the Masons' boat. That's cool—big group. Got it? I'm *not* an idiot."

She leaned back, smiling. "I'm sorry. No, you're not an idiot. Where are we going?"

"I told you. Diving," he informed her firmly. She glared at him, but when he told her that she was welcome to go aboard Manny's boat or one of the other three vessels making the run, she refused.

Amber was going to be aboard Hank Mason's boat, and that meant she was, too. Along with Jake and Ashley, who weren't just cops but excellent divers.

The trip started off well. The sun was out; there was a perfect breeze. Amanda was actually being a charming hostess, and Beth thought she might actually be sincere when she asked with concern if anyone had discovered who the prankster was who had left the skull on her desk.

"I bet he would have admitted what he did if the

police hadn't come in, making the whole thing such a big deal," she suggested, which made Beth wonder if the skull on her desk had actually been a prank, totally unconnected to the very real attack on her. Maybe someone had heard about the incident on the island and thought they were being funny.

"Well, we'll find out soon enough if it was a prank or not," Jake Dilessio said with a shrug.

"Really?" Amanda said. "I thought you were homicide. What are you doing investigating such a silly thing?"

"Hadn't you heard?" he asked her. "There's an APB out on the couple you all know as Brad and Sandy. They're suspects in the piracy that's been going on along the coast for over a year now, and they were recently spotted in Miami."

Judging by the shocked looks that greeted that statement, neither Amanda nor her family had heard a thing about it.

"Really?" Hank said. "We were sleeping right down the beach from them!"

"Let's hope to God they're apprehended soon," Roger said fervently.

"They will be," Jake said with deadly assurance.

There was silence for a minute. Then Amanda determinedly changed the subject. "You know, I've never dived this site before. Have any of you?"

The conversation turned to diving, and Beth half listened to the stories exchanged. Mostly she found herself watching Amber and being worried.

Hank decided to stay aboard while the others paired up and went into the water. Amanda immediately pounced on Ben, determined to be his buddy.

"Hey, Amber, can I be your buddy?" Jake asked, glancing reassuringly at Beth. "Ashley and Beth can go together."

Beth smiled at him. She could relax if Amber was with Jake.

Hank's boat was fitted out perfectly for diving, with stands and benches for easy access to enough tanks for ten. In fact, she was actually better equipped than many professional dive boats, with medical equipment on board, as well. She was surprised that he had decided to take on the role of dive master above board, since he loved to dive so much himself. Then again, he could head out whenever he chose, so perhaps he had decided that supervising the entire scene would be fun for a change.

It was hardly as if they had the area to themselves. Dive boats from the Keys, Miami and as far north as Palm Beach congregated here, along with private boaters like themselves. The wreck was a well-known and popular site.

It was fun being down with Ashley, and an easy afternoon, with so many divers present that it was almost impossible to be worried. In addition to the wreck, the area teemed with fish, anemones and all kinds of undersea life.

They had barely begun the dive when Ashley glanced at her compass, then beckoned to her. She led

Beth away from the wreck, into an area of reefs.

They came to a huge outcrop of coral. Next to the coral, there was a bed of sand and seagrass. There was a diver there, exercising perfect buoyancy, simply sitting on the sand.

Waiting.

It took Beth a minute to register who it was—people in tanks and masks were hard to recognize at first glance. But then she knew.

Keith.

She stared at Ashley, furious at both of them—especially Keith. This had obviously been arranged, even though she had told him in no uncertain terms that she didn't want to talk to him until he was willing to do some explaining.

Ashley was her dive partner, but their group wasn't far away. She could have turned and propelled herself right back to join them, and she was sorely tempted to do so. She didn't understand what his appearance here—twenty feet down—meant. He could hardly do much explaining where they were.

He gave them the divers' sign to rise, and Ashley nodded, then looked at Beth. Beth lifted her hands. Fine. They would rise.

They surfaced by a boat. Beth was startled to realize that it was Manny's. He and Maria were both there, as if they were awaiting their arrival.

She lifted her mask, held on to the ladder and pulled off her fins.

Keith pulled himself out of the water easily, then

reached down to help her and Ashley. Manny stood by, ready to assist, as well. "Welcome, gorgeous," he said, with a smile. "Let me help you with your tank."

"Wait . . . I need this tank to get back to the boat I'm supposed to be on," she protested, staring at them all one by one, confused and angry. Her last reproving glance was for Ashley. How the hell had this happened?

"No, it's all right. I'll radio over that you and Ashley decided to come up here and visit with Maria," Manny said. "Let me take that. We should go below."

She stared at the sea around them. There were a number of boats around. Dive flags littered the area.

Hank's boat was a good distance from them, no activity evident on board. Everyone must still be down at the wreck, she thought, and allowed Manny to help her with her tank.

"Come on down. I've got coffee and tea ready," Maria said, offering them towels. "Not that it's anything but a lovely day. Still, you're wet, and the air-conditioning is on in the cabin."

Beth followed the others down to the cabin. It was nice, not huge. Manny's boat could sleep two. There was a head, a small galley and a dining/living area, with a table against the port side. Beth stared at Keith, damning both him and herself. She'd hated herself for wishing he would reappear at any moment.

Now that he had, she just wanted to run over to him. But she couldn't let herself. She had to remind herself that the man had an agenda. An agenda that included disappearing whenever he needed to do so and it included spending all kinds of time with Amanda.

He stared back at her with no apology.

"Sit, please?" he said.

"I didn't know the three of you were so well acquainted," Beth said, speaking at last and looking from Manny to Maria and then to Keith once again.

"We've just recently become friends," Keith said.

"Interesting," she murmured.

"I didn't tell Manny anything," Keith said evenly. "He knew who I was."

"Clue *me* in, why don't you?" Beth said, her tone heated and her heart wondering if he'd reveal his secrets to her.

"I'm with a company called Rescue, and most of our contracts are military," Keith explained. "No one was supposed to know who we were or what we were doing," Keith explained.

"I see," she said, looking around at the group. It amazed her that even Maria was in on it, while she had been in the dark.

"Beth, you must understand. I already knew who he was," Manny explained.

"And Maria knew, too. But you couldn't tell me," Beth said icily.

"You didn't want to call the police when you were accosted at both gun- and knifepoint. If you had, they might have caught Brad and Sandy," Keith said. "There's plenty of blame to go around here."

Beth glared at him angrily. "Not fair. Amber's life

was threatened." She stared at Ashley. "And excuse me, but how the hell did *this* all come about?" she asked, gesturing at the group and their surroundings.

Manny cleared his throat. "I arranged for all this to happen today. You needed to see Keith."

She hoped she hadn't given away the fact that she'd begun to feel desperate to see the man. It felt as if her cheeks were burning.

"Why?" she demanded.

She didn't get the answer she had hoped for or expected.

"I need to be at your Summer Sizzler tomorrow night," he told her.

She almost laughed aloud—at herself. She managed not to, and instead stared at Keith, shaking her head. "You've gotten into the club on your own several times. Membership doesn't seem to mean a lot where you're concerned. You're best friends with Manny and Maria. And Amanda would be happy to invite you to the party. You sure as hell don't need me to get in."

"You need to tell her everything you've discovered," Manny said.

"Sit down, Beth. Have some tea. Please," Maria said. She flashed Beth an apologetic smile. "It's partially my fault that you're here."

"Oh?"

"Please, sit, Beth. I'll explain," Keith said.

She sat. He sat opposite her.

His eyes were on her, dead steady. "Beth, Manny knows me the same way Jake and Ashley do, through a previous situation here in Miami-Dade, that's all."

"And I know about him because Manny told me when I went to him for help," Maria explained.

"Wonderful," Beth murmured, still lost. She looked at Keith. "So you were never on the island looking for the Monocos from the start?"

"No."

She stared straight at him. "Then you were looking for the ship."

"What ship?" Maria murmured.

"La Doña," Beth said flatly, staring at Keith.

He stared back at her. She realized that no one had known what he was really doing—they had just known who he was. And he didn't appreciate the fact that she had spoken.

"It doesn't matter," Beth said, offering Maria a quick glance, then turning back to Keith. "Go on."

"The point is, I want to be at the Sizzler from the start. I need to *watch*. And I don't want anyone to know I'm there. I want access to your office, and I want to get behind the scenes, so I can watch what's going on. Matt and Lee will be there. We've all been invited already."

"The Masons?" Beth asked.

He nodded. "Amanda called and invited us," he told her.

She tried not to stiffen. "I don't understand what you want. You could have arranged this without me."

"Actually, no."

"Why?" she demanded. "What's so important about

you being there with my blessing?"

"I told you, I need free access. Everyone who was on the island will be there," Keith said.

She shook her head, a wry smile in place. "Not exactly. Brad and Sandy aren't invited."

"I have a feeling they'll be there anyway."

"They wouldn't dare be so obvious," she protested.

"I think they're confident enough in their ability to disguise themselves to risk it."

"Then the police should be there."

"The police will be there," Keith said, glancing at Ashley.

"Then they can arrest them the moment they see them," Beth said.

"They'll have to know who they are—but it goes beyond just identifying them. Beth, here's the thing. We don't think they're working alone. Or that they just want to get to you. They're looking to get paid."

"Paid!" she exclaimed.

"They disappeared really quickly after attacking you. I looked into the property surrounding your house, specifically at the block around the corner. Do you know who owns most of the houses in the area?"

"Who?" she demanded.

"Eduardo Shea."

Beth stared at him in surprise. "You think Eduardo is in on the piracy? I don't understand."

"Among Mr. Shea's investments are a number of boatyards on the South American coast," Keith told her. "We know that whoever is stealing luxury vessels has to be making them over somewhere. The police have investigated all the local facilities, and everyone comes up clean. It would also make more sense to get the boats far away from this country, where all of them have been registered."

"Now I'm really confused," Beth murmured. "I don't understand why Sandy and Brad would risk being at the club."

"I think that Eduardo was talking to them on the phone the other day," Maria put in.

Beth stared at Maria.

"Eduardo was distressed. He was threatening someone. Then, he said that he'd see them at the club. I told Manny," she explained. "Manny was very upset. He contacted Keith and said we must tell him."

"But . . . that's so . . . I mean, they must know that they'd be in danger of exposure at the club."

Keith shook his head, offering her a rueful smile. "How? They don't know the police will be there. They don't know that Eduardo Shea's finances have been investigated."

"Still, it would be a ridiculous risk!"

"Hide in plain sight," Ashley murmured, joining into the conversation at last.

"I'm sorry. I still don't get this," Beth said, eyes hard as she stared at Keith again. "What is your involvement? Because, according to what you've told me, you were never out at Calliope looking for the pirates."

He sat back. "My involvement is personal. I happen to believe that, if they're apprehended, Sandy and Brad can answer a lot of questions," he said flatly.

"I still don't understand why you need me—why you need to be out of sight," Beth murmured.

He lowered his head for a moment, then looked up. "There are a few other dynamics I need to keep an eye on. I'm asking you—no, begging you—to trust me. And not to demand answers that I can't give you yet. I had Manny set up the dive—and no, your brother doesn't know that Manny arranged all this on purpose—because I hoped that if you met with Ashley and Manny and me, you would be able to have faith in me."

"I wouldn't go so far as to say that I have faith in you," Beth told him. "But sure, be my guest. I still don't understand. You can have access to all areas of the club and hide out in my office or wherever." She stared at Ashley. "The more cops the merrier." She felt as if her head was reeling, and she didn't understand anything. "Commodore Berry knows the police will be at the club? And the board of directors are aware of what's going on, as well?"

Keith nodded to her.

"Then you really didn't need my permission for anything," Beth said.

He stared at her. "Yes, I did."

The tension seemed heavy. Manny and Maria remained silent. She didn't know on exactly what level he meant his words, or if being with her had been part of his undercover work or also something personal.

She just wanted to get away.

"I think we should join the others now," she said sharply. "The rest of the divers must be up."

Keith stood. "I'm going. I'll see you tomorrow, then."

"Right," she said stiffly.

He went topside with Manny. Ashley took his place at the table. "You've got to understand my position. Please, Beth," she said. "Trust me."

"*I* trust *you,*" Beth said, the implication that she didn't care not to be trusted herself quite evident.

Ashley flushed.

"You really need some tea," Maria said.

"I really need a drink," Beth replied.

BETH WAS FINDING IT impossible to sleep. Usually, the night after a dive, she crashed immediately.

Not tonight. She was at Ashley and Jake's place, the kids were sleeping. Ashley and Jake were sleeping. And she was tempted to join the crowd hanging out late at the restaurant.

There were sure to be cops among their number.

Then again, Brad and Sandy had apparently patronized Nick's, as well. Still, when she went to the window and opened the drapes, she could see the docks. As late as it was, she could see several people sitting on one of the ice chests on the walk, talking, beers in hand. She craned her neck to look to her right, toward the restaurant. People were still filling the patio seats.

Restless, she dressed and stepped out, locking the door, pocketing the key Ashley had given her. She walked toward the patio and took a seat, then ordered a beer. That might help her sleep. God knew, she needed to sleep.

People at Nick's were friendly. Several said hello. She was asked if she wanted to join in a game of darts but declined.

At last the crowd began to thin out. She rose, heading back to her friends' house.

As she walked, she heard the sound of a chair scraping. She spun back, cursing at herself for being such a goose.

But the feeling remained with her that she was being followed. She quickened her steps, turned back and saw a form.

All she had to do was scream. People would come running. But as she looked at the shadow of the man who had just left the light of the patio area, he was joined by a young woman. She caught his hand, and, laughing, they headed down toward the dock together. She let out a sigh of relief and turned.

She froze. And saw another shadow. It wasn't coming from the patio but from the parking lot. It shouldn't have been there. She stared, trying to figure out whether she was imagining it, maybe seeing the shadow of a large hibiscus. Her breath caught as the shadow grew. She stayed calm. All she had to do was turn around and head back for the patio.

She did so, walking quickly, to her dismay discovering that everyone had left. The serving staff couldn't all be gone, she told herself. Nick himself was in there somewhere.

She started to hurry after one of the waitresses, who was disappearing inside. The door closed as she reached it. She grabbed the handle and found it locked.

Panic was rising inside her. She lifted a hand to pound on the door.

Then she heard her name.

She turned.

Keith.

She gasped softly.

"What on earth are you doing, wandering around out here?" he demanded.

She couldn't breathe for a moment. "I was having a beer," she said finally. "What are you doing, wandering around out here?"

"I was going to have a beer—I guess they've closed," he said. She stared at him. She still felt so distrustful.

And so hungry, even though she loathed herself for it.

"Beth," he said.

She took a step backward. "I really don't know you," she said.

"Actually, you really do. And I know you."

He lowered his head for a minute. The light caught

the sun-bleached blond of his hair. He seemed very tall, a striking presence. She suddenly ached to be held, to feel as if she hadn't somehow made a disaster of her world.

To feel as if something was real and solid . . .

He looked at her again. "Let me just walk you back to the door."

She shrugged. "Tell me, Keith, what do you think you know about me?"

He looked at her, frowning. "I know I care," he said simply. "And I know you are who I want to care about."

He took her arms, turning her toward him. He appeared perplexed. "Please try to understand."

"There are things I can understand, and things I can't," she said.

"And exactly what does that mean?"

She shook her head, turned and walked to the door, then unlocked it. The damn hibiscus still made her uneasy. Or was that really it? "There's beer in the house," she heard herself say.

"Are you inviting me in?"

"Apparently you have as much right to be here as I do," she said, leaving the door open as she entered.

He stepped in behind her. She stopped walking, knowing that his hands would fall on her shoulders, that he would sweep her hair aside, that she would feel his lips and his whisper against her neck.

He didn't disappoint her.

But then he shocked her.

"I know that I'm falling in love with you," he said.

The door closed behind them. She turned in his arms, then wound her own arms around him as his lips found hers. But as the fusion of their mouths grew heated, she forced herself to pull away slightly.

"The . . . guest . . . room," she murmured. "They . . . have . . ."

"Kids. Guest room," he agreed.

He swept her up. For the moment she forgot that she still didn't know or trust everything about him. In the darkness, in the privacy that lay behind closed doors, she thought only of his naked flesh, the heated explorations of his tongue, the eroticism of his touch.

Miraculously, he had appeared, vital, like a fire, pulsing with life. She knew he would disappear by morning.

At the moment, all she longed for was the night.

HE STEPPED AWAY FROM the shadows at the side of the house and into the light, staring at the door. He had watched it close. Watched the two of them come together . . .

And it enraged him.

He'd been so close. . . .

And what?

Dare he make a move tonight? No, no sense in it.

He stretched his fingers, knotted them back into fists. This was insane. Just too tempting. He'd had a beer at Nick's. If anyone had seen him, so what?

Then, just when he had seen her really beginning to fear the shadows, to trust that niggling sensation at her nape, the one that sent chills down her spine and gave him such pleasure . . .

Keith Henson.

He swore softly.

Then he disappeared back into the shadows.

16

THE CLUB LOOKED EXQUISITE. The florists had arrived at the crack of dawn. The dining-room staff began at the same time, and soon after, electricians were out stringing the special lights. The theme was hot and tropical, and by afternoon, the place had been transformed.

Beth came at ten. She'd slept late, knowing she would wake alone. As she left the house, she glanced at the hibiscus bush.

She was tempted to ask Ashley to rip the damn thing out!

Nick's was already buzzing. Cheerful waiters and waitresses called a good-morning to her as she hurried around to her car.

She felt silly for letting herself get so spooked the night before. And elated because she'd been with him. Because he'd said he was falling in love with her. Angry . . .

Because even though she'd been with him, so little had really been said.

She told herself to forget him for now and try again for a little bit of dignity and distance when she saw him again.

Beth spent the day in an uneasy fog. She ran around as she was supposed to, ensuring that the flowers were right, the tables set and the dais specially arranged for the commodore. Champagne was chilled; the correct wines arrived.

At three she went up to her office, ready to lock her door for a few minutes and collapse into her chair.

She started when she walked in and discovered that Keith was there. She stared at him accusingly.

"You didn't lock it," he told her.

"I don't usually during the day, when I'm up and down. I can see now that I should have."

He heard her tone and ignored it, speaking crisply, "You'll need to lock it tonight, and I'll need a key."

At the moment he was in dock shorts and a T-shirt. There was a garment bag hanging off one of her shelves, next to her own.

"You're here for good, then—I mean, from now till the party's over?" she asked.

He nodded.

"I have one question for you," she told him, trying to keep her distance.

"And what is that?"

"Why isn't my brother in on what's going on?"

"I'm working on a need-to-know basis here," he

said, his eyes level upon hers.

"I see. Maria needed to know all about you, but my brother shouldn't?"

He sighed. "Beth, Maria knew from Manny."

"So because they knew who you are, they're in the clear?" she asked.

"No one is in the clear," he said grimly. "Beth—"

She took a step back. "I don't think today is really the time to get into a heavy conversation."

"You're right. Let it go. I'm not accusing your brother of anything. He just doesn't need to have anything more dumped on him right now."

She felt a twinge of irritation coming on. "That's a crock. You think my brother can't be trusted."

"Beth, do we have to do this?" he demanded.

"You asked me if you could be here, remember?"

Something hard touched his eyes. "I'll need a key."

"Top drawer, on the left. It's in a compact," she told him.

"Interesting hiding place."

"I never needed to be all that worried about hiding it before," she told him.

She no longer wanted to collapse into her chair. She left the office. Downstairs, she decided to grab something to eat in the kitchen. The chef asked her to taste the black-bean soup, which was delicious. She was so nervous, though, that she could only manage a few spoonfuls.

When she returned to her office, Keith was gone.

She called Ashley, who assured her that the man

watching Amber had called in. Her niece would be getting out of school soon, then heading home and getting ready to come to the club with her father. Beth decided to get dressed for the evening. She headed down to the women's lockers with her clothing.

Extra staff had been hired for the evening, and caterers were working on the patio and dockside bars and chair arrangements. All the permanent staff and extra personnel were wearing tuxedos for the evening, the men and the women. She nodded with approval as Henry waved to her.

There was a large man helping Henry. He seemed a little awkward. He noticed her watching him and came over to her. "Officer Greg Masters, Miss Anderson," he said quietly. "I just wanted you to know we're here. Blending in."

"Thank you," she murmured. Blending in? She wasn't so sure, but he was there, and that was enough.

She crossed the side patio and entered the hallway that led to the women's lockers.

No one was in the area. In the locker room alone, she felt chills along her spine. She went through the place, looking into every bathroom stall, every shower.

She was definitely alone, but she still had the eerie feeling that she was being watched. She showered and dressed quickly, then emerged, still with the uncomfortable feeling of being watched. She wondered why she was so nervous, knowing that the police had already arrived and Keith was there, as well.

What about Lee and Matt? she wondered. They had been invited by the Masons. Were they there already, too? And exactly where was Keith at that moment, and why had he been so determined that he needed to be there so early.

She made a few last-minute checks in the kitchen, the dining room and the bar. The band arrived to set up, and then Eduardo Shea appeared, dashing in an elegant black-and-white salsa costume with ruffled sleeves. She knew she had to behave naturally, and she managed to greet him with enthusiasm. All the while, though, it seemed that her blood ran cold.

"Has Maria arrived yet?" Eduardo asked her.

"No, not yet. But, please, come say hello to Commodore Berry and his wife, and I'll show you where your table is. The band is set up, and everything will be exactly as you requested." She smiled and took him by the arm.

Commodore Berry was standing outside, looking totally the part in his white suit and captain's hat. He was gazing out at the docks with pleasure. He turned to Beth, smiling. "Look, there's a group coming in from the Belle Haven club. Rumor says this is going to be the end-of-summer party to outdo all the others." He lowered his head as if he was about to whisper to her, then noticed Eduardo. "Good evening, sir. Welcome."

Beth fled. If Commodore Berry could carry off his part so well—knowing that police were watching his party for uninvited guests—surely she could carry it off, too.

Ashley and Jake arrived, and then Ben and Amber.

"You all right?" Ashley asked.

Beth stared at her friend. "I guess you saw Keith this morning."

"Yes," Ashley said, flushing. "But I wasn't referring to Keith. I was talking about this evening. But, um, of course, Keith is welcome in my home anytime. But . . . as to tonight . . . ?"

"As long as you stay right on Amber every minute," Beth told her, "I'll be absolutely fine."

"I'll be with her, I promise," Ashley assured her. She looked at Beth anxiously. "You know . . . nothing may happen. No one will act if they don't see anything out of the ordinary."

Beth nodded. "I almost wish something *would* happen. Something . . . so that I can stop feeling as if I were on pins and needles all the time."

"It will be all right," Ashley said, and squeezed her arm. "Everything looks fabulous, by the way."

"Thanks," Beth said wryly. "There's Maria. Lord!"

Maria was in a short sequined dress that hugged the perfection of her body. Her hair was swept back, and she wore a red rose tucked behind her ear. The dress sparkled with her every movement. Beth noted that the short skirt would swirl and glitter as she danced. Maria turned, saw Beth, and nodded gravely.

"People are beginning to arrive," Ashley said.

"Time to play hostess."

"Have you seen Keith?"

"Hours ago. I don't know where he is now. Excuse me."

For the next hour Beth was insanely busy, so much so that she nearly forgot that her sparkling contribution to the yachting club social season had become a charade. Despite the insanity, she found herself anxiously looking for Amber all the time. Her niece wasn't alone. Ashley was with her, as she had promised. Apparently Kimberly's parents had dropped her off to enjoy the event, as well. Both girls were stunning in their fancy outfits and heels.

She caught her brother watching her, as well. He still wore a look of accusation every time his eyes turned her way. They had been so close all their lives. She felt a pain in her heart because now he felt she had betrayed him. She longed to tell him she wasn't at fault, but she couldn't. Not yet.

The other dancers had arrived. Mauricio stood beside Maria.

The Masons were there, ringed around Eduardo, Maria and the dancers.

Then, in the crowd, she saw Matt Albright, and a small distance from him, helping himself to a glass of champagne, Lee Gomez.

Still, no sign of Keith. But then, he'd said he wanted to stay unseen, and apparently he'd meant it.

As she greeted some of the members, Commodore Berry came to her side. "Beth, this is incredible.

Already a hit, and we've hardly even started." He lowered his voice. "I know the place is crawling with police, but how can you tell who's who in such a crowd?"

He had a point, she decided. In a moment of panic, she excused herself and threaded her way through the crowd.

She breathed a sigh of relief. Ashley was still with Amber. Sticking like glue.

The band stopped playing just then, and the commodore asked everyone to start taking their places for dinner. People began to file to their tables. An older man, tall and well built, with thick white hair, beard and a mustache, and sea-green eyes, passed her and smiled. She smiled back, though she had no idea who he was. There were too many guests from their sister clubs that night, she decided. She watched the others file into the dining room and take their seats. The dance instructors were together at a table with Manny and Eduardo Shea. The Masons were all in attendance, including Gerald. They were at a table with Matt and Lee.

If Brad and Sandy were present anywhere, she hadn't seen them.

The commodore gave his welcome speech. Beth joined her own family at last. When she sat, she was at Jake Dilessio's side. Ashley was beside her husband, and Amber was on Ashley's other side, with Ben next to her, and Kimberly next to him.

She tried to relax, tried to eat.

Whoever the man was with the white hair and Colonel Sanders mustache, he must have been a friend of Commodore Berry's, because he had a seat on the dais.

The commodore announced the menu, welcomed the members and guests, and hoped that all the docking arrangements had gone smoothly. He thanked the chef and the staff, and made a special announcement, thanking Beth, as well, and introducing her. She was startled when he demanded that she rise, which she did, and she tried not to feel awkward as she received applause.

Her brother clapped with the others, politely, but he stared at her as if he felt he had nurtured a traitor. She wondered if she would ever be able to fix things between them.

Yet again, she wondered where Keith was.

Dinner was served, and it was as delicious as the chef had promised. Kim and Amber chatted; even Ashley and Jake seemed casual.

As courses came and went, people hopped sociably from table to table. Amanda joined them for several minutes, complimenting Kim and Amber, flirting with Ben. Hank dropped by, then Gerald.

There was a tap on Beth's shoulder. She nearly jumped a mile. It was Matt Albright. "Hi. I just came over to see how you're doing," he said cheerfully.

"Great. Good to see you," she told him.

"Have you seen Keith?" he asked her. "He was supposed to be here with us."

"No, I haven't seen him in here," she answered honestly.

"There's just no telling with that guy," he said, and shrugged. "Well, I hear there's dancing later. Save something for me, huh?"

"Sure. Though I hear it's salsa—and your best partners are over at that table," she said, pointing to Eduardo and his group.

"I have a feeling you'd be a great partner," he told her.

"Well, thanks," she murmured.

Roger Mason stopped by next to greet her brother.

Amber rose. "Where are you going?" Beth asked sharply.

Amber stared at her, surprised by the tone of her voice. "The bathroom, if it's all right."

"I'll go with you," Beth said.

"Aunt Beth, I know where it is."

"I know, but, um, I need to go myself."

"We'll all go," Ashley said cheerfully, rising. "Kim, join us?"

"I don't really have to go," Kim said, bewildered.

"But you don't want to have to go during the dancing, right?" Beth asked. She didn't know why; she just wanted the girls together, no matter what, and with Ashley or Jake at all times.

She didn't understand, either, why she was nervous all the way to the ladies' room and back. The place was swarming with people, guests, members, staff, everyone having a good time. Ashley was as casual as could be, making the girls laugh. Beth thanked God for her friend—and for the fact that her friend was a cop and married to a cop.

Back at the table, she sipped champagne, realizing that throughout the day she had become more tightly wound with each passing moment. She had to calm down or she would wind up jumping out of her chair and screaming.

Dessert was served, and as the flaming soufflés went around, Commodore Berry rose again, announcing their entertainment.

Mauricio escorted Maria to the dance floor out on the patio, open to the dining room and surrounded by additional tables.

The music began.

For several minutes Beth found herself as transfixed as the others. As she had felt earlier, it seemed impossible that anyone could move so fast, that steps could be so sensual and erotic, that anything could appear as miraculously, glitteringly swift and elegant, all in one.

Then the music broke, and Mauricio and Maria stopped dead, dramatically posed. The old cliché was true, Beth thought. She really could have heard a pin drop.

Then the moment was over. The music began again, and the dancers swirled into motion once more until at last the performance came to a halt.

Everyone in the room rose; the applause was thunderous.

Beth blinked. Eduardo was walking forward to

thank his dancers. He was carrying a cordless mike, and he announced that there would be lessons for the guests, then introduced the rest of his staff. He had been speaking for several minutes before Beth realized that he hadn't come from the direction of his table, he hadn't been seated during the performance.

Her heart thudded as she wondered if that meant anything.

She looked around. The big cop who was dressed like a waiter was standing by one of the serving stations.

He was still staring at the dance floor. Everyone had been staring at the dance floor. Had anyone seen Eduardo come and go?

"Miss Elizabeth Anderson."

She started when she heard her name. She looked around, certain she must seem like a stunned child to the spectators.

"Come on."

There was a roar of applause. Eduardo was looking at her, an arm outstretched toward her.

"Get up, Aunt Beth. Go!" Amber said.

"Go where? What?" Beth demanded.

"He wants to use you to show everyone how quickly they can learn," Kim told her.

"What?" Beth said. "After that—after Maria, he wants me to get up there?"

"Go on, sis," Ben said, staring at her. "You were the one with the idea to bring in Eduardo Shea, weren't you?"

He had no idea how true that was, she thought. She was the one who had insisted on prying, on putting his child in danger. She knew that somewhere inside, her brother still loved her. But right now he wanted her to get up there and trip over her own feet.

She had no choice. She rose, forced a smile and walked toward Eduardo. She tried to remember everything she had learned in her brief workout during Maria's practice session.

She met the man's eyes. Tried not to betray the fact that she knew he might be conspiring with murderers. He stepped toward her. Her fingers curled around his in proper rhythm form. The band began to play.

She was no Maria Lopez. But Eduardo Shea was good. No matter what else he might be, he was a great dancer. With him leading, she was shocked at how quickly she fell into the rhythm and how she could turn at his command without missing a beat.

Mauricio's voice rang out as he invited everyone to rise and join them. He walked to the dais and selected the commodore's wife. Maria beckoned to the commodore. The other teachers went to different tables, inviting the guests to rise.

There were evidently, and perhaps naturally, many people in the room with some knowledge of salsa. Soon the floor was so crowded, it was almost impossible to move. Dancers began to spill out onto the lawn, in front of the docks.

Dinner was officially over, it seemed. But the party had just begun.

She was breathless when Eduardo stopped, bowing to her. "Thank you for being such a lovely volunteer! Regretfully, I must dance with others now," he said.

"May I?" someone said behind her as Eduardo turned away.

She turned. Before she could protest, she found herself dancing with Hank Mason.

"Quite a party," he told her.

"Thanks."

"Are you doing all right?" he queried.

"Of course."

"You look a little nervous," he said. "I heard about the prank with the skull, of course. Did you really see a skull when we were on the island?" he asked her.

She shook her head, staring straight into his eyes. "Must have been a conch shell—that's what Ben said."

He smiled. "You still seem awfully jumpy."

"I've got a lot riding on tonight, you know." She looked nervously past his shoulder. Eduardo had led Amber out on the dance floor. "Excuse me, Hank."

She extricated herself from his hold and hurried across the floor. She needn't have worried. Jake had already cut in.

"Beth?" It was Roger Mason. "Do an old man proud, would you?"

Before she knew it, she was in his arms. He knew how to salsa, and once again she found herself moving at the speed of light. She tried to see where Amber was and frowned, unable to see Kim, her brother, Amber or Ashley.

The music suddenly changed, with the singer announcing that they were going to take it down to a rumba.

"Excuse me. If I may?"

Someone else was cutting in, neatly slipping her away from Roger.

Beth was startled to swirl into the arms of the white-haired man she had seen sitting with Commodore Berry.

To her surprise, he knew how to rumba. She knew the basics and was able to move, but she was so concerned about Amber, she was thinking only about escape. "It's all right. Kim's parents are coming for her. The girls are out front. Ashley's with them."

She nearly gasped. She never would have recognized him, as well as she thought she had known him.

She nearly said his name out loud.

"Close your mouth, please. Relax. You can't be that tense for a rumba."

She stared at him, amazed. She wondered where he had learned to do such an incredible camouflage job with makeup. It was impossible to tell that the beard and mustache were false, that the hair was a wig. He was wearing green contacts, she realized. "Your own mother wouldn't know you," she told him.

"That *is* the idea."

"Matt and Lee don't even know you, do they?" she asked.

He was silent for a moment. "No."

"Do you still think something's going to happen?" she asked him.

He shrugged. "Shea got up and started to disappear when Maria and Mauricio were dancing. I followed him. He was getting a beer." He shook his head, looking a little disgusted. "I hope to hell I wasn't wrong. It will be hard to swing law enforcement around to my way of thinking a second time. They can be pretty unforgiving. Like someone else I know."

She arched a brow. "Interesting. Let's see, I have no idea what you're really trying to do—ever. And I realize now that you're as much a chameleon as any criminal out there. I thought I knew you, at least a little bit, but now I don't know if anything I thought I knew is true."

"Could you trust me for a little while? Please?"

She tilted her head, staring up at him. "I just don't know how far you would go to achieve what you're really seeking," she told him. She became aware of a ringing as she spoke, then realized that it was her phone, clipped to her skirt.

"Excuse me, will you? I'm sure there are others you need to dance with tonight," she said smoothly, and stepped away, quickly slipping through the crowd to reach a spot on the edge of the dance floor, a breath of air and enough semi-isolation to hear.

She glanced at the caller ID and quickly answered. "Aunt Beth?"

"Amber, what is it? Where are you?"

She heard something that sounded like a sob.
"Aunt Beth, come quick. I need you!"

17

KEITH WATCHED HER GO, feeling an actual pain in his heart. Even after last night, she didn't intend to forgive him.

Had he been an idiot? he wondered. He'd spent the day in various forms of disguise, joining in with the electricians, the wait staff and then the guests. He'd listened in on conversations between the Masons, the dancers, and even Matt and Lee. There had been nothing to hear. The only moment when something might have been amiss had been when Eduardo Shea had risen, and he'd followed the man, only to see him with one of the waiters, getting a beer.

He'd studied every guest. No sign of Brad or Sandy.

"Hey there, handsome!"

He turned to see an attractive older woman in a stunning blue gown that was complemented by the blue tint in her hair. "Spare me a dance?"

He was about to find a way to beg off when he saw that Matt Albright was on the floor with Amanda. He smiled at the woman.

"You must be from one of our sister clubs," she said.

He introduced himself as Jim Smithson, friend of Commodore Berry. He whirled her on the floor, close to Matt and Amanda. She began to talk as they moved, complimenting the party.

She knew the steps; dancing was not a problem. She was very talkative, which was.

Still, he caught snatches of conversation.

". . . and just disappeared," Matt said.

"I had a lovely night. I told you, I really like boats," Amanda replied.

"I saw that," he heard Matt say.

"Don't you, Mr. Smithson?"

He looked down into the eyes of his dance partner. He hadn't the least idea what she had said.

"Yes," he replied, wincing, praying she wouldn't speak again.

". . . the boat . . . but not me, I take it?" Matt said.

"I had an appointment," Amanda said. "Forgive me?"

"What's not to forgive?" Matt said a little harshly. "You took the tender and left."

Amanda giggled. "Sorry about that. I needed to get back to the club. I was meeting—"

"I'm so glad, Mr. Smithson. I think you'll find I have a lovely home," the blue-haired lady said. He realized she was staring into his eyes, enraptured.

"Excuse me?" Keith asked his partner.

"And I'm glad that you feel the way I do about sex for our generation," she said.

"What?"

Matt and Amanda had rumbaed away. "And since we agree that when a couple of our . . . maturity feel such an urge, there's nothing wrong with acting on it . . . we can slip away right now," she said.

"I'm afraid I can't, ma'am. I have a commitment this evening. You'll have to excuse me."

Keith apologized, thanked her for the dance and left as quickly as he could. He wandered out to the edge of the patio. The music was loud, the lights brilliant. He saw one of the cops he'd been introduced to and nodded. The cop nodded in return, then accepted an empty glass from a gray-haired woman who was looking helplessly around for a place to put it down.

It appeared as if she was about to approach him. He turned, circling around, searching for Matt. At last he found him, standing out on the dock, staring out at the water.

He strode down to the dock to join him. "Evening," Matt said, though he didn't look as if he was eager for company.

Screw the disguise. "What the hell was that all about?" Keith demanded.

Matt stared at him. His eyes widened. He swore softly. "What was what about? And what the hell are you doing, looking like Colonel Sanders?"

"Watching," Keith said, eyeing him. "Listening."

Matt flushed a brilliant shade of red. Then he winced. "I—should have told you." His shoulders hunched down. "Lee went barhopping with Gerald. I . . . I wound up with Amanda."

"And you took her out on the boat?"

Matt hung his head and nodded.

Keith stared out at the water. "Well, did you learn anything?"

"I learned she knows how to spike a drink."

"So, you think she was prowling around?"

"God, I hope not," Matt said. Then he shook his head. "Yes, I think so."

Keith was silent for a minute. He felt Matt shuffle miserably at his side. He looked at him. "Did you say anything to Lee yet?"

"I was too embarrassed to say anything to either of you."

Keith nodded. "Keep it quiet for now."

"Now that you know, I feel like I should tell Lee, as well," he said with self-disgust. "Then I can get my feelings of absolute mortification over with once and for all."

"Let's just see how things progress for the time being, all right?" Keith said.

"You're the boss," Matt muttered.

Keith stared at him and wondered.

BETH'S SENSE OF PANIC GREW as she searched for Amber out in front, near the driveway, and couldn't find her. She tried Amber's cell phone and got voice mail. Just when she was about to panic, Ashley called.

"Ashley?"

"I'm here. Amber's phone died, and she wants to talk to you."

"What is it? What's the matter? Are you all right?

Where are you?" Beth demanded as soon as Amber got on the line.

"With Ashley."

"Are you all right? Is your father all right?"

"Yes."

"Then what's wrong?"

"Oh, Aunt Beth, you're not going to believe this."

"What?"

"Kim broke up with me."

For several seconds Beth stared at the phone blankly, wondering if she had heard correctly. "I'm sorry, what?"

"It was unbelievable. She was here, having a great night. Then, right before she left, she said that she had to talk to me. We came out here—it was all right, Ashley and Jake were nearby—and she told me that it wasn't me, it was her. But we had to break up."

Beth was silent for several long moments. The conversation was definitely startling. She wanted to shout at Amber that she was worried sick about her life and not petty problems, but she couldn't do that. She tried to focus on what her niece was saying, and that was even more confusing. "Um, was there something more to this relationship than I knew about?" she asked after a moment.

"No," Amber protested, and then laughed, the sound a little hysterical. "I mean, that's what makes it so bad. Have you ever heard of a *friend* breaking up with a *friend*? Like . . . don't even talk to me in the halls at school? I didn't believe her. I started laughing, at first.

But she was serious. I told Ashley after Kim left, and she thinks it's bizarre, too."

Beth could still hear the tears in her niece's voice. "Where's your father?"

"I don't know. Oh, Aunt Beth, I know that this is your big party, but . . . can . . . can you come out here? Can I go home with you?"

"I've been staying at Ashley's."

"Can I come to Ashley's?"

"If it's all right with her."

"I can't go home with Dad tonight. I just can't try to explain this to him. Oh, Aunt Beth, I don't believe this. I'm so upset."

"Honey, I'm right here . . . where are *you?*"

"To the left of the canopy."

"I'm over on the right. I'm coming. We'll find your dad . . . actually, he's not really happy with me right now. I'll have Jake talk to him. Tell Ashley that we need them to convince your father it's all right." She was walking as she talked. She still felt a slight sense of panic, she was so anxious to see Amber. Then, at last, she saw her. She breathed more easily, convinced she was creating demons where there were none.

She hurried over to the bench where Amber and Ashley were sitting. Ashley was looking lost and helpless. She stared at Beth with an I'm-trying-but-I-don't-really-know-how-to-handle-this-one look.

Amber looked absolutely stricken.

Beth reached down, pulling Amber into her arms. "We'll sort it out."

Amber looked up at her, her cheeks tearstained. She threw her arms around Beth.

"Have you ever heard of such a thing?" she whispered.

"It may be no big deal," Beth assured her. "She could change her mind tomorrow." She was trying to give Amber the attention she needed while looking around suspiciously. The three of them seemed to be alone in the driveway. No, they weren't. She could see the big cop down at the other end of the driveway, lighting a cigarette.

"No, it's serious, it's over," Amber said.

"But, honey, you weren't dating . . . you were friends. Friends don't have to have just one friend. Even if you're a little off right now . . . well, it can't be that bad."

"It *is* that bad. It's humiliating."

"You have other friends."

"We have all the same friends."

She squeezed Amber's hand. "We're going to have to see what happens, I guess. Remember, I love you. All my friends think you're the prettiest, most talented creature in the whole world. Honestly, honey, it will be all right. Someday you'll get to realize that most things that happen in high school aren't worth a crock of beans."

"That's true," Ashley told Amber, touching her cheek gently. "You're gorgeous, and you're talented, and we're all going to live our lives vicariously through you."

Amber stared at her, trying to smile, clearly not believing a word.

"Listen, honey, you know that I have to finish up here," Beth said. "I shouldn't be out here now, but—"

Amber let out a snuffle and a low wail. "I'm so sorry, Aunt Beth."

"Don't be sorry. It's all right. I'd ditch the job in two seconds for you, you know that."

"But I wouldn't want you to," Amber said softly.

"I know. So we're going to work this out."

"You go back in," Ashley said to Beth. "I can stay here with Amber for now."

"I just need to hang around the entrance, say good-night to people," Beth said. "They should start heading out fairly soon."

"Can we go to the locker room, Ashley?" Amber asked. "I've got to fix my face." She was trying to put on a brave smile.

"Absolutely. Meet you inside, Beth," Ashley told her.

KEITH HEADED BACK IN JUST IN time to see Eduardo Shea getting a beer from the same waiter—and handing something to the man. The waiter slipped an envelope into his jacket pocket and looked up. He had a black mustache, pitch-dark hair and appeared to be Latino. But there was something about him . . .

"Hey," Keith said, striding through the club. The waiter looked at him, then started hurrying through the crowd. "Stop him."

To his disgust, people just stared at him curiously but did nothing. Keith started to run after the man, who disappeared behind one of the bars and a huge arrangement of tropical flowers. Keith ran after him and nearly crashed into a man's back.

It was a different man. He turned, looking frightened. He began to speak in Spanish, protesting. Keith shook his head. "Where did the other guy go?"

The man shook his head blankly.

"The other waiter."

The man turned, pointing. There were waiters everywhere. As Keith stood there, his hands on the waiter's shoulders, Jake strode up to him.

"What is it?"

"Shea just gave one of the waiters an envelope."

"Which one?"

"I don't know. The one who's already half a mile away, probably," Keith said, and swore.

"Where's Shea?" Jake asked.

"Headed back inside."

"Maybe it's time to ask a few questions," Jake said. He went striding through the crowd, and Keith followed. Shea was heading for the exit.

"Mr. Shea?" Jake called.

Shea had definitely planned to make a break for it. It appeared as if he intended to keep going, at first. But then he turned, a brow arched as he waited. "Yes?" he asked.

"Let's speak outside for a moment, shall we, Mr. Shea?" Jake said.

"I'm sorry; I'd rather not. I'm quite exhausted by the evening."

By then Jake had produced his badge. "Police, Mr. Shea. Detective Dilessio, homicide."

"Homicide? Surely our dancing wasn't that bad."

"Very funny, Mr. Shea," Jake informed him.

Other people were beginning to note the conversation.

"Shall we go outside?" Jake suggested.

"I told you, I'm going home."

"I can take you in, you know," Jake said very politely.

"On what grounds?"

"Questioning. I've got twenty-four hours to hold you, sir, before I press charges."

"Charges for what?"

"Conspiracy to commit murder," Jake told him politely.

"We'll go outside—if you insist. You've got nothing on me, and trust me, I'll see you sued for false arrest," Shea threatened.

Jake took him by the elbow, leading him out. As he did, he said pleasantly, "Actually, I believe that a quick phone call to the FBI is all I need to assure myself that I can't be sued for anything, Mr. Shea."

They reached the outside of the club. "Mr. Shea, I believe you own a large amount of property on Mary Street. Would that be correct?"

"It's illegal to own property?" Shea said.

"And you have major interests in several South

American boatyards," Jake continued pleasantly.

Shea began to frown. "I don't know what you're suggesting, Detective." He nearly spat out the title.

"You know exactly what he's talking about!" They all started. Maria Lopez had come out of the club, a shawl clutched around her shoulders. "You killed Ted and Molly, you *bastardo*," she accused him.

"Maria, please," Keith said softly.

"I heard you. I heard you on the phone. You were yelling, saying they were not to be cowards, that they were to show up tonight, that they must not go near the studio to ask you for money. I heard you."

As he stood by, Keith looked out toward the parking lot. He saw a man in a tuxedo looking around furtively. "Shit," he swore, and he began to run.

The man turned, saw him and began to run himself.

But this time there was nowhere to disappear, no crowd in which to hide, no mass of tropical flowers to veer around. Keith was down the drive, shouting to the security guard. The "waiter" saw the guard and hesitated a split second too long before veering into the bushes bordering the park.

Too late. Keith tackled him. They both went down hard. The man stared at Keith, who was ready to rip at the man's mustache. Then he realized it wasn't a fake—the man wasn't Brad.

He stared up at Keith, wide eyed. Caught, he lifted his hands.

By then the security guard had come running. "What's in your pocket?" Keith demanded. He was losing his own mustache. He ripped it off, leaving only his beard. The man's eyes widened.

"Your pocket!" Keith said again, rising, grasping the man's arm, dragging him to his feet. He felt in the man's jacket. There was nothing there. It didn't matter. With panicked eyes, the man pointed at Eduardo Shea.

"That man should be arrested for assault and battery," Shea protested, staring at Keith.

"You're going in for questioning," Jake said firmly. "Feel free to call your lawyer."

One of the plainclothes officers was standing nearby. "I have a car, Detective," he told Dilessio. Jake nodded. "I think this silent gentleman needs to come in, too," he said.

"The man has nothing on him," Shea protested. "By all means bring him in. Let him file charges, too."

Keith suddenly felt an urgent need to get back inside.

"I can take them both in for questioning," Jake told Keith. "But I'm going to need solid evidence."

"You have Maria's testimony—"

"An overheard conversation. I'm going to need more. Unless you can get the feds in on this," he said. He followed the officer escorting Shea.

Keith turned to head back in.

THE BAND WAS PLAYING ON UNTIL the bitter end, and there were a few straggling members who intended to stay until that bitter end. Beth had a splitting headache

366

by then. She stood beside the commodore in the main dining room, feeling as if the salsa beat was now smashing into her head.

She was startled when Ashley came up to her, alone.

"Where's Amber?"

"With her dad. Beth, a man will follow you to my place. You have your key, right?"

"What's happened? Did—did they catch Eduardo . . . doing something? Sandy . . . Brad?"

"Not really, but . . . Eduardo Shea is going to be questioned at the station. I think Keith is calling his boss so they can come up with something to hold him on. Anyway, I need to get down to the station, as well. You have one of our friends, the big waiter, on guard duty. I'll be home as soon as I can get there."

"Ashley—"

"Beth, that's all I know right now. When I find out anything else, I'll call you, I promise."

Ashley murmured good-night to Commodore Berry and started out. Beth looked at him, ready to explain that she needed to be with her niece, then decided not to bother. He would know about the entire events of the evening soon enough, she was certain.

She walked outside. Her brother was nowhere to be seen. The party out here had broken up. A waiter was wandering around, picking up fallen glasses. "Ben?" she called.

Her brother didn't answer.

Panic seized her. "Ben!" she called again, louder.

Still no answer. She tried to calm herself. Amber was Ben's child. He might have insisted that they head home. She called her brother's cell phone. No answer. She tried Amber's, then remembered that Ashley had said it was dead.

She cursed, and tried her brother's phone number again. Still no answer.

Then she saw Amber. The girl was striding along the dock. Idly, it seemed at first. She looked up, seemed to see something and started to walk faster. And where the hell was Ben?

"Amber!" Beth called.

Amber apparently didn't hear her. She kept moving along the dock, her long-legged stride taking her quickly down to the farthest pier. Beth followed. Amber didn't stop at the dock that hugged the shore; she had seen something that had drawn her attention. In a minute she was almost running down the length of the dock that jutted out to the sea.

"Amber!" Beth called again, following as quickly as she could. It was hard to run in her ridiculous heels, and she wondered how on earth her niece was moving so fast. But then, Amber had mile-long legs.

Down the length of the pier, past sailboats, motorboats, big boats and small, Amber at last came to a halt. Beth had been running so desperately in her wake that she couldn't stop when Amber did. She nearly plowed into her niece. "Look," Amber said, pointing. "It's their boat."

Beth stared at the boat. It didn't look familiar at all.

It had a fresh coat of paint and was of moderate size, about twenty-six feet. She frowned, looking at her niece. "What are you talking about?"

"That couple who were on Calliope Key—they've decided to clean her up. She looks good, huh?"

Chills raced up and down Beth's spine. Amber was right, she thought, though she couldn't be a hundred percent sure. It looked like the same boat . . . but different. Fresher. It was the size and make of the beaten-up vessel they'd seen off Calliope Key.

"Amber, we've got to get out of here," she said urgently. As she spoke, she started to turn. Then she screamed as something wet and cold slapped against her ankle. She looked down just as a man sprang up.

It was Brad—or the man she had known as Brad. Bald now, clad in a drenched tux. He had managed to shed his shoes, and the dark toupee he had worn to blend in with the other waiters was askew. He must have seen Amber coming and slipped into the water. Maybe he'd intended to hide. Maybe he'd hidden intending to accost her the second he had seen her look down the dock and start toward his boat. She opened her mouth, ready to scream, determined to protect Amber no matter what.

"Don't do it," Brad said, producing a knife. He lunged toward Beth; in a second, he had pulled her tightly against him, the knife to her throat. She met his eyes. He smiled. They both knew it didn't really matter if she screamed or not—the band would drown out any sound from the docks.

Despite the blade against her throat, Beth ordered, "Amber, run."

"Amber, don't even think about it," Brad said harshly. "Move and she's dead."

"Amber, run!"

"Amber, step aboard the boat," Brad said. "Or she's dead."

"Amber, I could be dead one way or the other." Beth started to protest further, but her words ended in a little gasp when the knife bit into her flesh.

"No, don't hurt her!" Amber sobbed.

Brad just smiled into Beth's eyes as Amber hopped immediately onto the deck.

18

KEITH HURRIED INTO THE FOYER and then the dining room. He was certain he looked ridiculous without his fake mustache and beard, but he didn't really give a damn. He saw Commodore Berry, still smiling, still wishing his members a good-night and a safe trip home.

"Where's Beth?" Keith asked the man.

"I don't know. And quite frankly, this is all becoming a bit of a fiasco. Miss Anderson should be here, saying good-night with me. Whatever you people were so certain of tonight certainly didn't happen—"

Keith ignored him. "Where are Ben and Amber?"

"Mr. Henson, I'm afraid I don't know, and I'm still quite busy—and you look a mess."

Keith walked past him, continuing to search the area. His blue-haired dance partner glanced at him and gasped.

Shaking his head, he hurried to the patio, since the closest door led out in that direction. There was no one there, but the door to the men's locker room was ajar. Keith ran toward it and burst in.

He was stunned to see a figure on the floor. As he hurried over, he heard a groaning sound. He was stunned to discover Ben Anderson, struggling to sit up.

"Ben, what happened?"

Ben shook his head. "I was in here . . . I don't know. My head. I came in because I'd left my watch in my locker . . . must have tripped. I was walking toward it . . . look, it's open." His eyes widened. "Amber . . . Amber was waiting for me, by the door. I told her to wait—not to wander off. Oh, God, she didn't wait. She wandered. She didn't listen. She didn't realize . . . wouldn't believe it could be dangerous here!" He stared at Keith. "My daughter! You have to find my daughter."

Keith straightened. "Have you seen your sister?"

"No."

"I'll get you help," Keith said.

Then he was out the door, shouting. He ran into a waiter in the patio and grabbed him by the lapels.

"There's a man hurt in there—get help. Get the police."

The waiter paled and turned to do as he'd been told. Keith raced down onto the lawn. A few people were straggling out to spend the night on their boats. He searched through the crowds on each pier.

In the distance, he saw Amber Anderson getting on a boat. He frowned. There was someone else on the boat . . . and on the dock, but he couldn't tell who.

Amber probably knew most of the people who had boats here, he reminded himself. But even so, why wasn't she waiting for her father, the way she'd undoubtedly been told to do?

Amber's father was lying on the floor of the men's locker room, after being struck by someone, for some reason.

Keith started ripping off his dinner jacket as he raced down the pier.

"No! Don't listen to him. Get out of here," Beth insisted. She was terrified but trying desperately not to sound it. Her mind was racing. She knew that if she didn't somehow force Amber to escape, they would both be prisoners and probably end up murdered.

"She's already listening to me, honey," Brad said.

It was true. Amber was already on the boat.

At that moment Sandy came out of the cabin. She had stripped down to the white shirt worn by the caterers beneath their tux jackets. Tonight, she was

372

wearing a disheveled red wig, and she'd designed a perfect smattering of freckles over her nose. She wore big, thick-rimmed glasses.

"Brad, what—oh!" she began.

"Get on the boat," Brad told Beth.

"Amber, get off the boat!" she cried.

There were tears in her niece's eyes then. "Aunt Beth, he'll kill you."

"Amber, he'll kill us both!"

"No," Sandy protested suddenly. "Get on the boat. Please, just get on the boat. We've got to get out of here." She turned pleading eyes on Brad. "Brad, don't hurt her. Get on the boat, just get on the boat. Please, nothing will happen to either of you if you'll just get on the boat. Brad?" she implored.

"What the hell do you want me to do? They'll both go screaming for help. We've got to get out of here now—with them aboard," Brad replied roughly. "Get the lines, kid," he said, addressing Amber. "I've seen your dad's boat—I'm sure you know what you're doing. I don't want to hurt your aunt—Sandy there likes her a whole lot. But this is a pretty desperate situation you've caused for us. Tell your aunt to get her pretty rump on the boat so I don't have to kill her, and help us get out of here!"

Beth wasn't even sure that Brad cut her on purpose, but the knife moved against her throat, and she choked out a small sound of pain.

Amber jumped like a rabbit and did as she'd been told. Sandy stepped up to the rail as Brad prodded

Beth forward, forcing her to either step or fall onto the deck.

Once they were all on board, he grabbed Beth by the hair, dragging her down to the small cabin. "If you hurt Amber in any way, I swear I'll kill you," she said, her voice shaking despite the bravado of the words. She didn't consider herself a particularly brave person, but she had discovered a deep-seated maternal instinct. She would fight to her last breath for her niece.

KEITH GOT CLOSE ENOUGH to see the knife at Beth's throat before the boat headed out. He swore, weighing his options. If cornered, they might kill one of their hostages, as a warning to back off.

He reached for his cell phone; it was gone. He'd lost it in the scuffle out front. Swearing silently beneath his breath, he started to move again, kicking off his shoes as he ran to the end of the pier, then dived into the water. He surfaced, then paused briefly to reconnoiter.

The boat was just moving within the speed limit of the law and following good boating etiquette. They were obviously trying not to be noticed. That was his first piece of luck. He swam hard.

His second piece of luck came when he realized that they'd been in a hurry and careless of the lines. One was trailing in the water. He caught hold of it just as the boat began to increase its speed. He strained to pull himself up closer, fighting to clear the motor. As the boat began to scud across the water, he held on for dear life.

"TIE HER UP!" Brad shouted to Sandy.

"You are not going to—" Beth began. She stopped. The knife again. She swallowed hard. "I'll do anything if you'll just let her go," she said quietly.

"Sandy, quit screwing around. Tie the kid up," Brad insisted.

"No!" Amber shrieked.

"Shut up, kid, or I *will* kill your aunt."

Beth couldn't see what was happening, but she was surprised when the knife didn't bite into her flesh but instead eased away from her. "Stop," Brad hissed to her. "I don't want to hurt you *or* the kid."

"What makes us any different?" she asked.

"We haven't killed anyone," he said harshly. "Yet."

He sounded honest. Oddly, disturbingly honest. She held still. His hold eased again.

She heard Amber whimpering, but she didn't dare turn to look. "I swear, let her go and I'll help you do anything."

Sandy came into the cabin. "Is the kid tied up?" Brad demanded.

"Yes."

"Okay, now this one."

"Brad, this is insane. Why did we take them?"

"Are you nuts? They'd have had the cops after us in two minutes. They know, Sandy. That bastard was a liar."

"I don't know anything," Beth said. It was a lie—and yet, paradoxically, also the truth.

"You didn't get the envelope?" Sandy demanded.

"Hell, yes, I got the envelope. And if we're caught, so help me God, that bastard Eduardo is going down, too. He said the money would pass from hand to hand. In the end, some fool stuffed it into the pocket of the kid's father's jacket by accident. Can you believe that? I had to cream him to get it and get out. You know what's in the envelope?" he demanded of Sandy. "Do you want to know? Go ahead, look inside."

Beth wasn't tied up, and Brad was paying attention to Sandy. Beth tried to figure out how she could get the knife.

"Look in the envelope!" Brad raged.

Sandy did, then cried out in dismay, staring at Brad in disbelief.

He wasn't looking at Beth. She twisted, biting his arm as hard as she could. He dropped the knife with a loud scream. She shoved a knee into his groin, and he screamed again, doubling over in pain. Beth turned to run to Amber.

But Sandy was already there, and she had grabbed a frying pan. It cracked against Beth's skull, and she went down.

Lee had just brought the tender back to their vessel when he saw one of the little boats from the yacht club leaving, something trailing in the water behind it. He turned and hurried down to the cabin. "Matt? Matt, you back yet?"

He paused, stunned. Matt was back. But he wasn't alone. "What the hell are you doing here?" he demanded of their visitor.

WITH TREMENDOUS EFFORT, Keith made it over the side. Amber's eyes were wide as she watched him appear. Emerging from the surf and the darkness, he must have been a frightening sight. She looked as if she was about to scream, but he brought his finger to his lips to silence her and hurried to her side. She was tied up, her Summer Sizzler finery in disarray.

He worked hurriedly at the ropes Sandy had tied around her wrists and ankles. "Where are they?" he mouthed.

"In the cabin."

Keith judged the distance to the shore. It was becoming greater every minute. "Can you swim that?" he asked her.

She nodded. "But Aunt Beth—"

"I'm here, and we'll have a better chance of saving ourselves without worrying about you. There's a life jacket. Wear it. You're not afraid? You've got to get to shore and get help. From Jake, from the real cops, no one else, okay? Find Jake and tell him to get a hold of Mike. He'll know what you mean. They'll get everything on the water out after these guys. You can make it? You're sure? We're a half a mile out in night waters."

"I can make it," Amber swore tearfully.

"Then get out of here. Now."

He grabbed one of the life jackets and handed it to Amber. Looking down into the cabin he saw no movement.

That worried him.

"Go!" he told Amber.

She turned back once, her eyes tearing up.

"Honey, go. Get help."

She nodded. Apparently aware of the need for quiet, she slipped into the water. He afforded himself a split second to curse the fact that he'd sent a kid into the water at night, a half mile from shore. But if anyone could do it, it was Amber Anderson, he was certain. He turned, hunched down.

Beth was in the cabin.

And the cabin was far too quiet.

BETH AWOKE FEELING A THUDDING pain in her temple.

Memory flashed back. She remembered Sandy wielding the frying pan. She laughed inwardly at the irony.

She had eluded a man with a big knife, then been bested by a woman with a frying pan. She opened her eyes slowly, aware that she was still at sea and moving quickly. She was on a bunk.

She tried to move. Her hands were tied. She began working at the ropes with her teeth, then froze when she heard a racket topside.

"What the hell is that?" she heard Brad cry out.

"The kid?" Sandy suggested.

"You stay here and mind the helm. I'll go see," Brad said.

Then there was nothing. Beth remained dead still, listening in terror.

Suddenly there was a thump.

A moment later Sandy came rushing into the cabin where Beth lay. She reached into a drawer, drawing out a gun. Smith & Wesson .38—yes, the same gun Ben kept. The woman sidled over to the bunk and knelt down beside Beth, putting the muzzle against Beth's temple.

Beth swallowed, feeling the cold bite of the metal, imagining the bullet ripping through her head.

Amber? What had happened on deck? What about Amber?

After a while Sandy grew restless, tired of waiting. She stepped to the small doorway to the cabin, ducking. "Brad?"

Nothing. Sandy stepped out, but a second later she was backing into the cabin again. Beyond her, Beth could see that someone else was aboard the boat.

Her eyes widened. Keith. Soaked and dragging Brad by the collar.

"Brad!" Sandy cried out.

"I don't want to kill him," Keith said. "So you'll give me the gun, Sandy, and then you'll turn this boat around."

Again the gun was pressed to Beth's temple. She saw Keith's lips tighten, his flesh take on a paler hue.

But he held his ground. "Trust me. You shoot her, I'll snap his neck. I can do it, and I'm pretty sure you know it."

"I can shoot you and then her!" Sandy said, turning the gun on Keith.

"Do you really have the nerve?" he asked her. "And you know," he said, sparing a lightning glance at Beth, "Amber is on her way home."

"She'll drown."

"I don't think so. She's a strong swimmer. And she has a life vest."

Beth's heart took flight. Amber *would* make it. She was a survivor. She would get help. Adrenaline burst through her. She gritted her teeth and wrenched at the ties binding her wrists. She felt a surge of sheer joy and power as her arm swung free, catching Sandy right across the jaw. The other woman gasped.

And the gun went off.

"YOU ARE GOING TO EXPLAIN this, aren't you?" Lee demanded. They were already in pursuit of the smaller boat, but they were keeping their distance. Lee didn't want to alert them to the fact that they were being followed.

"Honestly, we were just talking," Amanda said, giving Lee her sweetest smile.

Matt was up, restless. "There's got to be more we can do," he murmured.

"You want to take a chance on spooking them, so

they kill Keith and whoever else they've got?" Lee demanded hotly.

Matt shook his head.

Lee looked at Amanda. "I'm really sorry, but you're here for the duration."

"I'm fine," she assured him, blue eyes excited. "Where do you think we're heading?"

Matt spun around, looked at Lee. "I think I know where we're going," he said. "The island."

Lee glanced at their headings. "Seems like a damn good guess to me," he said.

THE BULLET RICOCHETED WILDLY, hitting the brass lamp, a metal mirror backing and a bedside-lamp mounting, rather than thudding into the wood.

Then Keith let out an oath and, one hand to his temple, sank to the floor.

For a moment both Sandy and Beth were dead silent. The gun had fallen to the floor, forgotten.

"Oh, God!" Sandy cried out, rising.

To Beth's amazement, she raced over to Keith. Brad remained groaning on the floor while Sandy grabbed a towel, dabbing at Keith's head. She stared at Beth. "You might have killed him!"

Beth sprang to her feet, her heart in her throat. She pushed Sandy aside, falling to her knees beside Keith. He wasn't dead; he was breathing. His heart was beating. The blood . . .

Sandy dabbed at the wound. "Give that to me," Beth said. Taking the towel, she applied pressure to Keith's temple. She sensed movement around her, but she paid no attention, determined to stop the flow of blood.

Keith's eyes opened. One green contact was still in; the other had been lost somewhere. He stared blankly at her, dazed, and groaned. "What the hell happened?" he demanded. Relief filled Beth. At least he was still alive. His eyes closed. "Oh, yes. I remember. Bullet . . . out of nowhere."

"Sandy, can I have some water?" Beth asked.

A wet towel was stuffed into her hand. She washed the blood away and was relieved to see that he only had a surface wound. She looked around. The bullet had come to rest in the wood of the door frame.

"Can you sit up?" she asked.

Groaning again, he did so. Then he looked up. Beth did the same, then gasped softly, backing up against the wall. Brad was back on his feet, and he had retrieved the gun she had so stupidly forgotten.

"Brad . . ." Sandy said anxiously.

It was all . . . out of focus, Beth determined. In her struggle to help, she had nearly killed Keith. Sandy, who'd been acting like a cold-blooded killer, had been terrified that Beth might have killed the man she'd been threatening just seconds before. And Brad . . .

Brad looked really angry.

"Brad," Sandy said.

"What?" he snapped. "She bit a hole in my arm and nearly broke my Mr. Jolly. This asshole gave me a black eye and a knot on the head. And you want me to be nice?"

"They think we're going to kill them," Sandy said, fighting on their side, it seemed to Beth.

"I'd like to!" Brad muttered.

Keith was staring at them, a deep frown furrowing his features. A trickle of blood ran down his face. "What do you intend to do with us?" he demanded.

"Just hold you—until we get our money," Sandy said.

"Will you kill us then, the way you did the others?" Beth demanded.

Brad looked furious. "We didn't kill anyone! We take a few boats. We get them down to South America. And we get paid. That's all."

"You stole the Monocos' boat. And neither Ted nor Molly has been seen since."

Sandy was impatient. "They weren't anywhere near the boat. Brad and I went aboard, and they weren't even there. We took the boat, yes. We didn't kill them."

Keith studied her. "Where's your money?"

"Don't tell him," Brad snapped.

"What difference does it make? They're going to know anyway." She shook her head. "That bastard Eduardo kept telling us we could get it in Miami. But he's paranoid that he'll be seen. Tonight it was supposed to be in an envelope. And do you know what he sent us? Again? A damn note saying the money is in the clearing on the island. He's such an asshole."

"So that's what you were looking for," Beth whispered.

Keith, at her side, was silent, still studying the pair.

"Please, quit fighting. When we've got the money, we're leaving, period. And we'll let you go," Sandy pleaded.

"Tie them up, Sandy. And do a better job this time, please," Brad said wearily.

He turned the gun on Beth, smiling, but he addressed his words to Keith. "Let Sandy tie you up good and tight. Or else I won't kill Miss Anderson, I'll just see that she has a few shattered bones. How would that be?"

Beth winced.

"Get up," Brad told Keith. "Hands behind your back."

Keith obliged. Sandy shoved him toward the bunk. "Get in." She giggled. "It's actually kind of sweet. You can have your girlfriend just as soon as she's tied up, too."

A few minutes later, both securely tied—their bonds approved by Brad—they lay on the bunk, side by side, alone in the dark, while the little boat shot through the water.

For a moment they were silent. Then Beth exhaled. "I'm so sorry."

"Hey . . . you were trying to save both our lives," he said.

"But . . . in a way, I shot you."

"Yes, you did," he mused. "So much for my attempt to rescue the woman I'm falling in love with."

She was silent. "What constitutes love in your

book?" she whispered.

"Wanting to spend my life with you, every waking moment, you know, that kind of thing. The bullet-in-the-head thing . . . well, I'd just as soon not have that happen too often."

Tears sprang to her eyes suddenly. They might be about to die. She had to know.

"What about your work?"

"I like my work. Usually it involves saving lives," he said a little bitterly.

"But you were willing to do almost anything in this current . . . search."

She could sense him slowly smiling in the darkness. "Amanda?" he said. He turned to her. She felt the warmth of his whisper against her face. "I never slept with her. I wouldn't have slept with her. I spent time with her, talked to her—she and her family were on the island."

She inhaled. "If we survive . . ."

"You're going to owe me for this one."

"Do you think . . . could they be telling the truth? That they didn't kill anyone?"

"Let's hope so," Keith said softly. "Turn around."

She did so and felt him edging down her back. "What are you doing?" she demanded.

"Sorry, nothing erotic. I'm pretty good with my teeth, so I'm working on the knots."

She had no idea how far he had gotten when, what seemed like an eternity later, she felt the boat begin to slow.

"We must be at the island!" she told him.

"Turn around and hold still," he warned her.

The door to the cabin opened. The light was turned on again. They both winced against it. "Get up and behave," Sandy said. "We're taking you ashore. If you're good, we'll leave you alive and well on the island. Maybe we'll even leave you a little water. But move now. We've got to hurry."

Keith gave a pretense of struggling to his feet, giving Beth time to grasp her wrist bonds with her fingers, so no one would suspect she was free. She rose carefully, face forward, and stood in front of Keith. Sandy led them past Brad, who was in the main cabin, his gun on them.

They got into the tender, carefully.

Sandy took the gun. Brad rowed. They were all silent. Then Sandy said, "There's a boat coming . . . a big one, Brad."

"Nice? You think we can take her?" he asked.

"I think we need to find the money fast and get the hell out of here!" Sandy said.

They beached. Awkwardly, Keith and Beth got out. Brad turned on a flashlight. The moon was high in the sky, but not bright enough to light the interior.

"Let's move," Brad said.

"The boat is still coming. Hurry," Sandy urged.

They started walking. Apparently Keith wasn't moving fast enough, because Brad prodded him forward.

"Eduardo Shea is under arrest, you know," Keith

said over his shoulder.

"Good. I hope he rots."

"The police are looking for you, along with the FBI."

"We have plenty of places to go in South America," Brad assured him. "Move."

They reached the center of the island. Sandy ran ahead and started kicking palm fronds around. "Do you think the bastard stiffed us?" she wailed in dismay. "Help me, Brad. We've got to hurry."

Brad swore and headed across the clearing. "Stop running around like a headless chicken. Organize what you're doing. I'll come from the east, you start from the west."

In a minute the two of them were intent on their quest. Beth stared at Keith. He nodded to her, then inclined his head toward the west. She frowned, then understood.

Someone else was coming. Brad and Sandy were so intent on their quest that they hadn't heard the stealthy movement through the brush.

"Now," Keith mouthed, and he and Beth moved furtively, heading toward the barely discernible trail through the western foliage. Then they began to run.

"Hey!" Sandy shouted.

There was the sound of a gunshot. A bullet whizzed by Beth's head, so close that she felt the rush.

Brad hadn't been the one to fire, though. The bullet had come from the other direction. Beth kept running, tearing into the brush.

"Get down!" Keith warned her.

Brad screamed in agony after a second bullet burst loudly in the night. Sandy let out a horrible howling sound.

"What the hell are you doing?" someone shouted.

In the brush, blind, Beth nearly collided with Keith. Her hands were free, though, and she steadied herself, then started working on the ties at his wrists. She fell to her knees, tugging at the ropes, her heart thundering as she listened to the events in the clearing, far too close behind them.

She glanced up. She could see that Keith was tense, listening, and she suddenly realized that the man who had spoken was Matt Albright.

"Where are they?" another voice demanded.

Sandy sounded hysterical. "They're alive, I swear. You shot him! You shot Brad. My God, you've killed him!"

"Where are they?" Lee repeated. Then Sandy screamed.

Beth didn't want to think about what had happened to her.

"Dammit, Lee," Matt protested again.

"They took Keith, Beth and the girl," Lee said.

"They ran," Sandy cried, barely coherent. "They ran . . . except the girl . . . Keith got her off the boat. I don't know how."

"You're lying."

"I'm not."

"Keith?" Lee shouted. "Where the hell are you?"

Beth was certain he would step forward. He didn't. Instead, he looked down at her and shook his head. "No," he mouthed in the moonlight.

They crept closer, close enough to see what was happening in the clearing.

"Lee?" Matt said.

Lee spun on him suddenly. Raised the gun.

"What are you doing?" Matt asked, stunned.

The direction of the muzzle moved. Lowered onto Amanda Mason. "You just had to bring her on the boat, didn't you, Matt? Now I've got to kill her, too, and Hank isn't going to like it. I think it better look as if you killed her."

Beth's eyes widened in disbelief.

It was then that Keith moved. Like a shot in the dark, he catapulted himself out of the trees, slamming against Lee's back before the man could turn.

The two of them went down. Beth saw the gun go flying.

The fight was bitter. She saw Matt running to get in the midst of it. She saw the other two men rolling, fists flying viciously.

Beth rose, hurrying to the edge of the clearing to hide in the thick foliage. Just as she got there, Keith emerged victorious, straddling Lee Gomez.

But then another shot blazed through the night. Hank Mason came striding through the clearing, followed by Roger. Hank strode closer, aiming the gun at Keith's chest. Keith was breathing hard, his features stony. "Get up," Hank ordered crisply. He looked around. Brad lay dead. Sandy was bloodied and still sobbing silently. "Get up."

"Yeah, I'll get up. But I wouldn't trust him anymore. He was going to kill Amanda," Keith said.

"Like hell," Hank said.

"Daddy!" Amanda cried, seeing Roger. She raced over to him, and Roger stopped, uncertain. "What the hell is she doing here?" he demanded.

Lee stared up at Keith venomously. "She was on the boat," he said. "I had no intention of killing your daughter, Roger. Now get him off me!"

Hank didn't seem to give a damn about his cousin. He coldly eyed Keith, who rose slowly. Lee rose, as well, swinging a hard punch, belting Keith squarely in the midriff.

"Hey!" Amanda protested. "Dad, what are you doing here?"

"What are *you* doing here?" Roger demanded. He turned to Lee. "Well?"

"I saw Sandy and Brad taking off with our very own Jacques Cousteau here," Lee said, wiping blood from his mouth. "It seemed like the opportune time to do away with him and let the sea thieves take the rap. Should have been perfect."

"I still don't get it," Amanda said plaintively.

"Allow me to explain, Amanda," Keith said. "Brad and Sandy were working for Eduardo Shea, who had something more than dancing going on. He led them to the Monocos' boat, but they didn't kill Ted and Molly. And they didn't kill a good friend of mine, a great kid named Brandon. Nor did they kill a young diver who stumbled on something here recently. Brad didn't even know why those people died. But your father, Lee and Hank do. Hey, is Gerald in on this?"

"What do you care? You're a dead man," Lee told him.

"So humor me," Keith said.

"No, Gerald just comes around sometimes, and since he's innocent, he makes us all look good," Hank said.

Amanda gasped, staring at her father. "You . . . you pushed me into sleeping with Matt and exploring the boat because . . ."

"Your father is a pimp, Amanda," Keith said softly.

Roger stared at him coldly. "And you're a dead man. Hank, do it."

"Daddy!" Amanda cried in astonishment.

"Wait," Lee commanded sharply. "Beth Anderson is out there somewhere." He gritted his teeth. "That bitch stumbled on good old Ted's skull. I'd gotten rid of the rest of the rotting corpses when they washed ashore, but I hadn't been able to find that damn skull." He looked at Keith, shaking his head. "And that got you going, didn't it?"

"Actually, Mike has been suspicious for quite a while. After all, someone knew where Brandon was and killed him. It was you, you sorry bastard. You killed that great kid, just so you and your buddies could have the treasure all for yourselves."

Flat in the palm fronds now, lying dead still, Beth held her breath.

"Are you sure you know where to find it now?" Roger asked suddenly. He pointed at Keith. "He's the one who—"

"Found a coin. I know," Lee snapped. "I can take it from there."

"He can't dive worth shit," Keith said. Beth gazed across the clearing as Lee took another swing at Keith. Matt had been backing up, unnoticed. Now he saw her. He looked ill. He was unarmed, she knew, and he was stunned by the recent events.

Lee's gun was just inches away. She stretched her fingers, her arms, silently, desperately.

"I'm going to enjoy killing you," Lee told Keith.

"We need to find Beth Anderson," Roger reminded him.

"And you think he's going to go get her for us?" Lee mocked.

Hank took aim. But Keith was lightning fast. He grabbed Lee and thrust the man in front of him just before the bullet exploded.

In the confusion, Beth reached for Lee's gun. Matt raced forward, tackling Roger Mason's legs as the man fired off a round. Roger spun, noticing Beth, and tried to take aim again.

"No, Daddy!" Amanda cried, reaching for her father's arm.

Her action gave Beth time to grab the gun. As Keith thrust Lee's now-dead body forward, hard, at Hank

Mason, Beth fired at last. It was a big gun, heavy; she didn't even know what it was, and she was amazed that she could aim it. The recoil sent her sprawling into the bushes.

But she caught Hank in the arm.

He howled, and his gun flew. In a split second, Keith was on him. Moments later, it was over.

Suddenly there was silence. Dead silence. The smell of gunpowder filled the air. Then they heard Sandy, sobbing softly once again. Lee Gomez and Brad were dead. Hank was unconscious, and even Roger was dazed. Amanda began to cry loudly at her father's side.

Matt was the first one to speak. "Imagine. Amanda just came aboard to apologize, to tell me she thought she was really in love at last. With Ben Anderson."

"Beth!" Unbelievably, as if on cue, Beth heard her brother shouting her name.

Her knees gave out, and she sank to the ground just as the Coast Guard came bursting into the clearing, Ben running frantically in their wake, along with a tall, hard-bitten man in a camouflage suit, shouting orders.

Her brother reached her. She looked at him. "Amber?"

He smiled, but his smile faded as he looked around, then fell to his knees at her side. "She said you saved her life. You and Keith." Ben dragged her into his arms. She hugged him tightly, then drew away. "Brad said that . . . that . . . he knocked you out."

"I'm fine."

They both looked over at Brad and Sandy. She was keening softly, her eyes glazed.

Amanda was hovering over her father.

"Oh, God," Ben said.

"She was innocent. She helped save our lives," Beth said. Ben stared at her blankly. She smiled. "She's going to need a lot of help."

"I already have some help," she whispered. Ben nodded, stood and went over to Amanda. Beth smiled, feeling the hand that fell on her shoulder. She was drawn up, and strong arms came around her.

"We made it," he said simply.

SOUTH FLORIDA HAD SEEN PLENTY of bizarre scandals and mysteries, and far too many stories of greed and murder. But this one dominated the media for weeks, mainly because there was more to it than Beth had known the night she nearly died because of it.

Far more than Spanish gold had been at stake. Documents recently given to the American government by the German government told a tale she had never expected.

The crew of a German U-boat had taken refuge on Calliope Key when their vessel had begun to fail far closer to the American coastline than the government had wanted the public to know at the time.

The ship had carried the makings of a small atomic bomb, but they hadn't had all the time they'd needed to assemble it. Knowing that they were in danger of being taken by the Americans, the captain had ordered the components hidden before they attempted their escape.

Two men had been forgotten on the island. They had thought themselves dead, marooned. But their comrades had been blown up while heading north, and they had been rescued by British sailors. One of them had written a report for the German government, which had lain long forgotten in a secret vault. When it had been recently brought to light and given to the U.S., the American government hadn't known if it was a hoax or a strange and terrible truth. And Rescue had been brought in.

It was terrifying to know that a man like Lee Gomez had teamed up with a financier like Roger Mason to heist such a discovery. There was no telling where the bomb might have ended up, since their only concern had been the highest bidder.

A week after the rescue, Keith and Beth were finally back together again. She'd spent days trying to tell everything to the satisfaction of the officers with the various different agencies questioning her. It had been worse for Keith, since he'd had to file reports in any number of places.

At first, when she saw him, Beth had no desire to speak. She greeted him at her door. Whispered hello, dragged him in.

They didn't actually talk for hours. When they did, she asked him at last, "So what will happen now? Now that the world knows *La Doña* is out there, and that there's more on her than gold?"

He was silent for a moment, meeting her eyes. "I found the location."

"When?"

"Before the party. I knew that someone in our group was on someone else's payroll. Remember that I mentioned Brandon? He was like a kid brother to me. It was the worst waste in the world that he was murdered." He shook his head. "I kept making the connection to Eduardo Shea, but he was small time. The Masons were using him, though, getting information. Anyway, I reported exactly what I found to Mike, with all the coordinates. Lee and Matt knew I'd discovered a coin, but they didn't know that I'd figured out why we couldn't find the remains of the ship."

"And why couldn't you?"

He smiled. "Hide in plain sight," he said. "The ship had become the reef. Once you figured that out, you could begin to trace her timbers—and the cargo hold. I won't be going down on that particular dive anymore. They'll put other guys on it. I have some time off."

"I'm not sure if I do or not," she said ruefully.

He rolled over, staring at her. "Quit."

"Just like that?"

"If they can't give you time off for a wedding and a honeymoon, quit."

She fell into his arms again, smiling. "For you? Just like that," she whispered.

• • •

SHE WAS INCREDIBLY GRATEFUL to be alive. And so was Amber. But being grateful didn't always make living all that easy.

Despite surviving "Sail Into Terror!" as the newspapers had dubbed the event, Amber still had a serious dilemma.

"I think he's really falling in love with her," she told Beth, horrified.

"Well, she really did come through for us. She made a move against her own father. She helped save our lives."

"I'm trying not to hate her," Amber told her. "I mean, she might be my stepmother."

"You both have a lot of wounds to get over. But I think she's actually in love with your father and ready to change her ways. And you can always spend lots of time with Keith and me."

"I *am* in the wedding, right?"

"You bet."

THE WEDDING FELL IN THE MIDDLE of October, on a perfect fall day. The sun was brilliant, but the air didn't have the touch of fire that made the summer months so hot.

Beth couldn't have imagined anything more perfect, couldn't have imagined feeling a greater happiness.

They were married at the club, in a field of exquisite flowers. Everything was gorgeous.

After all, she did know how to plan a good party.

She was insanely in love with her husband, and when he looked at her, she still trembled, knowing he felt the same. They were married as the sun set in the western sky, surrounded by family and friends.

And when the champagne had been sipped, the toasts raised and the last of their excited hugs goodbye given out . . .

They chose not to sail into the sunset.

They honeymooned in Vermont.

Center Point Publishing
600 Brooks Road • PO Box 1
Thorndike ME 04986-0001 USA

(207) 568-3717

US & Canada:
1 800 929-9108